NOT
HERE
TO STAY
FRIENDS

Also by Kaitlyn Hill

Love from Scratch

KAITLYN HILL

NOT
HERE
TO STAY
FRIENDS

Delacorte Press

Text copyright © 2023 by Kaitlyn Hill
Cover art copyright © 2023 by Monique Aimee

Visit us on the Web! GetUnderlined.com

Educators and librarians, for a variety of teaching tools, visit us at RHTeachersLibrarians.com

Library of Congress Cataloging-in-Publication Data is available upon request.
ISBN 978-0-593-48370-1 (trade pbk.) — ISBN 978-0-593-48372-5 (ebook)

The text of this book is set in 11-point Maxime Pro.
Interior design by Cathy Bobak

Printed in the United States of America
10 9 8 7 6 5 4 3 2 1
First Edition

Random House Children's Books supports the First Amendment and celebrates the right to read.

For Brianna Hill, who has always been there. I still can't make you un-my sister, and I'd never want to try.

CHAPTER ONE

Life is all about beginnings. Every day you get a new one . . .
until one day, you don't.
—*THE COVE,* SEASON 2, EPISODE 6

Sloane

Pop music legend has it that when fellow Tennessean Miley Cyrus arrived at LAX many years ago, she had naught with her but a dream and a cardigan.

As I, Sloane McKinney, stand in the baggage claim area of the same airport waiting for my luggage to appear, I have only a backpack and a zit on my chin that I swear I could feel getting larger and angrier with each minute spent in recycled plane air. It's not exactly what I would consider a "Party in the U.S.A.," but that's the song my brain has chosen to play on repeat since the pilot announced we were preparing for landing.

If my life was a TV show, this would be the opening scene of the pilot episode. Fade-in: the camera pans over the masses of people rolling suitcases, talking on phones, hugging the person who came to pick them up. Cut to our plucky heroine standing in the middle of it all, watching with naive hope on her zitty face (*note—clear up her skin in post?*). Music playing softly in the background until now grows louder, slows down for dramatic effect. Camera zooms in on heroine to the sound of *It's definitely not a Nashville party.* . . .

Yeah, I should stop.

While I wait for my bags, I scan the room again for a recognizable head of blond hair and, finding none, pull my phone out of my pocket to see if he's texted an update. Nothing since he left his house.

That's fine. NBD. My hands are just shaking from fatigue, or low blood sugar after the only food provided on my two flights to get here was pretzels and peanuts. Definitely not because in a matter of minutes I'll be reunited with my best friend, Liam Daniels, for the first time in over two years. Nor the fact that we'll spend the whole summer together. Oh, and absolutely not because he lives in my dream city, which I desperately hope I'll love as much as I think I will, because all my hopes and aspirations are pinned on moving here after high school. In a lot of ways, this really does feel like the pilot episode of *The Rest of Sloane's Life.* No pressure.

I cut off my mental sing-along for the twenty-seventh time and slam my tapping foot flat to the ground. The sound draws the attention of a few fellow passengers waiting for their own luggage, and I smile in a way that I hope conveys harmlessness, maybe even charm. No one smiles back.

In my head, Miley taunts, *"She's gotta be from out of town."*

Somebody get this girl a nap.

Anyway, it wouldn't make sense to be nervous about seeing Liam. For the first twelve years of our lives, we were next-door neighbors in our hometown of Knoxville and hung out every day. Even after his dad's local TV production company went national and the Daniels family moved to LA, we stayed in touch via texts and video calls better than I keep up with any of the friends I see in person. He used to visit once or twice a year, to see his extended family around the holidays, and it was never weird to be around each other then.

But those visits fizzled out in the wake of his parents' divorce a couple years back, and something about Liam has been different ever since, too. Not a super-obvious something, as he's good at keeping his emotions in check, but I get the impression that his life out here isn't as rosy as he'd like me to believe. I want to have fun together, but I also want to be here for him, in real life rather than through a screen.

Which is only part of the reason I jumped at the chance to (and begged and pleaded for my parents to agree to let me) visit for the summer when Liam extended the invitation. I tuck my phone back into my pocket, thinking of the other reasons.

Even though I haven't left the airport yet, this city already feels so much bigger, more fast-paced and vibrant than anything I'm used to. It's like it's brimming with creative inspiration, with stories to be told.

I hope my story starts here.

My people-watching is interrupted when someone jostles my shoulder, trying to get past me to the baggage carousel.

"Oh, sorry," I say on instinct, even though I'm not sure what I have to be sorry for. But then I see what the guy is reaching for. "Hey, that's my suitcase!"

The stranger's big hands are hoisting up the L.L. Bean carry-on that the airline let me gate-check for free, its lavender color one I chose specifically to stand out at baggage claim and its front embroidered with my initials. It's unmistakable.

I take a step closer, eyes still trained on my bag like if I let it out of my sight it'll be gone for good, when the tall, broad-shouldered guy turns around.

And he isn't a stranger at all.

"Liam!" I squeal, my hand flying up to swat at his chest. A chest that seems like it's a foot higher than when I saw him last, not to mention wider and surprisingly hard. A girl could break something swatting that chest. I have to tilt my head back to look into his eyes, which twinkle with amusement, his mouth half smiling down at me.

"You were about to miss it. Thought I'd help you out," he says, his voice a soft rumble. Everything about him, this in-person Liam, seems so much more . . . grown-up than the Liam who lives in my phone. It's taking a minute for my brain to recalibrate.

When I notice his cheeks start to go a little pink under my attention, I force myself to speak. "It . . . it would've come back around. God, Liam! It's . . . you . . . wow! You're here!"

Impulsively, I stand on tiptoe and throw my arms around his neck, hugging him close. He smells like pine and clean laundry, all woodsy and cozy, and I feel the urge to press my face deeper into the crook between his neck and shoulder and inhale. An urge I suppress because *What the hell, creepy Sloane?* Liam bends and wraps his arms around my middle, then lifts me off the ground as he straightens back up, and I laugh through the fluttery feeling in my stomach.

What is my body even doing right now? He might smell like Hot Guy—and, okay, look more like it than I expected, too—but he's not. Or like, he *is,* but he's not—

"I'm always here," Liam says, cutting into my inner spiraling with a chuckle that vibrates through my chest. Liam's hugs have always been amazing, but they hit different with the addition of an altitude change. Good different, I think, but also weird different. "You're the new arrival. Welcome to the best coast, Sloane."

He sets me down again and I take a step back, watching a lock of his blond hair tumble down over his forehead before he pushes it back. My eyes track over his face again as I scramble for something to say—something other than *How long have you looked like* this?

"Some welcome. You scared me half to death," I tease, crossing my arms over my chest as I turn back to the conveyor belt to watch for my other suitcase. "I'd been in the big city for all of five minutes and thought I was gonna have to fight a luggage thief."

"Excuse me for being helpful." I think Liam means to lightly elbow my side, but the jab lands in the vicinity of my armpit.

"So, growth spurts, huh?" I say abruptly, because I can't entirely avoid the fact that the guy standing beside me is giving off strong Simba vibes, post–"Hakuna Matata" montage when he's all grown-up and weirdly attractive for a cartoon animal. I'm his shrimpy meerkat friend who still saw him as a baby lion until this moment.

Liam clears his throat, but I detect a laugh beneath it. "Yeah, I mean, we've mostly just seen each other's faces the last couple years, right? Felt weird to, like, give updates on anything else.

'Oh, by the way, outgrew my jeans again.' But that's happened. Several times. Think I've leveled out now, though. Six foot two." He pushes back the hair that's fallen over his forehead again, adding, almost to himself, "I don't know why I just told you that."

I roll my eyes, faking exasperation. "I'll remember it for the Tinder profile we're making you when you turn eighteen."

He coughs. "The *what* we're making me?"

"Oh look, there's my other bag," I say, shooting him a smile as I see it come around the bend. I'm about to lean over again when it's in front of us, but Liam steps around me and beats me to the punch, then hauls the hefty thing like it's a lunch box and sets it down beside him.

"'Able to lift at least fifty pounds, too—come and get it, ladies,'" I say slowly, pretending to type the words in the air.

Now he has the gall to give *me* an eye roll as he steers both bags away. "Whenever you're done, can you meet me at the car? We've got traffic to sit in."

"Wait. Is that *the* Hollywood sign? Like the real one?"

Liam chuckles at my question from where he sits in the driver's seat of his gently used Mercedes, which he describes as a "guilft"—a "guilt gift"—from his dad in the wake of the divorce. "As far as I know, there's only the one."

"You can just see it from your car? I feel like I should have to buy a ticket for this experience." I've been glued to the passenger-side window since we left the airport parking lot, entranced by everything new and shiny around me. Even the familiar stuff, like a McDonald's we pass, seems exciting—it's a *Los Angeles* McDonald's. That's *Hollywood* litter on the sidewalk. Even sitting in California traffic feels somehow more glamorous than sitting in Tennessee traffic.

I'm basically bouncing in my seat as I take in the palm trees that line the streets, their fronds spraying out like fireworks against the cloudless blue sky overhead. I've never lived anywhere that has palm trees. Is it weird to be so excited for that? To me, palm trees are like nature's party hats. When you live somewhere they grow, every day has to feel at least a little bit like a party, right?

My eyes are peeled for any recognizable celebrity faces. I make up backstories in my head for all the people in the cars around us—that lady in big sunglasses and a blazer driving a Porsche is probably a studio exec making a major movie deal over her Bluetooth headset. The town car with the blacked-out windows is probably carrying a pop star to her record label's office. I see someone waiting at a bus stop who sort of looks like one of the Avengers if I squint.

"I feel like the Avengers probably don't take public transit," Liam responds to my observation. He's been pretty quiet, driving with ease through this adopted city of his, but I can feel nervous energy radiating off him nearly as much as the Hot Guy scent. It's doing nothing to calm my own jitters.

So far, it's not hard to imagine this as a place I could call home. In my post–high school future, I could live in one of the trendy apartment buildings that we pass going down the free-way, if I don't live on campus at whatever screenwriting school I end up in. Later, I could work at a big TV studio in the area, on one of the shows advertised with massive billboards all over town.

This summer could be just the beginning.

We start winding up into steeper hills, slowing down through neighborhood streets lined with bigger and bigger mansions. I knew Liam's dad wasn't struggling financially, not by a long shot. But this area is nicer than I even envisioned.

"Dad kept the house, you know," Liam says with casualness that feels forced. "After. Mom moved to a condo downtown. She'll be away on business most of the summer, so we probably won't see her."

I nod, having kind of expected that based on how seldom Liam talks about his mom anymore. I don't know what her deal is. I can't imagine being so blasé about spending time with my only kid in these last years before he's grown up and moves out. But I'm glad he has his dad, and that he got to stay in a place he knows, where he's comfortable and feels at home and—

Holy shit, it's a castle.

Well, not a literal castle, but one big-ass, old-English-looking chateau in the middle of Southern California. Liam rolls down his window at the gates—the gates!—and scans a key card that opens them, then drives us on through so I get an even better view of one of the most beautiful houses I've ever seen.

It has honest-to-God turrets. Gorgeous gray stone covers the outside walls, with moss artfully scattered across a black slate roof. I can count three chimneys from this vantage point alone. The massive mahogany front door—featuring a wrought-iron knocker—looks like it should only be opened by a butler, and certainly shouldn't let in a peasant like me.

I don't realize that the car has stopped or that my jaw is on the ground until Liam nudges my shoulder. I look at him and he gives a short, quiet laugh, running a hand over his jaw.

"I know the house is, uh, a lot, but I promise it's comfortable. In places."

He looks more anxious than he has so far, which makes *me* even more anxious. I feel like I have to break this tension somehow but don't know why we're so tense to begin with, because *this is Liam.* We know each other better than anyone else in the world. Don't we?

"If my bedchamber doesn't have a wood-burning fireplace and formal sitting room attached, I'm getting a hotel," I announce before unclipping my seat belt and getting out of the car.

This time, Liam's laugh is loud and genuine. He takes both of my bags even when I try to fight him on it, then goes the extra mile to playact like a fancy servant as he gives me the tour. We cross dark hardwood floors, passing sconces and chandeliers that light up deep-jewel-toned walls and furniture that belongs in an oversized dollhouse. It all suggests that Mr. Daniels is living out his dream of being the lord of his ancestral home in the English countryside—and that he might be hiding his ex-wife in the attic.

"Your chambers, my lady," Liam says with his terrible attempt at a British accent as he opens a door off an upstairs hallway. At the face I give him, he scrunches up his nose and drops the accent. "Ick, yeah, I didn't like that either."

The guest bedroom they've put me in is definitely Brontë-ready. There's a four-poster bed with a chandelier hanging just past the foot of it, an elegant wardrobe, an en suite bathroom with a waterfall shower *and* soaking tub. My dingy purple luggage looks as out of place as a Taco Bell cup on the set of *Downton Abbey*.

"I'm afraid to touch anything," I murmur as I spin in a slow circle by the foot of the bed, taking it all in.

Liam leans a shoulder against the wall. "Don't be. This stuff doesn't get enough use. It's like a sad shrine to all the guests we don't have."

The room on its own wouldn't strike me as particularly sad, but Liam's tone has me reconsidering. Acting on the *FIX IT!* impulse I get any time Liam is giving off a less-than-happy vibe, I snap my fingers.

"Ooh, should I get out the list?" I ask with turbo-boosted levels of cheer.

"The list?"

I give him a mock-chastising look, setting my hands on my hips. "Yes, the *list*. Sloane and Liam's Summer of Fun! Your contributions have been scarce recently, I must say, but don't worry—I've thought of a few more." I unzip my backpack and dig through it for the notebook in which I've been keeping a handwritten bucket list of things we want to do this summer. "I know we had a hike or two on there already, but I've added one called Runyon Canyon, because apparently celebrities like to walk their dogs there? Sounds fun, right? And I've been thinking it could be cool to binge *The O.C.* again while I'm actually *in* Southern California. Also, I want to go to that museum with all the lampposts out front and take artsy pictures of each other. Is it pronounced *lack-muh,* or L-A-C-M-A? Dang, I packed more in here than I realized—"

"Let's wait on the list for now," Liam says. I stop trying to wrestle my notebook from my bag, sit back on my heels, and look up at him. His expression is tight and almost . . . uncomfortable? Maybe I'm going too hard on the tourist itinerary within the first five minutes of getting to his house.

"Okay, sure," I say as I get to my feet. I can be chill. *So* chill. "Should we move on?"

The strain in his face melts into a soft grin as he nods. "I think you'll like the next part."

"After you, Lord Daniels the Younger."

He guides me back down various hallways and staircases. His comments on the guest room have me noticing the echoes of our footsteps more than I did before, how they bounce off every corner of this huge, mostly unoccupied house. It feels almost eerie, the dark sitting areas and study and dining room more sparse and impersonal than homey. It's . . . lonely. *I'm* almost lonely by proxy, thinking of what Liam would be up to right now if I wasn't here, all the time he probably spends in this house by himself while his dad is at work and his mom is who knows where.

I'm about to broach the topic, probably not very tactfully, when he puts a hand on my back to nudge me toward a door off the Food Network–worthy kitchen, the only modern part of the house I've seen so far.

"This way," he says, opening it to reveal another set of stairs, which we take down to the basement—and the home theater of my dreams. In contrast to the rest of the house, it's super cozy, with deep blue walls painted in a starry pattern. A few track lights on the ceiling illuminate three descending rows of overstuffed recliners. There's a fluffy throw blanket draped on the back of each chair and cupholders in the armrests with trays that unfold from one side. A projector sits in a nook in the middle of the back wall, and most of the giant front wall is a screen.

I look to Liam, and the hearts in my eyes must be obvious because he laughs. "Should we watch something?"

He already knows the answer—it's why he brought me down here right away. While the amenities might be fancier than what I'm used to, *this* is familiar. This is Liam and me as we've always been—comfy, couch-hunkering TV bingers to our core. Despite all the rest of the changes around us, I feel something in me settle at the reminder that we're still the same people, the same halves of our best-friendship whole.

Warmth spreads through my chest as we both settle into back-row seats. I pull a blanket around me like a cocoon while Liam presses a button on the remote, bringing the screen to life.

"This. Is. Perfect," I whisper reverently.

"I thought you'd be a fan." He says it with a sheepish smile, looking straight ahead at the screen instead of at me. "Definitely thought about showing it to you over the phone a bunch of times, but—I don't know, I guess I knew you'd see it in person someday. The surprise was too good to spoil."

My smile is trying to outgrow my face as I look at him, and when his gaze finally shifts my way, his cheeks redden.

Maybe he's struggling to adjust to Real Life Sloane as much as I am to Real Life Liam. Grown-Up Simba Liam. Hot Guy L— Nope, gotta stop playing with that label. We'll get used to each other. There's nothing different between us just because there's no screen or phone line involved.

"You're the best friend I've ever had," I tell him, batting my eyelashes goofily as I reach out to clasp his hand. It's a thing we've always said to each other since we were little, back when we were each the other's *only* friend. But even as we've grown up and met new people, lived in different places, it's always remained true.

"Yeah, yeah," Liam answers with an eye roll, giving my hand a squeeze before dropping it to click around with the remote. But he adds, "You too."

I sigh as I settle deeper into the comfy seat and turn my eyes to the screen. He's pulled up the guide, and I gasp when a show catches my eye after less than thirty seconds of scrolling.

"We have to," I say, pointing at the listing on the screen for *The Cove,* starting in two minutes. "It's fate, right?"

With a smirk, Liam selects the channel. I gasp again when I realize it's a rerun of season one, episode one. There's barely a hint of teasing in his voice when he says, "Definitely fate."

The warmth spreads from my chest now, all the way to my fingers and toes as we watch the very end of some murder mystery show, then the ad proclaiming a marathon of *The Cove*'s first season, and finally the show's dramatic intro music.

Liam is the only person in my life who has never belittled my love of TV. It's why he knew this home theater would be so exciting for me, why he has no problem settling in to watch a show within our first couple hours of being reunited. We've binged all my favorite series in the soapy teen drama genre together over the years, from the classics like *Dawson's Creek* and *One Tree Hill*, up through *Riverdale* and *Outer Banks*. We'll video chat or text for hours through episode after episode, often while Liam studies or does woodworking projects and I take notes for possible fanfic or script ideas.

And our all-time favorite—the one we have to sync our schedules to watch live together each week, despite the time difference—is *The Cove*.

This is the show that got me into my other, even bigger passion—writing. I started with *The Cove* fanfiction, as a way to pass the time between episodes and fix things I wish the writers had or hadn't done. Before long, I moved into writing scripts myself, both for existing series and for original shows of my own. But both of my parents hate how much "trash TV" I watch, so I've taken to hiding my writing like a drug habit.

Only Liam knows my fanfic pen name, reads all my original work, helps me talk through ideas. He's always gently prodding me to be proud of my writing and make a real go at this thing I'm secretly passionate about. He's the first and only fan of the get-Sloane-to-LA-to-be-a-TV-writer plan.

That means more to me than he could know.

The opening shot of *The Cove* appears on-screen, and I sigh contentedly. "It's been ages since I've seen season one."

"Same," Liam answers. "I barely remember what happens."

"We should watch the whole marathon this week," I say, wiggling in my seat. To my surprise, he looks less enthused. He murmurs a soft "Maybe," but before I can ask about it, he turns the intense theme music up louder.

The main character, Dorian, sits on a cliff over the beach near his house, his legs hanging off the edge. The camera pans in from the side, getting closer until you're right up against his face, looking into one of his sharp blue eyes. He blinks. Fade to black. Fade-in the title: *The Cove.*

Like so many shows, *The Cove* has been through growing pains in the three seasons they've made so far and took a few episodes to hit its stride . . . but wow. The dialogue in this pilot is something. And overall, there's so much going on that I forgot was tossed at us in episode one. Already, we learn that Dorian has a crush on the cheerleader who is trying to get with his best friend and cocaptain of the baseball team, another best friend with an unrequited crush on *him,* a habit of cheating on calculus tests, and a target on his back from the local bicycle gang (*what?*). As if having the name Dorian wasn't unfortunate enough.

I can't even lie—I *live* for this shit.

When the credits finally roll on a truly wild hour of television, there are a few moments of silence before I blurt out, "Was there always that much happening in the pilot?"

Liam's answering laugh is loud, and when I look at him, he's slouched in the chair, more relaxed than he's seemed since I got here. "I definitely thought the bike gang wasn't introduced till later in the season."

"I almost feel bad for him, but the calculus thing is not a good look."

"But, Sloane, who has time for studying when he could be *pining*?"

"Ugh, poor Chelsea," I scoff, referring to the girl bestie who's had it bad for Dorian throughout the entire series so far. "She can do better. Dorian and Mara deserve each other."

Liam lays a hand over his heart. "R.I.P. Dorsea, gone before you even existed."

It's never made sense to us that the show puts its hero in an on-again, off-again thing with Mara, and they treat each other like shit about 90 percent of the time, while he and Chelsea could clearly be something beautiful. All my fanfic is Dorsea-centric, giving them the love story that I and most other *Cove* fans wish they'd had.

But part of the show's popularity comes from the fact that the cast is mostly made up of actual teenagers rather than twenty-something actors. With that has come plenty of fun speculation about the behind-the-scenes drama among the characters' real-life counterparts. They've all been known to tease fans with flirty Instagram interactions, or the occasional hand-holding paparazzi shots. Most famously, the teen heartthrob who plays Dorian, Aspen Woods, has been in a rumored on-again, off-again relationship since the show began with the actress who plays Mara, Evie Baker.

I guess it wouldn't be as exciting for Dorian and Chelsea to date on-screen if we all knew Dorian and Mara had the hots for each other in reality. But it does remind me . . .

"Speaking of weird romantic choices," I say, "have we learned anything more about that reality spin-off *The Cove*'s doing? I can't even imagine how a *Cove*-themed dating show is going to work, and they've kept it so hush-hush. You don't think it's really one of the actors, do you?"

The network that produces *The Cove* kept airing these weird, vague ads during the end of the last season about a "reality cross-over experience" and "unique opportunity to date the perfect leading man." They were seeking twenty-five girl contestants aged fifteen to seventeen from across the country but didn't make it super clear who the "leading man" in question would be. Curious when I first saw it, I checked out the website, but didn't get much more out of the bizarre application. The prevailing rumor is that Aspen and Evie, mirroring a Dorian-Mara breakup in the last season finale, might be over for good, and that Aspen is starring in his own dating show.

Liam is suddenly tense again. He clears his throat and shifts in his seat to face me. "Yeah, actually, about that . . . I have something I need to talk about with you. It kind of involves our plans for the summer, and in a weird turn of events, *The Cove*—"

"Well, if it isn't my two favorite kids in the world, back together again!" a booming voice interrupts.

I whip around to see an older, more distinguished-looking version of Liam filling the doorway. It startles me at first, how much stronger the resemblance has gotten since I last saw them. They're both tall, tanned, golden-haired California boys now. But there's a bit of silver threaded through Mr. Daniels's thinner locks, more lines creasing his forehead and the corners of his eyes and mouth.

His whole face seems to crease up as he looks at me with a

smile. "Sloaney, baby," he bellows, opening his arms. I untangle myself from the blanket and stand. Mr. Daniels wraps me up in a hug that makes me feel five years old again. "It's been way too long. How were your flights? Are your arms tired?"

I pull out of the embrace and return his smile with a hint of surly-teen-eye-roll, the reaction I think he was hoping for. "Flights were fine, but I'm really glad to be here. Thanks again for having me, Mr. Daniels."

He gives a hearty laugh, the one that always got us cackling with him as kids, as he leans against the doorframe. "Are you really still Mr. Daniels–ing me? Call me Spencer from now on. My ex-wife's the only one who ever cared about all that Southern-manners, respect-your-elders bullshit."

He says all this in the same jokey tone, but I know I'm not imagining the layer of contempt underneath. I freeze up—am I expected to openly shit-talk Mrs. Daniels with him now? Is that what happens when people get divorced, even if you're basically their pseudo-kid? I would look to Liam for guidance on this, but I'm guessing he's already uncomfortable, and I don't want him to feel responsible for my feelings to boot.

"I'll try that, but it'll take some getting used to. I'm a creature of habit, Mr. Dan— er, Spencer," I say, trying to sound light and breezy. *Subject change, subject change!*

Mr. Daniels smiles, glancing at the projector screen as he straightens back up, and his face gets even brighter. "Oh ho, there's our boy!"

My brows knit together in confusion, as the "boy" he's referring to could only be Aspen Woods as Dorian, jogging through a park as the second episode of season one plays. I didn't realize Liam's dad had ever watched *The Cove*. His company focuses on home improvement, DIY, reality TV stuff, so I've always assumed his interests would be geared more toward that than scripted teen drama.

He looks at Liam as he continues, "Doing some research, son?"

Liam seems to shrink into his seat, focusing intently on the screen again.

"Research?" I ask.

"Sure," Mr. Daniels says, as though this conversation should make any sense to me. "For tomorrow."

"Tomorrow?" Weird how the echo in this room sounds a lot like me.

Now it's Mr. Daniels whose forehead wrinkles in confusion. "Yes . . . Liam's first day. Didn't he tell you?"

Now totally lost, I swivel my head back and forth between the two guys. "First day of what?"

Liam's mouth opens, but his dad beats him to it.

"Liam's summer job! He'll be working behind the scenes of my company's new reality show." He hitches his thumb toward the screen, where Dorian is still running. "*Aspen Woods's Future Leading Lady.*"

CHAPTER TWO

Friends and family are what keep all the pieces of your world
stuck together, right? Some of them are the duct tape.
Others are half-chewed sticks of gum.
—*THE COVE*, SEASON 1, EPISODE 2

Liam

Today could be going better.

I take a bite of pepperoni from the slice on my plate, hardly
tasting it as I chew. Dad and I order takeout most nights, or I
order it for myself when he's working late. But tonight we're
eating it on real plates, ones Dad's assistant purchased after
Mom moved out and took the dishes from their wedding reg-
istry with her. Even weirder, we're sitting at the formal dining
room table, the fancy one long enough to seat twenty people.
But since it's just the three of us, we're in a small cluster at one
end.

Sloane hasn't made eye contact with me since we left the
basement.

Dad is going on about his day, how he would've been home
to greet us if it wasn't for the traffic (doubtful), and how some

higher-up at some network is pissing him off. But I'm hardly following as I run over my own mistakes in my mind.

I should've told her sooner—about the fact that dad's company is producing the new reality spin-off of *The Cove,* sure, but more importantly, how I got roped into working on it. Should've told her before she even flew out here, but I was afraid she'd cancel her trip if she knew I was going to be busy the whole time. Selfish as it was, I couldn't risk that. Couldn't imagine ruining our chance to spend the summer together, even if I'll have less free time than we originally planned.

At the very least, I *definitely* should have broken the news when I picked her up from the airport, or when we got home and she started talking about our Summer of Fun list . . . or at any point before Spencer Daniels announced it with all the finesse of someone driving a forklift under anesthesia. But from the second I saw her standing at baggage claim—waiting for the same suitcase she used to take on our combined family vacations to Florida in elementary school—it was hard to say much of anything. I was too shell-shocked by the live-and-in-person *Sloane.*

A person who is noticeably, unavoidably not *un*attractive.

So yeah, I was afraid of messing up now that we were face to face; instead of a calm "Hey, I actually have a summer job," I'd stupidly blurt out something like "Puberty, am I right?"

Dad claps a hand on my shoulder, yanking my attention back to him, but he's looking at Sloane. "So Liam failed to mention that we're working together, huh?"

Sloane gives a small, awkward smile, her eyes trained on her glass of water as she takes a sip and sets it back on the table. "He did, yeah. Kind of a big surprise."

I rub a hand over the tightness in my chest. Dad chuckles, seeming to think she means "surprise" in a fun way. I'm not so sure.

We've talked for months—*years*, really—about Sloane and Liam's Summer of Fun. The cheesy LA sightseeing. The lazy at-home movie marathons. Just being together, in person, 24-7.

And now she thinks I've traded it all for a day job.

"It's going to be a riot, isn't it, son?" Dad gives my shoulder a squeeze before picking up his beer and taking a drink. "Sloane, I think the show will be right up your alley. It's a refresh on the reality romance competitions but for the younger set, like *The Bachelor* if it ended in a guest role on *The Cove* and being the lead actor's date to the season premiere. Projections for audience reach are massive. You watch *The Cove*, right?"

Sloane nods, her eyes lighting up. No matter how blindsided she's feeling by me, the *Cove* superfan in her can't hold back her curiosity.

"So I'm told they ended the last season on a big breakup between two of the lead characters. The showrunners worry that fans are getting tired of that drama and want to get everyone excited for a new era. One of their people told one of my people, who told me, and I said, look, here's what you need: a reality dating spin-off. It's fresh, it's fun, it capitalizes on Aspen's celebrity, and engages his fans in the most hands-on way. *Genius.*"

Dad taps the side of his head before plowing on, giving more details about the premise of *Aspen Woods's Future Leading Lady* and how it'll work, a spiel I've heard at least five times by now—the casting process for "charismatic, diverse, and, of course, age-appropriate" girls, the filming schedule that's set to start in just a couple of days. He's ecstatic about his company branching out from their typical house-flipping, house-hunting, and other house-verb-ing reality content.

Thus, the show I have come to think of as *AWFLL*. Time will tell if the acronym shoe fits Aspen Woods's presumably pampered feet.

"Anyway, I'm very happy that I could get my boy to join us for this project," Dad says with another shoulder clap. This one comes as I'm swallowing another bite of the pizza I've hardly touched. I cough and barely avoid spitting it back out onto the table. That's just what I need—a regurgitated pepperoni nail in our fun summer's coffin. "Liam's never really had a chance to see what I do up close and personal, you know? It'll be good for him to get out of the house, see what an honest day's work at a real job looks like—not just playing with his Lincoln Logs up there in the attic, right? Ha!"

After hearing digs like this from him hundreds of times, I don't even feel the urge to hit back—it's a wasted effort. Instead, I sink down in my chair, giving up on the rest of the pizza slice. But I've forgotten that Sloane is not familiar with our standard dinner conversation.

"You mean his woodworking?" she asks, her forehead wrinkling in obvious confusion. I'm sending her strong *do not engage* brain waves, but they must be bouncing off the force field of a Spencer Daniels Soapbox before they can reach her.

"Sure, right," Dad says, taking the napkin from his lap and folding it on the table again as he looks to me. "You know, I'd almost rather you go into construction than try to get this custom woodcrafts thing off the ground—at least building houses is steady work. But you're too smart to waste your potential on any of that stuff, aren't you, kid? It'll be good for you to start to learn this business so you can see all the options at your fingertips if you just *try.*"

My smile is more of a grimace, but Dad doesn't seem to notice before turning his attention back to Sloane.

"What about you, Sloaney? What's on your agenda after senior year?"

I don't think I'm imagining the new tension to her posture before she answers. "Yeah, uh, I've actually been looking at screenwriting programs out here. That's what I want to study in college, and I hope to get a job writing for TV later on."

"Writing, huh? Well, I suppose that's a little more marketable than woodworking. Ha! I haven't worked with too many writers' rooms, what with the reality market, but that reminds me—a buddy of mine . . ." He trails off as he picks up his phone and starts to tap around on the screen. "I actually need to make a call for work, if you'll just . . ."

Dad mumbles this last part as he rises abruptly from his chair and walks out of the room, still staring down at his phone.

Sloane's mouth is agape as she stares after him.

"I think of it like filling out Mad Libs," I say to try to break the tension, picking idly at a bit of crust. "What was coming after 'a buddy of mine'? A verb, probably. I'm gonna go with . . . wheezed."

Sloane's expression shifts for a second to what I'd almost call a smile before her mouth snaps shut. "Oh, good—I love that I reminded your dad of his buddy who wheezed." She glances down at her plate, then back up at me. "Are you done eating?"

We clear the table of our dishes and leftover pizza in silence. After the kitchen is clean, I'm trying to decide what we can do for the rest of this awkward evening when Sloane speaks first.

"Can I see your workshop?"

It feels like an olive branch, a let's-stop-this-awkwardness signal. My shoulders relax for the first time tonight.

"Yes. Yeah, of course."

As I lead the way, I have the ridiculous urge to take her hand, an urge I obviously don't act on. We haven't been hand-holding friends since we were six or so, when someone—almost certainly the same kind of straight person who throws gender-reveal parties—called us each other's "little boyfriend and girlfriend." Until then, I don't remember being aware that Sloane was anything but my best friend.

Starting up the stairs, I find myself wondering if that's the source of all these new observations about Sloane being . . . aesthetically pleasing. I've simply internalized the knowing smirks and comments and feel like I'm supposed to find her attractive. Nothing more than that going on here. Nothing I can't snap out of.

That's the secret to overthinking everything—if you do it hard enough, sometimes you can undo the problems that your own mind created. *Genius,* I think in my dad's voice, imagining tapping the side of my head.

We walk down the upstairs hall until we reach the last door

on the right. I open it, revealing another staircase, this one small and spiral.

"Whoa," Sloane murmurs behind me when I flick on the lights. "If there's a spinning wheel with a particularly sharp-looking needle up here, I'm out."

"No spinning wheels, no needles," I answer, grinning with relief. It feels like we're returning to us. "Definitely some sharp objects—good rule of thumb to avoid those anyway."

At the top of the stairs, I open one last door and gesture for Sloane to go ahead. After letting it fall shut behind us, I lean against the door and watch as she takes in the space. I conveniently left a water bottle up here earlier, which—finding my mouth suddenly dry—I grab and take a greedy sip from.

My workshop is in one of the house's turrets. From the outside, the round, towerlike rooms that protrude from a couple of the structure's corners look almost like they're just for decoration. But each holds real useable space—space that was going unused until I asked Dad for permission to convert one of them for my woodworking projects.

It's still unfinished, the rounded outer walls a shell of wood and beams rather than drywall, the floor a bare, splintery ply-wood with a thin rug I laid down for a walkway. All the other available space is filled with my workbench, shelves holding my hand tools, my band saw, and assorted finished or in-progress projects. Sawdust stirs beneath Sloane's feet with each step she takes into the room, despite my efforts to frequently vacuum and sweep. I screw on and unscrew the cap of my water bottle a few times, feeling restless.

She runs her hands over a cuckoo clock I crafted but still haven't gotten the mechanics quite right on, a few wooden Christmas cookie cutters still waiting on their first use, a lap desk with a hinged top that opens to a storage space for paper and pens. She doesn't seem to notice the large sheet-covered pile on the floor to the side of my workbench, and I don't point it out. That work in progress isn't ready for viewing yet. I watch her eyes trace the curve of the wall up to the domed ceiling over our heads, back down to another small door to my left.

"Where does that go?"

I flip the lock and open it to reveal a narrow catwalk that runs along the roof of the house. It's accessible just from this turret room, and as far as I know I'm the only one who's ever been out there.

Sloane gasps. "Is that—can we walk on that?"

This time, I do offer her one of my hands as I step outside. As her palm slides against mine, I feel the contact like a shock through my entire arm. Okay, clearly not overthinking my escape route from the attraction thing quickly enough. I lead her about halfway out before releasing her hand and then turning to rest against the slanted roof and admire the view behind the house. Sloane copies my position a few inches from my side.

"Holy shit," she says on an exhale, and I nod at her appropriate reaction. From here, we can see over the hillside, and it feels like the whole city is spread out below us. Lights are starting to twinkle against the setting sun—perfect timing. It's glittery, colorful, beautiful, and one of the few things about this place that I really love.

"Yeah," I agree. "It's something."

I can practically hear the wheels turning in her mind. I brace myself, bringing the water bottle to my lips and taking a long drink.

"So how many of your one-and-dones have you brought up here for a romantic make-out sesh?" she asks.

The whole mouthful of water spews out like I'm a human sprinkler system. Sloane is already cackling by the time I recover. "I—wha— None! Zero. And stop calling them that! What is wrong with you?"

Still snickering, she replies, "I call 'em like I see 'em. Liam Daniels, One-Kiss Wonder."

My list of regrets in my young life is not very long. But telling Sloane that I'd had three first dates—and three kisses—in as many weeks during sophomore year? That's probably at the top.

Ever since, she's loved to tease me about my dating life, especially my tendency to end things after only a date or two. She refers to the girls—in what she has clarified many times over is a criticism of *me,* not them—as my one-and-dones.

"I've had second kisses before. And second dates," I say defensively.

"Mm-hmm." Sloane's tone reminds me that she knows just how few. "Mr. Love 'Em and Leave 'Em . . ."

"Stop."

"Mr. Pash and Dash . . ."

My brow furrows. "What is 'pash'?"

"Australian slang for kiss," she answers matter-of-factly. "Mr.—"

"All right, yep, I'm very aware." For some reason, the ribbing

28

irks me more today than it normally does. "As we've discussed many times, I just know early on whether there's a spark with someone and I'm never going to waste their or my time. Would it be better for me to drag things out for a year, trying to force a spark when it's clearly not going to happen?"

I give her a pointed look. Sloane's had a couple of long-term boyfriends, relationships that I think we all knew from the beginning weren't right for her. But she has a tendency to get comfortable with someone and convince herself she'd rather have their "meh" companionship than none at all.

Well, none but mine, from all the way across the country.

"Touché. We both have our damage."

We look out over the view in silence for a few minutes.

"It's nice," she says finally, nodding toward my workshop. "Really, really nice. I love it, actually."

"Thanks," I say, feeling my face heat. "It's mostly more guilfts, you know. All the tools and stuff. I've been accumulating them every time Mom or Dad slips me some cash with that wink-wink-nudge-nudge-I'm-the-better-parent look. It's the only way either of them is supporting this interest—without really meaning to."

I wish my short laugh didn't sound so bitter. Sloane crosses her arms over her chest.

"So what does your job on this show actually involve?"

I straighten my spine at the abrupt subject change. "Uh, yeah, so I'm a production assistant—a PA. And to be honest, I've gotten very little information past that. Dad says it's the way that anyone with an interest in TV production gets their foot in the door. Apparently I'll be doing whatever I'm told by anyone else on set—moving equipment, cleaning up messes, running errands, you name it." I shrug, palms held up to the sky. "I don't know. Trying to go in prepared for the worst so I can be relieved if people, like, don't spit on me."

"That's a high standard you've got there," Sloane answers with a laugh, but her face grows more serious then. "So, you think it'll work?"

I look to her in confusion. "Preparing for people to spit on me?"

"No, goober. You, being your dad's on-set servant boy for the summer. It's obvious you agreed to work on his new reality show to appease him."

I can't help the snark that enters my voice. "Yeah, good one, Sherlock. I want to make my dad happy. You figured it all out."

Sloane jabs my side with her elbow. "Don't sass me, Daniels. I get it. If you make it seem like you're actually giving the production thing a go, he might be more open to supporting your woodworking, knowing you've considered all your options."

That . . . is closer to the whole truth than I'd like to admit. I push a hand through my hair and release a long breath. "I know there's probably a better, more effective plan out there somewhere. Or that maybe I could have one brutally honest conversation with him and solve everything. But it's . . ."

"Complicated?"

"Yes." I sigh again. My dad's actually the reason I even got interested in making stuff. Years and years ago, before Daniels Entertainment really blew up, he was involved in their home-improvement shows in a more hands-on way. Some of my earliest memories are of going on the set with him and holding a hammer that was half my body weight, getting him to teach me how to swing it. It feels like a different lifetime. "I figure at the very least, being on set for the summer will give us more time together than we've had in years. But at the same time, he might see that his path isn't for me."

Sloane knows the plan, in essence—start selling some of my furniture and other creations online, build up a following, hope it takes off to the point that I can open up a physical storefront. But even she doesn't know the hours I've spent researching what makes a successful small business, the best online shop hosting services, what products might be the most lucrative to get sales off the ground. I try not to let Dad's comments like the Lincoln Logs thing get to me, because he doesn't even know as much as I've told Sloane. If he was aware of half the amount of work I put in up here when he thinks I'm just fooling around, well, I don't believe he'd talk about it that way. I can't let myself believe that.

Sloane turns toward me, tilting her head. "I get that," she says, taking away what feels like a hundred pounds of worry-weight from my shoulders. But then her face twists into a pout. "I just don't get why you didn't tell me as soon as you found out. Like, 'Hey, Sloane, I know we've talked constantly about all the fun we'll have this summer, but heads up that I'm gonna be working on a spin-off of our favorite show, and also you'll be spending most of the time on your own! Cool, bye!'"

I wince. "I was afraid you wouldn't come. Dad only asked me to do it a few weeks ago, and I've spent all my time since then trying to figure out things for you to do when I'm at work.

I know it was selfish, though, and stupid, and I'm sorry, Sloane. Really."

My pathetic explanation seems to crack some pieces off the hard shell she's been maintaining since discovering my apparent betrayal of Sloane and Liam's Summer of Fun. "All right, well, I'm not mad at you, Liam," she says. "You know I get the distant parent thing. It'll probably be another few days before mine even remember I left for the summer."

There's a painful pang in my chest. Sloane is the middle child of three. Franklin, three years older, is Mr. Perfect. Former homecoming king *and* class president *and* high school soccer superstar–turned–D1 college team starter. Liza, seven years younger, is a little princess—literally, as she competes in pageants across Tennessee and fills the McKinney house with crowns and sashes. In between them, Sloane has always—and wrongfully—considered herself unremarkable. Writing is her thing, a thing that she's amazing at and passionate about. But it's a quieter pastime than her siblings', and one that her parents haven't taken very seriously.

I wish she knew how good she is, how cool and talented, even if it's not always recognized by others. More than that, I wish I could shake her parents and make them give their second kid the time of day.

"I doubt that. You're highly missable, you know," I say.

"Yeah, yeah. Well, listen, I've got your back no matter what." Sloane's lips curve up in a half smile that sets off a confusing swooping feeling in my stomach. "And I hope it works—all the things you want to get out of this job. I'll find ways to stay busy—

maybe put a dent in some of my list items you seemed less thrilled about. Sneak onto *The Cove*'s set to snoop around and bug you."

"Seriously, please do," I say, putting my palms together in a pleading gesture.

After a pause, she asks, "So . . . how much did they have to pay Aspen Woods to get him to do a reality dating show?"

My laugh is tinged with relief. "Apparently, it's an image thing for him. There are enough rumors out there about him having a huge ego, being hard to work with, an overindulged child star, and Dad says it's cost him some roles. His 'people' want him to do damage control by showing that he's, like, down-to-earth. Thus, *Aspen Woods's Future Leading Lady*—or as some might be calling it for short, *AWFLL*—was born."

At the acronym, which I pronounce like "awful," Sloane doubles over laughing. I reach a hand out instinctively to grasp her by the elbow—there's a wrought-iron railing that would probably keep her from toppling off the roof in the worst-case scenario, but I'd prefer we didn't test its capabilities.

"Oh, that's amazing," she says once she's calmed down. "Are they actually using that for short? How did no one flag that in some marketing meeting?"

"*I'm* using it, at least in my head. Maybe they want to set the expectations low in a subliminal way." I release her elbow, but she surprises me by looping her arm through mine, settling back against the roof almost hip to hip with me and resting her head against my shoulder.

"I feel that," Sloane says on a sigh. "Expect awful, be pleasantly surprised if it turns out amazing. So wait—I guess we're supposed to believe Aspen and Evie are as done as Dorian and Mara, then?"

"I guess. Surely having him do this while in a relationship would be the opposite of helping his image."

She nods. "They always seemed kind of fake to me anyway. Like, way too many of their posts about each other would end with, *Don't forget to watch* The Cove *tonight at eight/seven central!* I'm not sure a reality dating show is actually gonna make him seem more authentic." She pauses, giving me a sly look. "But the going-to-the-*Cove*-premiere part of the prize would be cool. Think your dad has any strings he can pull to get me there?"

"I wouldn't hold your breath," I say through a forced smile. It's not like I've already thought about asking him the same thing as a surprise for her at the end of the summer. Definitely didn't play into my decision to work on the show and get me further in his good graces. Nope, no way.

"Come with me tomorrow?" I ask, both to change the subject and because I really want her to. "I'm nervous about the first day, and Dad seems to think it's fine for you to visit the set whenever. There are *some* benefits to being the executive producer's kid."

"Ooh, yes. Maybe I should bring my backpack so I can steal a prop or something." I laugh at the new eagerness in her voice. "I wonder how much I can get away with once you're filming. Guess we'll have to wait and see, huh?"

If that doesn't sum up everything about this summer job, I'm not sure what does.

CHAPTER THREE

You think because I have a nice house my life is perfect? Well,
it's not. My girlfriend's cheating on me, *and* I had to fish a frog
out of the infinity pool yesterday!
—*THE COVE*, SEASON 1, EPISODE 8

Sloane

I've been awake for about two hours and have yet to get my
hands on any coffee. Normally, this would have me sleepwalking
through the day and snarling at anyone who breathes in my direction. But today, the sun is out, the seagulls are squawking, and
I'm visiting the set of *The Cove*.

It's a beautiful time to be Sloane.

Sadly, that does not exactly equate to being *actually* beautiful
at the moment. Liam knocked on the guest room door at an un-
godly hour this morning and, after pointing out the drool hanging off my chin when I answered, informed me that Mr. Daniels
wanted to get an earlier start than we'd planned on. I barely had
time to shower and get dressed before we were hustled out the
door.

"*Please* let me go get you my sweatshirt from the car," Liam whispers for the third or fourth time. My hair is only a little damp by now, but he has the grandmotherly fear that I'm going to "catch a chill," which is not helped by the fact that I keep visibly shivering. In part because the AC in this massive mansion we're currently touring has to be set somewhere in the low sixties. But truthfully, I've had goose bumps since we pulled up to the cul-de-sac that houses the most iconic filming locale from my favorite TV show of all time.

We're at *The Cove*. The actual cove part of *The Cove*, where three big houses belonging to the show's three main characters sit on a cliff overlooking their own private section of beach. The seafoam-green mansion we're in right now is Chelsea's; next to it is a nearly identical house, except for its coral paint job, belonging to Dorian; and finally, a third navy blue rendition that is baseball team cocaptain Brock's. I took about a hundred pictures of the houses as soon as we stepped out of Mr. Daniels's car, including plenty of selfies that involved pulling Liam down to my level and are mostly of the two of us squinting against the bright morning sun with some blurry masses of beachy colors in the background.

"If you do, I'm not wearing it," I whisper back to him now, patting his shoulder without tearing my gaze away from the wall of artwork "painted" by Chelsea's artist dad on *The Cove*. "So don't waste your time."

"Oh, did you have a question, Sloane?" the tiny, perky producer walking ahead of us asks, turning to continue on her path backward as she smiles at Liam and me expectantly. She introduced herself as Kristi-with-a-K-and-an-I. Mr. Daniels tasked her with showing us around set while he went off to do whatever it is that the head of Daniels Entertainment does. Filming doesn't start until tomorrow, and while the set is a flurry of activity, Liam's dad seemed excited to give the two of us the chance to explore and take it all in rather than throw his son right into the deep end of PA grunt work. Thus, Kristi. It's unclear so far whether she's had coffee or if Energizer Bunny is her standard mode of operation.

"We're good, Kristi, thanks," Liam says with his sheepish smile, which seems to pack a more powerful punch each time I see it. I don't think it's intentional, this new-to-me, subtle smolder-y thing he does. I get the sense he doesn't even realize what he looks like nowadays.

"Okey dokey! Well, if you all wanna hop on up these stairs with me, we can see what's normally Chelsea's bedroom on *The Cove*. On *Future Leading Lady*, this whole floor is going to serve as bunk rooms for some of the girls," Kristi says, her long, shiny hair flipping flawlessly over her shoulder.

I turn to Liam, whispering as we follow a few steps behind her. "You're not hopping."

"Neither are you," he says, his lips flattening into an unimpressed line.

"I don't work here. I don't need to impress anyone."

To my surprise, he answers this by actually hopping up to the next step, landing with a thump that causes Kristi to glance back. I hide my laugh by coughing into my elbow.

On the second floor of the megamansion, we walk through a bright hallway into a room I recognize from the many times it's shown up on my TV screen: Chelsea's bedroom. The prop vintage movie posters and photos of Chelsea, Dorian, and their other friends still paper the walls, but instead of the queen bed that would normally take up much of the floor space, there are two sets of twin bunk beds, each mattress covered in a fluffy white duvet and bright accent pillows.

"So four lucky ladies will sleep here in Chelsea's room, at least to start out with," Kristi is saying. "There will be twenty-five girls in episode one—half will stay here and half in Brock's house. Aspen will be living in Dorian's house, right in the middle! *So* fun, right? Now if we continue on through this door, there's another bedroom. . . ."

Liam and I follow her wordlessly, both of us taking it all in. The next room is one I don't recognize from the show, but there are two single beds in here, and two more in the next connected bedroom we walk through. Each room is bordered on one side by large windows that look out over the incredible ocean view.

"So does *The Cove* own these houses? Or are there normally, like, people living in them when the show isn't filming?" I ask as we step out onto an upstairs balcony. This is some seriously prime real estate, the kind I imagine costs a fortune. Like, a several-million-dollars-plus-the-promise-of-Aspen-Woods's-future-firstborn-child kind of fortune.

"The show owns them, actually," Kristi says with a touch of pride in her voice, and I remember that Mr. Daniels told us she's a producer on *The Cove,* too. "That's not very common for shows like ours. A lot of times, the exterior shots for characters' homes are filmed at private residences, and all the interiors are built on a soundstage. I think it gives our set a much more authentic feel, both for the actors filming and for viewers watching. You know?"

I nod, leaning against the balcony railing and letting the salty sea breeze caress my face. Liam stands beside me. Overhead, a few birds twitter as they circle down to land on the sand below us.

"Do you ever think about how birds can go literally anywhere," I say, just for Liam's ears. "And some, like those smart ones, come to beautiful places like the freaking *Cove,* but others choose to hang out in, like, fast food chain parking lots?"

"You could've given me a hundred guesses as to what you were thinking about just now. . . ." Liam murmurs, shaking his head. "No, I haven't thought about it. But birds are allowed to love a good dollar menu as much as the rest of us."

"Fair," I concede. "But seriously, this is somehow even prettier in person than they make it look on-screen. If I was a bird, I'd never go anywhere else. The girls who get to live here don't know what they're in for. Almost makes me wish I was one of them." At Liam's pained laugh, I add with a wink, "Almost."

"Should we continue?" Kristi pipes up from behind us. Her tone implies she's framing it as a question only to be polite.

As Liam and I follow her into the house, back downstairs and through the luxurious living space, my mind has totally wandered. What *would* it be like to live here and take part in this reality show situation? I've never been too impressed by Aspen Woods, aside from his role as Dorian. He gives off the vibes of someone who knows he's hot, and knows you know it, too. Even in interviews where you can tell he's been trained with canned answers to promote various projects, he manages to make it all about promoting himself. It's hard to imagine how his relationship with Evie ever worked for so long. But maybe she's just as self-absorbed, and it balanced everything out in some weird, mutually apathetic way.

Still, living on this set sounds so beyond cool that it might almost be worth all the faux-mance stuff.

Again—*almost.*

Kristi leads us out to the backyard, which is really a series of tiered patios leading down to the beach. The uppermost patio has a pool and swim-up bar, there's a putting green on the next tier down, and on the lowest are several dining tables of varying sizes with tons of seating.

"The saltwater pool is heated, so it's perfect for swimming day or night. At all our season wrap parties so far, at least half the cast has ended the night by jumping in fully clothed," Kristi says with a laugh that sounds like it could come from a Disney princess. "This place has a lot of memories. Now, if we want to continue on to—ope, just a second."

She puts a hand to the headset she's wearing and listens intently. Liam and I look to each other with mutual patiently-awaiting-further-instructions faces.

"Ten-four, I'll be right there," Kristi says, then gives us an apologetic smile. "I actually need to stop by the production tent out front before we continue the tour. Why don't you all follow me, and I'm sure we'll be back on track in a sec!"

She turns and bounce-walks off at a brisker pace than before.

"What do we think's going on?" I whisper to Liam as we follow.

"I don't know—rushing home to make lunch for seven little old men before they return from the mines?" he deadpans.

"Really? I think she's more of a Rapunzel than a Snow White. Big I've-been-trapped-in-a-tower-and-never-learned-how-cruel-the-real-world-could-be energy."

Disney movies were the first media love that Liam and I shared as kids, and we still get passionate talking about them. Still think I'll keep my Hot Simba observation to myself, though.

"I guess," Hot Simba answers with a shrug. "But she would definitely sing while doing chores."

"Rapunzel does that too!" My voice is nearly a shout, and I feel my cheeks redden as I lower it. "That's, like, all she *can* do in the tower. There's a whole song about it."

Liam's lips quirk up on one side as he opens his mouth to respond, but before he can—and before I can examine the weird thump I feel in my chest at that half smile—we hear a voice that sounds a lot like Mr. Daniels's yelling, "Well, what the hell are we supposed to do with that?"

Liam's wide eyes meet my own. We pick up our pace behind a now-jogging Kristi and follow her to the big white tent in front of Dorian's house. Once there, we see his dad standing with a circle of other business casual–clad men who I assume are producers or otherwise important industry folk. Kristi has joined a group in matching headsets and harried expressions who are tapping furiously on laptop keyboards or talking on their phones. In the middle of the commotion, Mr. Daniels has one hand shoved into his hair and the other waving emphatically as he talks in hushed but still intense tones.

We approach with caution.

"What's the issue if we go forward with twenty-four?" another middle-aged white guy asks.

Mr. Daniels scoffs. "The issue is that all of our advertisements say twenty-five contestants, we've prepared everything for twenty-five contestants, and we will *not* be made to look like a bunch of idiots who can't count because *your people* dropped the ball. Fix it."

With that, he turns and stalks off to the other side of the driveway, staring down at his phone as if it's just pointed out his receding hairline.

Liam looks on with a grimace. "Maybe I should, ah . . ."

He gestures toward his dad. Even though I'm not entirely sure that he should, actually, I give him an encouraging nod. Who am I to get in the way of possible father-son bonding, I guess? He jogs over to Mr. Daniels, and as they start to talk I trail after him. No one seems to notice I'm here, and I feel suddenly, hopelessly awkward.

Deciding I belong closer to where Liam is than not, I start toward him slowly. When I'm a few steps away, Mr. Daniels abruptly picks up a phone call and Liam turns to me.

"What's going on?" I whisper.

Liam's face appears stuck in grimace mode now. "They're short a contestant somehow. The casting team made some changes to the list in the past couple weeks and somehow ended up with one less girl than they planned on. Which they only realized"—he checks the watch on his wrist—"twenty-eight hours before filming is supposed to start."

Oh my God.

"Yeah," Liam says, and I realize I spoke aloud.

Mr. Daniels hangs up the phone and starts pacing in a circle, pulling at his hair again. It's becoming clear how his forehead has gained so much real estate.

"I swear, these people are some of the most incompetent I've ever worked with," he rants to himself. "They say they want a reality show, but they cut me off at the knees at every turn. Twenty-four contestants! How the hell did they screw that up? And how the hell am I supposed to fix it? It's not like there are tons of teenage girls sitting around who can drop everything on a dime to come to LA for a month—not with parental permission and all the paperwork and shit, it's taken months of applications and vetting for everyone, and now—"

He cuts off midsentence at the sound of a fart. Or rather, at the sound of my flip-flops making one of those embarrassing squeak-farting noises when I shift my weight from foot to foot. Mr. Daniels's gaze lands on me for the first time in all this chaos, and my cheeks flush.

"That wasn't me," I blurt out, sounding very much like someone guilty of squeak-farting. "I mean, it was, but it wasn't. It was my shoes. Rubber, you know? What are ya gonna do?"

I shrug and put my hands out in a gesture that I hope signals Benign Weirdo as opposed to Guilty Gas Passer. Peripherally, I see Liam close his eyes and rub at the bridge of his nose, definitely signaling Not Responsible for This Dumbass.

But Mr. Daniels doesn't even seem to register what I'm saying, or get concerned about my bodily functions. Instead, he's looking at me with a glazed expression.

"Sloane," he murmurs softly, as if in a trance.

"Y-yes?" I stammer.

He continues in a stronger voice, "We might have a solution."

. . . *Might we?*

Again, I must say this aloud without meaning to, because Mr. Daniels nods emphatically. "Yes. Absolutely. This could be perfect."

"What could?" I ask at the same time Liam says in a wary voice, "Dad . . ."

But the man doesn't look at his son. "You could do it, couldn't you, Sloaney? You could be our twenty-fifth girl."

I make a noise that's something like *buuuhhhh,* offering a compelling case for what a graceful, poised addition I would be to his show. Because I think that's what he's suggesting. That I compete on his mother-effing dating show starring Aspen Woods.

"You're already here for the summer. And since Liam and I will be busy on set, what else are you going to be doing, right? It's perfect. Your parents would agree to it if I talked to them today. And honestly, this . . . this could be a big coup for me."

I tilt my head at him like a nervous puppy. "A coup? For you?"

Has the Cat in the Hat entered the scene? I almost let out a delirious laugh but swallow it.

"Yes—see, like I said, *The Cove*'s team has done all the other casting. And to be honest with you, I don't trust them, especially not with this mix-up." He paces in front of us again, eyes darting around the driveway. "But you—I know you'd be a great contestant, Sloane. I wouldn't have to worry about you causing any sort of mess for me. It would really help my peace of mind to know there's at least one good girl in this group."

I shake my head, trying to follow this runaway train of thought. "And that . . . that good girl is me? You want me to be the twenty-fifth contestant?"

"Dad," Liam says again, more strength behind it this time. "This is ridiculous. Sloane has no interest in doing that."

Don't I? I mean, I don't think I do. Or I didn't before visiting set. But I *have* been thinking all day about how cool it would be to live here, get a glimpse of what the experience of filming *The Cove* is like—even if I don't really want to date Aspen Woods. But this is a lot to process all at once.

"I . . . I don't know if I can do that," I say meekly.

Mr. Daniels steps closer and lays a hand on my shoulder. "You could absolutely do it, Sloaney. You're sharp, you're personable, you've got a good head on your shoulders. You'd give viewers someone solid to root for, even if the rest of casting's picks are duds. Oh, and of course I imagine you'll be a hit with Aspen."

He gives me a meaningful look with that last part, and I cringe.

"I don't think I want to be a hit with Aspen, though. I mean, I don't want to date him. So I'd be, like, faking." I'm grasping at straws to explain why I can't, shouldn't, won't agree to this. But it feels almost like fighting the inevitable already.

Mr. Daniels gives me a smile that straddles the line between caring and patronizing. "Welcome to reality TV, sweetheart. But you never know what could happen, how you might feel once you're in it. And regardless, you're there for a bigger purpose. You'd be really helping me out, being my handpicked competitor. I'd owe you big." Something else seems to occur to him then, as he snaps his fingers. "You know what, I can help you out too."

"Help me?" Guess I'm back to dumbly parroting him.

"I happen to know the dean of the Los Angeles Film Academy. You heard of them? Great screenwriting program. If you do this for me, I'll have him over for dinner with us once we've wrapped this season, before you leave at the end of summer. That's more or less a guaranteed admission for you next year. And I have some other contacts in the TV writing space who we could talk to about job shadowing, mentoring, you name it. All of that, if you'd be the twenty-fifth contestant and do your best to stick around awhile. Let's say . . . if you make it to the top four. How does that sound?"

I gape at him. I'm already starry-eyed just thinking about the list of opportunities Mr. Daniels rattled off. But surely he could pull these strings for me whether I do the show for him or not—whether I somehow make it to the *top four* or not. Right? The fact that he's not offering to pull them regardless makes me feel . . . weird.

My gaze snags on Dorian's house behind us, Chelsea's and Brock's on either side of it. It's the closest I'll ever get to being in *The Cove* in real life. And all I have to do is flirt with an admittedly superhot actor until I get to the final four, then I can dip out. That couldn't be so difficult, could it? It's not like I'd be losing out on much—Sloane and Liam's Summer of Fun list has already gone through the metaphorical paper shredder. I'll get to spend more time with Liam than I would if I wasn't on set. And at the end, I get a major kick start to all my dreams coming true.

What's the worst that could happen?

"Dad," Liam says, basically pleading. "I'll help you find someone else. I'm sure there's a girl from my school or something who could—"

"I'll do it," I say, turning back to them.

"You'll do it?" Mr. Daniels's face lights up.

"You'll what?" Liam sputters at the same time.

"Yeah. I'll be your twenty-fifth girl, and do my best to stay till the final four," I say, crossing my arms over my chest and trying to look like Someone Who Is Not Completely Winging It. "But you'll have to talk to my parents, like you said. And if they agree, get me the paperwork or whatever."

Mr. Daniels beams at me, and I wish it didn't warm up all my insides. I've always loved him like a second dad, but I can't decide how much I like him right now.

"You've got yourself a deal," he says, extending a hand to me. I shake it, watching Liam walk a slow circle in my periphery, his hands on his hips as he looks up at the sky. "I'll go tell the crew and start making calls. Stay close by."

"Sloane, you don't have to do this," Liam says, pinning me with a worried look as his dad heads back to the tent. "Dad is just freaking out right now, but when he settles down, I'm sure he'll see it's a stupid idea and—"

"Why stupid?" I cut in, surprised at how defensive I feel.

"You think I'll embarrass myself or something? Aspen won't be into me and I'll get my fragile heart broken?"

An exasperated breath puffs out of him. "Of course not. I'm sure you'll do great, and I don't see how he couldn't be into you. But I'm sure there's another way to make those writing connections happen. You don't need this 'handpicked competitor' thing to get you there."

He pushes a hand through his hair. Unlike with Mr. Daniels, it leaves his sticking up in a cute, messy way rather than contributing to a fivehead. I reach out and wrap my fingers around his, giving them a quick squeeze.

"Liam, it's fine. I think . . . I think I want to do this, honestly. It'll be an adventure. Living on set will be cool. I'll get more time around you while we're both here. And it'll require, what, a few minutes per episode of pretending to be impressed by a narcissistic child star whose name sounds like an air freshener? It may not be the start of the world's greatest love story, but it also won't kill me. Probably."

I add a wink at the last part, but Liam isn't looking at me. His gaze has shifted just over my shoulder, and he seems to have gone a shade paler.

Then it's a new voice that responds from behind me, one I've heard only through my TV screen for hundreds of hours before, and suddenly Liam's reaction makes much more sense.

"Well, you'll never know till you try, will you?"

CHAPTER FOUR

Style and class aren't everything, Chelsea, but you could
maybe try to act like they're something*.*
—*THE COVE*, SEASON 3, EPISODE 1

Liam

I don't know if I've ever cringed this hard.

It's like I saw it happening in slow motion—Aspen Woods climbing out of an SUV that just pulled up the drive behind Sloane, taking off his dark sunglasses and then tucking them into his shirt collar as he walked toward the production tent. Sloane rambling on in the way she does when she's freaked out by something but doesn't want to show it. Aspen, approaching from behind, then stopping as he hears Sloane say his name.

And the rest is history.

When she hears Aspen's voice, her shoulders jump up to her ears and she squeezes her eyes shut. She obviously knows she's just insulted the guy whose affections she's apparently supposed to be competing for in a little over twenty-four hours. As unfamiliar as the social norms of a reality dating show are to me, I can't imagine this would be considered a good first impression.

Sloane turns around slowly, arms crossed in a way that suggests she's self-consciously trying to cover up her "May the Forest Be With You" T-shirt from the Great Smoky Mountains National Park. She looks the actor up and down, and, inexplicably anxious all of a sudden, I do the same. His hair is dark brown and stylishly messy in a way that mine only gets when a barber puts a pound of gooey substances in it. His tan skin makes his blue eyes look almost cartoonishly bright. I recognize a good-looking guy when I see one, and, no matter what Sloane has said about him before, I know she does, too.

It occurs to me that maybe my duty as the best friend here is to throw out a life raft from the sinking ship of this introduction.

"Hey, uh, you must be Aspen," I say as I step around Sloane and extend my hand. "Liam Daniels. I'll be a PA on, uh—your show."

Barely stopped myself from calling it *AWFLL. Barely.*

Aspen raises an eyebrow as he shakes my hand. "Daniels? You wouldn't be related to . . ."

"Yeah, Spencer is my dad," I offer, almost embarrassed by the nepotism I never asked for, but the other guy's attention has already moved on.

He takes a lazy step closer to Sloane, eyes twinkling. "Hi," he says with a distinctly raspy quality that his voice didn't have when talking to me all of two seconds ago. "I'm Aspen. And you are?"

It's a struggle not to roll my eyes.

"Sloane," she says with surprising softness, shaking the hand he's now offered to her.

"So," he says, lips turning up as he holds her gaze a few seconds too long for my comfort. "Narcissistic child star, huh?"

Sloane grimaces. "I didn't mean—"

"No, no," he cuts her off with a laugh that feels practiced. "Don't sugarcoat anything for me, please. I love a good challenge. I'll do my best to surpass your expectations, Sloane, if you'll give me that chance?"

I watch a series of emotions play across Sloane's face as she tries to come up with an answer to that, before she settles on a hesitant "Sure."

"Good." Aspen smirks, turning on his heel to continue toward the production tent. "Guess I'll be seeing you both tomorrow then. Looking forward to it."

Sloane's shoulders descend to normal human level again while she watches him walk away. Her mouth falls open and slowly makes its way through a series of shapes, as if she's forming all the words she wishes she'd said.

It's starting to freak me out a little.

I clear my throat, trying to snap her out of it, and it works; her eyes dart to me and she clamps her mouth shut.

"Hey, that could've gone worse," I offer less than helpfully, but it's all I've got at the moment.

Sloane laughs, but it comes out sounding more like a wheeze. "Uh, how exactly?"

She drops her arms from their crossed position, which draws my attention back to her shirt, and I have to bite down on my lower lip to keep a laugh from bubbling up. Okay, ways her introduction to Aspen Woods could have been worse. I can do this.

"You could've said that it *would* kill you to date him?" She narrows her eyes at me, and I hurry to find something more helpful to add. "Uh, or you could've tried to impress him by doing a front flip and given yourself a black eye?"

A real thing that happened at Jesse Garnett's birthday party at the gymnastics gym in fourth grade. Sloane had a crush on Jesse; Jesse was good at gymnastics; Sloane was not. But, with all the confidence of a ten-year-old, she was like, *How hard could it be to do a front flip off the trampoline into the foam pit?* Bam. Knee to the face and a self-inflicted shiner, just in time for school picture day.

Her laugh sounds more genuine this time. "Wow, thanks. That's like punching my arm to make me forget I stubbed my toe. You're great at this." She bumps her shoulder to mine playfully, then sighs. "Well, who knows? Maybe my parents will tell your dad no, and then it'll be over before it begins. I'll become just another weird, non-famous-person encounter in Aspen Woods's distant memory."

&

Sloane's parents do not withhold permission. Ten minutes later, we've followed my dad into a trailer set up in the cul-de-sac, its walls lined with tables, chairs, and computer monitors that are currently blank but that Dad explains will eventually show all the live camera feeds. He calls it the "control room." Inside, he eagerly passes over a stack of forms with both Mr. and Mrs. McKinney's electronic signatures printed on all the designated lines. It has to be a new land-speed record for people signing their daughter's life away.

"Just like that?" Sloane says, the corners of her mouth tilting down as she eyes all the environmentally unfriendly forms.

"Just like that!" Dad says, snapping his fingers and looking gleeful. "You've got some easygoing folks, kid."

He goes on to explain the paperwork and point out all the places where Sloane will need to add her signature to the contracts. I'm distracted, though, watching her process her feelings in real time. She thinks she keeps them contained so well, but Sloane is easy for me to read. Even knowing how little concern her parents usually show for her, she has to be surprised at how readily they agreed to let her do the show. There's hurt in her expression, maybe a little irritation. She's definitely overwhelmed at Dad's information dump, too.

"Now, forgive me if this is too presumptuous," he's saying, and that's when I step closer to Sloane's side. I can only imagine how he's going to finish that thought. "But it seems likely that when you were packing for this summer, you probably didn't plan for the kind of wardrobe we recommended contestants bring with them. You'll see the list on this page here—you might be missing, say, evening wear?"

I relax a little. That's innocent enough.

Sloane considers the list with a bemused expression. "I'm not sure that I own any evening wear."

Dad nods. "Right, sure. Well, the first night is semiformal, as are most of the Casting Calls—the ceremonies at the end of each episode where Aspen announces who he's keeping and sending home—and possibly some of the dates you might go on, so most of the girls will have packed accordingly. We've also recommended various types of footwear, activewear, and well, you can read through it all there. Seeing as you've stepped up to help me out, I'd be happy to treat you to whatever you might need for filming. You and Liam can take his credit card this afternoon and hit some shops—how does that sound?"

Sounds like one of the last ways either of us would want to spend our time, up there with dentist appointments and watching one of Liza's pageants. "Oh, uh," I stammer. "I don't know if I'm, er, the best one to—to do that with. . . ."

Dad shrugs, considering. "I suppose I could send Kristi with Sloane instead."

He steps back and starts tapping on his phone, presumably to summon our tour guide from earlier. Sloane gives my arm a swift yank, pulling me in to her side.

"Liam Daniels, if you abandon me to that overeager human Furby, I swear to Darwin or whoever you believe in, I will deliver retribution," she whispers through gritted teeth. Her eyes promise said retribution will be painful. Definitely more so than spending the afternoon with her, even if shopping is involved.

I clear my throat to reclaim Dad's attention. "Actually, you know what, Dad? It's fine. I'll go with Sloane. It'll be, uh, fun."

༄

Which is how we end up in the cramped dressing room in a boutique recommended by the human Furby herself a couple hours later. I'm trying to get comfortable in a chair clearly not meant for actual sitting, having just watched Sloane disappear behind a curtain with her arms full of clothes. In the spirit of two birds, one stone, we've brought the show paperwork with us to go over while she shops. I pull the hefty stack from the manila folder in my hands, ready to start skimming for important information, but her voice stops me first.

"So it seems like my parents agreed to this way too easily, right?" she says, and it occurs to me that the curtain between us is not actually much of a barrier at all. Of course we can carry on a conversation like normal. This is confirmed when I hear the slide of a zipper as clearly as if she's right next to me.

For some reason, the sound makes my cheeks heat up. I want to smack myself, because this is not the physiological response we have to the thought of our best friend undressing nearby, dumbass. Actually, we don't think about our best friend undressing at all. God, what is happening?

"Uh, yeah," I say, shaking my head to stop those thoughts before they have a chance to go any further. "I mean, it must have been a pretty quick phone call."

I always feel like I'm hedging when the subject of Sloane's parents comes up. Because if I really spoke my mind, all I would ever do is tell her how much they suck. How she deserves better, more attentive people who recognize what an awesome middle kid they have. But you can't just say that about someone else's family.

"Like, they haven't even tried to text me. I keep checking, thinking surely I've missed it. But nothing—they signed on the dotted line without even talking to me."

"Are you not sure you want to do it?" I ask with more hope in my voice than I'd like to convey.

"No, I am, but like, it's the principle. Imagine if it was Franklin in this same position. They'd have some long, involved talks about the effects on his future, if he'd be missing anything for school, how it would look to potential employers. Or if Liza was tapped for some *Toddlers and Tiaras*–type cameo, there would be clapping and cheering because their baby is gonna be a star. But with me . . . nothing?"

She steps out from behind the curtain then, causing my eyebrows to shoot upward. I didn't know she'd be showing me the stuff she tried on, for one thing, but also she looks . . . well, really good in the strapless emerald-green dress. It's simple, just the solid color and all straight, clean lines, but . . . yeah, good.

"What do you think?" Sloane does a goofy, exaggerated twirl, almost plowing down a mannequin in the process.

"It's . . . a good color. I like it," I offer, trying to judge on the spot what my script is supposed to be in this scenario. I don't think we've shopped together since our Toys "R" Us days.

She looks down, smoothing the fabric with her hands. "Right? I do, too. Thank God, I don't want either of us to have to do this longer than necessary." As she heads back behind the curtain, she says, "Not that I'm not grateful to your dad for doing this! It's super nice of him. Honestly, enough about my parents, right? Mr. Daniels is the real one right now. He's here looking out for me."

I'm thankful she can't see my grimace. My dad isn't exactly Parent of the Year material, either, and I don't want Sloane to pin too many hopes on him for the summer. I know how he gets once he's in "production mode," and it isn't all take-Liam's-credit-card shopping sprees.

"Okay, what's next in that stack?" Sloane asks. "I think I left off at the page about communication."

I look back to the papers, running my finger down the one on top to find our place again. It's a variation on a nondisclosure agreement, with lots of details specific to the show and the ways Sloane will be cut off from the outside world during and after filming.

"You read the part about cell phones, right?"

"Mmphrmm" comes a reply muffled by what sounds like fabric entrapping her. I'm about to ask if she's okay or if she needs—actually, I don't even know what—when she continues more clearly. "How we'll turn them in to production when we arrive and are not to touch a cellular device for the duration of filming under penalty of death, et cetera."

I smirk at that. "Mostly right. I don't see anything about death in here."

"Reading between the lines, Liam. Oh shit, this is a romper! That's why I couldn't figure out which holes go where," she says as fabric swishes on the other side of the curtain.

"Is that a bad thing?"

"No, it's great! Well, mostly. They're comfy, because they're like shorts-slash-pants connected to a top. But less comfy when you have to get completely naked every time you use the bathroom."

My brain short-circuits. She keeps going. "Unfortunately, this romper also appears to have been made for some sort of woodland sprite. There's a wedgie situation that I don't need in my life. Continue, please."

Shaking my head as if to clear the Etch A Sketch of mental

images I never wanted to be confronted with, I return to the task at hand. "Okay, so there *is* a house landline that you can use for calls home, which have to take place with a producer in the room. You can't discuss your relationship with the Lead"—this is really how they refer to Aspen in all the paperwork—"during those calls and production reserves the right to take away phone privileges if you do so."

Sloane emerges again in a swishy, soft-blue dress and settles her hands on her hips. Despite the disgruntled expression on her face, I can't help but notice that the color makes her eyes a more vivid blue-green than I've ever seen them.

"Supervised calls on a landline? What are we, inmates?"

I swallow a sudden, confusing lump in my throat. "I'd, uh, avoid making that comparison around anyone but me."

"So do we think this means I can't take my laptop, even if I pinky promise not to use the internet at all? I'm getting Microsoft Word separation anxiety already."

I'm grateful for the excuse to look back down at the paperwork. "No laptops or tablets. Guess you'll have to write the old-fashioned way."

"Fine, fine. I'll be a good little glamorous mansion captive. Here, lemme sign that one." She chuckles as she leans down and takes the pen clipped onto the folder, then uses my lap as a desk to scrawl her name on the designated line. A sweet scent, I think it's vanilla, wafts around me from where her hair falls near my face. I detected the same thing when I hugged her at the airport yesterday, and like yesterday, I wouldn't mind if it lingered. If *she* lingered, I guess. But she straightens back up, taking the scent away with her as she holds her arms out at her sides. "What do we think of this one?"

"You look—" I start, and my voice comes out almost croaky. I swallow again, feeling strangely disoriented as my eyes dart from the dress to Sloane's face and back. "Cool."

She snorts, arms flopping down in a deflated posture. "Cool? What is that, a step above looking 'neato'?"

I pretend to kick her shins as she turns to step back behind the curtain. "I tried to tell you I wasn't gonna be good at this."

I'm even worse at it than I thought I was going to be. She shows me a few more dresses, shoes, shirt-and-shorts ensembles, and honestly, they all look good to me. I'm trying to offer any feedback I can think of that's more constructive than "It's nice," commenting on the ones with colors I think look good, or the flowy sleeves on this one dress that seem like they'd be comfortable and Sloane says would surely get "pit stains from stress sweat."

Weirdly enough, I feel myself starting to sweat as time passes, whether from the store being too warm or the pressure of helping Sloane decide what to buy, I can't tell. What I *do* know is that I've never spent so much time staring straight at Sloane and evaluating how she looks, well, ever.

It's strange.

So I try to focus most of my energy on getting through this paperwork. I read off the rest of the guidelines for what Sloane can and can't tell people (nothing and everything, respectively) during and after filming, then help her fill out some of the "About Me" information.

Eventually, she announces that she's on the last outfit she

picked to try on. I'm finishing a sentence she dictated to me about the superpower she would choose if she could have any—mind reading—so I don't look up at first as she comes out from the changing area.

When I finally do, about to put the period at the end of the sentence, my pen skids off the page, leaving a wild slash mark behind. The dress Sloane is wearing is the least Sloane-like thing I've ever seen her in. It's all tight black lace and a plunging neckline that puts a lot of normally-covered skin on display, the hem hitting high up on her thighs. I feel like I shouldn't be seeing her in this, then I feel like a creep for even noticing all the newly exposed parts of my friend who happens to be a girl, but *geez*. My brain has turned to mush while the rest of my physical self is a live wire, my eyes darting around in search of a safe place to settle.

I catch her eyes, and she looks nervous but also a touch confused, like she's seeing too much in my so-far-speechless reaction. She runs her hands from her stomach to hips and back in a self-conscious gesture. I let my gaze land at the top of her head. That's good. Nothing untoward here.

"Wow," I say for the first time since we got here, unable to think of a more fitting word. "You look . . . that is . . ."

"Boobular?" Sloane offers, and my eyes snap back down to meet her mischievous look. I can feel my face going up in flames.

"Wha— No, I mean—what's wrong with you!" I sputter for the second time in as many days, and she cackles. "I was going to say . . . sophisticated? And, um, pretty."

"Pretty boobular," she mutters. But she also ducks her head, and I see the color starting to stain her cheeks, too. "Thanks," she says as she returns behind the curtain.

I run my hands down my face, not sure why my hormones had to choose this week to start seeing Sloane as an objectively attractive member of the girl species. I wonder if that scrap of fabric that calls itself a dress is making it to the Yes pile. I kind of hope not. Then I feel like an ass, because who am I to hope for anything like that? Sloane can wear whatever she wants, decide on her own what she wants to show the world.

Yet there's still a voice in my head that has, for whatever reason, latched on to one specific thought—that I don't want Aspen Woods to see her in it.

About ten minutes later, we walk out with two full shopping bags of what we've started calling Sloane's TV Wardrobe, after I reassure her a good three times throughout checkout that this is not too much to get on Dad's dime. I know the old man will barely glance at the bill.

We pick up burgers and fries on the way back to the house and, finding that Dad isn't home yet, have a casual dinner poolside. Afterward, Sloane announces her plans to head up to her room and start packing.

"Not that I ever really *un*packed, but I need to shift some things around, figure out what I'm leaving here to make room for the new stuff in my suitcases. Then I might try calling Mom to see if she remembers she has a third child, then hit the hay early. So I guess . . . I should say goodnight here?" She pulls her bottom lip between her teeth.

I nod. "Sounds good. Let me know if you need anything else?"

"Of course," she answers with a small grin that sends a wave of warmth through me.

"I mean it. Not just tonight, but once you're on the show, too. I'll be around a lot, at least as much as Dad, but you can always come to me first. Okay?" I reach over and squeeze her knee, where it sits facing mine on the neighboring pool lounger. "I've got you."

"I know you do," she says softly. And if she doesn't know anything else about this bizarre situation, I hope she knows that's true.

After Dad gets home and I hand off Sloane's finished, signed paperwork, I head up to my workshop. There's too much anxious energy coursing through me to go to sleep anytime soon. I pull the sheet off my work-in-progress pile with care, as if I'm not about to make all kinds of other noise and mess up here. But this is probably the most special project I've worked on to date, and every part of it feels fragile right now.

I clamp the spindly piece of oak I've been working with into the vise on my workbench and flick on the lamp over my head. As I pick up the gouge and set to work carving, I'm ready to feel like I can fully exhale for the first time all day. Woodworking always does that for me. Whether the work is messy and strenuous or focused and tedious, my mind clears of everything but the feel of the tools in my hand and the wood on the bench. It feels like my own kind of magic, taking this material that grew out of the ground and shaping it into something practical or beautiful.

But today, that magic isn't working quite the same as it normally does. Even as I find my rhythm with the oak leg, my mind is spinning. It's not like I wanted Sloane to sit around at home while I was doing *AWFLL,* leaving herself available to hang out whenever I was done working or had a day off. But also . . . I guess I kind of *did* want that, as unfair as that sounds. The fact that she's going to be a *contestant* is something I hadn't even remotely considered, and it's thrown me. Add that to the things I kept noticing, the ways I was rattled throughout our little shopping trip, and, well, my quiet, contained world feels like it's starting to get knocked off its axis.

Eventually, feeling only marginally more settled than when I got started, I put my tools away, cover the project back up with its sheet, and close up the workshop for the night.

Hopefully it'll all be worth it for us both, Sloane and me. And by a month from now, our weird adventure in the reality show world will be over. We can spend all the time we want together for the rest of her trip, do everything we want or nothing at all. Reconnect face to face.

A few weeks. One little reality show. That's all this will be, in the end. What's the worst that could happen?

CHAPTER FIVE

*It's always alllll about Dorian. As if his life is a movie and he's
the star, while we're the extras they hired off the street.
But we don't even get paid!*

—*THE COVE,* SEASON 2, EPISODE 12

Sloane

The air is thick with hair spray and anticipation.

I'm standing behind an artfully sculpted hedge with Kristi, who they've assigned to shepherd me around tonight. We're currently waiting to get the go-ahead for me to make my entrance and meet Aspen for the first time on camera. They have him standing by the front door of the mansion that is Dorian's house on *The Cove,* and each of us girls is tucked away with a producer or PA in varying spots surrounding the house. One at a time in an order determined by production, we're supposed to walk out from our little hidey-holes and approach our target—I mean, boy. Suitor. Person.

But honestly, he has to feel a bit like he's under attack. Finely dressed girls popping up from all sides, Whac-A-Mole style, with no warning as to where to look next.

Thinking about what a mind-eff this must be for Aspen somehow makes me less nervous. And you know what? It's probably good for him to get a taste of the complete chaos of this experience from the girls' side. I hope he *is* a little overwhelmed so we're on equal footing.

I give the area I can see from here another quick scan but still see no sign of Liam. Is he hidden away somewhere being someone else's Kristi right now, hyping another girl up about how great she looks and how well she's going to do? The thought of him trying to compliment a stranger when he could scarcely tell me I looked "cool" yesterday makes me laugh.

I chose the blue dress for tonight from my boutique haul—no need to put all the goods on display from the get-go with Ms. Black and Lacy. I'm not sure I'll ever feel the confidence to bust that one out, though I did pack it, just in case. I feel surprisingly confident in tonight's ensemble, even teetering on the wedges I haven't worn since homecoming last year and only packed on a whim with all my casual, beachy clothes. I have on more makeup than I've ever worn, after I was warned yesterday that the lighting and cameras would wash me out if I didn't lay the makeup on thick. This makes me wonder if they've put Aspen in makeup, too. I sort of hope so. Anything to take his attractiveness to a less startling level.

"All right, you're almost up!!!" Kristi says, and I swear I can hear all three exclamation points she puts at the end. She double-checks the mic pack strapped to my back, under my dress, to make sure it's secure. Then she steps in front of me and starts fiddling with my hair without asking permission, twisting and adjusting the shoulder-length brown curls to her liking. Her face doesn't budge from its perma-smile, which is somewhat scary this close up.

When I guess I look satisfactory to her, she steps back and claps her hands together. "Gorgeous! Teeth check?"

I smile, but it probably comes across as more of a confused grimace. I *did* have a burrito a couple hours ago. And now I'm wishing I had a mint, dammit. Not that I'm trying to get frisky tonight, but I don't need to bombard anyone with my cilantro breath.

I feel the stress sweats starting in my armpits. Thank goodness I didn't go with sleeves.

"Perfect!" Kristi beams, and somewhere my dentist feels a rush of pride for no detectable reason. There's a crackling in the radio clipped to Kristi's hip, and she puts a finger to her earpiece, listening intently to whoever's on the other end.

"Got it," she says in the most serious tone I've heard her use yet, then she puts her hands on my shoulders and pushes me gently around the hedge.

"Off you go!" she whisper-cheers.

Turning the corner, I see Aspen for the first time tonight, standing between a pair of fancy topiaries at the house's entrance. He wears a black blazer open to reveal an oxford shirt with the top few buttons undone and skinny gray pants hugging his legs. On his feet are high-top sneakers so shiny they have to be brand-new. I couldn't begin to guess what designer names are getting all this screen time, but he looks expensive.

He hears my heels on the driveway, clomping more than

clicking, and turns in my direction, his face breaking out in a knowing, smirky smile. It makes me blush. I look down, both to avoid his gaze and to focus on not tripping, but whenever I think too much about walking, it's like my feet forget how to be feet. So I trip, just barely. But it's enough that he notices and starts to step forward as if he could catch me from twenty feet away. Fortunately, I recover and walk the rest of the way as proudly as a person can when they've almost bitten the dust during their first ten seconds on camera.

"Hey, beautiful," Aspen says when I'm standing in front of him.

Before I can school my features into a more normal reaction, a small laugh slips out. That wasn't the greeting I was expecting, and yet it so perfectly fits his vibe that I can't help myself.

"Hi," I say, sticking out my hand for an obligatory shake. "I'm Sloane."

The producers gave everyone the option of preparing a special introduction if they wanted to make an impression or show a bit of their personality, but I felt like doing neither of those things. I probably showed more than enough of my personality when I met him yesterday.

But he doesn't take my hand, instead touching my waist softly and then leaning in to kiss my cheek. The side effect is that my hand, still stubbornly stuck in shaking position, jabs into his open blazer like I'm trying to pickpocket him. *Oh Jesus, Mary, and—*

"Aspen," he says, leaning back and dropping his hand. He doesn't seem to have noticed my brief turn as a Dickensian street urchin. "I'm so glad you're here. I'll be sure to find you inside so we can talk more, yeah?"

"Sure," I say, and then that's it. He's opening the front door behind him and ushering me through it.

Just like that, I'm inside the house at the center of my favorite TV show, its super-famous lead actor shutting the door behind me. It's the first time I really feel like someone needs to pinch me. A gigantic portrait of Aspen-as-Dorian with his TV family hangs on the wall straight ahead. To my right are the stairs that lead up to Dorian's bedroom. And is this rug underneath me the same one that Chelsea vomits on when the police show up to bust a house party in season two? I know the vomit was fake, but still—has it been cleaned since then?

A sudden burst of clapping interrupts my very important line of mental inquiry, and I look up to see a producer standing in the foyer, holding a hand out to the hallway behind her. "Come on in and start to mingle! Help yourself to snacks, drinks, whatever you want. And welcome to the cove!"

It sounds like she's welcoming me to the location—*a* cove—not the show—*The Cove*—but I can't say for certain. *The Cove* is fiction, obviously. This show is supposed to be "reality." But the line between the two already feels blurry.

I mumble my thanks, start wandering in the direction she pointed, and soon find myself in another familiar room. The den in Dorian's family home always looked like one of those TV set rooms that no one's house would actually have in real life. But sure enough, here it is, with its big, sunken-in couch taking up most of the floor space, a few hanging swings in the corners of the room, and a gigantic TV. The back wall is all windows with a view of the ocean, but with remote-controlled blackout shades that roll down when Dorian and his friends have movie nights.

Scattered around the space are about a dozen girls, some in the swings, others in the couch pit. It seems like everyone has realized there's no way to really look classy and sophisticated while sitting among overstuffed cushions that are trying to swallow you whole. Some girls valiantly try to sit with good posture but just look like stiff Barbie dolls, while others have embraced the slouch. Try as we might to overcome its wiles, we are all the same brand of comfortable blob in the couch pit—the great equalizer of furniture.

"Hiii," they all call out with varying degrees of enthusiasm when I walk in.

I give a little wave like a competitor in one of Liza's pageants. "Hey, I'm Sloane."

There's some incoherent murmuring in response. I'm not sure what my move is now—am I supposed to jump in and start trying to make friends? I haven't watched many reality shows, but I know that it probably won't look good for me to be standoffish or a total loner. But I also don't want to pick a friend group too soon and inadvertently end up with the mean girls or something. Maybe I should sit back and—

"Grab a seat," calls out one friendly voice. I match it to a girl in one of the hammock-like chairs who could be Zendaya's little sister, all long limbs and brown skin that looks amazing against her shimmery white dress. Honestly, one of the most beautiful people I've ever seen in real life. I try to smile and follow directions like a normal human rather than letting my jaw hit the floor as I perch on the edge of the couch pit near her swing. I don't want to give myself fully over to blob mode yet.

"I'm Bree," she says, reaching out a hand. *Now* it's handshake time. "Where are you from?"

"Tennessee," I say, releasing her hand before smoothing my skirt around my knees. "You?"

"Portland. So like, Nashville? You like country music?"

A pretty standard connection people make when they hear Tennessee. "Knoxville, a few hours away. And country's fine." I pause, trying to dredge up some social skills to ask anything other than *you?* again. "Do you like . . . Oregon?"

Oh my God. Fortunately, she laughs, using her heels to push her swing back and forth. "I guess. I like California better, though. I'm trying to move down here next summer after I graduate if I can find a job."

"Hey, maybe you'll have a boyfriend who can help you out," I offer, nodding back toward the front door. Then I wonder if I sound too eager for someone *else* to end up with Aspen. I wouldn't say things like that if I really wanted him for myself, would I?

Bree gives me a curious look, lips tilting into a smile at the corners. "Maybe . . ." She trails off, and there's a brief silence between us. I'm running through ways to revive the conversation I've clearly killed when she continues. "This is so weird, right?"

Her voice is hushed, even though we both have mics on that will still pick up whatever we're saying. Before I can answer, another girl walks into the room—Ella—and it's our turn to do the *hiiii.*

Turning back to Bree after this bizarre little routine we'll no doubt be repeating another ten or so times tonight, I smile. "Super weird."

"Want to go see about some food?"

I think I'm halfway in love with her. I agree eagerly, and we make our way to the kitchen. The counters are covered with trays of hors d'oeuvres and dispensers of tea, water, and lemonade alongside plastic cups. I doubt the tea will be sweet, so I might as well get lemonade. Then I pile a plate with mini-quiches, pigs in a blanket, chips, plus a few veggies for the sake of aesthetics before locating Bree again.

She's taken a seat at a bistro table with two other girls, and they've pulled up a fourth chair to the already-too-small table, presumably saved for me. I take it with a grateful smile, setting my plate gingerly in the little bit of space left.

"Sloane, this is Alicia and Hattie." She gestures to the two girls, who wear open, friendly expressions. The first, Alicia, has dark, curly hair, big brown eyes, and wears hot pink lipstick better than I've ever seen anyone wear hot pink lipstick. Hattie is super pale and freckled with long blond hair braided over one shoulder; even though we're sitting down, she has the kind of 90-percent-legs frame that tells me she's tall. I don't know if I'll have anything in common with these girls, but the fact that we've all hit the refreshments so early is a good start.

Shortly after the introductions are made and I've started to eat, a camera operator appears with a producer. The latter, dressed in a tight black T-shirt and artfully faded jeans, with an earpiece poking out from his slicked-back brown hair, interrupts Bree. He introduces himself as Ty before politely asking if we could shift our chairs so they can capture our conversation in one frame. We comply somewhat awkwardly, smooshing together like we're in a stage play. Which I guess isn't so far off from reality.

The other girls are better at acting natural in the presence of the camera than I am. I learn that Hattie lives on the beach in Georgia and her family has a new golden retriever puppy, Darla, who she was sad to leave behind. Alicia is from Chicago, a first-gen child of Mexican immigrants who already knows that she wants to be a doctor and is, per my estimation, way too smart to be within a hundred yards of a reality TV set.

Just as Bree's starting to speculate on the flavor of the mini-quiches, Ty jumps in again.

"All right, ladies, this is all great, but I'm gonna stop you right there for a sec and ask some questions, okay? We call these on-the-fly interviews, or OTFs. Just checking in to see how everyone's feeling, clips we can cut in with the action. And any question I ask you, you'll want to restate it when you're giving your answer. Viewers don't care to hear my voice in there. Sound good?"

We all nod, as it doesn't seem like he's proposing something optional.

"Okay, awesome. Sloane, you've been pretty quiet over there. How are you feeling so far?"

I shrug. "Not bad—"

"Remember, restate the question."

My cheeks flush. "I'm feeling . . . pretty good so far? It's nice getting to know people?"

Ty smirks. "Are you asking? Try that again."

Honestly, feeling worse the longer I talk to you, Ty! I clench then relax my jaw before doing as he says. "I'm feeling pretty good so far! It's nice getting to know people."

"That's great. But what did you think of Aspen? First impressions?"

It occurs to me that I haven't talked about Aspen with any of these girls since we got here. The meeting-Aspen part seems a long time ago already. Even longer if I'm counting the actual first time I met Aspen, when he overheard me calling him a narcissist named after an air freshener. How do I expect him to keep me until the top four again?

"Oh, um. My first impression of Aspen is that, uh . . . he's obviously very good-looking," I say, then realize how incredibly shallow I probably sound. But, like, what else do I know about the dude? Besides an unflattering reputation that's part of why he's even doing this show, that is. "And he's . . . charming."

Great work, Sloane. The producers are going to be devastated to lose such a compelling orator whenever I go home.

Ty blinks at me, then turns his attention to Bree. "What about you, Bree? What have you been thinking about Aspen so far? Did he meet your expectations?"

"Aspen seems chill," she says, already giving a usable quote without sounding like a robot. "I've seen him on TV a lot and thought surely he'd seem different in person, but he's about what I expected, in a good way. Hopefully the more I get to know him, the more impressed I'll be."

Her entire vibe says that Aspen would be lucky to get to know her better and not the other way around. I envy this level of cool that I will never achieve.

Before our first foray into OTFs can go on, we hear clapping coming from the den. Ty stands up straighter and gestures for us to follow him. "Everyone must have arrived by now. They're about to bring Aspen out."

We all stand and start picking up our cups and plates, but one of the younger, more harried-looking crew members I've seen running around the set rushes over and takes them from us before shooing us onward. A peek at the Daniels Entertainment badge clipped to the girl's belt confirms my suspicion that she's one of Liam's fellow PAs. I wonder if Liam is doing the same thing for a different group of cast members in a different spot around the house right now.

Back in the den, all the girls who were in the couch pit have now climbed out and are being shepherded like an obedient flock onto the back patio. I meet Alicia's gaze. She shrugs and blows out a breath in a move I interpret as "Welp, here goes nothing." We fall into line behind the other girls and leave the house through the sliding back doors.

Dorian's house doesn't have a pool like Chelsea's, but the uppermost deck does have a hot tub—one that has featured heavily in some blush-inducing Mara-Dorian scenes on the show. I feel like I can barely look at it as we pass, it's seen so many things. We continue down the tiered patios toward the beach, passing a big firepit surrounded by benches, then all kinds of beautiful plants and fountains set up in ways that make for lots of private alcoves with tables and chairs.

When we step off the lowest deck and onto the sandy beach, I toe off my shoes and leave them in a pile on the sand with everyone else's fancy heels and flats. As I turn around, I see what

Kristi and other producers and PAs are handing out to everyone—freeze pops. The fangirl in me can't help myself; I gasp. So many of Dorian and Chelsea's most meaningful best-friend moments and deep talks on *The Cove* occur while the two of them sit on the beach eating freeze pops. I accept one of the cherry-red tubes from Kristi, both because it's Chelsea's favorite flavor and because it won't turn my mouth too funky a color for the rest of the night, then survey the scene around me.

Mr. Daniels and another one of the producers come out from wherever they've been hiding to take a look at everything while preparations are made for Aspen's entrance. The rest of the girls have formed a semicircle facing Dorian's house, each holding her own rapidly melting freeze pop in its plastic tube. As Bree, Hattie, Alicia, and I slowly make our way toward the pack—inhibited by the many people and cameras bustling around along the way—I feel a hand on my elbow.

"Hey," Liam says in a low voice. I smile, throwing my arms around his neck before I can stop to think that maybe I shouldn't do that while he's working. He huffs out a soft laugh and pats my back before I release him and step back to take in his whole PA getup, which is the same T-shirt and shorts he had on earlier with an added Daniels Entertainment PA badge and the headset-radio combo that all the crew members have. It's been only a few hours since I was with him, but seeing his face again in the midst of all this chaos makes me feel weirdly emotional.

"You feeling okay so far?" he asks, reaching out to catch a drop of red juice I didn't notice was about to drip onto my hand. He licks it off his finger before giving me a smile.

"Of course," I say breezily, taking a discreet sip from the top of the freeze pop tube. "If I had a nickel for every time I've been on a first date with a guy and his twenty-four other girlfriends at the beachfront mansion owned by his fictional alter ego . . ."

"Then I'd be fascinated to see what you could get for your five whole cents in an economy that's quickly rendering small change useless," Liam replies.

"I love it when you talk inflation to me." I bat my eyelashes up at him.

He snorts before continuing in a softer, more serious voice. "But really. You good?"

I give him a small smile and nod. "I'm good. It's weird but I'm having fun? I think?"

Liam doesn't make Ty's are-you-asking joke, just reaches out to squeeze my arm again before he steps away. "Hang in there. You're doing great, and you look amazing."

My mouth turns up in a smile, because *aw* but also *amazing?* Amazing feels like a strong word. But I have no time to investigate the comment further, as the producer standing with Mr. Daniels starts talking.

"Okay, girls, everybody have a pop? Aspen's going to come in and give a toast to kick off the night, everyone cheers with your freeze pops, then there will be time for him to mingle and get to know you all. I know everyone will want their chance to talk to him, so don't be afraid to be assertive in getting your time. Now, make sure we're standing up straight, big smiles, the camera sees everything, remember?" I don't know if he means for that to sound as vaguely threatening as it does. "Here we go."

He mutters some other stuff into his headset, probably something like "The eagle is flying." The noise on the beach fades to nothing, just the gentle crashing of the waves in the background. Then as the man of the night—week? month?—appears from behind the potted plants that line the lowest deck, cheers and applause take over.

I offer the awkward kind of clap you give when you're holding a red liquid you don't want to spill on your blue dress, which is to say I'm basically soundless, but it'll look like I'm trying. I do feel an odd flutter of . . . *something* at the sight of Aspen again. It's like now that he's here, down on the beach with the rest of the girls and crew and cameras, it's *really* real.

And he's still *really* hot.

"Ladies," he says, clasping his hands around his own purple freeze pop—Dorian's favorite. "Thank you all so much for being here. I am stoked to get started on this journey with you, to find out more about each and every one of you—what we have in common, what makes you special. My life can be hectic and move so fast, but I'm ready to open my heart to you all. I hope there's a girl here who I can share this wild ride with, who will care about me for me. And I hope you are ready to open your hearts to me, too."

At this point, he raises his freeze pop, and we all mimic the movement. "Cheers to finding my ride or die."

Oh no. Am I supposed to repeat that? I don't know if I could without laughing. Fortunately, Bree kicks off the response with a loud and succinct "Cheers." We all echo her as we tap the flimsy plastic tubes together and spill artificially flavored fruit juices in little colored droplets on the sand.

"Aspen." Alicia surprises me when she steps forward, her voice soft but confident as it cuts through the gathering. "Want to find a place to chat?"

Respect, girl. Aspen clearly respects it, too, one brow lifting and a pleased grin forming on his lips as he takes her in. "I'd love that. You lead the way."

She gives a coy smile back and turns, nodding in the direction of the house. Aspen falls into step beside her, resting a hand on her lower back as they start up onto the deck. I peer around at the remaining girls and see their eyes tracking the two, expressions ranging from wistful to judgmental to envious. Here we go indeed.

I wonder already if that should've been me—if I should have tried to pull him away first, knowing I have a lot of ground to make up. I should probably figure out some way to apologize for what I said yesterday, but without also making it clear that we met before the show started. Is it possible to do that? Will he even want to talk to me more tonight? Have I already been written off as potential ride or die? Is that for the best?

Before I can fully panic, Hattie starts bouncing up and down, gripping Bree's and my forearms.

"OhmyGodohmyGod! How much would I have to pay y'all to play with me?"

I follow her gaze to the volleyball net set up in the sand behind Brock's house, a few yards away from us. Then I look Hattie up and down. "You're gonna be really good, aren't you?"

She smirks. "I meeean I'm not, like, the best. We can just hit around a little, no getting sweaty in our nice clothes."

Bree and I exchange skeptical looks, then she shrugs. "I guess we've gotta pass the time somehow."

I decide that I don't particularly like my odds even in a casual game with these two tall, athletic-looking gals, so I settle into the referee's chair while they start to pass a volleyball back and forth. A camera hovers nearby, and I imagine this is the closest I'll ever get to Doing Sports on ESPN.

The cameras don't come too close to us until they follow Alicia our way. She fills us in on her talk with Aspen after sitting down in the sand to the side of the court. Hattie and Bree don't seem to be in any rush to get their face time with said Lead, but I'm starting to feel itchy for mine. Anything to get it over with—whether it goes well or poorly.

Looking around from my perch, I don't see Aspen. He could be tucked away in any number of quiet spots around the expansive backyards of these three houses. Will I even have time to find him? The more I think about it, the more I chew on my bottom lip. R.I.P. nice lip gloss.

"Sloane, who was the blond guy talking to you before the toast?" Bree interrupts my worry spiral as she bumps the ball over the net with a fist.

"What?" It takes me a moment to realize what she's talking about. "Oh, that's my friend Liam. He's a PA."

I don't miss the quick appraising look she tosses my way. "Oooh. He giving you all the inside scoop?"

There's no judgment in her voice but I squirm a little anyway, casting a glance at the camera guy. I mean, I didn't promise anyone I wouldn't talk about how I got on the show. But is it weird to mention it? Is it weirder if I *don't* tell them? Ugh, I should have asked Mr. Daniels more than, like, two questions about the entire gig.

"Ha, I don't think he has any of that himself," I hedge. "But he's the son of Spencer Daniels, one of the EPs. I was supposed to just be visiting him for the summer, but casting found out they were short one contestant at the last minute, which is actually how I ended up doing this show."

Hattie catches the ball and pauses, holding it in her hands as she looks up at me with a confused expression. "Wait, how last-minute?"

I grimace. "Yesterday."

There's a pause before they all crack up. "Holy shit!" Bree says. "That's one way to get here. Do you even know who Aspen Woods is?"

I scoff, but I'm trying not to laugh too. "Of course! I'm obsessed with *The Cove*. I'm, uh, curious about Aspen. I just . . . didn't really go through an application process to get here. And, um, it's probably best if that stays between us. I don't know how everyone else would feel about it."

"But you *are* interested in him?" Alicia asks.

I find myself answering honestly—maybe too much so. "I don't know? I mean, I've always gotten a weird vibe from him. I'm not sure if we'll be a good fit at all. But I'm . . . open to seeing how it goes."

"Fair enough," Hattie says, her blasé tone surprising me. "And

I won't tell anyone, but I don't think it's a big deal that you didn't apply."

Bree nods her agreement. "And *I* think that if Aspen doesn't work out for you, Liam is hot and you look cute together."

My cheeks feel like they catch fire, and I try to cover the blush with my hands, shaking my head furiously. "*Nooo,* that's never, ever gonna happen."

"What's never gonna happen?" a new voice cuts in, and I nearly tumble out of my chair. Aspen stands beside me, looking at me with a curious gleam in his eyes. We have to stop meeting this way.

Bree covers her laugh with a cough. "Oh, Sloane said she's never gonna play volleyball with us."

Hattie is bouncing on her toes again, clearly enjoying this. Aspen nods like he didn't hear the discussion of how I got here or my best friend's hotness.

"Well, since you're not playing, could I steal you away for a few, Sloane? I've been looking forward to talking with you." He holds out a gentlemanly hand.

That makes me feel like tumbling out of my chair again. *He* sought *me* out? What in the unexpected hell?

Behind Aspen, Bree is nodding emphatically, drawing hearts in the air. She's just starting in on gestures of the lewder variety when I look away.

"Sure," I answer, grabbing his hand. "Let's go."

It occurs to me as we walk that this is the first boy who has held my hand—in a romantic way, not a Liam way—in about a year. Since my last boyfriend, Patrick. But Patrick's hands were always sweaty, which made me self-conscious that maybe it was really *my* hands that were sweaty. This is a very dry, comfortable handhold, if I can set aside the fact that a real-life Hollywood star is the one doing the holding.

"Having a good time so far?" Aspen asks.

"Uh, yeah," I say, probably betraying too much surprise. "Are you?"

We get to a bistro table on the lower deck, hidden away from most of the backyard's view by some of the potted plants, and he drops my hand to pull a chair out for me.

He sighs as he takes his seat opposite me. "A little over-whelmed, if I'm honest." He gives a stiff, quiet laugh. "I've never been around so many beautiful girls in one place."

I can't help the extremely dubious look I give him, letting his words hang between us.

He tilts his head and smiles. "Okay, maybe I have. But usually they're not all there to get to know me."

I'm still skeptical, but I fold my hands on the table, trying to look thoughtful. "Maybe it would help to pretend we're all extras on *The Cove*. Dorian has no time to be nervous about people's beauty while he's trying to, like, take down drug cartels and be the prom king all at once."

His laugh this time is loud and all the way real. He reaches out to put his arm around the back of my chair, leaning closer. "You're funny, you know that?"

I squirm, uncrossing and recrossing my legs. I'm very aware of the camera that followed us over here and now homes in on our expressions. "Gotta compensate somehow."

Then I want to smack myself, because oh lord, I am not about to be the insecure weirdo fishing for the cute boy to tell me I'm just as pretty as every other girl here even though I'm fairly positive that I'm not. And humor has always been my fallback when I'm not the prettiest person in the room, or smartest, or most talented—even when that room was in my own home with my family. But I am not digging into my issues with Aspen Woods, of all people, and definitely not on national television.

He looks at me with concern. "Compensating? For what?"

My answer can only be blamed on my discomfort and inability to think on my feet. "I have a truly terrible personality."

If Liam was around, his eyes would have rolled out of his head by now at these shenanigans. Fortunately, Aspen laughs again, and I'm surprised by how relieved I feel. I haven't done anything to make up for what I said about him yesterday, even though I was fully prepared to grovel so that he would keep me around. But he's acting like we're totally cool. It can't be this easy, can it?

He reaches into his pants pocket and pulls out a folded-up piece of paper.

"I'll have to be the judge of that—and somehow, I think I'm gonna disagree with you. Listen, Sloane, I think you're gorgeous and so easy to talk to, and I'd love if you stayed another week. This is the paper where I'll fill in the 'Cast List' at the end of tonight, with all the girls I want to stay. But I get to put one name on it before the Casting Call as soon as I know I want to keep that person, and if you're interested in sticking around . . ." He takes a deep breath that I'm sure is for dramatic effect, because the only other cause would be nerves. And there's no way this guy is nervous because of me. I feel my stomach churning as I wait for him to go on.

"I'd like that name to be yours."

CHAPTER SIX

You have to find your passion to be successful in life.
His passion is watching himself work out in the mirror —
and those biceps are a success.

—*THE COVE*, SEASON 1, EPISODE 17

Liam

This is a plot twist I did not see coming.

I hover behind Kristi, who I've been charged with shadowing for the evening as I learn the production ropes, and we both stand behind the camera guy filming off to Sloane and Aspen's side. Sloane doesn't seem to have noticed me, fortunately, so she didn't see my look of shock at Aspen's list announcement.

My main responsibility thus far has been toting around an "apple box"—a rectangular wooden box on which the camera operator nearest to me now sits. When Aspen pulls a girl aside, or vice versa, for a private conversation, there are usually multiple cameras covering different angles. Sometimes, like now, one of them will sit to be on Aspen and the girl's level.

I'm the guy who places the box seat.

Holding the entire production together in my capable hands,

I know. It hasn't been as painful as I was expecting—doing the PA thing, running around a set, seeing Sloane in the periphery—but something about this particular moment has my stomach sinking, as if I've suddenly remembered how badly I don't want Sloane or me to be here.

In contrast, Kristi is whispering something excitedly into her headset about the Cast List. Most of the things Kristi says sound excited, but this one especially so. I suspect it's as big of a deal to everyone else as it is to me personally, the fact that Aspen has chosen Sloane as the first girl he wants to continue on the show for another week.

A "week" that, in reality show terms, equates to an episode of television, however many days are involved in filming it. It could be two more days or eight, depending on the schedule of dates and other activities for Aspen and the girls. But regardless of the specific amount of time involved, it means that he's interested in spending more of it with Sloane.

It's not that I didn't expect him to like Sloane, of course. She's extremely likable. I think it's more that I'm protective of her—that I question his sincerity and I don't want her to get hurt. But I guess that's a thing that could happen only if she likes him. Which she doesn't yet. Does she?

Sloane looks at least as caught off guard as I am. She looks between Aspen, the gold Sharpie he's holding, and the paper on the table a few times, her mouth seeming to try to form words.

Please, please, don't let her embarrass herself, I will the universe.

Finally, she seems to shake herself into action. "Oh, uh, sure. Yeah, go ahead."

I bite back the laugh that threatens to burst out. Is that part of the appeal for Aspen? The pursuit, chasing after someone who, at best, thinks dating him "won't kill me"?

He smiles, teeth as white and big-screen-ready as ever. There's something else in his expression—relief maybe? It's a little satisfying to see from a guy who's probably never heard the word "no" in his life.

But the satisfaction ebbs as I continue to watch them, as Aspen writes her name down on the first line of his Cast List, as he leans in, bringing his face closer and closer to hers, and oh no, this guy isn't really going to—

Looking very obviously at her lips, he says softly, "Sloane, can I kiss you?"

Which is when I jerk back in surprise, knocking right into something behind me. I whirl around, relieved to see it wasn't a person I collided with, but less pleased to see a leafy monstrosity in a plastic planter go toppling over, sending dirt spilling out onto the ground and onto the shoes of the camera operator.

Because he's a total pro, he doesn't falter or stop rolling, just shoots a brief annoyed look in my direction. I scramble to pick up the planter without making any more of a scene. In the process, I'm vaguely aware of Sloane and Aspen having stopped to watch the chaos I've caused, but when I straighten and resume my unobtrusive position, Aspen shakes his head and returns his attention to Sloane. The girl he was just trying to kiss about two seconds after meeting her.

Not that this upsets me.

"Let's try this again," Aspen says with a laugh before schooling his voice back into what I guess is Romance Mode. "Sloane, can I kiss you?"

Her startled gaze, which had been on me and my plantastrophe, darts back to his face, and she blanches. Once again I find myself begging whatever higher powers are listening to not let her say something emb—

"I can't," Sloane blurts out.

I bring a hand up to cover my mouth, unsure if I'm about to gasp or laugh.

Aspen looks flummoxed. "You *can't*?"

She closes her eyes and shakes her head, as if that could shake away her words.

"I mean, I *can* kiss, obviously. Like, my lips work." All right, that's one way to course correct. "But I . . . don't typically do so, uh, this . . . early. In a—a relationship. I like to take things . . . slow."

I imagine Aspen doesn't get rejected often. But especially not by someone who then goes into so much detail about her physical kissing capabilities. After another moment, though, he wipes his face clear of any confusion and smiles at her.

"Absolutely. Sorry for being so forward. I'm not used to feeling this much for someone so soon, either. But of course we can wait."

Did she say that she was feeling that, buddy? Sure isn't what I heard. But whatever—at least he isn't being a dick about it.

"Okay, great!" Sloane says in an overloud voice, slapping a clumsy hand down on Aspen's shoulder and bringing her own face forward so her right cheek presses to his left. The only natural option for him is a polite air kiss.

My heart is pounding as if coming down from some adrenaline rush. Was I really so panicked over the thought of him kissing her? Once again, my physiological responses aren't making sense to me.

But just then, Aspen is whisked away by another producer. Sloane looks around uncertainly but smiles when her eyes meet mine. Actually, her whole body kind of sags in relief, and I feel a pang in my chest. But before I can go to check in on her, yet another producer leads her off in a different direction.

In the silence, Kristi and the soil-covered camera guy stare at me. I grimace and look down at the pile of overturned dirt. "I'll go find a broom."

When my mess has been handled, I return the cleaning supplies to the closet I found them in and head toward the firepit, where Kristi told me she was heading. But Kristi's nowhere to be found. I scan my surroundings for any producers or camera people who look like they might need help with anything, trying to look like someone who *does* have a purpose but finding none. I'm about to give in to being fully useless and, I don't know, find some grass I can watch grow, when the distinctive sound of wood being cut catches my attention.

I whip around to see a man crouched at one end of the circle of benches that surrounds the firepit. He's setting up some kind of platform behind it, several wide, flat lengths of wood arranged in a semicircle. I approach carefully, already able to hear the guy muttering curses to himself as he works. When I'm about to gather up the nerve to say something, a hammer that was bal-anced precariously on one of the boards falls to the ground with a loud clang.

I hurry over to pick it up just as the man raises his head from his task.

"Need any help?" I offer, wishing my voice came out sound-ing a little more confident.

He squints up at me from his spot on the ground. He looks like a slightly younger Harrison Ford, weathered face framed by short, graying brown hair and a day-old beard. His button-down work shirt is sweat-stained and flecked with sawdust, and his hands stay locked on the wooden leg of the platform that I as-sume he's keeping upright. In general, he also seems about as Over It as Harrison does when promoting *Star Wars* movies.

"You know what you're doing with that?" he asks, nodding to the hammer now in my hand.

I clear my throat, anxious under his stern gaze. "Yeah. Yes, I, uh, build things."

Great work, Daniels. More convincing by the second. But to my surprise, there's a twitch in not-Harrison-Ford's cheek that almost looks like a grin.

"You do, huh? You work here?"

A fair question, given most everyone my age on set is a girl or Aspen Woods. "Yes, sir. I'm Liam. I'm a PA, but they don't have me working on anything else at the moment if there's anything I can do to, uh, assist."

"Garrett," he says, taking one hand from the support he's been holding to offer it to me. I shake it quickly so this whole structure doesn't collapse. "I build sets on *The Cove,* normally, but they called me in here to do some stuff around this new show as needed. And they needed it. Badly."

Garrett says "stuff" as though censoring himself for my benefit, looking at the semicircle of wooden platforms disdainfully.

"Somebody from that reality TV crew allegedly built this for easy setup and teardown, but the workmanship is shoddy."

"What is it?" I ask. I lower myself to a crouch a few feet from him.

Garrett uses his shoulder to wipe sweat from the side of his face. "They're supposed to be risers for this whole ceremony they're doing later tonight. Half the girls are gonna sit on the benches that are already around the fire, and they want the other half in director's chairs set up a little higher behind the benches, so everyone can be seen by cameras. But they also think risers visible behind the benches during the rest of filming are an eyesore, so they have to be able to be set up just before the ceremony—now—and taken down again right after. Then do it all again for the next episode.

"But the way they built these, I'd barely trust them to hold the chairs, let alone people. So I've been trying to make 'em safer, but I've also been prohibited from making any noise with that"—he nods to the hammer—"until after the ceremony, when they're not filming anymore. You know, when I won't even need it."

I nod. "Well, whatever you need, I'm here. I kind of mess around with woodworking." A different craft from the kind of construction he's doing now, but no need to split hairs. "I've built some furniture and stuff."

I don't think I'm imagining the increased respect in his eyes as he looks at me again and nods before passing me a handsaw. "First thing I've been doing is trying to get all the pieces to fit together more sturdily by making these notches. . . ."

So begins the most enjoyable time I've spent on a TV set to date. Under Garrett's direction, I follow his method of cutting out notches in various spots on the platforms, the rails underneath, and the legs to get them to sit steadily without being able to nail or screw them together at the moment. After that, we do our best to make all the legs level with one another so the whole structure doesn't wobble. Then we make sure that everything holds up to our combined weight standing on top.

"That should be it," Garrett finally says after what could have been five minutes or two hours. Judging by the way the sun has fully gone down and all the patio lights have been turned on, I'd lean toward the latter. "Appreciate the help, kid. Might not have finished in time on my own."

"No problem at all," I say truthfully, shaking the hand he's offered. "I love this stuff."

I almost add that I'd rather be doing this than literally any other job on set but don't know if it's too soon for that kind of honesty.

"Well, I'll be around," he answers gruffly. "If you ever see me working on anything on set, just assume you're free to join me."

A feeling like hope swells up in my chest. I don't think Garrett's the kind of guy who would say something like that to be polite. And if I get to do more of this kind of work in the day-to-day, well, the job may not be so bad after all.

"There you are!!!" Kristi's squeal has me jumping out of my shoes as she arrives seemingly out of thin air. "Liam, I'm so glad you met G—he's a total teddy bear! Okay, they're about to gather everyone up for the first Casting Call, where Aspen announces his whole Cast List. So let's go grab those director's chairs!"

Garrett follows too, grumbling about Kristi's teddy bear comparison in a way that tells me their friendship—however unlikely—is real, and the three of us are able to bring all the chairs in one trip. We set them up on the risers Garrett and I fixed up as more crew members start to filter into the firepit area and get the cameras and lighting ready. Producers gradually bring the girls over from where they've spread out around the grounds and position everyone in their spots.

Eventually, the producer named Ty calls out a literal "Quiet on set!" which I sort of thought was a thing that only happened in movies. But from my few observations of the way he saunters around set like he owns the place, Ty strikes me as the kind of guy who would take any chance he gets to boss people around. The girls and the crew quiet down, everyone standing at attention as my dad comes walking out of the mansion alongside Aspen. He leads him behind some trees, and once Dad steps out of sight, Aspen reemerges for his official "entrance," golden boy smile plastered on his face.

The girls clap and cheer as he comes to stand in front of them, waving his hands in that *oh-stop-it* fashion as he leans against a podium that's been placed on the other side of the fire. I spot Sloane in the front row of girls, on one of the benches.

"Ladies," Aspen says solemnly. "Thank you again for coming

all this way, putting yourselves out there, and giving me the privilege of getting to know you. It has been a pleasure and an honor, and it pains me to say goodbye to any of you tonight. But I'm here to find my one and only, so hard decisions must be made."

I feel a touch on my arm and turn to see Kristi motioning at me. I follow her to the far edge of the set, where the crew is circled up around the firepit. A guy whose badge identifies him as a "lighting tech" appears to be wrestling with one of the metal C-stands that Kristi explained earlier are used to hold various mics, silks used for filtering light, flags for blocking light, and more. It looks like this one is supposed to be holding a silk, but the extendable arm isn't staying up.

"Here," Kristi whispers, unclamping the silk from the C-stand and then pushing the material toward me. "Liam, hold this."

My brows lift, but I hesitate for only a second before taking it from her hands above my head, making sure not to move its position in any significant way. I feel like that guy in the '80s movie who holds a boom box over his head, but 100 percent less romantic.

Kristi steps off to my side. "Keep it right there until I tell you to stop, okay?"

"Ten four," I whisper back without even thinking about it—she's getting to me, clearly.

Now that we've found a lighting work-around, I return my attention to the action at the Casting Call, where things have briefly paused while someone dabs a makeup brush on Aspen's forehead. I glance over at Sloane, surprised to find she's looking at me. And clearly trying very hard not to laugh.

She's probably loopy, still jet-lagged and up way later than she'd ever be otherwise. But I'm also aware that I look a little ridiculous, holding up a gray rectangle the size of my body. Her struggle not to laugh only makes *me* feel like laughing, and I'm certain that's not an option right now. So I give her the sternest eyes I can and flick them toward Aspen.

Biting her bottom lip and not looking the least bit sorry, she refocuses on the guy at the podium.

"I have the Cast List here," Aspen goes on with more than enough drama in his voice, tapping the podium surface. "And as you may or may not know, I was able to ask one girl to stay on before we got to the Casting Call tonight. That girl was Sloane, and she's accepted her spot in the cast for another week."

There are some murmurs and mild applause from the other girls. The one sitting on the riser behind Sloane pats her back.

Aspen clears his throat. "With that, the next girl . . ."

For a second I think he's experiencing a brain lapse or something—his pause is so uncomfortably long. But then I see another producer off to the side of the girls, in Aspen's line of vision, holding his hand up.

The producer's hand shifts to a thumbs-up, and Aspen goes on. ". . . who I'd like to add to the Cast List for next week . . ."

Palm out. Pause. Girls shift in their seats. Someone coughs. Then, finally, thumbs-up. ". . . is Alicia."

A short girl with an amazing mass of brown curls steps down from one of the benches and walks up to Aspen with a wide smile. He takes one of her hands in one of his, a gold marker poised over the Cast List in his other.

"Alicia, will you stay another week?"

She nods. "Of course."

Aspen scribbles down her name before leaning in to give her a kiss on the cheek, and she heads back to her spot. This process repeats, and I've accepted that my arms might be stuck in this outstretched position indefinitely. I can feel the strain on my muscles and wonder if Kristi ever intends to return and relieve me. Eventually, all the girls I've seen Sloane hanging out with tonight make it through to the next week, and only five are sent home.

I feel for the girls being led out to the mansion entrance by another PA. But I don't have much time to linger on their sad expressions, as Kristi finally returns and takes the silk from my hands. I nearly gasp in relief when I'm able to put my arms down, but she immediately pulls me away for instructions on gathering everyone's mic packs and shutting things down on set for the night.

That's a wrap on our first "week" of *AWFLL*.

Plastic bin cradled in my, yep, definitely sore arms, I walk over to the remaining girls. They're talking among themselves, not a single one looking my way. I don't think I've ever had to command the attention of a group both this large and this good-looking.

"Okay, I'm collecting mics," I shout, and twenty startled faces turn to me. I clear my throat. "Uh, so, if you can help each other take them off, or let me know if you need my help, that would be great. Then hand them to me. Please."

I look to Sloane, and she gives me an exaggerated thumbs-up, one that says she's definitely making fun of my lack of smoothness.

"Great use of your authoritative voice," she says with mock reverence as I approach her. "Those two weeks you spent on the Hallway Safety Patrol in fifth grade continue to pay off."

"I was uncomfortable with my role in the elementary school's punitive system. No matter how much you make fun of me, I'm never gonna regret handing over my badge." I wave a hand at her. "That said, I have no problem ordering you, specifically, around. So get moving. That mic isn't gonna take itself off."

She looks like she's about to snap back at me, but another girl steps up beside us, turning so her back is facing me.

"I wouldn't normally ask a guy to unzip my dress so early in the relationship, but could you? My mic is stuck on it."

My cheeks redden instantly, but I nod and reach for the zipper.

"Bree! No hitting on the PA," Sloane scoffs, a hint of real displeasure in her face.

"Ooh, can the hot guy help with my mic next?" another girl pipes up. I think I remember her from the Casting Call as one of two Ellas.

"Me too!" calls someone else. "Are you single?"

Are they being serious? Is this a we're-all-exhausted-and-don't-know-what-we're-saying thing? I look around almost frantically, trying to figure out who actually requires my help and who's just piling on.

One of the girls appears in front of me then, pulling her long red hair over one shoulder and looking at me over the other.

"Sorry, but I actually do need help," she says with an easy laugh. "I'm not sure if they sewed it on there or what, but it feels pretty stuck."

"No worries." I smile back as I start to examine what her pack could be caught on. "It's what I'm here for."

"I'm Peyton, by the way," she continues, watching me with something unreadable in her eyes. Unreadable but not un-interested. She looks like she could be sisters with Riley Cart-wright, the stunning redhead who plays Chelsea on *The Cove*. Sloane's and my shared crush on Chelsea might be more to blame for our Dorsea fandom than a pure concern for Dorian's best interests.

"Oh, uh, I'm Liam," I say belatedly, adding, in what I think to be an under-my-breath mutter as I work on her mic, "Not 'Hot Guy.'"

But of course, because it's Embarrass Liam Hour, Peyton hears, letting out a soft, Disney-princess-perfect laugh. "No, you're definitely 'Hot Guy,' too."

Just then her pack comes off in my hand. I look up in time to see that she winks—fully *winks*—as she leaves me with a "See you around, Liam."

I think I need to wear a ski mask around these girls from now on. Anything to keep them from reading my flushed face like a book.

When everyone's mics seem to be dealt with, I search out Sloane again. She's standing a little apart from the rest of the group with her arms crossed over her chest, gazing out in the direction of the ocean. Worry settles in my stomach, and I set the box down on one of the benches before approaching her.

"Hey," I say, and she whirls around so fast she almost falls in her tall heels. I steady her with my hands on both her elbows. "Whoa. You okay?"

Sloane's expression is stormy at first before she obviously tries to clear it with a shake of her head. "It's been a long night."

Realizing my hold on her has probably lingered too long, I drop my hands, curling them into fists against the odd tingling in my palms. "Are you sure? You seemed kind of upset about that stuff with the mics."

Her chin lifts stubbornly, smile turning more toward a smirk. "I don't know, it seemed . . . weird to me. Like they shouldn't be harassing you like that."

I reach up to scratch the back of my neck. "I didn't exactly mind it."

Sloane laughs, but it sounds cold. "Of course you didn't. It just seems inappropriate when we're all supposed to be here to date someone else. They're not about to become your one-and-dones." I rear back at the snappish comment, and she instantly looks regretful. With a sigh, she says, "Sorry, I think I really am just tired. Being grouchy for no reason."

She looks up at me with genuine apology on her face, and it makes my chest feel tight.

"Don't worry about it." I want to pull her in for a hug but settle for a soft squeeze on her upper arm. "The show's not called *LDFLL,* after all."

I pronounce it like "lid-full," and it takes Sloane only a moment to get that I've swapped my initials for Aspen's. Her head falls back on a loud, full laugh that brings out an answering smile from me.

"You know," she says through the last of her chuckles. "You've gotten funnier in your old age."

Before I can respond, likely to point out the fact that she's two months older than me, one of the producers claps her hands together and announces that the girls can go to their assigned houses, find their luggage, and pick their beds. You would think she'd announced a winning lottery ticket was up for grabs, the way the whole group scrambles toward the two neighboring mansions.

But Sloane doesn't rush; she turns to me with uneasiness in her expression and arms wrapped tight around herself again.

"What is it? Don't like where you're assigned?" I'm already considering the odds that Dad could pull rank and put her somewhere where she'd be more comfortable. I'm about to tell her that when she shakes her head.

"No, I'm at Chelsea's house. I don't really care which bed I end up with. I just . . . I don't know, I'm gonna miss you. It's weird not having my phone and texting you about everything that's happening all the time, even though I know you're always somewhere nearby in person. It seems like we might be doing totally different things a lot of the time we're here. I wish there was a way to keep in touch."

I try to put aside the strange but not unwelcome warmth that fills me at her words and peer around the backyard area, waiting for a solution to come to me. Smoke signals? Carrier pigeons? Messages in bottles?

"Did you bring your notebook?" I say with a snap of my fingers.

Sloane gives me a sardonic look. "Obviously."

"Why don't we pass notes? Old-fashioned, I know, but we can have a drop-off spot somewhere around here where we can both leave messages whenever we're able to."

A smile spreads slowly across her face. "Okay. Yeah, let's do that." She peers over her shoulder at the patio area, where crew members are roaming around and cleaning up for the night. Garrett has reappeared by his risers, making all the noise he wants as he takes them apart. "I should probably get going. Where's our secret mailbox going to be?"

I haven't actually gotten that far in the plan. "I'll find a place and let you know tomorrow."

"Sounds good," she says through a yawn, backing away toward Chelsea's house. "I'll see you tomorrow then?"

"You got it," I say. Then add impulsively, "And Sloane?"

"Hmm?"

"I'm gonna miss you, too."

The last smile she gives me is tinged with an emotion I can't quite interpret. Then she turns and strolls away. I blow out a long breath, looking at Chelsea's house even after Sloane disappears from sight.

Finally, I start off toward the front of Dorian's house, then nearly jump out of my skin when I hear a voice behind me.

"Forgetting something?"

Turning around, I'm startled to see Aspen standing behind me, hands in his pockets. I don't know where he came from, but the cuffs of his pants are rolled at the ankles and his shirt is unbuttoned farther as if to firmly signify "off the clock." His stance is casual but there's a watchfulness in his expression that gives me pause.

"Wh-what?" I ask.

He gives a jerky nod toward the box of mics that I have indeed forgotten on the bench. I scramble to pick it up, cradling the box in my arms like it will forgive me for nearly leaving it to get rained on or snatched by enterprising raccoons or whatever else.

"Thanks," I say, meaning it. Another day-one screwup narrowly avoided.

"You're welcome," Aspen replies. For whatever reason, it feels deliberate—not a casual *no worries* or *not a problem,* but a *yeah, we both know I saved your ass and you're welcome.* His narrow-eyed gaze moves from me back to Chelsea's house over my shoulder, and I suddenly wonder if he's been there longer than I realized. Watching me watch Sloane.

Seeing too much.

I feel like I should say something else, but I don't even know what. Fortunately, he breaks the silence first.

"I'll see you around," he says, nearly echoing Peyton from earlier before he turns and continues down the decks toward the beach, disappearing into the night.

Maybe it's the drama in the air of a reality TV set getting to me, but the way Aspen said it? It felt like a warning.

CHAPTER SEVEN

The past can teach us a lot about the future, you know?
Like how you start and end life in diapers.
—*THE COVE*, SEASON 2, EPISODE 5

Sloane

The first script arrives when I have a mouth full of Cocoa Puffs.

"We got a script!" squeals a cute brunette named Chandler. We met in line for the bathroom last night and shared the sink while brushing our teeth. I was impressed by everyone's patience around bathroom usage. The room of four bunks that I'm sharing with Bree, Alicia, and Hattie shares a bathroom with four other girls, but things moved pretty politely and efficiently the first night. I can only hope for this positive of a shared bathroom experience in college.

I wipe rapidly at the chocolatey milk dribbling down my chin as a camera operator and Ty, the producer, follow Chandler into the kitchen, where most of us are eating breakfast. The girls from Brock's house are here, too; producers herded them over in their pajamas about twenty minutes ago, presumably so they'd be around for this.

A script? Are we gonna have to memorize lines now? I guess I've always heard speculation that some of the most dramatic reality shows are scripted.

Chandler holds a paper up in one hand and an envelope in the other, then clears her throat. A crease appears between her brows.

"Wait, why does it say 'awful' at the top?" she murmurs, her confused gaze darting to Ty. I nearly spit out my cereal, then mentally curse myself for even trying to eat right now.

"It's not 'awful,' it stands for *Aspen Woods's Future Leading Lady*," he answers a bit snappily. "Go on and read it."

Chandler faces the rest of the room again, shaking her head. Then she starts to read.

"'Ladies, I'm happy to be sending you your first script! You will get these each time there's a new date planned. The scripts will either be for an "Ensemble Date," meaning a larger group will go with me, or a "Scene Partner Date," meaning only one of you is invited. The script will tell you who is going on the date (the characters), where we're going (the setting), and an opening line from me about what we'll be doing. See you soon! Xo, Aspen.'"

There are some cheers from around the room. Chandler bounces on the balls of her feet as she tucks the envelope behind the paper, pushing her hair over her shoulder as she reads.

"'Characters: Meg, Jada, Ella C., Aubrey, Chandler—yay!— Isabel, Sloane, Peyton, Ella M., Alicia, Olive. Setting: Memory Lane. Aspen: Get ready for the ride of a lifetime. . . . Today I'm gonna show you *my* Hollywood story.'"

The producer behind the camera waves his hands, signaling

to us that we're supposed to be excited now. There's a collective *wooooo* around the room before he tells us that the girls going on this date have forty-five minutes to get ready and meet in the front driveway.

I gulp down the rest of my breakfast, then follow the stampede of girls upstairs.

Alicia falls into step beside me up the staircase and leans in covertly. "Was that script supposed to give us any helpful information whatsoever?"

I laugh. "You mean you don't know how to dress for the ride of a lifetime?"

"If I didn't know this show was supposed to be PG, I'd think that was a euphemism."

I'm glad I wasn't the only one thinking it.

Bree and Hattie join Alicia and me in our room to help us get ready, and they don't seem at all bitter that they weren't invited on this date. Bree insists on touching up my naturally wavy hair with a curling iron while Hattie helps Alicia debate over sundress versus shorts and cute shirt. We're ready just under the wire, but when we get out to the driveway in front of Dorian's house, we're somehow still the first ones there.

The first of the girls, anyway. There are already plenty of cameras and production staff bustling around the circular drive, and right in the center of it all is what I'd wager is our ride for the day. It looks like an especially souped-up Jeep, long enough to hold seats for our whole group but also high off the ground and open-air, reminding me of the vehicles on the safari ride at Disney World.

I'm jolted out of my car inspection at the feeling of fingers brushing the strip of exposed skin on my back.

"Sorry," Liam says, and my shoulders relax at his voice. "I'm supposed to check everyone's mic packs."

My eyes roll before I can stop them. "Have they made you the sound technician or something?"

He frowns. "Does someone need more sleep?"

Ugh. He's right. I don't know why last night rubbed me so wrong, the way everyone was flirting with Liam. It's not like I can fault anyone for not being 300 percent devoted to Aspen from night one. I was just . . . irked. I felt like covering Liam with caution tape that reads "OFF LIMITS."

Still kind of feel like it.

"Hey, Liam?" the cute redhead named Peyton cuts in as she appears beside us. "I think my pack is falling off. Could you help me—"

"Of course," he says, practically jumping to get away from me and go help her. She "needed help" last night, too, and when she looked at the rest of us while he worked on her pack, she was totally smug. I didn't hear what she was saying to him, but it all seemed a little *too* friendly. But so what if it was, I guess? He can be interested in whoever he wants. That's always been how we've operated, even when I tease him about his many first dates. And I'm trying to "date" Aspen, anyway, until I make it to the top four at least.

Apropos of exactly that, I catch sight of Aspen strolling onto the set alongside Mr. Daniels, who's leaning into the younger boy as he talks and gesturing enthusiastically. I wish seeing Aspen made me feel better, but it just takes me back to our extremely awkward one-on-one time last night, when I rejected his kiss and possibly screwed up my chances of going any further on this show.

I don't know if I can recover that ground today—or honestly, if I should. Maybe this is all the evidence I need to prove that I'm not cut out to pretend-date this guy while who knows how many millions eventually watch.

Aspen doesn't approach the group, and once all the girls are out in the driveway, we see why. Production rolls the *AWFLL*-mobile back around to the start of the driveway so they can film our mostly faked reactions as it drives back up to us with Aspen hanging out of the passenger seat, a winning smile on his face.

"Laaadies," he says, all drawn out with a wink at the end. "Hop on up, grab your seats, and let's go for a spin."

He jumps down from the passenger seat and opens the door to the back rows, holding out a hand that each of us can take for support as we step up into our ride. Since we're standing closest, Peyton goes first, followed by Alicia and me, and we fill in the very back row. After everyone else files in, Ella M. and Olive are the lucky leftover two who take the seats in the front row beside Aspen. He turns to face us as he leans against the passenger seat with a mic in his hand, looking very much the seasoned tour guide.

"All right," he says, his voice suddenly booming through speakers placed throughout the rows. "Welcome to our first date! In any good love story—whether on *The Cove* or a romantic movie or book—one of the first things you learn is the main character's backstory. Where they came from, what has made them who they are, all of that. So today is all about our backstories, starting with my own. We're taking a tour of the greater LA area, but it's not your typical Hollywood tour. This one is specific to the life of *me*, Aspen Woods. Let's make this a really fun day together!"

One of the first things I realize as we coast through the hills, and even more so once we're on the highway, is that doing anything to my hair was a waste of time. With no windows to speak of in the back rows, it's like one big hair tornado here, our locks whipping around our heads and tangling with each other in the most ridiculous way.

By the time we've pulled off the freeway and are winding back through quieter areas, most of us have created makeshift solutions to the hair problem. A few—myself included—had the classic Wrist Ponytail Holder on hand, so there are a lot of messy buns. Alicia has unwound the skinny cloth belt from her dress and fashioned it into a headband that has no right to look as good as it does. A girl named Jada has creatively tucked her long curls under her bra strap. All told, I think we're only a little worse for wear by the time Aspen turns to face us all again.

"Everyone having a good time so far?" he asks.

Wooooo!

"Awesome. Well, we're coming up on our first stop on the backstory tour." He gestures to the right of the quiet street we're cruising down, and our truck rolls to a stop at the curb. "See this office building, behind the bus stop over there?"

He points to a nondescript two-story block of gray concrete, then looks back to us with the eagerness of an Instagram influencer about to push some multivitamins.

"That office building used to be a park where my mom took me to swing as a baby. And it was at that park that I was scouted by a talent agent for a baby food ad, which was my first-ever paid acting job. They tore down the playground and built over it a few years ago, but I still drive past here from time to time to remind myself where it all started."

He looks toward the building proudly, a king surveying his domain. After a beat of silence, in which I think we're all waiting for a punch line, a couple of the girls give an "Aww" or a "That's so sweet." On my right, Alicia snorts and tries to turn it into a cough. I have to bite my lip and grip the seat to try to stop the laugh that wants to break free. Peyton shoots us both a stern look. As the truck starts moving again, Alicia says, "Was that story kind of sad to anyone else?"

"Maybe he's warming up for the good stuff?" I speak out of the side of my mouth, worried that the road noise won't be enough to prevent our mics from picking up this conversation.

"We gotta work on our reactions just in case," Alicia says, clearly still trying to keep the giggles in check. "Otherwise, we're locking ourselves into the villain edit, no question."

Aspen was not, in fact, warming up for the good stuff. The next few "stops" on our tour are the Montessori preschool that Aspen attended for two weeks before dropping out when he got his first recurring role on a sitcom, a billboard for *The Cove* with a large spot of bird feces on Aspen-as-Dorian's cheek, and the In-N-Out where his assistant would pick up food for him when he didn't like what was in craft services on the studio lot. It's the weirdest tour I've ever been on, a mix of vain humblebrags and mildly depressing glimpses into child star life. A lot of the stories that I think he intends to be neutral-to-positive end up almost making me feel sorry for him. He's had such a weird, bubble-enclosed existence for as long as he can remember.

I entertain myself by thinking about what this date would look like in the TV show version of my life. Maybe a montage of our tour stops with quirky background music, signifying that this is not the romantic rendezvous the viewer was expecting. Maybe the cameras would zoom in on my face, breaking the fourth wall with a deadpan look like a character on *The Office*.

Alicia's eyelids droop like she's struggling to stay awake as we continue on through the city, and honestly, same. But just when I'm pinching my own leg to keep from drifting off, the truck stops again and Aspen stands to face us, clapping his hands. "Okay, that's about it for my portion of the backstory. Now I'd like to know more about yours. What do you all say to dining beachside?"

My *woooo* this time is more authentic and comes straight from my grumbling stomach. Our little urban safari concludes outside a restaurant that appears to be closed down for us. Producers meet us inside and lead us out to a spacious patio with views of the beach below.

Our late lunch/early dinner spread is a buffet with as many options as I could've hoped for, and I end up with a plate piled with steak and plenty of sides. Back at the table, I'm about to dig in when Aspen clinks his knife on his water glass. My stomach growls its dissent at the delay, so I stuff an entire dinner roll into my mouth to try to appease it.

"I hope everyone is satisfied with their meal," Aspen says with a dazzling smile that almost makes me forget that I am 0 percent satisfied yet and would very much like time to eat. "I have a bowl of backstory-related questions here. I want us to pass it around, and when it gets to you, take one of the questions out and share your answer."

He passes the bowl to his left, thank God—I'm two seats away on his right, so I'll have time to continue stuffing my face before I have to talk about myself. As the other girls start sharing, I find that I actually enjoy the little glimpses, however trivial, into who they are.

So far, I've only really spent time with Bree, Hattie, and Alicia. But some of the other girls here seem cool and funny, too. Like Ella M., whose favorite trip she's ever taken was to Dublin for an Irish dance competition she was in. Jada's story of her biggest "accomplishment"—trading places with her twin sister so the sister could go to sleepaway camp in Jada's place—has us all laughing, Aubrey so hard that water comes out of her nose. Which Aubrey then uses for the backstory prompt she draws from the bowl, most embarrassing moment. I'm not especially impressed by the most difficult decision Peyton has had to face in her life—when she was voted both Most Likely to Succeed *and* Best Dressed for the yearbook and had to choose which title to accept—but I guess there are only so many tough decisions most of us have made in our short lives, so whatever.

When it's finally my turn, I am pleased to be a member of

the Clean Plate Club, and my stomach is finally content. I take the bowl from Alicia with a smile and pull out the second-to-last slip of paper.

"What is your happiest memory?" I read aloud, and immediately forget everything that has ever happened in my whole life. I worry the paper between my fingers, giving an awkward laugh. "That's a tough one to think of!"

I look out into the distance as I try to jog my memory, as if anything in this random restaurant in California is going to do the trick. But then, it actually does. Liam leans against a far wall, off to the side of a camera operator. I've glimpsed him a couple times since we left this morning, but this is the first time we actually make eye contact. He stands up straighter, offering me an encouraging little half smile and nod. Something about his face just then looks so boyish, so much like who he was when we were little. And the memory clicks into place like it was sitting right there in my mind, a framed picture waiting for me to pick it up and dust it off.

"Okay, so my family used to go to the beach with my best friend's family. I've never been a big beach person—I'm not into swimming or deep water or anything—and this one year, we all went to a water park for the day." I'm even less of a water park person—too many opportunities for drowning. But I probably shouldn't get that far into Sloane's Dark Psyche in my happy memory story. "My friend could see that I was completely miserable and freaked out and didn't know what to do with myself. Bear with me, it gets happier," I interject with a laugh.

"So even though he loved all the adventurous water park

stuff, he hung back with me. First we ate Popsicles by the pool, but eventually I agreed to float in the lazy river with him in a double inner tube. And once we got going, I had more fun than I did the whole rest of vacation, floating in circles on the lazy river for hours, laughing with him about who knows what. I don't know if it's, like, the happiest I've ever been or anything, but it turned what could've been a depressing, lonely day into something that still makes me smile."

The other girls offer polite smiles at what was probably, on the surface, an underwhelming story, and while my eyes want to stray back to Liam, I force my gaze to Aspen first. He's looking at me in this way that makes you feel like you're the only girl in the room. It would feel more special if I hadn't seen him look at each girl before me the exact same way, and I want to shrink away from the intensity of those icy blues.

"That's really sweet, Sloane. Sounds like a good friend," he says.

I swallow down an unexpected swell of emotion in my throat before answering, "The best."

Everyone's attention then moves on to Olive, the last girl to share, and I discreetly glance over to Liam. I inhale sharply when I find his eyes fixed on me, an emotion in them that I can't read. His smile has faded. Is he worried that everyone will know he's the friend from the story? Should I not have told it? I give him a questioning look, and it's like it shakes him out of a dream. He gives me a tilt of his chin and an everything-is-okay smile, and I try to make myself believe it as I return my attention to the table.

After the show-and-tell portion of the evening ends, produc-ers set Aspen up for one-on-one time with some of us. The first one chosen for the honor—whether by him or producers, we can't be sure—is Jada. Her eyes widen as Liam whisks her away on Aspen's behalf to some cozy corner for a "private" chat. With cameras and mics, of course.

One by one, girls come and go from their alone time with Aspen while I keep eating desserts. At some point, I'm surprised to realize I'm the only one who hasn't been pulled away for a chat yet. The restaurant has gotten quieter as everyone gets more and more tired and conversations peter out, and I wonder what it means that I've been left for last.

Aspen seemed so into me last night, like, a weird amount seeing as I've given him the bare minimum so far. But today we've scarcely made eye contact. His attention, all that flattery last night, felt . . . not bad, just confusing. If I can't take a super-hot actor's interest in me and even halfway reciprocate, what's wrong with me? What am I even doing here?

There's a hand on my shoulder, interrupting my spiral, and I turn to find Liam there.

"You're up," he says with a tight smile. He starts to lead me to the spot chosen for my talk with Aspen, down some patio stairs and onto the beach, but I'm still occupied by my own discomfit-ing thoughts, which aren't helped at all by the tension in Liam's face and body language.

"Producers are picking the order," he murmurs softly before I can ask how he's doing.

"Huh?" I whisper back.

"Producers have been choosing in what order to pull girls aside. They saved you for last since you were his first pick last night. They don't want it to look like he's too interested too early. Probably also why you didn't get your own date this episode."

He says this all with such swiftness and softness that I know he doesn't want us to be heard. He's not mic'd up like I am. Trying to take in . . . whatever that means, I reply carefully in case anyone is listening to my mic feed.

"O-okay, good to know."

Then we're stepping onto the sand, and I pause to slip my shoes off.

"Also, I found a spot for notes. Blue flowerpot on the lower-most patio at Dorian's house. You'll see what I'm talking about."

Liam's voice is quiet and almost businesslike before he passes me off to Ty without another word. I look back at him, trying to catch his eye, but Ty urges me forward with a hand on my back. He tells me where to sit on the blanket beside Aspen, who smiles when he sees me. Based on what Liam said, it wasn't Aspen's choice to leave me for last and doesn't mean he's any less interested. Why doesn't this make me feel better?

"Don't be afraid to get a little closer," Ty adds, waving his hands to signal that I should move in toward Aspen. That feels . . . not necessary. But Aspen has scooted in, so I do too, and now our thighs are touching. The positioning must be satisfactory, because Ty finally motions that we're rolling.

"I've been looking forward to this all day," Aspen says, shifting his upper body weight. The result is that his face is super close to mine, all that pristine dental work staring me in the eyes.

I lean back on my palms, trying to regain a little personal space and fighting the urge to say that after paved-over playgrounds and billboard bird shit, I'm honored to be considered such a highlight of the day. "Same here."

He reaches up and tucks a wisp of hair that fell from my bun behind my ear, and the feeling of his hand brushing my skin is startling. A we're-not-on-this-level startling. Nothing like the comfort I feel when Liam is near, fixing something in my hair or giving one of his supportive arm squeezes.

Wait, why am I thinking about Liam again?

"Tell me something about you that I don't know," Aspen says, and I don't think I'm imagining his eyes flicking toward my lips and back up.

"That leaves most everything about me," I say. *Impeccable social skills, Sloane. Great job showing him how much you want to let him get to know you.*

Aspen smirks. "Lots to choose from, then. Pick anything."

"I have two siblings," I say almost automatically. "An older brother and a younger sister."

I always default to talking about my family. In a lot of cases, it's because they're who people ask about, when I run into acquaintances around town. When most people look at me, my family is where their minds go. I guess at some point, I started defining myself by them, too.

"Middle child." He nods, like this tells him everything he needs to know. To some extent, that's accurate. "I have an older brother, too."

I was vaguely aware of this, and the fact that big bro is an actor, too, though mostly in indie, artsy films. I wonder how he feels about the fact that Aspen is making bank on the most commercial kinds of productions.

"Are you guys close?"

Something hesitant flashes behind his eyes before his chill face is back on. "Close enough." He shrugs. Whatever that means. "What's your favorite thing about California so far?"

I look around the beach, being very deliberate about letting my eyes drift past the cameras without looking directly into them as I want to do every time. My casual perusal falters when my gaze lands on Liam, a few yards away. I probably can't answer, "The guy I came out here to see in the first place," though that would be the truth, wouldn't it? Liam can't be the answer to all my favorite things today.

"Um, probably the . . . palm trees?" Wow, she is eloquence personified. "We don't have those where I'm from, and they've always been something I only see when I'm on vacation. Waking up to them every day still feels special."

Aspen nods as if I've hit on the most important feature of his homeland, not grasped at the first thing that came to my mind. "Palm trees are great. My parents live right on the coast, and their backyard has a bunch. And I love the ocean." He gestures to the water in front of us. "It looks so peaceful but, like, there's so much going on under the surface that we can't even imagine. You know?"

I squint against the sun as I nod, a bit taken aback. I'm probably too hung up on the "my parents live" part, wondering why this seventeen-year-old *boy* is living somewhere different from his parents, but I'll probably sound like a sheltered baby if I ask that. I'm trying instead to think of something deep to say about ocean life when he turns his head back toward mine, somehow even closer than he was before.

"You're so beautiful, Sloane. And there's so much more beneath the surface of you, too. Everything I learn about you has me wanting to know more."

My eyebrows rise involuntarily. That's what he's gotten out of the three (3) details about myself that I've shared today? Which, if we want to be technical, aren't really about me—they're about my best friend, family makeup, and the Californian landscape. I have depths like the ocean?

I mean, it's flattering. I'd like to think I have more going on under the surface. Maybe Aspen's just on some other level from me, feeling this connection that I'm not worldly or cool or experienced enough to feel just yet. Or maybe it's the windswept train wreck of my appearance that's put him under my spell.

"Have you had a good time today?" he asks, whisper-soft, with a sparkle in his blue eyes that's communicating something more like *Let's kiss each other's faces off, Sloane.*

"I have," I answer, which is true. Even if it was more because of Alicia and the other girls than his skills as a tour guide, it's been a pretty decent day. "It was fun to learn a little more about everyone from those questions."

He laughs, and the puff of his breath on my own lips causes my head to jerk back. How did we get so close again? "Uh-huh, sure."

I frown as his words register. Was that sarcasm? "What do you mean by that?"

Aspen blinks, his expression shifting to a conspiratorial smirk. "You can be real with me, Sloane. I was fighting to stay awake for most of that dinner. I mean, I didn't expect to hear about any major movie gigs or whatever, but we don't have to pretend Irish dancing and summer camp stories rocked our worlds."

My eyes widen. Did he just drag the other girls to my face? Girls who have dropped everything and come from all around the country to open themselves up and date him on TV?

"Your story, though, it was so sweet. You're a naturally gifted storyteller, you know. I was so swept up by you. . . ."

This time, he's very obvious in his intent to kiss me, after being kind of a dick about a bunch of perfectly nice humans and the things they've shared with him. He brings his face to mine, angling his head to the side, eyes trained on my lips. But instead of the sweeping romantic music he must be hearing, there's a record-scratch sound in my head.

"Okay, back up, buddy," I say, scooting my whole body a good two feet away on the blanket. I bring my fingers up to my temples and rub, looking past the camera and crew in front of us and out to the ocean.

"What?" Aspen asks, confusion clear in his voice.

For a moment, I consider not answering. It's not my job to explain to him how he's being an asshole. But if I don't do it, will anyone else?

"You just—that was . . . not a nice thing to say about the other girls here who just shared some personal stuff with you and the many strangers who will watch it all on TV later. And then you try to kiss me after I told you no, like, not even twenty-four hours ago?"

Damn upspeak habit. That wasn't a question, but I'm too flustered to repeat myself.

"Sloane, calm down. Let's rewind. I didn't mean—"

Still not looking at him, I get to my feet, dusting some sand from the blanket off my backside and shaking my head. "No, I think you did. You're not exactly proving what I said that first day wrong, you know."

I turn and nearly run into Ty, whose hands are out in a placating gesture. "Come on, Sloane, let's calm down and talk this out with Aspen."

"If one more man on this beach tells me to *calm down*, I swear," I mutter before marching off in a direction unimpeded by a dude-bro producer.

I know I probably look dramatic—ridiculous, even. But this just feels like a wake-up call. A big, noisy alarm clock blaring, *"Time for Sloane to GTFO!"* I don't know why I thought for a second that doing this show was a good idea. Aspen Woods is even more self-obsessed than I thought. I can't pretend anymore that he's the type of person I'd be into, no matter what I might get out of it in the end. I wonder if I should go find Liam and—

"Sloane," an out-of-breath voice says behind me, but unfortunately it's not the crew member I was hoping for. I stop and let Kristi catch up.

"Whew, okay," she says, briefly resting her hands on her knees and taking a few deep breaths. I realize I'm breathing heavily, too, and feel a little impressed with myself. I didn't know I was moving *that* fast. "Look, I know that was bad, but let's see if we can work it out. I don't think you really want to walk away right now."

I've liked this woman well enough so far, but that gets my hackles up. "I don't think you know anything about what I want, Kristi."

She nods, studying me with a more serious expression than I thought she was capable of and still breathing hard. Then she walks behind me and sticks her hand up the back of my shirt.

"Girl, what the—" My freaked reaction is cut short when I realize she's just turned off my mic. Okay, reasonable.

"Sorry, I figured you'd want this off the record," she says in a quieter voice as she faces me again. "Look, Sloane, I know that wasn't great. But I genuinely think he wasn't trying to trash the other girls so much as compliment you, in his own clumsy way."

I can't help it—that gets an eye roll out of me.

Kristi goes on, starting to sound more urgent. "Okay, even if you don't believe that, walking off now is not gonna look good. I know I'm new to the reality TV game, but I've watched a shit ton of *Love Island* and *The Bachelor,* and I know how editing works. They're never going to let Aspen look like a bad guy. If you leave, that whole conversation will be edited so that you look like 'the crazy girl.' I know you might not want to give Aspen another chance, but at least give yourself one—a chance to stay around, leave on better terms whenever you go, and not be made a punch line when the show airs."

I don't know if I'm more shocked by the actually reasonable point she makes or the fact that she says the word "shit." Regardless, it resonates.

I heave a deep sigh and turn to look back at the beach behind me. Aspen is shielded from my view by Ty, who is crouched down in front of him saying who knows what. Most of the crew around them are clearly trying to act like they're not extremely curious about what Kristi's doing with the flight risk.

And then my eyes find Liam, standing a little off to the side from the others and very much looking at me with not curiosity but concern. For some reason, it brings the smallest smile to my face. He tilts his head, probably wondering what the hell I'm smiling about in the middle of my apparent breakdown, but then his lips turn up on one side.

And I feel . . . something. A little flutter of nervous, excited energy in my stomach that's nowhere near the trepidation I felt at almost being kissed by Aspen. But that can't be right; the two guys are in totally different categories in my life and mind. Why am I even comparing these feelings?

And why am I trying to analyze this right now, when I have a jittery producer waiting on me?

"Okay," I say before I really know what I'm doing. But I guess that's just how I operate these days. "I'll stay."

Kristi's relief is palpable. And when I return to the blanket, Aspen is deeply apologetic, ensuring me that his words came out all wrong, that he gets nervous around me, that he only meant to demonstrate how much he enjoyed listening to *me* rather than speak poorly of anyone else here. I'm not sure I'm sold on it, but I could also believe that his people skills truly are that bad. I saw the evidence of his out of touch childhood all day, after all.

I let him hold my hand as we walk back up to the restaurant a few minutes later. He doesn't exactly ask, but neither do I slap him away. It all feels very maturely settled, smoothed over. Aspen and Sloane have made peace.

Now if only the pit that seems to have taken up permanent residence in my stomach would get the memo.

Back inside, producers convene with Aspen to get his decision on which girl on our date he wants to add to the Cast List early. I highly doubt it'll be me two episodes in a row—especially because after this whole mess tonight I highly doubt I *am* the favorite. Even if he could overlook how I've rejected his kiss attempts two times and counting.

That's why I'm not at all offended or even surprised when he announces to the whole group he's decided to add someone from our date to the Cast List early this week—aka episode—and it's Ella M. Not surprised or offended, but perhaps less sure than ever that I'll hold up my end of Mr. Daniels's deal.

CHAPTER EIGHT

Sure, sometimes I wish I could un-dad him, but I can't.
That shit's biology.
—*THE COVE*, SEASON 3, EPISODE 2

Liam

I try not to regret my decision to ride with Dad to work before the crack of dawn. He offered, even though we'd been driving separately since filming started, and I appreciated the idea of spending some time together. I've been abnormally stressed since the drama of the Ensemble Date yesterday and thought it might be better to have his company than be alone with my thoughts.

I just hadn't anticipated the pre-daylight wake-up nor his extra-bad road rage. By the time we get to set, the tension in my body is so high that it doesn't feel like rolling my shoulders or neck around are doing much. I need a cooldown from the full body workout of carpooling.

It's a sad state of affairs that I'm actually relieved to be put on trash duty straightaway. As I walk around the whole set emptying all the smaller bins into one large bag and collecting miscellaneous debris from Hurricane *AWFLL*, no one on the crew

bothers me. It's almost meditative, being on my own with a focused task. I am one with the garbage. Call me Liam the Grouch.

But as I start to come down from the day's rough start, my
thoughts return to their Sloane McKinney spiral—a spiral I've
been trapped in since the moment I saw her at LAX, if I'm being
honest with myself. After last night, I can't ignore it anymore.

I'm her happiest memory. Which I can appreciate, since she's
at the center of all of mine. But hearing her tell that story and
thinking about how simply, consistently happy she makes me . . .
Yeah, I'm a little off-balance.

Are these normal best friend feelings? Or something alto-
gether bigger, more life altering? I keep telling myself the former.
But there's evidence to the contrary to be found in, say, tight
black dresses and the amount of time I've spent lately contem-
plating her eyelashes.

And that's not even factoring in the feelings I had when she
and Aspen got into it, when she stormed away from him and I
started to follow before Kristi stopped me with a hand and went
instead. There wasn't another chance for me to talk to Sloane
after that, to get a sense of where her head was or why she decided to stay. If only I could—

That's when it hits me. The notes.

I use the pretense of looking for more trash on Dorian's back
deck to slip away. I should've written her something that I could
leave there today to kick us off, but my mind's been a little preoccupied. What would I write? "Hey, Sloane, not much new here.
Trying to figure out if there's anything happening between the
two of us aside from friendship. So is there? Check yes or no."

Yeah, no.

I walk down the tiered terraces behind Dorian's house till I reach the big blue flowerpot, ensuring that no one around is watching me before I crouch to check it. There are these little cut-out pockets all around the side of the pot in addition to the main planter in the middle, where smaller clusters of flowers and greenery stick out. I didn't have time to explain the specific drop-off point to Sloane, and I guess I hoped she would figure it out without my telling her—and sure enough, she did. There's one cut-out pocket that doesn't have anything planted in it, just a little dirt at the bottom where it connects to the main body of the pot. I smile when I see the folded-up piece of paper left there, then pull it out to read.

Dear Liam,

Excited to be exchanging our very first secret message! Should we create some kind of code to write in, like in that Benedict Cumberbatch movie? Jk I just won't write anything incriminating in case these communications are intercepted. Ten-four, over and out. (You've heard Kristi say ten-four into her headset, right? I laugh every time.) Anyway, I don't have a whole lot to share. Bree, Hattie, and Alicia are great roommates. There's kind of a funny divide that seems to be forming between the Chelsea's House Girls and the Brock's House Girls—choose your fighter (Team CH 4evr!). There was a game of Disney-themed charades last night (really scraping the bottom of the barrel for entertainment w/o phones or a working TV) that got a liiittle heated. Each team wrote prompts for the other team members to act out and Team Chelsea's House might've dug a lil too deep with our Disney references, like The Three Caballeros and The Black Cauldron, while Team Brock's House gave us stuff like Sleeping Beauty, Mickey Mouse. . . . Miscalculations were made on the intensity of each team's charade game.

What are you up to when you're not here? Anything new? I like seeing you the little bit that I get to. Still so weird to be hanging out irl right?? Like to see your real live face and freakishly tall bod right in front of my eyes? (Are you uncomfy w/me using the word 'bod' hehe xo) Anyway, don't know when I'll see you next, so whatever you're up to, I hope you have a wonderful day! Remember that you're smart, funny, a super-talented woodworker, the nicest person I know and all-around greatest human there is! Okay? <3 you!

                                        Sloane

I know there's a stupidly big smile on my face; at the same time, it feels like someone's taken my heart and squeezed it in their fist. Now I'm really glad I didn't write the first note. It would've looked like shit next to this. No new intel on her talk with Kristi last night, or how she's feeling about all things Aspen, but she seems pretty upbeat in general. That eases some of my worry for her.

I came prepared to write her back, so I pull out the pocket-sized notepad and pencil from the back of my jeans before sticking her note in my pocket in their place. Then I get to work quickly writing my response.

When that's done, I start to jog back to the production tent out front in the cul-de-sac but stumble upon my new friend Garrett before I get there. He's about to head to Brock's house to reinforce some shaky bunk-bed frames, and he seems happy enough to get my help with the task. Now that we're here, my job appears to be handing him tools, holding up various pieces of the beds as he asks me to, and staying as unobtrusive as possible.

"So you said you're into woodworking, eh?" he asks through a grunt as he wrestles with a particularly stubborn stripped screw.

"Oh. Yeah, I am," I answer, not sure how much information he expects in return, but maybe I'm a little starved for conversation that's not about reality dating, so I go on. "I love it. So far I've only really made things for fun, or that I give to family and friends, but I . . . Well, I kind of hope to open up a real shop eventually. Sell my stuff, if it's good enough, make custom orders, all of that."

Garrett grunts again, but this time I think he's trying to communicate something. I wonder if Google Translate has a setting for this. Then he speaks. "Don't sell yourself short before you even get started. You want to try opening your shop, you should do it. Not so hard to set one up online these days, as a start. I freelance a little on the side, hired a website guy who knows about 'SEO' and all that shit. Been able to bring in enough business to cover my utilities and groceries every month. You ever thought about working for anybody else to get started, though? Apprenticing, anything like that?"

It takes me a minute to digest all of that, more words than

I was expecting to hear from Garrett in one go. And he has his own woodworking business? Okay, focus, he asked me questions.

"Yeah, I've thought about it," I answer, trying to hedge without getting smacked with a selling-myself-short reprimand again. "I guess still being in high school and not having any on-paper experience yet, I worry about no one wanting to take me on. I also don't want to be choosy when I don't really have the room to, but, well . . . I'm mainly into woodworking for the artistry of it. I love working with hand tools, feeling the shape of the thing beneath my fingertips, taking my time with it. I don't have much interest in working in a big industrial setting on cabinetry or stuff like that. So I know my thing is kind of niche and it'll be hard to get off the ground, but it's what I want to try for. And my parents aren't especially supportive, which makes things harder until I'm eighteen."

Garrett stands up straight, and I put the last screw into the bunk, then face him. His arms are crossed, and he eyes me skeptically.

"And what is it till you turn eighteen, a year? Less?" I nod. "So now's the time to lay the groundwork. Figure out what you can do that'll work in tandem with your real passion, until you can get that passion to make you money. Which you're starting to do by helping me here, a practical-construction, handyman-type role you could find in a lot of places. But I'll give you some names to look into, people and workshops that do the kind of artistic and custom work you're looking for. You can come see my shop sometime, though there isn't much to it, if I'm honest. Just a garage. It's all more possible than I think you think it is."

That last sentence sticks with me as we go back to working.

We head over to Chelsea's house to go ahead and fix up their bunks while all the girls who live there are hanging out by the pool. All the while, the wheels in my head are turning over the possibilities.

When the job is done and I help Garrett take his tools back to his truck in front of Brock's house, I thank him, adding that I do want to see his workshop sometime. And when we part ways, I feel reinvigorated to get home, work on my projects, plan for the future. I'm more hopeful than I have been in a long time.

෫ఏ

When I make it to the production tent, an EP is splitting up the crew into different assignments for the rest of the day. Some will stay here with the girls at the mansions, while the rest will join Aspen on his first Scene Partner Date.

You know, what us normal folk call . . . a date.

To my surprise, I'm put in the smaller, latter group. The girl who receives today's script—aka invitation—is Sloane's friend Bree, and the setting is "Up in the air."

They're going parasailing. The date is inspired by an early episode of *The Cove* in which Dorian and Chelsea go parasailing together and, while in the air, spot a sunken sailboat. They later scuba dive down to check out the wreckage and find both a suitcase full of gold . . . and a dead body. Because of course they do.

I feel less flattered by my placement on the exclusive Scene Partner Date crew an hour later, as it's an overcast day and the waters of the Pacific are especially choppy. It's all I can do to try to hold on to my breakfast while getting tossed around on a tiny boat that holds most of our film equipment and crew. Clutching at my life vest, I take slow breaths, in through the nose, out through the mouth. A dozen yards away, Aspen and Bree are getting buckled into some complicated harnesses connected to the parasail on another speedboat like ours.

Turning to Kristi, I try to sound composed and not panicky as I ask, "How long are they going to stay up there?"

She shrugs. "Oh, half an hour or so. Have you ever been parasailing?"

I shake my head.

"It's the coolest thing—once you're actually in the air, you can't feel the rocking of the boat or choppiness or the waves or anything at all. Smooth sailing, as they say, right? Ha!"

I'm close to asking if Aspen needs me to act as his stunt double. For, you know, insurance purposes.

After what feels like half a day, the parasailing portion of the date ends and our watercraft return to shore, sans any sunken treasure or dead bodies. I still feel like the earth beneath me is rocking in the hour or two afterward that we spend filming Aspen and Bree having a picnic on the beach, but I manage to stay upright.

Once we've wrapped up the date production and brought everything back to the set, it's early evening. I'm ready to find out if I'm released for the day, say hi to Sloane and/or check for a new note, track down Dad, then hightail it out of here. But when I start to look for Kristi, I hear an unexpected voice call my name.

"Hey, it's Liam, right?"

I turn slowly to stare at Aspen Woods with more than a little surprise. We haven't interacted since the first night when he crept up on me after the Casting Call, which has been fine with me. What could we possibly have to talk about?

"Uh, hi. Yes, that's me."

"Hey, man, how's it going?" He claps one hand on my shoulder and uses the other to grip my hand in a familiar shake. Way more familiar than I thought we were.

"It's . . . fine?" It comes out like a question, because it sort of is. Am I fine? Is this fine?

"Glad to hear it, glad to hear it. Look, I wanted to talk to you about something. You free to come on a run with me? I just have to stop by my place—well, Dorian's house—and change clothes and then we can hit the beach."

My brows feel like they have to be somewhere in the vicinity of my hairline. "Oh. I, uh, don't really . . ." *Run? Because I'm more of a chair-sitting person? Hiking person at my most active?* These seem like things I shouldn't admit to this guy. "Have running clothes with me. Sorry. And, uh, my dad drove me to work today so I probably shouldn't leave—"

"You can borrow my stuff," he says, looking me up and down. "And my guys can drive you home."

I don't know who these "guys" are, but between them and his commanding tone, Aspen Woods is giving me serious mob boss vibes. It feels like he's about to make me an offer I can't refuse.

Pushing a hand through my hair, I scramble for any more excuses he might accept but come up empty. "Sure, yeah. I'll go."

Which is how I end up feeling like I might be sick for the second time today as I chase a child star down the beach in a too-tight T-shirt and shorts I borrowed from his closet.

"So. You're pretty good friends with Sloane, right?" he asks, voice as level as if he was strolling down the sidewalk, not running a brisk pace on the sand.

The wheeze I let out is mostly due to the fact that I'm currently exerting myself far beyond my normal limits. But also, *Sloane?* Really? There will be no mercy for Liam today.

"Uh, yeah," I pant, pressing a hand to the cramp already forming in my side.

Aspen nods, unaware of—or just unconcerned by—my struggle to keep up. "Right. I've seen you all talking on set, and of course you were there when I met her that first day. So, we both know she never intended to come on the show and date me."

I grimace, unsure if this is a thing that's supposed to be out in the open. "Oh, well, I don't know that she—"

He waves a hand. "No, I know, and I'm fine with that. But I want her to be my last girl standing."

Now I'm choking. Jesus, this is too much for one day. I have to stop, bending over to rest my hands on my knees as I try to resume normal breathing patterns.

Casting my eyes up briefly, I see that Aspen has stayed close, jogging in place while he waits for me to work through my respiratory crisis. Very generous.

"I didn't think that would shock you so much," he says with a hint of teasing in his tone.

I hold up a hand while I finish coughing, then straighten

back up. "I just don't run that often. Can we pause for a sec? You want Sloane to be what now?"

He slows his jogging-in-place speed, which feels as close to a compromise as I'll get. "I want to pick her in the end."

My chest feels like it might collapse, in ways both literal and metaphorical. "You still have, like, twenty girls left. You haven't even gotten through the second episode, to the second Casting Call. Isn't this a little early to decide?"

Aspen shrugs, the movement extra bouncy. "I know what I want, you know? Trust me."

The incredulous look I give him likely conveys that I have literally no reason to do that. But I think of Dad, of my position on the show—and, most importantly, of Sloane. I know I have to play this carefully. Get to the bottom of this declaration and do what I can to make all parties happy.

"Okay. So, not to be completely obtuse, but why are you telling me this? What does it have to do with me?"

He cocks his head, letting out a measured breath. It's the first sign he's shown of anything like exertion, not that I'm bitter.

"You were on the date last night. You heard our conversation, how it didn't go so well. I don't think her opinion of me has improved at all since we've been together, and I don't like that. I want your help winning her over."

All right. Yep, it was a mistake coming here. He really is a mob boss, trying to kill my sanity. I can picture it now, any last shreds of cool and composure I had before this summer off to swim with the fishes. I lean my head back so my next words are directed at the sky. "Win . . . her . . . over?"

"Yeah, man. We both know she's not that into me right now, for whatever reason, right? I mean, I guess I'm not everyone's type. And I said some dumb shit I shouldn't have, but I didn't mean anything by it and hate that she was so upset. I care about her, and I want her to want to stick around. So I need your help with the wooing. You can tell me what she likes in a guy, what kinds of dates she'd be into, what I should talk to her about, definitely what *not* to talk to her about, all that stuff. Then maybe she'll come around to liking me, too."

My head is spinning, and for once, I actually *want* to run. In the opposite direction of Aspen, and *AWFLL,* maybe even through the space-time continuum to warn Past Liam not to take the job on this show, no matter what he thinks he'll be getting out of it.

"Why would I do that, though?" I ask. "Help you show Sloane a fake version of yourself to trick her into liking you?"

"No, no, that's not what it would be. Look, man, I'm an actor. Most of what I show the world is fake in some way. This wouldn't be me acting, though. I would just be emphasizing the parts of me that she'll like the best. Being the best version of me for her." He pauses, a more forced solemnity taking over his features. "And I'd look out for you in return, bud. Put in a good word with your old man, pull any other strings for you that I can, whatever it takes. I mean it. I'd owe you big."

I feel slimy for even considering it. And on top of that, I feel something harsher, sharper at the chance of Aspen and Sloane actually becoming a couple—at hearing for certain that she's the one he wants. I don't want to call it jealousy or possessiveness;

that feels dickish. I have no claim over her. I've been fine with her past boyfriends. Haven't I? Well, I mean, I've never especially liked anyone she's dated, but only because they weren't really right for her and she knew it as well as I did.

"Hey, do you care if I run a little farther and meet you back here?" Aspen points to a pier, probably less than a mile down the beach. "I won't be long, but I can give you some time to think and, you know, chill."

I nod, waving him away before going to plop down at the edge of the water, where the waves don't quite reach my toes as they lap at the shore.

Is there any way that Aspen could be right for her? I'm not sure. I mean, he's good-looking, hardworking (I assume), and talented. Kind of into himself, but I would be too if I was that famous and successful. It's possible he really was just trying to compliment Sloane when he bad-mouthed the other girls. I have no idea what kind of boyfriend he'd be, especially after the cameras are gone. But Sloane deserves the best. Someone who would want to be everything he could be for her, ready to cheer her on and watch her shine. Someone who would recognize how lucky they were to have her, because she's so kind, funny, selfless, beautiful, special—

Oh, shit.

I'm really into Sloane.

The revelation doesn't feel as earth-shattering as I would've expected it to. It's like my heart has been aware for a while, and my brain only just caught up. But the knowledge settles in me like the last piece of a puzzle clicking into place. Of course I never liked her boyfriends. Of course I've never made it past two dates with another girl. Obviously our friendship is amazing, but I have plenty of other strong friendships with people who aren't the most important person in my life.

I don't know how I didn't see it earlier, when, now, it's like it's always been right in front of me. But does this even change anything? I rub at an ache in my chest, right in the vicinity of my heart.

Would I actually be looking out for Sloane if I stopped Aspen from winning her over, or would it be my own self-interest talking? Besides, I don't have any real reason to believe there'd be anything more between Sloane and me if she wasn't with Aspen. I know I have feelings for her, but who knows if we'd actually have that elusive spark if we ever tried to take things further? And most importantly, I don't even know if she has a remote interest in seeing me as anything other than her best friend.

My head is spinning trying to work it all out, when I hear the muffled pounding of feet in the sand, slowing as Aspen gets closer to me.

"Well?" he says through barely strained breaths as he resumes jogging in place.

I drag both hands down my face, kicking at the sand with one sneakered foot. "You'd better not make me regret this."

CHAPTER NINE

I'm like coal. Put me in the heat, under pressure,
I become a diamond, baby.
—*THE COVE*, SEASON 1, EPISODE 10

Sloane

The day after Bree's Scene Partner Date is wide open until that
evening's Casting Call. There are no more dates this "week," and
the cameras are only hanging around to film "B-roll," or glimpses
of what's going on at the mansions when we're not out with
Aspen. Unfortunately for me, most of the girls have decided that
means spending all day in and around Chelsea's house's pool.

It's not that I can't swim, like I told Aspen I can't kiss. Or
I don't think it's like that, anyway. I could swim once upon a
time, and I assume it's something you don't forget how to do.
But the last time I went, aside from lazy-river floating with Liam,
Liza was a baby and Mom took the two of us to the neighborhood pool. Mom, like usual, stayed occupied with Liza in the
baby pool while I went off to find new temporary friends to play
around with under the lifeguard's supervision.

It was during a particularly rousing game of sharks and minnows that I went rogue, paddling on my kickboard away from the other younger kids toward the deep end. I was at the ten-feet mark when my grip on the board slipped and it flew out from under me, then landed a few yards away. Even though I knew how to swim, I was so startled when I dipped under the surface that I gulped in water. From there, my memory is a blur of flailing limbs and attempts at crying out, but I just kept drinking in more water and sinking deeper.

It was a few seconds that felt like hours before the lifeguard turned his gaze from the game at the shallow end and jumped in to save me, but it was enough to instill the lifelong fear. All these years later, I feel more foolish than ever.

But I also know it wouldn't have happened to me if I was Liza, because Mom would have been watching her like a hawk. It wouldn't have happened if I was Franklin, because I'd be a stronger swimmer, more capable and levelheaded in general. I know it's no one else's fault but my own that I almost drowned that day. But it doesn't stop me from feeling like I could be "drowning" in all sorts of ways, any time in any place, and the people who are supposed to be there for me the most wouldn't even glance at the deep end.

A couple girls squeal as another one cannonballs in and splashes them, the sound bringing me back to the present. *Yeesh,* what is wrong with me today? The Ensemble Date set me off, to be sure, but all the downtime since then has me practically writing emo ballads. I think it was the right call, staying here. But the time away from Aspen and the intense filming atmosphere has meant a lot more time to think, and I still wonder how much longer I'll last. I don't *want* to be some big, dramatic Character on the show with a big, dramatic Departure. But I also don't want to sit around listening to a whole TV season's worth of Aspen telling everyone how great he is, and pretend for the cameras that I'm super into that kind of guy. Surely there are better ways to make connections for my future. I can't imagine that Mr. Daniels would be losing out on much in my absence; as far as I can tell, casting did a great job with the rest of the girls they have.

I look around me at my fellow "cast," all swimsuit-clad and sunscreened up, most alternating between tanning on the lounge chairs and floating around the pool. A few hit a beach ball back and forth in the shallow end. In general, everyone looks like they're relaxed and having a good time. Hell, they're way better reality show contestants than I'll ever be. Is anyone else struggling with being here at all?

I sigh as I lie back in my lounge chair under the shade of a big umbrella on the pool deck. I'm in a T-shirt and shorts, my notebook and pencil in hand. It seemed like a good compromise when I came out here—I'm being social *and* I have a non-pool-related activity. But now that I'm here, I feel like the sore thumb of *AWFLL*. Sticking out in ways I'd rather not.

There's only one person I really want to talk to about this, but I've barely caught a glimpse of the back of his blond head since the Ensemble Date. I thought about working through some of my panicked thoughts in my first note to him, but it seemed too risky to put them in writing. Now, I might be getting desperate enough to do just that.

I pull out Liam's note that I grabbed from our hiding spot

earlier. I wanted to read it right away but didn't have a good excuse for why I would be chilling on the patio outside Dorian's house first thing in the morning. We're technically allowed free rein of the three backyard/deck areas, but there seems to be this unspoken agreement that it's weird to hang out outside of Aspen's place. So I had tucked the paper into my notebook and tried to look inconspicuous as I headed back to Chelsea's house.

With one last scan of the pool area, I get the sense that no one is really paying attention to me, so I pick it up and finally read.

Dear Sloane,

Did you just refer to the life's work of literal genius and war hero Alan Turing as "that Benedict Cumberbatch movie"? I found that a little too appalling to read the rest of your note, sorry.

Fondly,
Liam

P.S. Okay, I actually read the rest. And I can forgive you for that callous misrepresentation, only because I know how important Cumberbatch's bone structure is to you. Moving on, yes, I hear Kristi's "ten-four" about 10 x 4 (aka 40) times a day, because most of what I do is follow her around. The humor's worn off a little, but Kristi herself is growing on me.

I am 0% surprised at your Disney charades drama. If you'd given me ten guesses as to "ways Sloane would be most likely to stir up controversy," taking an innocent game too seriously would probably be #3 or 4. I mean that with all the fondness in the world. Have the Brock's House Girls forgiven you yet? Do I need to keep an eye out for anyone with an anti-Sloane vendetta?

Honestly, what I do so far when I'm not here is sleep. I've made some progress on a woodworking project that I'm excited to tell you about eventually, but my on-set hours have been longer than I expected. I am curious as to how they're getting around labor laws, etc., but I think my dad being in charge of my schedule means anything goes.

It's definitely weird to hang out in person but good-weird. How would you feel if I referred to your freakishly short "bod"? Exactly. (I don't actually think you're freakishly short.)

You're the one who's too nice around here. I don't know what I did to warrant all those compliments, but thank you, and I hope you're feeling pretty good today. You are funny and kind and way better at writing letters than I am. Ever thought about doing this writing thing long-term? Maybe you should.

Love you too,
Liam

"Have you put on any sunscreen today? These umbrellas might not have UV protection, and your face is starting to look a little tomato-y." Hattie's sweet, concerned observations startle me, and I slam my notebook shut on Liam's letter, swing my legs to the ground, and sit up straight.

As her words sink in, I put my hands to my face, feeling the heat there. But I know it's not from the sun. It's this inside-out kind of warmth from reading Liam's words and imagining him writing them for me. He's just the best there is.

But explaining to Hattie that I'm blushing at a completely innocent note full of platonic messages from my friend who happens to be a guy—well, I'd rather not.

"My moisturizer has SPF in it," I blurt out gracelessly. "So, uh, I think I'm just getting too warm out here."

"Want to get something to drink and dip your feet in the water with me?" she asks. She's also in shorts and a T-shirt. I'm itching to write a note back to Liam, like a text I can't bear to leave on read. But it does sound nice to hang out with her.

"In a minute maybe? I'm gonna finish something up here." I tap my pencil against my closed notebook. Hattie smiles and nods before heading to the other side of the pool, where the swim-up bar is. I hear her order "two ice waters with lemon, please, and can I get those little paper umbrellas?" It makes me smile.

Between the light tone of Liam's note and the time crunch I've just put myself in, I decide that pouring all my angst onto the page is not the move right now. I speed-write my note back to him, as if trying to scribble out funny observations and stories I would have texted him over the last couple days. It doesn't take too long; then I drop my notebook and pencil on the chair and sneak—as much as one can sneak in broad daylight—over to the lowest deck at Dorian's house and stick my note in the flowerpot.

As I make my way back to the pool at Chelsea's house, I

notice that the sounds of splashing, laughter, and voices have gotten louder. Stepping up to the topmost deck, the first thing I see is more cameras rolling than when I left—and then I realize why.

Aspen Woods in all his shirtless glory, right there in the middle of the pool.

He smiles winningly at the growing circle of girls around him, greeting everyone with hugs. By the looks of the wet hair he flicks back with a toss of his head and more water coursing down his tan, toned chest, he must have jumped right in.

It's not a bad look, by any stretch. There are uglier people to compromise your dignity on national television for.

I cross to where Hattie is perched on the pool's edge and take a seat beside her. She smiles and passes over a cup of water with a lemon wedge and—sure enough—a small pink umbrella in it.

"He showed up right when you left," she says, and I await the obvious *Where did you go?* question. But it doesn't come. "Apparently this is a *real* pool party now. If you don't like lemon, I'll take yours!"

"This is great, thank you," I answer, taking a sip. I look out at Aspen again, taking advantage of the moment to watch him.

He looks more relaxed here than ever, his smile natural as he absently scoops up water in his hands and lets it drop back into the pool while he listens to a girl named Raya talk. I wonder if he thinks *her* story is boring or unimpressive. You wouldn't think so, from how interested he looks right now. This guy appears softer, more approachable than past Aspens I've encountered. Or is it just the shirtlessness that makes him seem more human?

My eyes drift down to the flexing biceps as he stretches his arms out at his sides. Nope, I take it back—that is not exactly humanizing. He's a steamy Dorian-Mara hot tub scene come to life.

I realize I've finished all but the ice in my cup. Hattie's water is still half full, so I excuse myself from sitting here feeling confusingly turned-off and -on all at once, and I walk over to the pool bar to request another. While the PA there fills my cup—*How can Liam get* this *job?* I wonder idly—I hear my least favorite producer's voice coming from the nearby cabana.

"Ella, would you consider yourself a front-runner?" Ty asks, and the bluntness surprises me. Aside from night one in the kitchen with the other girls, I've only had one other OTF, and Kristi was the one questioning me. We talked about only the positives—what I'm enjoying about my time here, what I like about Aspen. Nothing too personal or that made me uncomfortable.

I thank the PA as she hands me my refill, then find myself lingering in this spot as I sip. It's not really eavesdropping if it's happening in earshot of myself, the bartending PA, and a lot of other cast around the pool, right?

I can hear the discomfort in Ella M.'s voice as she answers. "Um, I don't know that I would call myself a front-runner? I really like Aspen and think we have a great connection so far."

"A better connection than he has with the other girls, then?" Ty persists.

"Uh, I don't know?"

"Restate the question, please."

"I don't know if we have a better connection than he has with the other girls."

"Oh, yikes. She gave 'em a sound bite," whispers Alicia, and her sudden presence at my side makes me jump.

"What do you mean?" I whisper back, wiping at the water I just spilled on my shirt.

"Editing could chop off the beginning of that sentence easily, then it's just: *We have a better connection than he has with the other girls.*"

My mouth falls open. Damn, does everyone here have a better awareness of reality TV editing possibilities than I do?

Well, Ella M. clearly doesn't.

It gets harder to hear the conversation in the cabana as a game of beach ball keep-away starts up, but I tune in again as Ella is saying, "Kissing Aspen was really good . . . definitely the best kiss I've ever had."

I swallow down a gasp. Other girls have kissed him already? When? Is this what happens in others' one-on-one time? I guess it's no wonder he keeps trying with me, then. *Ugh.* I'm gonna look like some prude-y freak for putting him off, aren't I?

Admittedly, there's been a little voice in my head, one that sounds like all the *Cove* fans across the world, hissing, *What the hell is wrong with you?*

I've missed whatever Ella M. said, but I hear Ty shoot back, "So you'd say you deserve to be here more than anyone else, then?"

"What? No!"

Oh, yikes.

"I'm just repeating what I heard, Ella." Ty's tone is patronizing.

"That's not what I— You twisted my words," Ella M. replies, her voice starting to wobble.

"Ty, that's enough." Kristi's voice, sharp and loud enough to turn some heads from the pool, catches me off guard. "Ella, you're free to go, honey."

"What the hell, Kristi?" Ty scoffs. Ella M. emerges from the cabana right beside Alicia and me, but she doesn't look at us as she heads straight for the house. Alicia and I exchange grimaces as the two producers continue squabbling, only bits and pieces audible over the murmuring of the spectators and the cast still playing in the water.

We start to creep away toward the other end of the pool to sit with Hattie, when Ty storms out right in front of us. He stops in his tracks, cutting a suspicious gaze our way. We're probably the most obvious snoopers to ever snoop. But I'm surprised when his face turns into a smirk.

"Oh, Sloane, I was looking for you earlier," he says. I feel a chill run through my body, like I've dumped the whole cup of ice water all over myself.

"Y-you were?" Did he see me sneaking around on Dorian's house's deck or something? I haven't really done anything wrong; there's no need to act like I'm on trial.

"Yeah, I found this on a chair over there." It's only then that I first see what he's holding and, yep, I go full ice cube. My notebook. The one with a note from Liam still sticking out of the top. There's also a lot of random notes for story ideas, Sloane and

Liam's Summer of Fun list, scenes I've written, and other things that I don't especially care for Ty to have perused. Most recently, I've been toying with a new pilot premise, sort of a meta TV drama that centers on the behind-the-scenes relationships of the cast and crew on a show like *The Cove*. The villain, as far as I've gotten, is a particularly unpleasant producer.

"Looks like it's yours?" he asks.

"It is," I say, pleased that at least my voice doesn't shake.

Ty nods, holding the notebook out to me and tapping the cover before I snatch it back from him. "Wasn't trying to spy on you or anything"—meaningful pause, pointed look at Alicia and me—"just to see where I should return it. Must say, I found some interesting stuff in the process, though. Is that *our* Liam?"

He gestures to the folded note where it's tucked between some pages. I balk at the use of "our," and almost laugh at the thought of telling Liam about it later. But then I refocus: Ty has had my notebook in his clutches for a not-insignificant amount of time. What does he know—or think he knows?

Most importantly, what will he do with that knowledge?

Somewhere behind us, another crew member calls Ty's name. Before he makes a move toward them, he delivers an ominous "We'll talk soon, Sloane."

He walks away looking a little too much like the Grinch plotting to steal Christmas. Not sure what Christmas would be in this case, though—my intellectual property, my secrets, my future happiness? Time will tell, I guess.

"Okay, that was weird as hell. He read your diary or something?" Alicia's face is screwed up in confusion.

"It's not really a diary." I try to play it off casually, but my hands shake where they grip the book. "Just where I do some writing, rambling really. And I have a note from Liam in here. I don't love that he looked through it, but—" I gesture to the cabana. "Who am I to talk about getting into other people's business, right?"

She gives me a sardonic look and crosses her arms over her chest. "It's different and you know it. I don't trust that guy."

I definitely don't either, but I swallow down the words. I don't say much of anything for the rest of the time I stay by the pool hanging out with Hattie and Alicia. I haven't even talked to Aspen yet when I excuse myself to go inside, blaming a headache.

Safely ensconced in my upstairs bedroom, I open up my notebook and try to do what normally calms me when there's too much going on in my head—I write. My pencil and paper and a whole slew of ideas suck me in for what has to be hours after that. I'm so in the zone, switching between drafting a few scenes and dialogue and doing some of my own journaling, that I don't even register when other girls start to come up and get ready for the Casting Call. It's only when a hand appears in front of my face and snaps its fingers that I come back to the present.

"Last call," Bree says, and I get the feeling she's been trying to get my attention for a while. I look up at her, embarrassment creeping over me as I snap my notebook shut. "You going to get ready for the evening, or is this what you're wearing?"

❧

I thank her about six more times over the next hour for saving me, as I shower and attempt to make myself look halfway decent.

I land on a red romper that I got on Mr. Daniels's dime and my wedges, my hair twisted into a fancy bun by Alicia with a couple of curls framing my face.

There are some nerves in the air, since Bree and Ella M. are the only ones of us on this week's Cast List so far—Bree having been added at the end of her Scene Partner Date yesterday. I'm still unsettled by Ty, wondering what he read—or read *into*—while he had my notebook, but I'm trying to refocus for the night. I need to figure out what I'm really doing here, and I'll only get there by spending time with Aspen.

When we make our way down to the beach behind Dorian's house for our pre–Casting Call freeze pop toast, I'm not thrilled to be greeted by a) zero freeze pops, b) zero Liam either, and c) Ty standing there with a camera operator.

"Who's ready for some OTFs to start out the evening?" he asks, Grinchy smile lighting up his face. There are a couple of half-hearted *woo*s from the group that's gathered around in the sand, probably because rumors of the Ella M. Inquisition from earlier today have made the rounds, but Ty claps as if we've all just done a choreographed dance routine. "Awesome! How about we start wiiith . . . Sloane."

Somehow, I knew this was coming.

I submit to getting the mic strapped on me by one of the nice PAs before being led off to a more private area behind a dune, where they spend a few minutes readying the lighting and camera placement. When Ty gives me two thumbs up, I return the gesture, and he starts in.

"Sloane, how have you been?"

The question surprises me, though I guess I shouldn't have expected "Is your fictional TV villain based on me, and also, do you want to fight right now?" as a lead-in.

"I've been . . . pretty good? It's a lot to get used to, being here, living with all the girls, all the cameras and stuff."

"Sure, of course." He nods. "You've been making friends in your house, though? Settling in okay?"

"Yes, I'm settling in, and all the girls are so great." A little bit of a stretch, but saying *most* of them are great would obviously invite a follow-up question I don't want. "I'm probably closest to Bree, Hattie, and Alicia, my roommates."

"Very nice, very nice. So as you get to know the other girls, what do you think about their reasons for being here?"

That one gets a head tilt out of me. "Um. What?"

Ty adjusts his stance, crossing an arm over his chest and bringing the other hand up to start stroking his chin, a caricature of Pensively Thinking. "You know, everyone has their own reasons for coming here. But mostly, it's because you all want to date Aspen, right?"

I nod, and it doesn't even occur to me that I didn't get his usual "Restate the question, dummy" reprimand until he's nearly through his next sentence.

"Or that's what we hope, anyway. But has anyone given you reason to doubt them, to question what they're really doing here?"

"I don't . . . I mean, no?" I blink in bewilderment. "I don't question what anyone else is doing here."

"Nobody's said anything about being here to . . . advance

their own ambitions, or chase fame? Nobody has, say, some-one else in their head or heart while they're supposedly here for Aspen?"

Oh. This is what we're doing. I'm getting a sense of what Ty thinks he got out of his little journey into my personal belongings today. I'm being cornered here—he thinks he's caught me, and I'm guilty of . . . what, exactly? Wanting to get famous from this show so I can turn it into a screenwriting career? Having some kind of relationship with Liam? Neither of those is an accurate conclusion, so nice try.

Okay, so they're not super far off base, either.

But not accurate! He's still got nothing, not really.

"I haven't gotten the impression that anyone here has shady motives. These are all good girls who genuinely care about Aspen, as far as I can tell." I take a deep breath and let it out. "And why are we talking about them, anyway? Shouldn't we be talking about Aspen and my relationship with him?"

"Sure," Ty says, still looking all narrow-eyed and skeptical. "Why don't you tell me about your *relationship* with Aspen? You hit a bit of a rocky patch the other night, didn't you?"

I give him my most serene smile, newly resolved to prove him wrong. "We're just starting to get to know each other and figure out how we communicate, you know? Aspen is . . . really something. He's cute, obviously, and sweet. He's been caring and concerned with my feelings, which I appreciate. I think I need more time with him, you know? If I'm really going to know if we connect and—"

"While I'd love to hear the rest of that sentence," I hear from behind me, "I think I can help with the more-time thing." Aspen gives Ty and the rest of the crew his most endearing, who-could-say-no-to-that-face smile. "Care if I steal Sloane away?"

Ty's smile goes tighter, his disappointment clear, but he nods jerkily. "Of course! Go for it. We'll follow, right, crew?"

Aspen doesn't wait to hear anyone else's answer before offering me his hand, blue eyes twinkling in the fading daylight. I'm surprised that when I smile back, it feels genuine. It's mostly relief at him getting me out of that mess of an OTF unscathed. But there's also the memory of seeing him in the pool, all relaxed and easygoing and, okay, not-bad-looking in swim trunks. And, honestly, the proximity to Ty makes any other guy look amazing. I don't know if it's the batshit concept of this show getting to me, but I'm resolving to give him a clean slate tonight—to stay more open-minded, give him a real chance to show me who he is.

I take his hand and let him link our fingers together as he leads me to the lowest deck behind Brock's house. I haven't been over here much beyond taking a brief look around, and it's quiet and empty while everyone else is at Dorian's. He takes me down a flagstone path toward the outer edge of the backyard area. Per usual, cameras follow us the whole way.

"Did I miss the freeze pops?" I ask. I was kind of looking forward to trying an orange one tonight.

Aspen gives my hand a tug that draws me in just enough to bump our shoulders together playfully before separating us again. "Nope. I wanted to come grab you before the night officially starts, if you don't mind. I was sorry I missed you earlier today."

An unexpected bloom of satisfaction fills me at that. "Oh, that's—that's so sweet. Yeah, I'm sorry, I think it was too much sun and I—"

"Hey, no worries. Are you feeling better now?" Those icy blues are filled with something that looks like real concern.

"I am," I say truthfully.

"Good," he says, and *oof,* that smile. It may be practiced, but practice has indeed made perfect. "Hey, I have a little something I wanted to show you. . . ."

When we reach the middle deck, he takes me to an opening shrouded by palm trees that I hadn't noticed before. Through it is a small offshoot—a low, isolated balcony off the deck's edge, hidden from view. There's a wooden swing looking out toward the ocean where the sun is setting over the horizon. Though we're not far from the rest of the party, it feels totally secluded here.

Aspen leads me to sit down on the swing beside him and the two of us start to gently sway, Ty and a camera crew setting up off to our side.

"Wow," I say, as close to a loss for words as I get. I look out at the pinks and oranges of the sky. "This is gorgeous."

"Yeah," he says, and when I turn my head, I confirm my suspicion that he is looking at me, not the sunset. Cheesy Hallmark movie, party of two! But I feel my cheeks go hot anyway, and I have to hold in a laugh because what in the actual hell is my life right now?

I look back out at the ocean, because I'm not sure what else to say, but Aspen leans away from me, bending over the swing's arm to reach for something on the ground. When he sits back up, I'm surprised to see he's holding two servings of my favorite beverage in the whole world—glass-bottle Coca-Cola.

He hands one of them to me with a smile. "Hopefully you're a Coke fan?"

"Um, yeah," I say, my brows still lifted in astonishment. "Glass-bottle Cokes are only my favorite drink *ever*."

"No way," Aspen says with a laugh, putting a hand to his chest. "Seriously? They're mine, too!"

I laugh, too, surprised at this turn of events. "Like, the glass is the superior way to drink it, you know? It feels like it keeps it extra cold without ice that'll eventually melt and water it down."

He nods his agreement. "And this might sound weird, but I always feel like the glass fits my hand better than a can or plastic bottle."

I swat at his arm without thinking about it. "Oh my God, I say the same thing!"

It's not that Cokes in glass bottles are some super-exotic, original preference, but it's kind of a cool coincidence that we're both so into them, right? It feels like one of my first glimpses of Aspen as just . . . a normal guy. A guy with the same specific soda preferences as me. And this is an objectively sweet thing to do, pulling me aside and getting me a treat before even going to the rest of the group. It makes me a little gooey inside, thinking that he planned this bit of quality time out with me in mind.

"Let's toast," he says, tipping his bottle toward mine. "To sunsets, good drinks, and the beautiful girl beside me."

I give a small laugh and clink my bottle to his before taking a sip.

We sit, sip, and swing for a few more minutes. He tells me what an average day for him looks like when I ask, and I tell him the same when he returns my question, though my answer is a lot more on the "average" side. His relatability kind of stopped at the glass-bottle-Coke thing, but what did I expect? He can't help that he comes from such a glamorous background.

Still, I find my mind wandering as we talk. I think about the last time I sat and watched a sunset with someone—with Liam, at his house just before everything about our summer turned on a dime. What would it be like if I hadn't decided to do this show? Would I have seen him today? Could I be at home with him right now, watching this same sunset from his rooftop, talking and laughing together with the ease that comes only from knowing someone as well as you know yourself?

I think of Bree's offhanded comments about being able to see Liam and me as a couple. Is there something to what she's saying? Is that why my mind seems so fixated on him these past few days? Or am I just missing him? I'm in an unfamiliar setting, and he's the most familiar and comfortable person to me. Is that all this is about?

"Well, I'd love to sit and do this for the rest of the evening." Aspen interrupts my thoughts with a sigh as he finishes up a story he was telling, and I feel guilty that I haven't really been listening. "But I should probably go get the party started. Shall we?"

He stands and offers me his hand, which I take as we head back through the palms and down the steps all the way to the beach, continuing toward Dorian's house.

"Thanks for this," I say, holding up my now-empty bottle. "It was nice of you to get me something."

Aspen smiles, tugging me to a stop beside the last dunes that hide us from the larger group. "Anything for you, Sloane. I want you to know that you're special to me, okay?"

He leans in, and before either of us has time to even think of another option, my head turns to offer him my cheek again. He plants a peck on it before squeezing my hand and then walking away, trailed by Ty and the crew.

I notice idly that Aspen took only a few sips of his Coke, which he hands off to a PA as they leave. Guess he's more responsible with his caffeine intake than I am.

Meanwhile, I'm buzzing the rest of the evening, filled with sugar and confusing trains of thought. I wish I could just see Liam, and for more than the brief moments we get in passing as one or both of us is pulled in different directions for filming. I need to feel out if there's something real shifting around in the space he occupies in my heart, or if I'm just high off the love fumes in the atmosphere on set. But something tells me that won't be easy.

I get an orange freeze pop and hang some more with Bree, Hattie, and Alicia by the volleyball court before the producers start to gather us for the Casting Call. It's another long ordeal of getting set up, dividing us between the benches and the risers rebuilt behind them, making sure all the lighting around the firepit is right, waiting for Aspen to show up. When he finally does, the process from the first night repeats, with him calling out the names of the rest of the girls who are safe this week, one by one. My name is first, and Hattie and Alicia are on the list, too. In the end, five more girls go home—Piper, Ella C., Lindsay, Meg, and Kenzie.

Getting ready for bed a short while later, I look at myself in the mirror as I take my makeup off, wash my face, brush my teeth. I made it through episode three. Aspen seems to be trying so hard with me, making me feel like his interest is genuine. Like I could reasonably make it to his final four, in spite of our shaky start.

And for my part, I feel better about him than I have in all the time we've known each other so far, like I see him for the well-meaning, flawed, fully human boy that he is. Between that, the plan with Mr. Daniels, and this new, deep desire to prove one gigantic asshole of a producer wrong, it's enough to keep my hands full and my head spinning for as long as I'm here.

CHAPTER TEN

I left the cucumbers from my spa treatment on the counter for
too long, and we got fruit flies. Take it from me—you can't
avoid your problems forever.

—*THE COVE*, SEASON 2, EPISODE 15

Liam

I really wish I'd never given Aspen Woods my phone number.

Actually, while we're making wishes, maybe I'd start with
wishing I'd had more of a backbone and hadn't agreed to this
job this summer. Or wishing that my dad gave a shit when I ex-
pressed my actual interests, which have nothing to do with working on a TV set. Would I go back so far as to wish my parents had
never separated? I'm not sure, though it was clearly when they
both started to go off the rails.

But presently, I absolutely wish I'd turned the movie star
down, or told him I didn't have a phone or something. Anything
to stop him from texting me his stream-of-consciousness-style
musings about my best friend he's trying to win over.

I was doing pretty well tiptoeing around yesterday like a double agent. It was an off day from dates, Kristi had the day off

entirely, and I was only scheduled for the morning, so I was instructed to "float" and see where help was needed. I had clamps clipped to my T-shirt sleeve if any grips or camera operators needed them, I set up apple boxes as required by camera operators, and in my back pocket were some batteries I traded out for dead ones in mics and walkies. All in all, I succeeded at avoiding Aspen so he wouldn't make me talk about Sloane and avoiding Sloane so she wouldn't try to talk to me about Aspen.

Up until I got to the parking lot, about to leave for the rest of the day, and Aspen finally tracked me down. He wanted to get a present that he could surprise Sloane with before the Casting Call, so he asked me if she has any favorite foods or drinks. Cokes in glass bottles came to mind, and he loved the idea.

And immediately asked if I could go buy him some Cokes in glass bottles.

That's how I, an idiot, spent my time off still working for my dad—not that he knew. I guess when you're one of the biggest celebrities in your generation and happen to be starring in your own reality show, it's not so easy to inconspicuously pop over to the grocery store. Or that's what I'm choosing to believe, anyway, as it's better than the alternative scenario, in which I've actually become Aspen Woods's servant boy.

I hauled my ass to three different stores before finding what I needed, then carted the bounty all the way to the set, snuck the six-pack into a bush outside Dorian's house, and got back out as quickly as possible.

Hopefully it was worth it.

But what would constitute "worth it" in this case? This is what I'm wondering as I pull into set the next day, feeling my phone buzzing in my pocket and somehow knowing that it's Aspen. Do I hope the Cokes made Sloane happy? Sure. So happy that she actually starts falling for the guy, or decides to kiss him or something?

I don't think I'm that evolved yet. I let my head fall to the top of the steering wheel with a thud.

But I wallow in place for only a moment before cutting the ignition and pulling my phone out of my pocket. Sure enough, a series of texts from Aspen awaits, telling me how well the Cokes went over and thanking me repeatedly. Good to be an appreciated servant boy, I guess. He also asks if I can meet at his house tomorrow—he'll be off on an Ensemble Date all day today—to talk about an idea he has.

It's always ominous when someone won't just tell you the thing that they want to tell you over a text. I feel like I should be able to install an app on my phone to block those sorts of messages, the ones that will just make me anxious all day. Something to work on when my reality TV career is up.

When I eventually make it to the morning huddle with the crew, I find out that I'm one of two PAs and a camera operator getting left behind at the mansions with the two girls not going on the Ensemble Date. Those two girls are going on Scene Partner Dates in the coming days, a term that would be less troubling if we hadn't gotten into the habit of saying so-and-so is "getting an SPD."

"You feel ready for that, Liam? Think you can handle the responsibility, pal?" Ty—who is far from what I would call a pal—asks me with a patronizing look.

I'm about to confirm that I am qualified and comfortable

with being a pseudo-babysitter for two girls my own age when Kristi beats me to it.

"Of course he's ready. Liam's got this!"

She gives me a pat on the shoulder before bouncing off to wherever she's needed next, dragging Ty behind her even though he's twice her size. Kristi may be intense, but at least I know she's on my side. Ty is just a dick.

One of the EPs finishes reading the meeting information off his clipboard. "So let's see, it looks like the SPD girls staying back today are gonna be Peyton aaand . . . Sloane!"

Ah, shit.

Sure enough, it's not even an hour later that all the other cast, producers, and cameras head out for the Ensemble Date on which they're hiking to the Hollywood sign and having a picnic. All the girls are taking a change of clothes for a "mocktail" party at some restaurant overlooking the city in the evening, so we'll be on our own here until after dark.

In other words, so much for my attempts to avoid Sloane.

Once everyone else has left, I look around the empty house, unsure what to do with myself. As I turn to face the backyard, it occurs to me that I haven't checked for a note in the flowerpot in a while, since before I started talking to Aspen. My head isn't sure it's such a good idea, but my heart and feet are not on the same page, the latter already taking me outside and down the steps.

Sighing as I get to the flowerpot, I crouch down to reach into the little pocket.

I'm surprised to find several notes inside. The first is long, rambling, funny—a lot like the very first note Sloane left me here. The subsequent ones are shorter, more pointed. Similar to actual texts I'd get if I hadn't been answering Sloane in a while.

Helloooooo Liam, where are u Liam

ARE YOU AVOIDING MEEEEE

Pls I'm bored

All Peyton has said to me today is "your hair looks weird."
Send help

All right, I'm officially feeling guilty. With a reluctant laugh, I tuck the notes into my back pocket and stand. This probably calls for an in-person apology. I'm still wary as I skulk around Dorian's back patio and over to Chelsea's house's, eyes peeled for a small, cute brunette. Damn, no—not cute. We need to cut off that line of thinking.

"Liam, could you help me with something?"

I whip around, surprised to find not Sloane but Peyton. Apparently she insulted Sloane's hair, but she hasn't been anything but nice to me. Okay, maybe a little nicer than nice. She's smiling at me with that extra glint in her eye like she knows I think she's cute and wants me to know the feeling is mutual.

"Yeah, absolutely," I say, jogging to her. She leads me into the kitchen at Chelsea's house, where a whole mess of yogurt, milk, and fruits sits out on the counter beside a half-full blender.

"I think I'm doing everything right, but for some reason, it isn't blending. Could you take a look?" Peyton tilts her head, wide blue eyes blinking up at me. She really doesn't have to lay it on so thick, but also, who am I to stop her?

"Let's see," I say, pushing the sleeves of my shirt up as if I'm some blender mechanic about to get down to business. Of course, all I really know to do is look at the thing, peering through the glass at all angles and deciding that, yep, looks like smoothie ingredients in a blender. I secure the lid on top then push the pulse button. There's a loud, miserable grinding noise and no real movement inside.

"Well, that's not good," I say, stating the obvious.

She purses her lips in a cute little pout, shaking her head. Okay, Daniels, you can save the day here. It can't be that difficult.

After opening a few different drawers, I find the silverware and pull out a spoon. My only idea is to mix things up so there's more liquid on the bottom than solid fruit, to see if that might make it easier for the blades to turn. Is that even how blenders work? I give it a try, digging the spoon down deep and giving it a stir, then take it out and put the lid on again. I also move the setting on the blender up to puree for good measure, then hit the pulse button.

Movement! And no grinding noise. All the separate layers in the blender are pulled together quickly and smoothly, just like they're supposed to be.

Peyton is suddenly right beside me, gripping my arm and squealing, "Yay! Oh, thank you so much, Liam."

I will not flex my arm right now, I will not—ah, okay, that felt involuntary. But this attractive girl is looking up at me like I'm her brunch hero, and I'm feeling pretty good about this bare minimum effort I put in. Definitely not just trying to divert my romantic attention from the Sloane direction.

"Hey, there you are."

At the sound of Sloane's voice, I jump away from Peyton, sending any semblance of cool I had for a second there out the window. Peyton shoots me a hurt look and narrows her eyes at Sloane before turning to pour her smoothie into a tall plastic cup. Sloane stops a few feet away, looking between Peyton and me with a small wrinkle of confusion in her forehead. She's holding a half-eaten chocolate muffin, a smear of chocolate lingering in the corner of her mouth. I should not find that so adorable, damn it.

"Here I am," I say, continuing to act totally natural by making jazz hands at my sides.

She tries to hold in a laugh and ultimately fails at it. "Right. Can we talk?"

God, I've missed Sloane. Seeing her face has already eased this tension I didn't realize I was feeling in my chest and replaced it with something new, something warmer. If the universe didn't want me to spend time with her, well, it probably should have stopped them from leaving us alone together on set all day.

"Yeah, let's go," I answer, refraining from any more awkward hand gestures as we leave the kitchen for the back patio.

I follow her lead, the two of us strolling side by side on the path that winds its way through all three backyard wonderlands. It's sunny out, and as we walk, it feels like I'm able to breathe for the first time in days.

Then Sloane breaks the silence, nearly taking all the breath back out of me. "I've really missed you."

My eyes dart to her and thankfully my feet keep moving without even tripping over each other. She doesn't look back at me, just keeps walking and shoves the rest of the chocolate muffin in her mouth, but is that a flush rising up her neck? Could also be a sunburn—probably a sunburn. But she goes on. "It's weird, because obviously, like, we spend most of our lives physically apart now. But something about knowing you're close by, that we *could* be hanging out and *would* if not for this weird plot twist, it makes me feel . . . clingy. Needy. Like I wish you could spend all your time on set hanging out with me, even though I know you have an actual job to do. I don't know, I'm rambling. But I've just . . . missed you."

My heart is pounding so hard in my chest, it feels like she should be able to hear it. Or see it, like I'm a cartoon character. But I think I do a decent job keeping my voice steady when I reply, "I've missed you, too. But hey, you've got me now. All day to hang."

"Yeah, if Peyton doesn't need anything else."

My laugh is an anxious one. "That's not—she was—wait." The thought seems almost too ludicrous to voice, but . . . "Are you . . . jealous?"

She throws her hands up in the air, still not looking at me as we walk. "I don't know, maybe! Would that be so weird? Ugh. I told you I'm being needy. I don't like it."

She may not, but the implication that she feels needy *for me*—I like it a little too much. I'm having to try harder and harder to keep my smile locked down.

"You have nothing to be jealous about," I say as Sloane comes to a stop beside the pool. She sits cross-legged at its edge, and I drop down beside her. "I was just helping Peyton to get the blender working."

There's so much unspoken there—like the fact that Sloane and Peyton are both here to date Aspen, so it's not like Peyton was trying anything with me. Or that Sloane and I are *friends,* so what even is there to justify if Peyton *was* trying something?

Sloane's laugh is quiet. "Right, and I always thank the blender maintenance guy with my whole body," she says, exaggeratedly throwing her arms around my neck and plastering her front to my side, nearly toppling me over.

I laugh, putting a hand to her waist to steady us both, but then we fall silent as we lock eyes and it becomes clear how close our faces are. So close that I can feel her breath on my lips, see the sprinkling of freckles on her nose that will soon get darker like they do every summer. The chocolate is still smudged in one corner of her mouth.

"You, uh, have something . . ." I trail off, gesturing in the vicinity of my own mouth.

Sloane lets out a soft exhalation that I feel on my lips even as she jerks back, wiping a hand across her whole face in a way that drags the chocolate out. Now it stretches toward her chin. "Better?"

I shake my head, lean in, and raise a hand to her face before I can think about what I'm doing. "Here, let me—"

I press my thumb to the corner of her mouth, the realization hitting me as I feel her suck in a breath. This is oddly . . . intimate for us. But I've already started, and I can't make it weird now, right? Or make it weird*er*, I guess. So I keep swiping my thumb down, a little bit at a time. Trying not to notice that her lips, now slightly parted, are the prettiest shade of pink I've ever seen, or that her skin feels impossibly soft. Or that in my periphery, it feels like I can sense her studying me back—eyes tracking over my face and lingering, if I'm not mistaken, on my mouth.

But I have to be imagining that. Or it's coincidence. My mouth is probably about level with her eyes right now, so where else is she going to look?

Clearing my throat, I swipe up the last of the smudge and pull away, fighting every instinct in my body.

"I didn't remember you being such a messy eater," I say with forced lightness as I wipe my thumb on my shorts.

Sloane scoffs and the tension is broken. She scoots back even more, turning to face the pool again, and I already wish I had . . . I don't know what. Hauled her even closer? Kissed her like I think I may have wanted to for a long time now? Unlikely.

"I've lost my dining etiquette since I've been in here, along with most of my other social skills, apparently." She gives a self-deprecating laugh. "Sorry for being weird about whatever that was in the kitchen—"

"Which was nothing," I interject, and she waves me off.

"—I just think I'm losing it a little, being in this bubble. Do you think you could, like, get me out of here somehow?"

"Get you out of here?" I drop my voice to a whisper, my eyes darting around as if one of the other crew members might be hanging out in the bushes somewhere, ready to report us to the rest of production. But as far as I can tell, we're totally alone.

Sloane sits up on her knees and faces me, her eyebrows doing their conspiratorial, wiggly thing as she tries to convince me. "Only for a little bit, and we can be back before everyone else gets home. I want to spend time together away from the set, get some fresh air. I want to feel, I don't know, *normal* again."

Warmth spreads through my chest at the idea that being with me is her touchstone for "normal." If she only knew the very not normal directions my thoughts have taken as of late. But since she doesn't know, can't and won't know . . . I consider what she's suggesting.

We should have at least another five or six hours before the Ensemble Date crew is back. I know this is probably rule number one of what not to do the first time you're trusted on your own as a lowly PA. It could probably get me fired or at least in big trouble with my dad.

But do I honestly care about any of those things when I could make Sloane happier?

"Let's go. We can get to my car if we cut around the side of Chelsea's house and walk behind the production trailers to crew parking. *Act natural.*" I infuse the last bit with mock sternness, but I also mean it. I don't want us to get stopped by anyone before we have a chance to escape. Ask forgiveness and not permission, or something like that.

Sloane and I play it cool as we cross the patio to the side of the mansion, but once we're around the corner, we pick up the pace, running on tiptoe through the side yard, down the street to the small gravel lot where my car is parked.

"Please don't let a freak hiking incident send everyone back here early," I whisper once I'm in the driver's seat and Sloane is buckling herself into the passenger side. She reaches over and gives my shoulder a squeeze, and I almost swerve into the only other car in the lot as I maneuver toward the street.

I breathe easier once we pull onto the freeway. We talk along the way, but it isn't quite as easy as it was earlier today. Sloane seems preoccupied with something, and I wonder—probably selfishly—if it has to do with the moment we had by the pool. Face touching. Mouth gazing. Again, wishful thinking.

When we get to one of my favorite diners, Sloane's face lights up and she bounces in her seat in delight. We both order burgers, fries, and shakes to go. I almost request two glass-bottle Cokes, but that feels too tied to Aspen now. We get cups of ice water instead.

Then we load all the food up in my car and continue to wind our way up the hills to a lookout with one of my favorite views in the city.

After grabbing the food out of the back, I shut my car door with a bang and move to the hood, where I set it all up like a picnic before hopping up to take a seat and patting the spot next to me.

"This feels a little like defiling the Mercedes," she jokes.

I smile as I dip my fry in ketchup and pop it in my mouth, turning to look out at the city lights beginning to sparkle in the evening sky. "I always thought I'd have a truck once I learned to drive. When I was little, anyway," I muse. "One with a big, flat bed in the back where I could sit and stargaze at night. But I also thought I'd still be living in Tennessee, so. A lot's changed."

Sloane hums her understanding as she takes a couple bites of her burger. After chasing it with some water, she looks to me. "Do you miss Tennessee?"

I shrug before looking away again. "Some things about it."

It feels like I'm hiding in plain sight. Like I've been anything but subtle since figuring out my feelings for her. Does she notice at all?

The silence lingers, and when Sloane speaks again, once we've each nearly finished our meals, it's a total subject change.

"I'm nervous about going on a date with Aspen."

Aaand that's what she was preoccupied with, I guess. Nothing to do with me or any "moment" I thought we might've had. But fine, I've been here plenty of times before, a sounding board for her relationship stuff. And she's done the same for me.

It doesn't usually feel so much like getting socked in the stomach, though.

I take a long sip of my chocolate shake, trying to think of how to play this. "Good nervous or bad nervous?"

Chancing a look at her, I see her nose scrunch up. "I don't know. I go back and forth, because he's grown on me after that rough first date, and he seems to *really* like me, but I still barely know him. And nothing about it feels natural, and I—" She huffs out a breath, her shoulders falling. "I think I should kiss him."

The socked-in-the-stomach feeling quickly turns into something more like being pushed off a diving board into a wave pool of all my insecurities. But I try to keep my tone even when I answer. "You think you should, or you want to?"

Sloane lies back against the windshield, stretching her legs out across the whole hood. "I don't know! I feel like a broken record, but I don't know. He's tried a couple times already and I've rejected him, but last night a bunch of the girls were talking, and more than a few have kissed him already. It's apparently kiss central around there. So I think it's kind of now-or-never if we go on a date this week, right? And it's just a kiss, so it shouldn't be any big thing, but I . . ."

She trails off, and I'm not sure what to do with that. I gather up all our trash from the hood of my car and walk it over to a public trash bin nearby. There's only one other car up here tonight, far enough away from ours that I can't even see if there's anyone in it. Now would be a great time for them to barge in on our conversation with a request for jumper cables or something.

When I walk back, I reclaim my seat on the hood beside Sloane, slightly closer this time but definitely not touching. She has an arm thrown dramatically over her eyes when she speaks. And I'm so glad I don't have any milkshake left to sip on, because her words would have sent chocolate spewing from my mouth across the windshield.

"I'm worried I've forgotten how to kiss."

CHAPTER ELEVEN

I know that I have heart-feelings for Dorian, but it's time to
explore my pants-feelings for Brock.
—*THE COVE*, SEASON 1, EPISODE 5

Sloane

"Y-you think you've forgotten?"

I nod, letting my forearm fall from my face. Liam brings a
hand up to wipe across his own face slowly, and I find myself
noticing the nice things the movement does for his arms. Then I
wonder why I'm noticing Liam's arms, or talking to Liam about
kissing. But in for a penny, in for a pound and all that.

"It's been a year. Since Patrick."

He lets out a laugh that sounds pained, then tries to play it
off as a cough, which only makes it worse. He answers wearily,
"Trust me. You don't forget how."

I give his leg a gentle nudge with my own. "How can you be
sure about that? Have you ever even gone more than a month or
two without a new girl in your life, Mr. One Kiss Wonder?"

A flush rises up his neck, invading his cheeks. For all that I
tease him about it, Liam is fairly tight-lipped—no pun intended—
on his own, er, experiences nowadays.

"I don't know, Sloane," he says, starting to sound almost annoyed. "There have always been, uh, gaps between when I've k— I mean, sometimes I go awhile, and— You just don't forget. Okay?"

Oh my. I feel my own cheeks getting flushed now. *Sometimes he goes awhile* . . . without kissing anyone? "Sometimes"? I'm reminded that Liam is definitely more experienced than I am. Significantly so, it seems.

"What if I'm bad at it?" I blurt out, starting to fully spiral at this new information that, theoretically, has nothing to do with kissing Aspen. "Aspen's probably super experienced, and there will be freaking *cameras*—oh god, and *microphones.*"

He rubs at the bridge of his nose, looking like he wants to launch himself off this overlook with a T-shirt cannon. "I'm sure you're not bad at it, Sloane."

"You can't know that!"

"Yeah, I'm aware." The sharpness in his tone seems to surprise him as much as me, and it shuts me up quick. His eyes meet mine with apology in them, though I'm not sure for what. We hold each other's gazes for a few seconds before he looks away.

I keep watching him, though. This renewed sense of something *different* that I've been feeling around Liam lately comes back with a vengeance. Only a couple hours ago, the same feeling hit me when he was wiping chocolate from my face, when I felt the path his thumb left like it had burned me for minutes after it was gone. I had a closer view of all his features than I'm used to and found myself noticing things I haven't before. Like his lips, and the small scar on the lower one. *A kissing injury???* my snarky brain wonders now.

I study those features again, in profile. I wonder for what feels like the hundredth time in days why the full force of Liam's handsomeness never hit me through a screen. I wonder if anything could've prepared me for seeing him in person, noticing all the things I do now that I never did before. Feeling the strange, confusing feelings I do now, every time I look at that face, those eyes, that mouth.

"Liam," I murmur softly, speaking as the idea hits me. The stupid, reckless, impossible, irresistible idea. "What if . . . what if we practiced?"

Liam's knee seems to give out. His leg collapses against the hood of the car and the arm that was resting on it goes flailing out to the side. "W-we *what*?" he chokes out.

My spine straightens and instinctively I clamp a hand on his knee as if to keep him from running away. I can't backtrack now. He knows exactly what I'm suggesting. "Yeah, you and me. Just—just once, to see. Um, if I still know what I'm doing. Or if I should cut my losses and quit before I humiliate myself on national television."

I can see the wheels turning in his head, his eyes blinking rapidly. "You want *me* to kiss *you*? For—for a *practice run*?"

Ouch. I lean back and cross my arms over my chest, tipping my chin up in a way I hope looks confident and not petulant. Anything to distract him from the panic surely showing in my eyes. "Okay, you don't have to sound so disgusted by the prospect."

He pushes a hand through his hair as he processes this bananas turn of events. "I'm not disgusted, Sloane. But we're *friends.* Friends who don't just . . . do stuff like this. I'm not your acting coach or your—your escort service, or whatever the hell."

His voice grows louder as he goes on. This was a bad idea. I feel small and stupid in a way I don't remember ever feeling around Liam. I don't know what came over me, suggesting something so outrageous. He's right—we are friends, *best* friends, friends who have never thought about doing anything like this and for good reason. But also friends who have had a lot of intense eye contact lately, at least from my perspective. And at least one friend who's been noticing the other's grown-up hotness in a big way. A friend who is, yes, nervous about kissing the big movie star on TV but also, if she's being totally honest with herself, wouldn't mind an excuse to find out what the other friend's lips feel like on hers.

I am such an idiot.

I squeeze his leg and he nearly jumps away. Wonderful—he's terrified of me now.

"Of course I don't think you're any of those things, Liam. You're my best friend in the world and I—I'm embarrassed, and we should probably pretend this never happened. Let's forget it, okay? The Ensemble Date should be over soon anyway, so we should head back to set."

I start to scoot toward the edge of the hood, ready to hop down and buckle myself into the passenger seat and commence the most awkward car ride of my life. But before my feet can hit the ground, a hand lands on my shoulder.

Liam gives it a squeeze, pulling me back toward him. His hand continues down my arm, eventually circling my wrist with his fingers. When I turn to face him, his eyes are squeezed shut.

"Sloane, this is . . . more than a little nuts," he says, opening his eyes and bringing them hesitantly to mine. "But I—I'll do it. To help you, or whatever. Just this once, so you feel better about"—he swallows heavily—"about kissing Aspen. But we can't let anything get weird. After the fact. Between you and me. Deal?"

I'm shocked by the words coming out of his mouth, and he seems shocked too. It probably shouldn't sound appealing—the way we've both framed this as some massive favor he's doing for me out of the selflessness in his heart. But that's fair. Because we're friends. Nothing more. My curiosity can stay quiet, kept to myself—it'll likely be satisfied with this kiss, hopefully along with my concerns about my own abilities, and Liam will never need to know I had any other motivations for this wacko proposition.

"Deal," I say, giving a decisive nod.

He lets go of my wrist, extending his hand to mine for a shake, which I return. But instead of releasing me, he pulls me closer, until we're sitting face-to-face on the hood of the Mercedes. My legs are pulled up underneath me so I'm at his eye level, his legs stretched out and framing my own. I blink a couple times, noticing that our faces are only a couple inches apart.

"Oh," I say, more breath than sound.

That gets a small laugh out of Liam as he whispers back, "What, did you want to do stretches first or something?"

I roll my eyes, pulling my hand from his. "No, you just changed your mind so quickly. I didn't think you necessarily meant, like, *now* now, and I wasn't gonna assume—"

I'm cut off midsentence by the press of Liam's lips to mine.

His eyes are closed, his kiss is soft but sure. There. He's kissing me.

And it only takes a second of hesitation before I close my eyes and kiss him back.

Liam's kiss is like nothing I expected, but everything I needed. It starts off gentle, a soft brush of his mouth on mine, until I meet him with more pressure. At my response, his hands come to my waist and pull me closer until our torsos are basically aligned. I feel a soft gasp leave me as his lips open over mine and I answer in kind, the kiss deepening until I can't tell where his mouth ends and mine begins anymore. One of his hands moves to my hair while the other glides down my back, and both of my own grip his T-shirt like a life raft.

I'm not thinking anything but *Yes, this, more,* as he draws me gently toward him, urging me to lean forward into his hold until he's lying back against the windshield and I'm mostly on top of him. Liam's long, lean figure stretches underneath me and he supports my weight with his hands on my hips. At some point, one of his legs folds up in a way that means I'm straddling his thigh with both of mine, but I'm too caught up in what's happening between our faces to be concerned that I'm essentially climbing him. I wrap my arms around his neck as I fall deeper into the kiss, as we explore each other with teeth and tongues, puffs of breath coasting over my lips, his jaw, my neck.

It could be minutes, hours, days that pass before I'm startled into opening my eyes by a bright light somewhere in the distance. I'd almost think it's some higher power coming to smite me for falling into a lusty haze with my closest friend, but I imagine that'd look more red and hellfire-y.

"Shit," Liam says, raising his head and blinking against the blinding interruption. He eases up and away from me, and we both turn to see that it's only the headlights of another car pulling in a few spots over.

His eyes meet mine and he looks dazed, but there's also something heated, heavier behind that gaze. We sit there for a few moments in silence except for our panting, motionless except for the rising and falling of our chests.

"You pass," Liam announces abruptly.

"I p-pass?" I sputter back, brows raised.

"Yeah. You get an A. Gold star. You're good. You're not a bad kisser. Aspen will be, uh, very . . . satisfied. You feel better now?"

I swallow the lump in my throat, trying to process the twists and turns that have taken place since I found Liam in the kitchen at Chelsea's house earlier today. Also processing the fact that my legs are still surrounding one of his like a sloth who's found a particularly comfy tree branch. "Yeah, I feel good."

An understatement. What I'm feeling is much better but also much more complicated than "good" would suggest.

"No more worries?" he asks, tone as casual as if we've just played a game of Scrabble, not kissed the ever-loving shit out of each other. As if we're not intertwined like mating seahorses.

"No worries," I answer, and that's the last thing we say on the matter before we mutually decide to extricate our limbs from each other, get in the car, and make our way back to set.

Liam cranks up his music on the drive back, and I roll my window down to try to let the breeze cool off my flushed face, clear my kiss-addled mind, chill out my wildly agitated body. With all the noise, we don't really talk.

But I've got worries, all right, and they're no longer about whether I know how to kiss Aspen. If that's ever really what they were about in the first place. Nor do I have any questions left in my mind about whether or not Liam knows what he's doing, that's for damn sure. *Whew.* Is the open window actually making it hotter in here?

I promised I wouldn't let it get weird between us after. But now, in the "after," I'm not sure I can keep that promise at all.

We say our goodbyes as soon as we get back; Liam says he's going to go find the other crew members and make sure our absence wasn't noted, and I head upstairs to get ready for bed. I pass Peyton on my way to the bathroom, and I don't think I'm imagining her giving me an extra stinky stink eye. Is this about thwarting her blender flirtation? Or do I have Guilty Best Friend Smoocher written all over my face?

I don't have long to dwell on it. Soon the Ensemble Date gets back, and I listen to my roommates tell me all about their day of outdoorsiness followed by a fancy dinner party.

But all the while, I'm trying to hide the fact that my world has shifted on its axis. After today, I know a few things to be true:

1. There is no "maybe" about my feelings for Liam. More-than-friendship feelings, want-to-kiss-him-and-be-around-him-always feelings.

2. Judging by his reaction after our world-rocking kiss, he does not feel those same things back.

3. There's no way any kiss from Aspen could compare to the one I experienced today.

It's a small mercy when the next day's script comes and it's a Scene Partner Date for Peyton. I'm gonna need more than twelve hours to get myself ready after last night.

Liam is on the production team assigned to Peyton and Aspen's date, so I see him for only a second in passing before he heads out. A second that does not include any poignant eye contact, declarations of love, or generally any sign whatsoever that he's been obsessing about our kiss, too.

I'm at loose ends, unsure what to do with my face or hands or life after the revelations of our time off set. It feels like surely everyone should be able to see there's something different about me, a kind of I-did-something-terrible-but-also-awesome glow. But no one says anything, and since I'm certainly not trying to kiss and tell on myself, I grab my notebook and pencil. Time to write through some feelings.

I settle into a lounger near the pool again and let the sounds of splashing and chatting and everything else fade out as I settle into the fictional world I'm building.

I don't know how long I've been at it before a voice at my side pulls me back out.

"Daaamn, making out on top of a car? This is some spicy stuff."

I whip my head around to see Bree smirking at me from where she leans across the back of my chair, clearly having read a bit of the scene I'm writing. I close the notebook and lightly smack her arm with it.

"Excuse you, did I say you could read over my shoulder?" I snap, but there isn't much actual irritation behind it. Mostly, I'm trying to cover up the flush that's risen in my neck and cheeks, hoping she'll think it's anger rather than . . . well, what it is.

I didn't fully realize what I was writing until she said it like that, but yep, looks like I have been reliving my Liam interlude through fictional characters a bit more realistically than intended. Embarrassing.

"Yeah, sorry, shouldn't have done that," Bree says, looking chagrined as she plops down in the lounger next to mine. "I've been curious about what you're always writing in there and didn't mean to peek, but when I saw the words 'lips' and 'tongue' my eyes just kept going, you know?"

That makes me laugh but also only worsens my blush.

"Why do you look so guilty?" Bree goes on. "Were things about to get X-rated in this story? Don't let me interrupt. Or wait—is all that going in one of your love letters to PA boy? Like some old-timey sexting?"

I drop my notebook to the ground. "What? No! How do you know about that?" I sputter, my heart beating faster. "I mean— I haven't been writing love letters to anyone, first of all."

She raises an eyebrow. "No? Just secret *friendship* notes exchanged via flowerpot?"

"Yes, actually," I shoot back, while trying hard to repress the memory of a very friendly sucking of faces. "It's a fun thing Liam and I have been doing since I don't have my phone in here and we don't always see each other. Just . . . little updates."

"Mmhmm." She gives my notebook a wide-eyed, pursed-lips look.

I roll my own eyes, gesturing to the book. "*This* is not *that*. I also write, like, for fun. Just for me. I like to write screenplays, scripts for TV shows. That's what I want to do, uh, with my life."

"Well, I think it's great," Bree declares. "What kind of script are you writing now?"

Not exactly prepared to talk about this with an audience, even a friendly one, I shift anxiously in my seat. "Oh, this one's not that far along yet. But I like the teen drama genre, shows like *The Cove.* I've only started this since being here, but it's a little bit of a story within a story, about the drama between young actors on a *Cove*-ish show when the cameras aren't rolling. My main character is an actress, and she kind of has this on-again, off-again thing with her costar. But she also starts to have feelings for her assistant, which gets complicated because they've been friends for a long time, and she's figuring out w— What? Why are you looking at me like that?"

The pointed look of a minute ago intensifies. "This story sounds familiar."

"Oh my God. Did I steal it from somewhere by accident?"

"I don't know, your own autobiography maybe?"

I groan. "Ugh, *nooo.* What's the disclaimer that's like 'Any resemblance to persons living or dead is coincidental'? That's my statement on *that.*"

I swallow down the rest of the words I'd normally say, arguing that Liam and I are just—and will only ever be—friends. Is that really true anymore?

And have I been working out my own romantic issues through fictional characters before I even realized it?

Shit. Friends-to-lovers has always been my favorite trope.

"Hey, it's fine," Bree says, placing a soothing hand on my back as she sees the emotional crisis playing out on my face. "I'm teasing you about Liam. If you say there's nothing more there, then there's nothing more."

My head bobs in a nod that hopefully looks more decisive than I feel.

"But just so you know . . . ," she adds, "Peyton was telling people last night that you disappeared for a while during the day. And that Liam did, too."

"She *what?*" I feel the beginnings of a cold sweat break out over my body. I didn't think Peyton gave a shit about where I was or what I was doing yesterday. The stink eye should've told me otherwise, I suppose.

Bree holds her hands up. "Hey, I haven't heard any more than that. And you don't have to tell me what happened—"

"Nothing—" I interrupt, but I cut myself off before I can finish the lie.

"You don't have to tell me," she repeats, voice dropping to near a whisper. "But be careful, okay? Your business is your own, as far as I'm concerned, but clearly not everyone here has that same policy."

I nod, trying to swallow down the lump in my throat. Someone in the pool yells for Bree, and she gives my back one last pat before heading over to them.

"Ugh," I say again under my breath, flopping dramatically against the chair and covering my face with my hands. What am I even doing here? Ty thinks he knows something, and he might not be so wrong anymore. Peyton is suspicious. With all of that and what I'm feeling for Liam, how can I keep doing this?

I wish I could talk it out with friends, but Liam is not an option for obvious reasons.

I wonder . . .

Standing up, I tuck my notebook under my arm and then hurry back toward Chelsea's house, flagging down a producer whose name I haven't yet memorized on my way.

"Hey, could I use the phone to call my mom?"

The producer answers in the affirmative and leads me to the kitchen, directing me to the phone attached to the wall by a long curly cord.

"I'll be in the next room," she says with a wink, giving me a bit more freedom than she's supposed to.

I dial my mom's cell number and wait as it rings. Mom and I aren't typically the heart-to-heart type of mother-daughter bonded, but desperate times, et cetera. I'll take any kind of sounding board at this point. Maybe I'll hint around the possibility of me leaving the show, see if she thinks it's the worst idea I've ever had. Plus, I haven't checked in with her since I moved on set. It might put me at ease, having a chat with my mom.

"Hello?" her familiar voice answers. There's a lot of background noise, and it sounds like she's nearly yelling to be heard.

"Hey, Mom, it's Sloane." I find myself talking extra loud back, even though Chelsea's house is silent around me.

"Sloane? I didn't think you'd be able to call. Are you off the show already?"

Well, hello to you, too! I frown into the receiver. "Uh, no. There's a phone here. I thought I told you that?" I definitely told her that when we briefly talked the night before I came here. "Sorry I didn't call sooner, though—it's been super busy."

"Oh, that's fine, honey. Hang on a sec, I'm at a dress fitting for Liza." There are some muffled sounds on her end, and I can picture her holding the phone to her chest as she weaves through the crowded fitting area at Fancy Clancy's, the store where most of Liza's pageant clothes come from. When she speaks again, it sounds like she's stepped outside. "Did you need something, Sloaney?"

That almost makes me smile. But it also makes me feel like I'm interrupting her in the middle of something more important than my problems.

"Oh, um, nothing too big. I just wanted to talk to you for a minute, if you have the time. Being here, it's a little stressful, you know? I guess I just felt like checking in back home, getting some reminders of . . . reality."

I cringe as it comes out. Also cringing at all my hedging, my "just"s and "if you have the time." Why did I think my mom and I would ever discuss something like my romantic issues? It's not her problem.

"Well, of course it's stressful, honey. Especially for you."

"It's— Wait, what? Why 'especially'?"

Mom gives a short laugh. "You've never done well in the spotlight. Remember your first and only dance recital? It's just not you, having a camera on you, microphones, some big movie star's attention, all of that. To be honest, I'm surprised you've stayed this long, sweetheart. I don't think anyone would blame you if you decided to leave. It's not your thing, and that's okay. Not everyone's center-stage material, you know?"

My mouth drops open, the words stinging more than they

probably should. More than I should let them. And I hate that I'm surprised.

The dance recital she refers to ended with me leaving the stage in tears midperformance and begging to quit dance lessons right after, ending Mom's stage mom dreams for a few years before Liza came along. But that wasn't because I don't "do well in the spotlight," was it? I was just super uncoordinated and hated dance class.

It's the "center-stage material" comment that's echoing in my head, though. Is that really how she sees me? Maybe I always knew it, at least a little bit. I just never expected her to say it out loud.

"Sure" is all I can murmur, trying to decide if it's worth putting up any kind of fight. But before I get there, Mom cuts in.

"Liza, honey, I thought you were going with the blue—oh, hang on, I'll be right there," she calls out. "Sloaney, I'm gonna have to let you go, okay? Tell Spencer if you need anything, all right? Love you!"

She's gone before I can say it back.

I try to tamp down the surge of emotion in my chest, but I can't help it. I'm *pissed*.

Not center-stage material? Okay, so sure, I might've agreed with her not that long ago. I've certainly let myself take a background role for a long time, especially in our family. But I don't like the idea that my own parents think I'm so not-special that I don't belong on a reality TV show, dating a cool celebrity.

Maybe this is my time to show everyone—show myself—that I can do things that are big and scary and out of character, things that force me to be the center of attention.

I can stay here, continue to explore my feelings for Liam while also giving Aspen and his show a chance. I can face down Ty and Peyton and not let them intimidate me. And most importantly, I can give my own dreams a chance. What if I *can* have it all?

As I go back outside, there's some chatter about Aspen and Peyton getting back from their date soon. My gut reaction is excitement at the thought of seeing Liam again, which probably says a lot about where my priorities lie. But I'm also nervous about facing Peyton, who might pose the biggest risk to everything I have going here. Plus the jitters-inducing fact that I'm still going on a Scene Partner Date with Aspen. And, oh yeah, that I need him to keep me until the final four. And that I have to decide if I'm going to let him kiss me?

I guess this is what a life in the spotlight is like, and I resolve to do my best to embrace it. I can only hope it embraces me back.

CHAPTER TWELVE

Putting others before yourself is important, but, like, imagine if
any of those tech geniuses had put their wives and families first.
We wouldn't have smartphones or two-day shipping.
—*THE COVE,* SEASON 3, EPISODE 2

Liam

Despite spending the bulk of his day busy riding horses with
Peyton—some date premise about "getting lost together," though
the horse ride was led by an experienced guide—Aspen still found
three different opportunities to pull me aside and remind me to
come to his place after filming was up. I imagine this is the kind
of thing that would be super flattering if we were romantic pros-
pects for each other, but as things stand, it's just annoying.

For better or worse, I had a lot of other things on my mind,
keeping me from getting too irritated by the overbearing actor
while driving a golf cart of camera equipment behind his romantic trail ride. Thoughts of Sloane, of last night's unexpected turn,
have made it hard to focus on anything else since I dropped her
off back at the set.

To think, I wasn't sure if there would be a spark.

There were definite sparks between Sloane and me when we kissed. So many sparks I'm shocked my car didn't burst into flames. It was almost an out-of-body experience, the way pure instinct took over as we explored each other in those . . . Seconds? Hours? Days? I honestly couldn't tell you. But I was also very much in my own body. *So* in it. I still feel a phantom grip on the back of her hair, the smooth strip of exposed skin by her hip. Her lips on mine.

God, I need to think about something else. As we arrive back on set after the SPD, I think about taking a running leap into the ocean to cool off physically and mentally. Because I'm here, on the set of the reality show on which the girl I made out with last night is dating *someone else*. If that isn't a massive sign with blinking lights that says "She's not into you no matter what you got up to on the hood of your car, so quit pining over your best friend, you dumbass," I don't know what is.

But there's no time for a swim, because I have to go meet Aspen. I check in with a producer who releases me for the day before heading toward Dorian's house. Before I even hit the driveway, Aspen calls out to me.

"Liam! Glad you could make it, man."

I look up and see Aspen shutting the front door behind him and sauntering my way. Judging by his clothes, he's about to go on a run.

Please, universe, do not let him ask me to join.

"This'll only take a second." *Yes!* "So I'm thinking of taking Sloane to the studios where we film some of the other parts of *The Cove*, like the school set, the café where Dorian and Chelsea hang out a lot, things like that. She's a big fan of the show, right?"

I nod. "Yeah, definitely. She would actually love that. You could also, I don't know, show her the writers' room? Or something like that? She's really into TV writing. Loves to write her own stuff, too."

He nods contemplatively. "Oh, sweet. Yeah, that's good. I bet we could get one of the writers to meet us on set to talk. Man, I knew you'd have something awesome for me."

He gives a few more canned lines of effusive praise before literally running off toward the beach, and I set out for my car in the other direction. The flattery doesn't do much for me, but it's good he's happy. And that he's doing something that will hopefully make Sloane happy. I feel for the poor writer who's going to get dragged back to work during the show's hiatus, but I guess that's not my problem.

What *is* my problem is that kiss. That girl. I don't know what got into me.

Well, actually, I do know what got into me. Of course I do. Wouldn't kissing her once still be better than never kissing her at all? Would I be a bigger dumbass if I did or didn't do it? I could've had to spend years wishing, dreaming, waiting for that very thing to happen, instead of the few days it took after realizing my feelings for her. I mean, in said wishes and dreams, she wouldn't have been "practicing" to kiss another guy.

But it was still a hell of a practice.

I know I can't be imagining how much she enjoyed it, too. We were both seriously freaked out afterward, barely talking the whole way back. I can still feel her hands pressed against my neck, pulling my shirt toward her, her lips chasing mine the few times I tried to pull away. It was beyond anything I could have expected and God, do I need to *stop*.

This is going nowhere. She's not with me, never will be.

And not even a full day later, I'm smacking myself for being such a sucker—for being so desperate to make her feel better while also getting whatever pieces of her I can that I'll send my own peace of mind careening off one of these oceanside cliffs.

But I guess if I'm going down, I should enjoy the hell out of the fall.

෨

The next day, I find myself doing something I've somehow avoided thus far in our near-lifelong friendship—third-wheeling on Sloane's date with another guy.

A guy who happens to be one of the most famous actors of our generation and has a face that's rumored to be insured for millions. This is going to be fun.

We've just finished filming the segment of Sloane getting her script, and her excitement at the date's premise seemed real. So real it almost stings a little, but I guess I have only myself to blame—I encouraged Aspen to take her to *The Cove*'s studio. I told Sloane she should kiss him.

I'm mentally kicking myself as I head for the driveway to help load up the vans for the day. But I'm stopped before I get there by a hand on my wrist.

It's like my body knows it's Sloane before I even turn, little electric shocks already shooting up my arm at her touch. Her expression is unreadable as she whispers, "Hey, can we talk for a second?"

I look around at the crew members passing through the foyer of Chelsea's house, barely even registering our presence. But still, this feels especially indiscreet.

"Uh, sure, but maybe we should . . ." I hold a hand out vaguely to indicate something like "find somewhere quieter" or maybe "run away from here and never look back."

She goes with the former. Before I can think about where to go, Sloane's already tugged me into a tiny half bathroom a few feet away and shut us inside. I stand there gaping as she spins to face me, pressing her back against the door, our bodies only a couple feet apart. My hands hang limply at my sides even though they want to reach for her, my blood heating at her vanilla scent filling the air in here.

"I just wanted to make sure you're okay," Sloane blurts out.

While it sounds nice on the surface, yeah, no. That cools the ol' blood right back down. Make sure *I'm* okay? Because *she's* so unaffected, so completely fine, and I'm the sad sack who might be reeling from yesterday, might have thought for two seconds that it all meant something? This is some strong "I hope we can still be friends" energy.

Cool. Cool cool cool. This is what I expected, isn't it? So why does it still gut me?

"I'm fine," I answer, striving to make my expression and voice as clear of emotion as they can be. She looks like she's waiting for something more, but I don't know what else I can give at this point. After a few seconds of silence, I ask, "Is that all?"

Sloane's head tilts, her mouth opening and closing a couple times before she retorts, "I don't know. Is it?"

What are we doing here? Keeping up the Liam Is Totally Fine act, I shrug. "I don't have anything else to talk about. You should probably get ready for your date, right?"

And if the word "date" is imbued with a little extra snark, well, I don't think I can be blamed. Sloane's lips press into a flat line, and something flares in her eyes. But she just opens the door again and walks out, leaving me to tend to my bruised feelings on my own.

My spirits stay low over the next couple of hours as we load up people and equipment and caravan to the Burbank studio. Kristi blasts '90s boy band music the whole way, as if she can feel my sulky energy permeating the back seat and has to obliterate it with sweet, sweet harmonies. But I'm unmoved.

If anything, as filming kicks off on the soundstage where many of *The Cove*'s interior sets are located, I only feel worse. They've put me in charge of a boom mic today, this big, fuzzy thing that hangs off the end of a pole and gets positioned over Aspen and Sloane whenever they're stationary, picking up any sound that might be muffled or missed by their individual mics.

Sloane hasn't even looked my way since the bathroom at Chelsea's house. It chafes at me.

I miss whatever Aspen just said as we walk through a hall filled with fake lockers, me trying to keep from banging the unwieldy mic into them while it's not in use. But it must have been funny, because Sloane is giving him her loud belly laugh, and that chafes, too. She's already given him a lot of those today—more than he could possibly deserve. I've never heard Aspen be funny. Even he seems surprised by her reactions, but pleasantly so.

My jealousy spikes each time. I feel a weird possessiveness over that laugh, even though I'm aware that I'm objectively not that funny either. I still want to be the only one who elicits such a reaction from her. Even if it's because I did something dumb and she's laughing *at* me.

I've been doing a lot of dumb things lately.

She also seems more engaged in their conversation than ever before, as if she's interested in every single thing he has to say. It could be that she *is* interested—in *The Cove,* not in Aspen. But I know how good it feels to be on the receiving end of those smiles, that deliberate, unwavering eye contact. I kind of hate him for getting to feel it.

Trying to ignore the romance playing out in front of me, I look around. Most of the soundstage sets we've walked through so far have been part of the school that Dorian and friends attend. I'm not immune to the novelty of being in a place I've seen on one of my favorite shows a million times. I could do without all the cameras, producers, and one particular actor, though.

As we enter a classroom, Kristi directs me on where to stand and hold the mic. This thing is heavier than it looks. Being a PA is a better workout regimen than I've ever had.

Aspen pulls Sloane to the front of the room and grabs a piece of chalk from under the chalkboard, holding it out to her.

"Want to draw something?"

She smiles and takes it from him. "Is that what you spend your downtime on set doing?"

He laughs. "Sometimes. These boards have seen a lot of tic-tac-toe. But mostly, I hang out around craft services." He runs a hand over his flat stomach, drawing Sloane's attention there, and she gives him a flirty smile.

"Oh, it totally shows," she teases, stepping closer to him and running her own hand over abs that I'm sure he's flexing for her. They both laugh. *Ha ha! The guy who can afford any personal trainer he wants and whose job is mostly to look good is super ripped! Hilarious!*

I nearly roll my eyes, but not before catching Sloane's. Our gazes lock for only a second, but I see a flash of . . . Defiance? Mischief?

Is she completely messing with me?

Aspen goes on about himself, as he so often does, while the two of them start to draw on the board. I faintly register that he's sharing some story about his childhood artwork, but I'm more focused on Sloane's reactions. Okay, and on not dropping the mic, but I tighten my grip and resume studying Sloane's face.

Maybe she's not as genuinely engaged with him as I thought. There's distraction in those eyes, a tightness to her expression that says her good mood might not be completely authentic.

Iiiinteresting.

"That's so sweet," Sloane says to Aspen's latest monologue, her voice startling me out of my thoughts. She reaches out and takes one of his hands in hers. I flinch, and the mic sways in midair. Kristi and another producer both cut sharp gazes at me and I mouth a sorry before looking straight ahead again.

"You know what, Aspen? This is something I appreciate most about you—that you're always so *open* with me about how you're *feeling*."

Okay, interesting emphasis there, McKinney. Maybe I'm a real self-centered ass, but I can't help but feel like that wasn't said for Aspen's benefit. What, does she think I'm not open with her? Did she want me to pour out all my feelings when she deigned to ask if I was *okay* after we kissed, so she could pat me on the head and let me down gently?

Whatever. She can send all the not-so-subliminal messages she wants. I'm as open with my feelings as she is anyway.

Sloane keeps drawing while Aspen gazes at her like she hung the moon. *I know the feeling, bud.* He reaches out and puts a hand to her lower back, stepping closer to her. His hand rubs a slow circle as he starts to say, "Sloane, I—*ow!* What the hell?"

All right, so I whacked him with the boom mic. A gentle tap, really, before I swung it back up.

"What?" Sloane says, twirling to face the crew in confusion.

Aspen straightens and rubs the back of his head. "Did you just . . . ?"

His face twists in bewilderment, and I feel a twinge of guilt, because I guess he thinks we're friends.

It's possible I'm a terrible person.

"It slipped," I say, since this segment is probably going to the cutting room floor anyway. They don't like when equipment gets in the shots. "My bad, man."

Sloane's mouth drops open in shock as she looks to me, the mic, Aspen, and back.

"Let's cut for a second," one of the producers calls out before walking over to inspect the back of Aspen's head for damage. He's clutching it as if there was a knife on the end of the pole in my hands. Kristi scrambles over to me and suggests I trade places with the PA who's floating today.

"Hey, Kristi?" Sloane calls out from the corner of the classroom, where she's begun pacing. "My mic pack keeps poking me—could you adjust it?"

Kristi, who's in the middle of giving the other PA the rundown on the boom mic, starting with how not to wallop your show's star while operating it, looks to me. "Liam, could you help her?"

"Of course."

Sloane crosses her arms with obvious displeasure as I walk to her. When I'm standing right in front of her, still taking the brunt of her Angry Eyes, I bring a finger up and twirl it, indicating she should turn around so I can fix her mic. She does, but immediately resumes glaring at me over her shoulder.

"Hitting him in the head? Really?" she hisses.

"It was an accident." I feign innocence as it occurs to me that this is going to be an under-the-shirt task. A task that feels a little different considering the last time I had a hand under her shirt. Heat rushes to my cheeks.

"You've always been a shitty liar."

Oh, Sloane, if you only knew. I lift the bottom edge of her T-shirt ever so slightly to reveal the elastic belt that holds her mic pack. Reaching for it, my fingers brush her lower back, and

I hear her suck in a sharp breath. Feel the goose bumps under my hand. See a blush rise in her own cheeks before she turns her head away.

But it's too late. I feel like I've seen . . . everything. Or, at least, I've realized that Sloane's not so unaffected by me after all.

It has me considering our talk this morning differently. What if . . . ? No, it's too much to hope that I completely misinterpreted her intentions. But what if . . . ?

"Did you fix it yet?" she asks, her voice soft, breathy.

I feel my pulse pick up in response, but the sound of the crew moving around behind us reminds me this is not the time or place. Kicking my frozen fingers back into gear, I find the wire that was prodding her, then get it to lie flat before settling the belt and her shirt back into place. When Sloane turns, she doesn't make eye contact as she mumbles a thanks, but it doesn't feel like an angry avoidance anymore. No, it feels . . . vulnerable. Exposed. Pretty much how I've been feeling for days now.

She returns to Aspen's side at the front of the classroom, now that he's recovered from that brutal blow I dealt, and everyone gets back into place to film. The two of them are instructed to resume drawing and talking as if we never stopped rolling.

Sloane clears her throat. "So, do you hang out with your costars much outside of filming?"

Her voice is quieter now than it was before the break, and I think I can still detect some pink in her cheeks. Surprisingly, that question gets a matching blush out of Aspen. "Uh, sometimes. Some of them. Like Nash, and Lane . . . Evie, and uh—" he coughs. "Riley. Hey, how about we keep going?"

"Did someone say my name?" a new voice asks, and all heads

in the room turn to see the actress who plays Chelsea, Riley Cartwright, leaning in the doorway. Sloane gasps and I get it, because *wow*. Real-life Riley is somehow even more stunning than the knockout she plays on TV. In spiky heels, high-waisted jeans, and a leather jacket, with bright red lipstick matching her long shiny hair, it's like she's walking around with one of those flaw-eliminating photo filters over her.

It also seems as though the surprise may not be as exciting for Aspen as it is for Sloane. His tan appears to have faded in seconds, and the smile he gives is more nervous than cocky.

"Riley, hey! What a surprise," he offers through a false laugh. He looks not only like he's flustered by her presence but like he wants her to explain it. Or am I reading too much into this?

"Aspen." The poised actress inclines her head and puts a hand on her hip. "Heard through the grapevine that you'd be around the studio today, so I thought I'd drop in and say hi to you and your *date*."

She says the last word with some bite to it. I narrow my eyes, looking back and forth between her and Aspen. Most of the crew have perked up at Riley's appearance, as if we're filming a nature documentary and have stumbled upon a lion about to pounce on its dinner. Kristi is the only one who looks chill—or as chill as Kristi is capable of looking—making me wonder if she's the so-called grapevine.

After a brief, awkward pause, Sloane steps forward with a hand outstretched before Aspen can pull himself together to make introductions.

"Hey, I'm Sloane. It's so wonderful to meet you—I'm a big fan of your show! Chelsea is definitely my favorite character."

Riley gives Sloane's hand a brief shake. "Pleasure. Things going well with you two so far?"

Sloane gives a nervous laugh, looking to Aspen. Seeing he's still frozen—why is he so frozen?—she answers for them both. "Sure, yeah. It's been fun getting to know each other, and Aspen's been so great."

"He is, isn't he?" Riley says, her tone frosty. "*So* great. Well, I guess I'll let you all get going . . . if you don't have anything to add, Asp?"

Weird nickname, but whatever works for them.

Although I can't tell if it actually "works" for Aspen, who is still acting like a malfunctioning robot. I swear his eye twitches as he answers her with a tense smile. "Nope, I'm good, Ri. Thanks for stopping by!"

Riley's red lips twist into a smirk as she backs out of the room. "Good luck," she adds, her eyes on Sloane.

Strange. It's all strange. I wonder if Riley is good friends with Evie or something. If she's less than thrilled, on behalf of her friend, that the friend's ex is rebounding with a couple dozen girls at once.

Sloane seems to take the surprise guest in stride, tossing out a thanks before following Aspen out of the same faux classroom door that leads to the next set. They turn in the opposite direction of Riley, who has since disappeared. Our whole crew follows a few steps behind.

I can see the stars coming back into Sloane's eyes as she

walks down the hall where so many pivotal making-out-against-fake-lockers scenes have taken place. God, why am I thinking about fake make-outs? Getting way too close to mental territory I should not be treading, especially not today.

"I've got one more surprise up my sleeve here, just for you," Aspen says, reclaiming my attention and, seemingly, his cool. He pushes open a door that looks like it should lead to a classroom at the end of the hall, but when I make my way through a few moments later, it turns out that it's the set for the café where Dorian and his friends hang out.

My eyes track over the colorful bistro tables, the counter with a display case full of presumably fake food, the area behind it where the snarky middle-aged café owner, Peg, makes coffees and rings up Dorian's and Chelsea's orders and gives them shit about their relationship. Sloane always jokes about Peg being the voice of the Dorsea stans on the show.

Kristi has Aspen and Sloane pause as the crew readjusts the room's lighting. I help set up one of the silks again, and fortunately the C-stand is functioning correctly, keeping me from having to hold anything.

Once everyone's satisfied with the setup, Aspen and Sloane can proceed into the fake café to a table with a woman sitting at it, her hands wrapped around a mug, and two identical mugs set out by the two empty chairs at her side. I don't recognize her as an actor for the show, so I wonder . . .

"Sloane, this is Priya, one of the writers on the show. I know you're into writing, so I thought you might be interested in talking to one of the people who makes the magic happen here."

Aspen gives her a self-satisfied smile, and I have to admit I'm impressed that he was able to actually follow through on such short notice. I guess that's what star power does for you.

Sloane's mouth hangs open and she claps one of her hands over it, clutching Aspen's arm with the other.

"Oh my God," she says, eyes wide and voice muffled until she lets her hand drop. "I mean, wow, it's so good to meet you, Priya! Aspen is right—I'm a huge fan of *The Cove* and, uh, it's kind of my dream to write for a show like it. Basically, I want your job. I mean not, like, literally *your* job—I wouldn't try to take that away from you, not that I am even remotely qualified to do so, but—well. It's nice to meet you."

I bite my lip to halt the laugh that wants to come out. She wasn't anywhere near this nervous to meet Aspen, the actual star of the show. It's pretty adorable.

Priya actually does give a little laugh. "It's great to meet you, too, and to see you again, Aspen. Do you all want to sit and chat for a few?"

They fill the other seats at Priya's table and start sipping from the mugs, which Aspen informs Sloane do hold actual lattes. Then Sloane proceeds to pick Priya's brain for the next thirty or so minutes about everything pertaining to her writing career and working on the show. Her face is lit up like a Christmas tree the whole time, and Priya seems to enjoy it, too. Suddenly Aspen is the third wheel on this date, and I'm not mad about it.

His face remains casually pleasant, but he never looks especially engaged in what either of them is saying. But then Priya shifts the conversation in a way that was clearly preplanned and scripted for her.

"You know, one of the best parts about writing for *The Cove* is working on the development of all the characters' relationships with one another, giving them meaningful conversations and connections, and creating these powerful love stories that fans can relate to. How have you two been feeling about the progression of your relationship so far?"

Yikes. I hope Priya is getting paid the big bucks for this.

Aspen slings an arm over the back of Sloane's chair, letting his hand brush her shoulder and giving both ladies his winning smile. "It's been amazing, from my perspective anyway. I think Sloane is used to taking things a little slower—which is totally fine—but I can already feel myself falling. When you meet someone so incredible, how could you not, you know?"

God, are his answers scripted, too? I realize my hand is clenched in a fist around the C-stand pole and have to deliberately release it, afraid I'll accidentally send something toppling again. In front of me I watch Sloane try to relax her own posture, which has gone tense while Aspen was talking. She gives an anxious, closed-mouthed grin, and while I'm relieved she's done with the over-the-top smitten act from earlier, I'm angry at Aspen, at this show, the producers, for causing this change in her from a couple minutes ago. I wish they'd let her keep on talking to Priya about things she actually cares about, rather than try to force the romance narrative.

Speaking of, did he really say he can "feel himself falling"?

The awkward, contrived relationship talk continues for a few more minutes before Priya announces that she'll "leave them to it" and gets up to leave the set. Sloane looks bummed as they say their goodbyes, and it gives me an idea. Once Priya steps out of camera range and a producer helps take her mic off while filming pauses to rearrange the setup for a one-on-one Sloane-Aspen talk, I move. I wind through the small group of production staff and intercept Priya outside the café set, back in the now-empty fake school hallway.

I clear my throat so I don't sneak attack her. "Excuse me, Priya?"

She turns around with a blank expression. "Did I forget something?"

"Oh, uh, no. Sorry, it's just—I'm Liam Daniels, and I'm a PA here, but I'm also a longtime friend of Sloane's. I was actually wondering . . ." I shake my head, suddenly nervous, but work up the nerve to continue what I started. "I know Sloane would be really interested in talking to you more. She wants to seriously pursue screenwriting, like go to school for it and everything. Do you, um, have a business card I could get for her? If you wouldn't mind, that is. If she reached out to you. At some point. I think it would . . . it would make her really happy."

I swallow the nervous lump that's formed in my throat. Priya's brows rise, and I worry she's thinking, *I would not like this strange boy to have my contact information now or ever,* but then her face breaks into a warm smile.

"I'd be happy to talk to her more, anytime she wants." She reaches into her purse and pulls out a card. "And you're a very good friend for looking out for her."

With one last look—one that might be saying, "Yeah, sure you're her 'friend,' buddy"—she walks away. I'm about to rejoin the rest of the crew when a different voice says quietly, "She's your friend, then?"

I whirl around to see Riley Cartwright, who is even more beautiful from just two feet away. She now has an iced coffee in one hand, car keys in the other, and sunglasses pushed up on her head, as if coming to set today was one of many errands on her to-do list.

I summon up all the confidence I can in the face of her intense gaze. "Sloane?" I point with my thumb in the direction of the café set, and Riley nods. "Yeah, she is."

Riley nods again and purses her lips thoughtfully. "Got it. Well, for what it's worth, if she was my friend, just . . . I'd tell her to be careful."

I swallow heavily. "You—what?"

She looks at me almost sympathetically. "I know I'm on the outside of all this, but I know Aspen. He can be charming, and sweet, but there's always an agenda underneath. He's calculating, and I don't know, I'd be worried she's not getting to know the guy she thinks she is. I could be wrong, though, about what Aspen wants here. Certainly wouldn't be the first time."

With that cryptic and wildly unhelpful statement, Hollywood darling Riley Cartwright turns on one spiky heel and saunters off down the fake high school hallway. I stand there gawking after her, unsure what to do with her warning. It was a warning, right? Again, cryptic.

I return to my spot in the café set. As I watch the last of

Sloane and Aspen's date, though, I find myself studying him more than her, wondering about what Riley said.

He's calculating.

His smile is Cheshire cat wide when Sloane says yes to his request to put her name on this episode's Cast List, his hand steady as he writes her name in bold, gold letters.

Is there any authenticity to what he feels for her? Or is Aspen Woods a better actor than I ever could've imagined?

CHAPTER THIRTEEN

Sorry, secondhand clothes give me hives.
—*THE COVE,* SEASON 2, EPISODE 7

Sloane

"Why do I feel like I've stumbled onto the wrong reality show set? I am *not* gonna be one of the Friends of Flavor."

Bree's grumbled words make me laugh, and I turn to see her gingerly holding an olive oil bottle between two fingers and drizzling it into a skillet. I give the pot of water in front of me a stir, trying to look busy while I wait for it to boil.

"At least you look good," I tease back. She strikes a pose in the same one-size-completely-swallows-all white chef's coat we're all wearing today, sending a couple drops of olive oil flying to the counter. While she scrambles to clean that up, I look around at the rest of the bustling kitchen.

We really do look like an episode of *Chopped,* or maybe more accurately *Hell's Kitchen.* It's chaos as girls move around, crack open crab shells, peel shrimp, mix spices, preheat this, melt butter in that. This is my second Ensemble Date, and we're at a real working restaurant that they've used for scenes from *The Cove* before. The owner, a kind older man named Chef Jeff, shut it down for our use today. He—and Aspen, but mostly Chef Jeff— is teaching us how to make some of Aspen's favorite dishes: crab cakes and shrimp scampi.

The crowd of oversized white coats is a lot less dense after the last Casting Call a couple nights ago, when five girls were sent home. Eight of the ten of us remaining are on this date, and we've divided into two teams, each to cook one dish. The mood at Chelsea's house has been somber since our numbers dwindled by a third, everyone kind of doing their own thing on our day off yesterday. I spent the time writing, mostly, but also feeling like a broody character on *The Cove*, repeatedly getting lost in thought while looking out over stunning ocean views. I'm still trying to work through all my feelings since my Scene Partner Date—about getting to know Aspen better, about meeting Priya and looking to my future, but mainly about where I stand with Liam.

"Are you gonna make the noodles, or should I just do it?" The disdain in Peyton's voice, matched in her eyes when I turn around to look at her, makes me feel like she can see straight through me. Last I saw her, she was at the far edge of the room, having what looked like a serious conversation with Aspen. Now she's standing over my pot of water I didn't notice had started to boil, peering into it like a witch over her cauldron.

Not to be dramatic, or anything.

I give her a saccharine smile as I pick up my box of noodles and open it. "I've got it, but thank you for your concern!"

She rolls her eyes, but instead of leaving to do . . . whatever it is she's supposed to be doing other than pestering me, she leans back against the counter and crosses her arms. It might look more threatening if we weren't all the same variety of baggy-sleeved marshmallow right now.

"Where's your guy Liam today?" she asks as I'm pouring the box out into the water, causing my hand to jerk and fling a few noodles across the stove top.

I shake my head, trying to stay composed and keep my voice down, even though there aren't any cameras trained closely on the two of us right now. "Not sure what you mean by 'your guy,' but I don't know where Liam is. Maybe he has the day off."

Peyton's pretty face is less pretty in a sneer. "You know exactly what I mean. I know you two snuck off together that day we were alone at the mansions. I've seen you both sneaking little folded notes to each other. And even if I hadn't, anyone can see how he looks at you."

As I collect the rogue dry spaghetti pieces and add them to the pot, my gut impulse is to ask how she thinks Liam looks at me. I mean, I've caught flashes of what might be more-than-friend feelings there. Definitely in a certain sequence of events on the hood of a Mercedes. But also in the close quarters of the hall bathroom I pulled him into, when he looked like he wanted a Practice Kiss, Round Two. But then his whole demeanor changed after I asked if he was okay.

I'd thought maybe that was my chance to start to feel things out with Liam, see where his head was at. But all I got was a completely robotic I'm-fine-why-wouldn't-I-be? routine that made me feel foolish for ever considering there was more there between us.

But if he didn't feel anything for me, why would he have childishly—but, okay, hilariously—knocked Aspen over the head with a microphone? Why does it feel like there's an electric current running between us now whenever he's nearby?

Which, since our kiss, hasn't happened much.

"Well?" Peyton prods impatiently, and I realize I'm doing myself no favors by drifting off into Liam dreamland in the middle of her confrontation.

"Well what? I don't know what to tell you. We're friends. We look at each other like friends do. People write notes to their friends. I don't know why I have to convince you of anything." I keep my eyes trained on the water and my noodle-stirring like this conversation is completely inconsequential to me.

She scoffs. "I don't believe you. And I don't trust you at all. The rest of us are actually here for Aspen, you know. I care about him, and I want to protect his best interests. And if I feel like someone here is threatening those, well, I might be inclined to tell him."

That gets me to look up at her, narrowing my eyes. "There's nothing here to tell, Peyton."

Peyton returns my glare, flicking her long red hair over one shoulder. "It's a damn good thing you're not trying to get into acting, because you seriously suck at it."

With that, she strolls off toward the other end of the counter, where the shrimp are being cooked. I watch her for another moment, and despite how unsettled she makes me and how little I want to give her credit for pretty much anything, I can't help but grudgingly respect what a killer line of dialogue she just delivered in the TV show of my life.

I shift my attention to Aspen where he stands at the crab cake station, chatting up some of the other girls. He and Jada have the group around them in stitches from using the empty crab shells like puppets to talk to each other.

A sizzling noise startles me, and I look down to see my pot of water boiling over under my lackluster supervision. I scramble to turn down the heat, then stir the noodles until the bubbling water calms. As I do so, my thoughts naturally drift to Liam again. What *is* he up to today? Is he still being a grump?

Is he still thinking about our kiss as much as I am?

"What've we got going on over here?"

Aspen's voice makes me drop the wooden spoon I've been using to stir. Instinctively, I reach for it, but stop myself just before plunging my hand into the pot of third-degree burns waiting to happen. My family has a motto, "No trips to the emergency room," which I've yet to break, and it'd be embarrassing to start with something so stupidly self-inflicted.

"Ah, my bad," Aspen says with a chuckle. I feel his hand rest on my back as he leans past me to grab some tongs, then uses them to fish the spoon out of the water. When I turn my head, his face is only a few inches from mine, his body still pressed close even after he's set the spoon on a trivet. I can feel his breath on my face, his eyes trained on my lips, but other than that, I feel . . . nothing.

I turn and step back so I'm leaning against the counter, trying to look unflustered after a jump scare from Hollywood's hottest seventeen-year-old.

"Oh! Just, uh, cooking some noods." Mentally smacking myself—because when have I *ever* called them "noods"?—I correct, "Noodles. What's up?"

So chill. So natural. So not thinking yet again about a hot make-out sesh with my best friend while I'm supposed to be TV-dating someone else.

But Aspen smiles as though I'm not looking more unhinged by the hour. "I wanted to check on you. You've been a little quiet over here. Anything on your mind?"

Of course that's when my heavy swallow goes down the wrong pipe. Aspen eyes me with concern as I cough, raising his hands like he might need to start CPR at any moment. Fortunately, Peyton cuts in before I have to explain myself. I never thought I'd be thanking the lord for Peyton's interruptions.

"Aspen, want to try our shrimp?" she asks in her sugary-sweet tone. Aspen's attention moves with the cameras to where Peyton stands over a skillet filled with sizzling shrimp, and Kristi takes the opportunity to hand me a water bottle. Even though my coughing has ceased, I mouth a thank-you and sip.

Aspen's easy smile returns now that he's not solely facing a jumpy weirdo trying to hack up her lung. "Ooh, those look delicious. Hey, I have an idea! Have you all ever been to a hibachi grill?"

He looks around at all the girls nearby. Some nod, me included, while others shake their heads. He goes on, smile growing. "At my favorite hibachi place in LA, the guys always flip food at guests with their spatulas and try to get you to catch it in your mouth. Should we try it?"

It's a question that clearly calls for a *woooo*, but having just resumed normal breathing, I'm not all that happy to oblige. Still, Aspen gets enough of a positive response to take the skillet and spatula from Peyton's hands, trading places with her at the stove.

"All right, who's up first?"

Bree raises a hand. In the blink of an eye, Aspen has flipped a shrimp through the air. Bree bends her knees only slightly, opens her mouth, and *boom!* The shrimp lands perfectly on her tongue. She raises her hand in the air like a gymnast who's stuck the landing, giving us all a closed-mouthed smile as she chews.

My own mouth drops open, and I give her a wide-eyed what-the-hell look. She shrugs. "My secret talent."

The game continues, largely devolving as only a couple of the girls are actually able to catch the shrimp. A lot end up on the floor, to the point that I'm questioning if one can have scampi without the featured ingredient.

By the time I'm taking the cooked noodles off the burner, there aren't many shrimp left uneaten or undropped, and the only girl left in the whole kitchen who hasn't yet participated in the game is me.

"Okay, Sloane, let's see what you've got," Aspen says with challenge in his voice, deftly twirling his spatula in one hand. He hasn't shown this much personality since the pool party. Even though said personality is that of a hyperactive hibachi chef, I like it. I don't have much confidence in my ability to catch flying food in my mouth, but his enthusiasm and the fact that everyone else has participated make me feel like I have to try.

I finish pouring the noodles into a colander before turning to face the group. All eyes are on me.

With his teasing expression, Aspen kind of reminds me of Liam right now, in the midst of one of our many playful competitions over the years. Incidentally and entirely unrelated, Aspen is more attractive to me in this moment than he's ever been.

Not wanting to examine that any further, I reroll one of my baggy sleeves that's fallen down before widening my stance and rubbing my hands together. "Bring it, Woods."

He laughs and tosses the shrimp in an arc my way. I track it with my eyes and open my mouth, lunging forward and tipping my chin up at the last second. I am still utterly shocked when I feel it land on my tongue.

"I got it!" I call through the mouthful, and the whole kitchen gives an answering cheer. We may be about to enjoy a nearly shrimpless scampi, but at least the game ended on a win.

After that, Aspen drifts back toward the crabby side of the kitchen and Chef Jeff comes to help my group with the sauce and putting the finished product all together. After a few minutes of this, I start to feel flushed. It hasn't felt hot in here so far, but maybe all the burners and people have raised the temperature more than I've realized. I reach for the bottle of water Kristi gave me earlier, which sits on the counter beside Bree. But after a few sips, I only seem to feel warmer, and my skin is starting to tingle. And am I imagining things, or is my tongue feeling somehow heavier in my mouth?

"Hey, Bree?" She hums in response as she plates the pasta. "My face feels kind of funny. Does it look weird or anything?"

Bree nudges a shrimp away from the edge of the plate with

her spoon before looking up at me, at which point her eyes go as big as saucers. "Oh my God. Okay, yeah, something's up with you. Kristi!"

Panic rises in my chest. "What? What is it?" I reach up and put my hands to my cheeks, and only then do I feel it—the weird, hot, bumpy texture my skin has taken on. I run my fingers up to my forehead and down to my neck, feeling the bumps everywhere. My pulse picks up speed and my tongue is definitely some kind of swollen. Is it getting harder to breathe?

"Oh my God!!!" Kristi echoes Bree as she appears in front of me, and the multiple exclamation points are the wrong kind of excited this time. "She's having an allergic reaction!!!"

Suddenly, a handful of producers and PAs surround me, all lobbing questions and directions. Is my throat closing up? Drink some water. When did I first notice the hives? Does anyone have an EpiPen? We have to call an ambulance!

That last one pulls me out of my own dazed panic. "No! No ambulance—that really doesn't feel necessary," I say, but my credibility takes a hit since I sound like I have cotton balls stuffed into my mouth. "If someone can just drive me to, like, a clinic or something . . ."

"Honey, we've got to get you to the ER," Kristi says, already reaching to unbutton my chef's coat.

So much for that family motto.

The next hour is a blur as I'm bustled out of the restaurant, then into a car that Kristi drives like a bat out of hell to the nearest ER entrance. I try to count the hives on my red, puffy arms to pass the time on the way, but it gets upsetting when I pass a hundred. When we pull into the hospital, the car screeches to a stop and Kristi throws it into park at a curb that definitely isn't a legal parking space. It's only when she greets the nurse inside by yelling, "WE NEED SOME EPI!" that it occurs to me that this woman has seen too much *Grey's Anatomy.*

The nurse must be used to grand entrances like ours, though, as she only hands us a clipboard full of paperwork to fill out and asks us to take a seat. The wait goes on long enough that I decide I'm not actively dying—my condition seems to have plateaued at swollen tongue, shortness of breath, full body hives, and swelling. My throat isn't closed up and my heart isn't stopping and, most telling of all, no one rolled out a gurney within the first ten seconds of our arrival and rushed me to an operating room. In fact, the clock on the waiting room wall tells me we've been here for twenty minutes when my name is finally called.

From there, it's clear that the hospital has seen my situation a million times before. They ask me all about what I ate or drank (shrimp, assuming my allergy is not to water) and if I've ever had this happen before (no) before hooking me up to an IV and explaining all about the drug cocktail getting pumped into my veins to make me all better.

When the kind nurse says, "This one's gonna make your heart race," she isn't lying. And, as she attaches the next line: "This one will make you really sleepy."

Boy, does it. But due to said heart race-y feeling, I'm still fighting to stay awake. I blink at Kristi in the chair beside my hospital bed through heavy lids. "Is Mr. Daniels coming? Or Liam? Could I text Liam maybe? I . . . I need to tell him. . . ."

I realize that I don't know how to finish that sentence, and that my scratchy, swollen-mouthed voice makes it sound like I'm a decades-long chain-smoker on her deathbed, so I let the sentence trail off.

Kristi presses her lips together, her eyes still full of worry. "I don't know about Spencer. I did text Liam for you, though, and I think he's—"

"Here," calls a breathless voice, and it takes all my remaining energy to turn my head enough to see Liam filling the doorway, one hand on the jamb and the other pushing back his messy hair. "I'm here."

His eyes look me all over as he walks into the room and sits at the edge of my bed opposite from where the nurse is still shooting me up with who knows what. Panic and stress are written all over his face, same as everyone who's looked at me since I uttered the words "My face feels kind of funny," but with the influence of all these drugs, I can no longer be bothered to care. I smile at him in what feels like a serene way, but for all I know, I look like a misshapen tomato on psychedelics. Liam's concern doesn't lessen.

I try to tell him not to worry. "What?" he asks. "Sloane, how are you feeling? I'm sorry I didn't get here sooner, traffic was . . . well, you know. But I can't believe this happened. A shrimp allergy? We used to eat all kinds of shrimp at the beach, right? But I looked it up—sitting in traffic, not while the car was moving, don't worry—and apparently your allergies can reset every few years? So this isn't uncommon, but it's still scary as shit. And your reactions can get worse each time, so we'd better get you an appointment with an allergist and see if you can get a prescription for one of those pens in case of anaphylaxis. That's the kind of reaction where you stop breathing. Thank *God* this wasn't that, I don't know what—"

My hand on his arm stops him. The effort pretty much wiped the last of my will to stay awake.

"Liam," I whisper as my eyes fall shut. "I'm okay now."

And as sleep claims me, with my favorite person's fingers lacing through mine, the words couldn't ring truer.

CHAPTER FOURTEEN

*Holding her makes me feel happier than I did when we won
the state championship. Or at least happier than when
we won the county.*

—*THE COVE*, SEASON 3, EPISODE 3

Liam

"Do you think Chef Jeff's parents knew he'd be a chef? Like, what if they'd named him Joctor or Jawyer?"

When Sloane poses this question from beneath the fluffy duvet in the guest bed at my house, her eyes are closed. I'm not sure if she's asking me or some person in her drugged-up dreams, but I feel obligated to answer.

"The name Sawyer was right there, you know."

She waves away the suggestion with a limp hand, still not opening an eye. "Sawyer's a hot guy in a romance novel, or on a TV island where a plane crashes. Sawyer wouldn't be let into law school."

"Okay, sure. Jawyer definitely would, though," I say, tucking her rogue arm back under the covers and pulling them up under her chin. Before I draw back, she turns her head, a peaceful smile coming over her face as she rubs her cheek against the back of one of my hands.

"Mmm," she hums. "This . . . is . . . good."

Then I no longer have to question her level of consciousness as her mouth parts and a soft snore slips out. I've never known Sloane to be a snorer, but after today's events, I feel like I should be grateful that she's breathing at all.

I pull my hand carefully out from under her, then run it over my own face wearily. I didn't have an almost-breakdown today when I heard what happened on the Ensemble Date and immediately raced to the emergency room, nor did I nearly pass out upon first seeing her in a hospital bed, puffed up like a balloon and tethered to an IV bag. Nope, couldn't have been me.

But I think I hid my panic well enough, given the circumstances. Before a few hours ago, I'd never seen someone have an allergic reaction worse than a small rash or something. Sloane looked like she'd stumbled into a hive of radioactive bees.

Not that I'd ever tell her that. The first time she had the opportunity to look in a mirror was when we got home tonight after the drugs had done a lot of the heaviest lifting, so I don't think she realizes how bad it really was. Not having a phone—and therefore a phone camera—on her was good for something after all. Now she's left with only a mildly puffy face and an inability to stay awake for longer than the five minutes it took to get from my car's passenger seat to the guest room (with my assistance), put on some pajamas (without), and let me tuck her in to bed.

As I head back downstairs, I hear the garage door closing again and know Dad must be home. Nice timing, after all the actual work is done. He wasn't at filming or back at the *Cove* set when a producer let him know that Kristi was taking Sloane to the hospital. But he'd already decided by the time we talked that if she didn't stay at the hospital overnight, we should bring her back to our place. Meaning that *I* should bring her back to our place, because he was caught up dealing with "studio business."

She's not his actual daughter, and obviously Kristi and I had everything handled with getting her discharged and safely home. But I guess I would have expected a little more concern from Sloane's temporary guardian for the summer. In general, he's been less present than I expected as filming has gone on. I can't tell what kind of impression he's getting of my work, the effort I'm putting in, from his drop-ins to the set between all his other Important Business. He mostly stays in the control room, and when I see him, all he wants to do is rant about various producers and how hard they're making his life, and have I noticed how they always screw up this or take too long with that?

I find him in the kitchen, ironically finishing up a phone call with "Those shitheads are lucky we ever decided to work with them and their kiddie soap opera. They'll see when we air! They'll see!"

Dad slams his phone down on the counter, jumping when he notices me standing off to his side.

"Oh, Liam. You're home! I take it they kept her overnight then?"

I give him a confused look as I go to fill up a glass with water. "No, Sloane's here. They decided she was all right to go, gave her a prescription, and sent us on our way. I texted you."

He flips his phone over and peers down at it. "Did you? Oh, I see now. Well, she's gonna live?"

His teasing tone and blasé attitude aren't unlike the ones Sloane has been sporting about the whole situation, but from Dad, it hits different. Responses like *No thanks to you* come to mind. But I know that's the lingering stress talking, and I'd probably regret the words as soon as I said them.

"Yeah. It was a bad reaction but not anaphylactic shock or anything. Steering clear of shellfish and seeing an allergist when she can."

"So she can go back to set tomorrow?" he asks, already glued to his phone screen again.

"What? No!" I blurt out a little too quickly, causing Dad to look up with a dubious expression.

"No?"

I try to sound as dispassionate as possible, because I *do* believe sending Sloane straight back to set is ridiculous, all personal feelings aside. Though, I mean, are we sure she really needs to go back to *AWFLL* at all? Her health comes first. "At least give her another day to rest. The stuff she's taking to make the hives and swelling go away makes her super tired—she wouldn't really be able to do anything anyway."

Dad's mouth flattens into a line, the corners pulled slightly down and the parentheses bracketing his lips becoming more defined. "Son, I've wanted to talk to you about this for a while now."

I try to ignore the prickly feeling at the back of my neck, the one that says, *We're not going to like this.* "About what?"

"I know you care about her a great deal."

I wait for him to say more, wondering if this is how Aspen feels waiting for his producer cue at a Casting Call, but the glance Dad throws my way tells me I'm supposed to respond somehow.

"Uh . . . yeah, of course. She's my closest friend."

His frown deepens. "Yes, well . . ." Another heavy sigh. "You know, your mother and I started as friends."

Oh, God. This is gonna be worse than I thought.

"And looking back, I think we should have stayed that way. When you're friends for that long without becoming anything more, there's probably a good reason for that, you know? I think your mother and I tried to force something because we felt like it was the natural thing to do—we liked each other so much as people, so why not give love a try? But it just—it wasn't the right move. We were best friends, we tried to turn the platonic love into a romantic one, but it was never really there. And now we're here, halfway through our adult lives, and are nothing at all to each other anymore. Makes you wonder how we each might've ended up if we'd held out for the right person, for real love. Would we be better off now? I think it's possible."

Again, I wait, feeling sure he'll add some reassuring, *Of course, then we wouldn't have you, my beloved son, and that would be terrible.* But no such statement comes, and the sinking feeling in my stomach is unbearable. I am not going to do something like cry in front of my dad right now. He'd think it had to do with Sloane, most likely, rather than his uncanny ability to casually break my heart all on his own.

I clear my throat, willing my voice to stay steady. "What does this have to do with Sloane? She and I aren't—we're just friends, Dad."

I'm less certain about this than I've ever been—at least, I'm less certain that I *want* it to be true—but I'll do anything to head off this ridiculous warning he's clearly trying to give me.

Dad shakes his head. "I see how you are together. There's at least a curiosity there, whether either of you would admit it or not. There's a reason you've never brought any other girls home to meet me. But you'd be wise to leave it at friendship. Don't let your own feelings interfere with this opportunity for Sloane, and don't let them keep you from exploring better options for yourself. You're both young and have so much life ahead of you. Don't jump into something you'll regret just because you latched on to this one person from a young age."

I rub at my forehead, not even sure where to start. I probably should've faked my own freak allergic reaction, so we could still be in the ER right now.

"Are you implying that you think Sloane and Aspen will— what—fall in love and live happily ever after?"

He waves a carefree hand. "Oh, who knows? Probably not, but I'm saying that you should let go now, anyway, before you hold her back from the possibility of that real, great love. If it's with Aspen on my show, all the better—it'll be great TV! And she'll more than fulfill her end of our deal. But if it isn't him, it'll be someone else out there before long, when she goes off to college and starts seeing more of the world and you do the same. You'll each come to find there are better options than each other, once you actually start to look for them. Trust me, son. I know better than anyone."

The certainty in his voice says he really believes this. Spencer Daniels, All-Knowing Relationship Deity. I know from experience that it's easiest not to argue, even if I think he's way out of line for suggesting what Sloane and I have is anything like him and my mom. Or that his nearly-twenty-year marriage was such a massive mistake. So I just nod.

I'm not even sure where this is coming from. Does he think I've been holding Sloane back? It sure doesn't seem like it. She's dated in the past, just like I have. Maybe he's reading a lot into her uncertainty about Aspen during filming, but that has nothing to do with our friendship. The guy's just kind of shallow and vain and she knows it, even if Aspen seems to be into her.

I guess I know all about reading into things that might not really be there, though.

Dad's eyes narrow now as he looks me over. Whatever he sees must not completely say *heartsick boy angling for maximum time with one true love away from cameras and hot actor competition,* because after another moment he nods. "Right, well. Sloane can stay here tomorrow, just to be safe, and we'll see how she's doing by the evening."

"Okay." I nod back, crossing my arms over my chest. "Good."

"And you can stay here to keep an eye on her, but don't make me regret that call." Another pointed look. "Liam, you can take or leave my advice. But if you do anything that interferes with the success of my show . . ."

I frown. "Of course I wouldn't do anything to interfere. Dad, we're fr—"

"Friends. I know, I know." Then he has the audacity to give *me* an eye roll as he turns and leaves the room. Not for the first time today, I wonder which one of us is really the parent.

When I ask Sloane what she'd like for breakfast the next day, she finds it hilarious to answer, "Shrimp biscuit."

Her laughter follows me down the stairs as I go to make us pancakes.

As much as it makes me feel like the worst person ever to think of anything good coming from Sloane's medical emergency, well, I'm grateful that it seems to have erased whatever weirdness there was between us since the kiss. I'm selfish, and terrible, and completely loving this time to be normal with my best friend again.

When I return a while later with a tray carrying a stack of blueberry pancakes (Sloane's favorite) plus a few chocolate chip (mine), mugs of coffee, and glasses of water, Sloane appears to be asleep again. I release a quiet sigh, figuring I should take breakfast to sit on the stovetop to keep it warm.

Just as I'm about to back out of the room, her nose twitches ever so slightly and then her eyes pop open.

"What? I wasn't asleep. Blueberry pancakes!" The combination of her groggy voice and bright smile makes me smile in return.

"No, you definitely weren't asleep," I say, approaching the bed and setting the tray down beside Sloane before I perch on the edge of the other side of the mattress.

"I was resting my eyes," she shoots back. "And you can sit on the bed, you know. I don't think an allergic reaction is contagious."

No, I wasn't concerned about catching her shellfish allergy. It's the feelings I've already caught that make hanging out in a bed with Sloane feel entirely too intimate. If sitting on the hood of my car led to what it did, this would be asking for trouble.

"I know, but I'm not staying for long," I hedge. "I've gotta go, uh, do some stuff."

The "stuff" in question is probably just going up to my workshop and hammering shit in an attempt to seem busy. As much as I don't want him to think he's right, I also don't want Dad to think I'm clinging too hard. Or—God forbid—"interfering." In the time I've had overnight to think about it, I've convinced myself that I can't sit here and let my heart eyes for her grow any bigger. She's going back to the show, still vying for Aspen, likely by tomorrow morning.

And I don't want to feel even more bereft than I already will when she's gone.

So the plan is to maintain some distance today. If I'm not physically around her, how could my feelings grow any stronger, right? So, distance. Boundaries. Restraint.

"Awww, no! I was hoping we'd get to hang out. I don't want you to go anywhere. Stay with me, Liam, pleeeease?" The face she gives me looks like a sad kitten.

Welp, guess I'm staying. Great job, willpower.

"Okay." I try to sound like it's going to be difficult working around my busy schedule of not doing anything. "For a little while."

A couple hours later, Sloane and I have our heads resting on the same pillow, both of us under the covers as we watch the credits of *Mamma Mia!* start to roll on my laptop between us.

"I won't lie," she says through a yawn. "Colin Firth in metallic spandex could still get it."

I laugh so hard the laptop bounces on the mattress beside me, the three male leads of the movie still dancing and singing in said metallic spandex on-screen.

"Have you been objectifying an old man for this whole movie?" I ask in disbelief, still chuckling.

"He has aged like a fine wine."

"One you aren't old enough to drink."

Sloane scoffs. "Harsh. Funny, but harsh. I can window-shop at the Firth liquor store as much as the next gal, though, and you can't stop me."

"This analogy has taken a weird turn."

"Whatever. Time for *Mamma Mia! Here We Go Again*?"

This last bit comes out through another yawn, and I narrow my eyes at her. "Sure you don't need a nap first?"

"I'm fine." She yawns. "This is just the remnants of the sleepy-making drugs getting out of my body. Like burping when you have a lot of gas."

"Aaand we're back to weird analogies."

"Better start the next movie if you want to shut me up."

I don't want to shut her up, actually; I'd sit here and talk with her all day. All week. I'm more at ease than I've been since she first got to LA; it feels like this is what we're meant to be doing. What our summer could have consisted of.

But I can also tell she wants to watch the next movie, so I queue it up. When I lean back against the pillow again, Sloane surprises me by scooting—arguably, snuggling—closer, resting her head on my shoulder. I try not to tense up even though the feeling is lighting up my whole body. The last thing I want is for her to feel that and, well, to make things weird.

"Thank you for staying," she says softly, and it feels like my heart has to be expanding, glowing enough to light up the room from my chest. But glancing down at my T-shirt, nothing visible is going on there.

"Anything for you, Sloane," I say almost without thinking, the words a little more honest than I'd have liked. She doesn't say anything, though, just snuggles even closer and drapes an arm around my waist.

The position feels very . . . girlfriendy. I'm distracted as the movie gets going, more beautiful people singing ABBA songs in beautiful places. So distracted, so hyperfocused, really, on the places where her body touches mine that I notice when, not half an hour into the movie, her head and arm both feel heavier. Her breathing has slowed, and even though there's no snoring this time, it's clear that Sloane is asleep again.

I circle my arm around her shoulders, letting my own eyes fall closed and absorbing the comfort of the moment. Before I know it, the rhythm of Sloane's steady breathing mixed with seventies disco pop has me drifting out of consciousness, too.

CHAPTER FIFTEEN

Time is fleeting. Tell people how you feel when you can, because
tomorrow they could get kidnapped by a bicycle gang.

—*THE COVE,* SEASON 1, EPISODE 3

Sloane

The first thing I notice when I wake up is that my forehead is hot.

So is the whole left side of my face. Do I have a fever? Does
an allergic reaction to shrimp give you a twenty-four-hours-
later fever? Wait, why would only the left side be feverish? That
doesn't seem right.

Next, I gather that my arms and legs are wrapped around a
hard, not especially comfy body pillow.

Wait, body pillows don't have arms that wrap around you in
return.

My eyes snap open, and I have the blessed presence of mind
to lie completely still while I survey the circumstances. The body
pillow in question, of course, is Liam. I knew it was probably
a little reckless to let myself lean on him during the movie, no
matter how much I wanted to enjoy being close with him while
I could. But I couldn't have predicted that my sleep-self would

be some kind of thirsty spider monkey, ready to climb the tree of hot best friend. I'm fully plastered to his side, one leg thrown across him at about hip level and the arm that started out casually draped on his flat stomach now clutching his shirt like my life depends on it. My head is solidly resting on his chest, and the heat I was feeling seems to be the puffs of his breath across my forehead and the side of my face getting cozy with his pectorals.

But sleep-Liam isn't so innocent either.

One of his hands is clamped firmly on my rib cage, awfully close to boob territory if we want to be particular about it. But making my heart race even faster is his right hand, which holds my bare thigh that stretches across him, just below where the hem of my pajama shorts ends. Each point of contact between us sends tingles across my whole body, a fluttery feeling taking root in my stomach—and there are many points of contact. Like, if my body was the board in that old game Operation, Liam would be setting off all kinds of buzzers.

From the slow, steady rise and fall of his chest beneath my cheek, it's clear that Liam is still fully asleep. I mean, no way he'd do anything like this if he was awake, right? But my brain quickly reminds me that he was wide-awake when he was kissing me like there was no tomorrow, and his hand slid onto my leg in a way not unlike this at some point during that whole fiasco.

But then he went right back to normal friendship mode afterward. Even distant, shut-off robot mode. Until now. So what does that mean? Is sleep-Liam doing what awake-Liam wishes he could do?

All right, I'm getting seriously overheated now, and I don't think it's from Liam's mouth-breathing. I consider how to extract myself, not coming up with any good ideas that won't wake the sleeping Sloane-snuggler. So I decide to take it one body part at a time, inching ever so slowly away from this living-romance-novel-cover tableau. But before my left foot has made it very far, all my efforts at sneakiness are thwarted by the boom of something heavy hitting the rug under the bed. I squeeze my eyes shut. Shit. The laptop we were using to watch the movies. Pretty sure I just kicked it off the bed.

Liam's whole body—still mostly wrapped up by mine—jerks. I manage to lift my head from his chest, but his hands don't immediately release me, so I can't untangle myself any more before his eyes are open and he starts to register our position. The hand at my waist flexes as his blinking gaze darts around, from my face to my whole torso pressed to his to the hand on my leg. His lips part, shaping soundless words I can't decipher. And then his eyes lock on mine.

For a second, I wonder if he's going to kiss me again. For way more than just this second, I want him to. But as quickly as his gaze meets mine, it darts away again, and even more disappointing, his hands let go. He raises his arms in the air, almost like he's trying to show he doesn't have a weapon on his person. Then, just as ridiculously, he rolls away from me until he's tumbling off the bed entirely. He lands with a louder thud than the laptop before hopping to his feet.

"Whoa! You okay?" I ask, proud of the lack of shakiness to my voice. I sound totally normal, if a little sleepy.

Liam nods but he doesn't make eye contact, looking anywhere else in the room but at me. His cheeks are flushed, his hair adorably rumpled. I imagine I look similar, if less adorable.

"Yeah, I'm good. I, uh, sorry . . . about, uh—well. Yeah," he breathes out the word then takes another deep breath, in and out. I don't know what to say or do next. But then he goes on, "I'm gonna go get something to eat. You want something to eat? We never really had lunch, so I'm starving. How about an early dinner? I'll just—"

Liam's rambling is interrupted by a knock on the door, and his eyes go comically wide. He looks to me as if I should know who the hell would be at the door. I shrug cluelessly and call out, "Come in!"

I guess it shouldn't be all that surprising, but somehow Aspen Woods is the last person I would have expected to come walking into my temporary bedroom. And naturally, he's trailed by a camera crew that appears to be actively filming. I don't even have to feign my jaw drop or look of genuine shock.

"There she is," Aspen says, making me feel like this is a nature documentary and I'm the rare species of braless bedheaded shrimp-reactive girl for whom he's been searching far and wide.

I give him a tight, I-wish-you-weren't-filming-this-but-I-guess-I-signed-up-for-it smile as he crosses to sit at the edge of my bed. And somehow, that seems to be the first time he notices Liam. His professional smile falters for half a second, his eyes flitting over Liam's tousled appearance then to mine and back. It occurs to me what this probably looks like and, well, I can't exactly say, *It's not what it looks like.*

"I'm so happy to see you," I say instead, recapturing Aspen's attention and regaining the full force of his perfect smile. Just like that, it seems Liam is forgotten.

"Yeah?" he says with a sheepishness that doesn't seem as genuine, because Aspen can't do sheepish. "Well, I'm happy to see you too. I've been so worried about you, Sloane. How are you feeling today?"

We talk like that for a few minutes, me updating Aspen on my Delicate Condition and him expressing appropriate-to-borderline-excessive amounts of concern. As always with him, it's hard for it all to feel . . . well, real. He says all the right things, but I never know what he's saying that's for me versus what's for the cameras—and the hypothetical audience eventually watching, who he wants to think he's sweet and down-to-earth.

As he's telling me about the rest of the date after I left, movement by the door catches my eye. When I glance over, I see Liam about to leave the room. He looks back at me once more, surprise in his gaze when he sees I'm already looking at him. Surprise followed by something else—something wistful.

That look stays with me, tattooed on my brain like his sleeping handprints feel they have been tattooed on my body. As I say goodbye to Aspen, as Mr. Daniels and the other producer who brought Aspen and the camera here talk to me about returning to set, as I shower and pack up my few things before setting off in Mr. Daniels's Mercedes without getting to say goodbye to Liam. Even returning to Chelsea's house and telling the other girls about my adventure, it feels like Liam's face is all I can think about.

But I don't feel like telling anyone else about it yet. I want to live in the comfortable bubble of the memory shared just by him and me for a tiny bit longer.

When I go to sleep, I resent the memory foam cased in cotton where my head is resting, wishing I had a hard, uncomfy body pillow instead.

∞

"If I get bruises on my back from these hardwoods, y'all are to blame," Bree says as she, Alicia, and I lie on the living room floor at Chelsea's house, watching the ceiling fan blades spin overhead.

"You suck at meditating," Alicia says, but I hear the suppressed laughter in her voice.

I can't hold back my own giggles. "This really is the least cushy area rug I've ever felt."

"Well, be mindful of that. Think about the way it feels under each of your body parts, one at a time. . . ."

Alicia continues on in her soothing voice, making a valiant attempt at guiding her two easily distracted roommates in meditation. It's a few days after the last Ensemble Date, since which we've all had a little too much downtime. While we still had the numbers for it, there were some pickup volleyball games and an impromptu mini golf tournament. We even tried Marvel charades, which, while less heated than Disney charades, proved too challenging, as we found ourselves making the same superhero power poses for every character.

But last night was the fourth Casting Call, where Aspen sent five more girls home, and we haven't been in a game-playing mood ever since. It's only our room—Hattie, Alicia, Bree, and me—plus Peyton left, with Peyton in her own room two doors down from ours. I heard Hattie offer to stay there with her from now on, but Peyton said she was fine with some "peace and quiet."

Apparently even more so than we thought, as none of us have seen her since breakfast. Hattie is on her first Scene Partner Date with Aspen today, and Chelsea's house feels empty and quiet enough that it could be an actual meditation studio. Alicia must give up on Bree and me, though, as I feel her roll over to her stomach and she and Bree begin to talk about dinner options for this evening.

I wonder what Liam is up to. He's been out on the dates or helping around with the set designer, Garrett, so much that I've scarcely laid eyes on him since leaving his house. There haven't been any notes either. I feel itchy, and not in the shellfish-reaction-hives way. Itchy to see Liam, hear his voice, talk to him, maybe even more. . . .

"Sloane?" Bree's voice cuts off my dangerous mental trajectory, and it sounds like it isn't the first time she's tried to get my attention.

"Yeah?"

"Just wondering where your head was."

The ceiling fan is starting to make my head spin, so I sit up straight and look around the room.

Bree takes a deep breath and continues on. "What's got you so spaced out?"

I feign offense. "I'm not spaced out."

"Are you thinking about Liam?" Alicia is the smartest person on this set, I swear. Her out-of-the-blue question makes my jaw drop, and she adds more quietly, "Sorry, that wasn't very tactful of me, was it? I just . . . You can't tell me there's nothing there at all."

I consider deflecting, but under the fixed raised eyebrows already calling my bluff, and the pressure of keeping everything inside for what feels like years instead of weeks, I finally give in.

"All right. There . . . might be more truth to your speculation about Liam and me than there was at the beginning of this." I'm met with two gasps and expressions ranging from excited to scandalized. "I just don't know what I'm feeling. I've never felt anything more than friendship for Liam before this summer, but now I feel it so much, I can't ignore it. And I don't know if he feels it too. Part of me just wants to give in and go for him, but I made a commitment to be here and see this through, and I don't know how I can walk away from it when I'm not sure where Liam's head is at, or if I'm giving Aspen and the show enough of a chance. But do I even want to give that more of a chance?"

"Hey." Alicia scoots closer and starts to rub my back. "Listen, first I think it'd be helpful to remember that Aspen's been dating twenty-plus other girls. I think it's okay if you're conflicted about one other guy. Not worth sending yourself into a guilt tailspin over it."

"Yeah, honestly, as much as I'm Team Liam for you"—Bree cuts off when Alicia elbows her—"I mean, no pressure. Forget I said that. What I meant to say was that I think it's fine to still be here exploring your feelings for both guys until you're sure about who and what you want. You're not about to accept a marriage proposal from either of them, you know? And there are still five of us left. You have time to figure it out."

Just then, we hear the front door open and fall shut again. There are footsteps on the tile floor, and all three of us turn to see Ty come into the room, heading toward the stairs. He stops with a hand on the railing, giving us a sympathetic smile.

"Ladies. Hope you've had a good day. I have a little bit of news for you—I'm here to get Hattie's things. She's been sent home from today's Scene Partner Date."

We give a collective gasp, my hand going to clutch Alicia's while she puts her other arm around Bree's shoulders. Not only is this the first time anyone's been sent home from a Scene Partner Date, but it's *Hattie*. And this means . . .

"Congratulations to you all. You're now in the top four!"

Not reading the room at all, he gives a few claps before continuing upstairs to get the suitcase Hattie packed this morning in preparation for her date, which we all assumed she would come home and unpack tonight.

"Oh my God," Alicia breathes out.

"Poor Hattie," Bree adds.

She and Alicia speculate on what this means for the timeline of the remainder of the show, while I really start to spiral.

Top four. I've made it to the top four. This means I've officially held up my end of the bargain with Mr. Daniels, right? I should feel like celebrating. I did it! He's going to help me make my dreams happen, and I should be so happy. But it feels all wrong.

"It should've been me," I murmur.

Both turn to me with confusion. "What?" Alicia asks softly.

"Hattie should have made it to the top four. Aspen should've sent me home by now. Hattie wasn't thinking about another guy. Hattie wasn't *kissing* another guy while dating Aspen"—my friends gasp, but I plow on—"or sneaking away with him, or watching movies in bed with him while Aspen probably thinks she's totally focused on *their* relationship. And it's just hitting me how close we are to the end now, how many girls have already left who were way more into Aspen than I am, and I feel like the worst kind of faker. What am I still doing here, you know?"

"I'd like to know the same thing," a new, sharper voice says from the staircase, and all of our heads whip around to see Peyton standing there looking like she's sucked down a lemon and been punched in the stomach at the same time. "What the *hell,* Sloane? I knew there was something up with you and the PA, but you're worse than even I thought. Why are you here if you're not sure you like Aspen at this point? *And* when you're apparently off making out with someone else? How dare you?"

My mouth opens as if to defend myself, but nothing comes out.

"Peyton—" Alicia starts, but the other girl holds up a hand.

"Save it. You all knew about this too, which means you're almost as bad as she is. I don't even want to be near this house of liars right now." She shakes her head in disgust. "I'm taking my stuff to Brock's house. And remember when I said I'd tell Aspen if I thought anyone was going to hurt him? That wasn't an empty threat."

"Oh, get over yourself, you low-budget Cheryl Blossom," Bree shoots back with an eye roll. "This isn't your business."

"I strongly disagree," Peyton answers, and huffs an actual *hmph* sound as she marches out the front door and slams it behind her.

And as much as I hate to say it, she has a point.

CHAPTER SIXTEEN

I'd do anything for Mara. I got *shot* to keep her safe. It was a
paintball gun, but still. Those things hurt like a bitch.
—*THE COVE*, SEASON 2, EPISODE 17

Liam

"You're going about this all wrong," Garrett's gruff voice says
from behind me.

For a second, I look at him wide-eyed, wondering how he
can hear my thoughts, which for days now have all been centered
around Sloane, our relationship, and what I should do with all
these feelings I have. I start to feel eager for whatever brilliant
relationship wisdom the older man is about to impart.

But then he takes the putty knife from my hands and nudges
me out of his way where we stand by one of the bedroom walls
in Brock's house. All the girls who lived here have now been sent
home, and Garrett and I are in the process of putting the house
back together for normal filming on *The Cove*. Garrett has been
taking apart bunk beds, mostly, while I've taken down a couple
temporary shelves they put up for the girls to store their stuff. I'm
starting to fill in the holes they made in the walls—and apparently I'm not doing a very good job.

"Sorry, I've never spackled anything before," I say, even though I know by now he doesn't mean to chastise me. He seems to genuinely want to teach me what he can, and when it comes out harsh, well, that's how Garrett talks to everyone. I'm pretty sure he likes me.

"It's fine, you're just not layering enough on here to actually fill it in. Don't worry about it looking rough and sticking out—we'll sand it down after."

Garrett finishes showing me what he means before handing the knife back to me. I interpret his grunt as one of approval when he walks back over to his own task and leaves me to mine. *Nice.* At least I can do this right.

"Liam," a voice barks from the doorway a little while later, pulling me away from the spackling stride I've hit. I turn, surprised to see Aspen standing there.

"Aren't you supposed to be on a date?" I ask before realizing that's kind of a rude greeting. Whatever. I've lost some of my niceness filter when it comes to this guy.

"It ended early." He crosses his arms over his chest and leans back against the door frame. "I sent Hattie home."

I fumble and drop the putty knife. Hattie was Sloane's friend, and I feel bad for her getting her feelings crushed so abruptly, of course, but she was also the fifth girl remaining. Which means . . .

"So now I have my top four, and I'm planning another Scene Partner Date with Sloane for tomorrow that I wanted to run by you."

Sloane is in the final four.

In my dream version of the situation, this is when Sloane

would interrupt everything to make an announcement worthy of the reality-TV-drama hall of fame—that she was only ever here because of a deal with my dad, she was never conflicted about her feelings at all and doesn't care for Aspen one bit. She'd run all over the set to find her one true love, Liam Daniels, and we'd ride off into the sunset together.

Instead, I get Aspen Woods breaking the news while he taps around on his smartwatch and looks vaguely annoyed that I'm actually trying to work.

"I was thinking through everything you've told me about Sloane, trying to figure out what to do with her," he says, his nonchalant attitude more grating than I've ever found it. "Production's real into shit that ties into *The Cove,* and there's a whole corny recurring theme of Dorian and Mara 'facing their fears' together."

He looks my way, his air quotes and tone making it clear that he's unimpressed by said corniness.

"Anyway, you said Sloane doesn't swim, or like, she can, but it scares her."

"Uh, no," I say quickly, not liking where this is going at all. Did I actually give him that information? I guess I did, intending to dissuade him from any swimming dates—definitely not to *encourage* them.

"Yeah, you said that. And she said something about it too, on the first Ensemble Date. So my plan is to have us face that fear together."

"No," I say more firmly, stepping away from the wall and walking toward him, trying to impress the gravity of this upon him. But Aspen keeps looking around the room and talking as if he doesn't notice.

"I'll take her on a yacht, have a nice dinner and chat, then we'll get into our swimsuits and—wait, what?"

He looks back to me, totally baffled.

I shake my head and slash one hand through the air to drive home the point. "Bad idea. Definitely don't try to make her swim. She won't do it."

He scoffs. "Well, you don't know that for sure—"

"I do. She'll hate that kind of date. She's not wild about boats and absolutely won't want to swim in the open ocean. Anything else, man."

His eyes narrow as he studies me for a few moments, and it only now occurs to me, a dumbass, that he didn't want constructive criticism here. Only validation that his idea was a good one, when it was actually the opposite.

"You're not even listening to me," he says, his voice turning flinty.

Still, I know I have to stick up for Sloane on this one. "I promise, I am. I've heard plenty to know that Sloane would be really upset if you tried to force her into 'facing this fear.'"

I even imbue my voice with the same mocking tone he had when saying the same words, as if to show we're on the same team. We are obviously not, though, and Aspen isn't fooled.

In fact, he steps closer and says, "Are you sure there's still nothing between you two?"

My head jerks back as if this is the most bonkers suggestion I've ever heard. *No, man, definitely not! We for sure didn't make out as "practice" for the kiss you two still haven't had, not that I've been paying super-close attention to that fact!*

My laugh sounds croaky. "No way. I mean, yes, I'm sure. All of this is coming from my concern as her friend . . . and as yours."

The last bit comes as an afterthought, a last-ditch effort at the buddy-ol-pal routine. Aspen's posture relaxes ever so slightly, and he steps back again. At least I know he's not about to haul off and hit me. But with his next words, he might as well have.

"Well, we're doing it. I've already cleared it with the producers. We'll see who's right about Sloane." He pauses before turning on a heel then walking out into the hallway. "You can get back to . . . whatever it is you're doing."

My mouth drops open at his cold dismissal, and I'm left with a sick feeling in my stomach. Regardless of everything else happening in my mixed-up heart and mind, I know one thing to be true.

I can't let Sloane get on a boat with this asshole—at least not without me there, too.

I find Garrett where he's moved on to another room of bunk bed disassembly and let him know I'll be right back, suddenly very grateful that he's not the type to ask questions. When I'm almost to the sliding back doors of Brock's house, I nearly run smack into another unexpected visitor.

"Peyton," I say, bringing a hand to my chest. Then I notice that she has all her luggage in tow and a confused frown pulls at my lips. "What are you doing?"

Rather than the charm and flirtation I've come to expect from her, the look she gives me is pinched and cold. "Relocating

246

due to extenuating circumstances. Have you seen Aspen? Ty said he saw him heading here. I need to talk to him."

I try for a second to parse her words, then decide I have bigger priorities right now. "Yeah, uh, he was just here. He might've gone out the front, if you didn't see him on your walk over here. Good luck."

"You should probably keep your luck for yourself," she mutters before flicking her hair back from her face and marching away.

"Okay, sure. Cool. Got it," I say under my breath, shaking my head as I leave Brock's house and start jogging toward Dorian's.

I have to find Kristi. But a scan of Dorian's backyard area yields no evidence of the short, perky producer. Heading inside, I finally locate her in the entryway of the house, having a hushed but heated conversation with Ty.

Kristi says in a pleading whisper, "I just don't think it's a good idea to—"

"Well, frankly, Kristi, your opinions don't carry much weight here." Ty talks over her.

I retreat into the hallway, shocked to hear him speak to her like that. But is it really all that shocking? This doesn't sound like the best conversation to interrupt, either way. But if I don't try to talk to Kristi now, I don't know when I'll get the opportunity.

"Hey, Kristi?" I say overloudly as I turn the corner. Both producers turn to me, irritation on Ty's face and a redness rising in Kristi's—embarrassment, maybe, that I've overheard? I want to tell her she doesn't have anything to be embarrassed about, and I want to call Ty out for being a dick, while I'm at it. But we're so close to the end of filming. So close to me finishing this job without causing any major conflict or chaos on Dad's set. I can't screw it up now, can I? "Could I talk to you for a minute?"

She nods quickly, already stepping away from Ty without another glance his way. "Sure, Liam, of course. Let's go out back."

I let her lead the way until we've stepped outside and she slides the door shut behind us. Facing her, I'm suddenly nervous. "What's up?"

Her face is relaxed now, no longer red. I'm in awe of that kind of composure. Meanwhile, very-much-not-composed me scratches the back of my neck, barely able to make eye contact.

"I was wondering if you know what crew I'm supposed to be on tomorrow. If I'm going along for Sl—I mean, the next Scene Partner Date or not."

Kristi bites her lip, and I don't have a good feeling about the anxious eyes she's giving me. "Yes, so, um, no. You're supposed to be staying here. Maybe helping Garrett out some more? That'll be fun, right?"

I swallow heavily, already shaking my head. "I need to go on this date. Aspen—he's gonna try to do something dumb, and I . . ." I trail off, unsure what to reveal. But who am I kidding? She's probably seen it all, anyway. Everyone else seems to. "I'm worried about Sloane."

Kristi nods, giving me an expression not unlike the one she gives girls who have been sent home. Ironic. "I know, Liam. I was talking to Ty about the SPD plan for tomorrow. But listen, I'll be there and won't let anything happen to Sloane, okay?"

"Please, Kristi. If there's anything at all you can do to get me on that damn boat . . ."

She looks as if she's considering whether to say something, then sighs into her next words. "Your dad spoke with me, and made it clear he wants you distanced from Sloane as much as possible."

My stomach sinks. *Shit.* Well, that's going to make this difficult, isn't it?

Pushing a frustrated hand through my hair, I pace in a slow circle for a few moments as I try to come up with a good argument.

"Kristi, I'm begging you." Okay, not my best work. "We can completely blame this on me when he finds out—*if* he finds out. He's barely ever there on dates anyway. We'll tell him I snuck into the vans, and onto the boat, whatever. I'll take the fall. Throw me to the wolves."

So much for my not-causing-chaos-this-close-to-the-end thing. But desperate times, desperate measures. Kristi's clearly trying to hold back a smile, so I push on.

"I'll owe you big-time. You can collect some massive favor from me in the future, whatever I can do for you—I'll put it in writing. And you'll be my favorite person in the whole world."

Her lips reluctantly tip up on one side. "I think that position's already taken," she says with a raise of one eyebrow.

Now my cheeks are flushing again, and I look down as I put my hands in my shorts pockets. "Possibly," I admit, then look up at her again. "But if you know that, then you understand why I want to be there so badly, right?"

We stare at each other for another minute. Finally, she lets out a sigh, closing her eyes tight and nodding.

"Okay. I'll get you on the date." I pump my fist in the air and she adds in a softer voice, "But keep it on the down low until then, okay?"

"Absolutely." I nod, then lean in to give her an impulsive hug. "You're the best producer there ever was."

She laughs, patting my back before we part. "I'm glad someone thinks so."

CHAPTER SEVENTEEN

I'd ask if you wanna take this outside,
but I have seasonal allergies, bro.
—*THE COVE,* SEASON 2, EPISODE 21

Sloane

There are many reasons I regret not leaving the show in a blaze of glory immediately after making the top four. Said reasons begin with my feelings for Liam, feelings that I'm more sure of by the minute. And today, they are joined by the fact that I'm on a motherfucking boat.

In the middle of the ocean.

In a bikini.

I wore the swimsuit out here under my clothes, and only after a lot of puppy-dog eyes from Kristi. I've felt for her ever since I saw Mr. Daniels chewing her out for lord knows what the other day, and if my scantily clad ass on TV will make her life a little easier, then whatever. I'm here.

But I don't have to be happy about it.

And I think it's pretty clear that I'm not, as I sit opposite a bare-chested, swim-trunks-clad Aspen, eating some ice cream out of a fancy dish. I'm less enchanted by him than ever, despite his impressive swimsuit bod. It would be more impressive if it wasn't presented against a backdrop of rolling ocean that keeps appearing then disappearing behind the edge of this yacht's upper deck. I'm getting a little seasick on top of hating my life.

Seriously, the only way this date could get *less* up my alley is if—

"What do you say we take a dip?" Aspen says with a smile that hits as more slimy than charming today.

"Wh-what? No thanks," I say quickly, dropping my bowl and spoon to the table with a clatter. He's really done it—found the antithesis of Sloane's Dream Date. Am I being punished? Did Peyton really go tell Aspen everything she overheard, and this is his retribution? I cross my arms over my bare stomach as Aspen gives me his best smolder. It doesn't suggest anything nefarious going on in his mind—not obviously, anyway.

"Not even with me?"

I shake my head vigorously.

His smile falters slightly before he corrects it, then reaches out to try and take my hand. I allow it, as if allowing a dog to have a saltine cracker when he was begging for bacon.

"Relationships," he begins softly, and I feel some philosophizing coming on, "are about growing together. And part of growing together is facing our fears together. I want us to be able to conquer anything, Sloane, side by side. Will you at least think about it while we're out here?"

So he definitely does remember that I'm afraid to swim. And, if I'm not being made to pay for my misdeeds, then I'm not sure whether to think his reasoning is sweet and meaningful . . . or if he's just trying to make a good TV show. Today, I'm feeling less generous than I have so far in our relationship, and therefore I'm leaning toward the latter.

"I'll think about it," I offer, because I will think about it. Think about how mad I am that he's brought me out to the open ocean and tried to manipulate me into plunging to my likely death.

Making everything a dozen times more tense and confusing, Liam is here for our date. It's not the world's largest yacht, nor does *AWFLL* have the world's largest crew, so I'm aware of where he is at all times. Trying to avoid looking right at where he is at all times.

But I slip again, my eyes darting over to him. He's already gazing intently at me. Embarrassingly, I blush.

Stick to one family of emotions at a time, McKinney. Right now we're stressed, tense, edgy.

And possibly a little lovesick.

No, seasick. I meant seasick. Aspen, appearing pleased with himself, encourages me to get up and follow him to the lower deck, the crew following behind us. There's a place near the back of the boat he wants to show me, where you can step on a little ledge that gives you the best view of the water below, uninhibited by a wall or railing. I definitely wouldn't step up here if the boat was moving, but anchored as we are, I feel able to stay balanced.

"See, the water doesn't look so scary from here, does it?" Aspen chides, clearly still not getting the concept of a phobia or, I don't know, childhood trauma. "See the fish down there? They're having a great time."

"Yes, well, they have gills and fins, so," I answer flatly. No more saltines for you, Rover.

He laughs and goes on pointing out various things on the horizon, while I'm expending all my energy trying not to freak the hell out. Surely we won't be here longer than another hour or so. I can make it that long.

"Oh my God, look!" Aspen says on a gasp, pointing into the water below us.

"What?" Cautiously, I lean down, still careful to keep my balance.

And I would have done so just fine, had a hand not pressed against my back and pushed, sending me over the boat's edge in a free fall that ends with a splash.

From there, it's a terrifying, panicky blur. Of course the first thing I do upon going under is gulp in a bunch of seawater. My vision goes spotty, glimpses of blurry bubbles and deep blue alternating with endless blackness as I tumble and turn, limbs flying in all directions. Anything I ever knew about swimming has fled my brain, replaced by a feeling of helplessness, paralysis, and above all, a sureness that I'm not going to break the surface again.

But then something bands around my waist, and the water around me starts rushing downward. No, I'm moving upward, propelled by something outside myself. When my head breaks the surface I gasp, cough, sputter, almost afraid to open my eyes at the risk of finding out this is in my imagination, that I'm still underwater. The force that brought me up is now tugging me backward across the surface. I think I almost hear my name being called above the roaring in my ears.

Then all at once, I feel myself being hauled fully out of the water, something warm and solid holding on to me, and I open my eyes.

It's Liam. I'm back on the boat. Liam is holding me, and we're not underwater. He looks down at me with an intensity I've never seen, water dripping off his eyelashes and the lock of hair hanging over his forehead. Everything else comes to me slowly. Liam gripping me tightly, carrying me somewhere, setting me down. Kristi appears with towels, and I'm bundled up with them while I sit on some sort of bench. The roaring in my ears is replaced by a rapid clacking, which I realize after only a moment is my teeth chattering. Liam's nice Henley shirt is soaked through with the rest of him, even the tennis shoes he still has on, but he appears to decline a towel, still checking me over while I just stare at him.

Then he's gone, and my narrow focus widens. I hear everything, see everything again.

"Sloane, you're okay, honey," Kristi is saying in my ear, her arm now wrapped around me. "Can someone go find her clothes?"

Frantically, I seek out Liam again, but it doesn't take long to spot him. He's striding across the deck with purpose, paying no mind to the cameras still rolling. He doesn't stop until he has a firm grip on Aspen Woods's shoulder, then he's slamming Aspen back against a wall.

For a second, I think the water affected my vision. I can't possibly be watching my gentle, soft-spoken best friend roughing up a Hollywood actor. But then he starts talking.

Yelling, more like.

"What the *hell* is wrong with you?" Liam barks, louder than I think I've ever heard him, trying to give Aspen's chest a shove with both hands even though Aspen's back is still pressed to the side of the boat's main cabin. "She could have drowned! She's clearly not okay, and that's one hundred percent on your shoulders."

Aspen sputters, "Look, Ty told me to do it—"

Liam whirls around to where Ty is standing by one of the cameras. "*You* told him to push a girl who doesn't swim into the ocean without a life jacket on? You want a lawsuit on your hands, you absolute prick, because that's—"

Ty seems unable to form words for once, but Aspen keeps trying. "It was—well, Peyton told me some stuff and then Ty said that Sloane . . . well, that you and she—listen, we thought it was only fair to mess around with her a li—"

"No," Liam turns back to Aspen. "I don't care who told you what, and you weren't messing around. You were being a selfish, reckless asshole who doesn't respect people's boundaries even when they tell you over and over! She told you, I told you. You should have listened."

Something about that has sparked more confidence in Aspen, or at least more indignation. "Yeah, well, you've told me a lot of shit since we've been here, and has any of it actually worked for me?" he yells back, stepping into Liam's space. "Clearly not! It was time to listen to my own gut instead of someone who obviously doesn't even know what it takes to win his 'best friend.' If you did, you might've gotten her by now!"

Liam lunges for Aspen again, but he's pulled back by another

PA before he makes contact. Aspen gives him a smug smile and starts to walk away, but not before I process what he's said.

"What are you talking about?" I croak out, voice raw from my unintentional saltwater gargle. My teeth are still chattering and I still feel unsteady, but I shrug out of Kristi's grip to walk closer, keeping the towel wrapped around me. I look back and forth between Liam and Aspen as they turn to face me, and both of their expressions are guilty now. "What do you mean, Liam's told you a lot?"

"Just—"

"We've talked—"

"Sort of become friends—"

They fumble over each other in vague nonanswers until I shake my head. "Don't bullshit me. What's going on?"

Liam and Aspen lock gazes, both grim-faced but in a weird sort of solidarity. It's Aspen who finally speaks up. "Liam has been . . . helping me. Telling me some stuff about you, stuff that might help me, uh, relate to, or, er, appeal to you. Likes, dislikes, things you might want to do on dates. I was interested in you from early on, but I didn't get the impression that you were especially interested in me back, so I asked for Liam's . . . assistance."

I feel my face twisting with more and more confusion and something else, something sharper—hurt. Liam grips the back of his neck, barely able to look at me. Aspen clearly knows he's just screwed everything up, too.

"The—the whole time, you've been working together behind my back?"

They don't answer, but they don't have to. I feel like I'm sinking all over again.

This whole time, Liam was pushing Aspen and me together. Was anything between us real? Why would he help Aspen if he wanted anything more with me?

The words "not center-stage material" drift through my mind in my mom's voice. Being on this show hasn't made me any sort of main character, not really. I've been a prop in other people's plans and lives, maybe more than ever before. I don't know why I thought this was some big step forward for me just because there are mics and cameras.

I feel deceived, betrayed, and most of all, ready to get off this damn boat.

"Sloane—" Liam starts, but I push past him. Past them both.

"No, I think I've heard enough," I say, then walk through the sliding door, planning to find a place inside to dry off and hide away until we're back to land.

I pull the door firmly shut behind me.

CHAPTER EIGHTEEN

You deserve someone who will choose you first every time,
Chelsea. There's at least a billion guys in the world, and if half of
them are single, and a third are an appropriate age, well . . .
I'm not good at math.

—*THE COVE,* SEASON 3, EPISODE 16

Liam

One would expect all hell to break loose—or continue breaking
loose, I guess—following the revelations on the yacht. But as it
turns out, hell has nothing on a disappointed Kristi.

"Stop rolling," she tells the camera operator as soon as Sloane
shuts the cabin door behind her.

"But—" he starts to protest, probably under instructions that
the messiest footage is the best.

"I don't care. No more filming. Shut it down." Her tone
invites no further argument. "You two"—she points to Ty and
Aspen, who look like scolded schoolboys—"go to the upper deck.
Stay there until we're on land. I don't want to hear anything
more out of either of you."

That gives me a moment of satisfaction, until Kristi turns on me with the same stern expression. "You—stay back here. Don't go upstairs, don't try to talk to these guys. You all stay with him."

"These guys" are, of course, Aspen and Ty, who have avoided eye contact with me since Sloane left and are now moving toward the stairs to the upper deck. The "you all" seems to be the rest of the crew, save for another PA who Kristi takes with her into the cabin where Sloane disappeared.

I feel like I'm in time-out as I sit on the bench at the very back of the boat's lower deck, waiting to return to shore. I should probably be filled with dread at whatever awaits me when we get back to set, especially once my dad catches wind of this. But all I can worry about is Sloane.

She looked so hurt. And it'd be one thing if that hurt, that betrayal, was entirely from Aspen. But he's not the only one to blame.

Someone offers me a towel again, and this time I take it and wrap myself in its warmth while the rest of the crew packs up cameras and equipment. By the time we get back, my clothes are no longer dripping—though my shoes still squish when I walk—and everything is ready to be off-loaded into vans and driven back to set. Note to self for the next time I have to rescue the most important person in my life from drowning—take the half second to kick off the sneakers.

Once we're docked and some deckhands put out a gangway, Kristi comes out back to let us know we can follow her off, calling up to Aspen and Ty to do the same. I assume Sloane must be leaving from the front of the boat with the PA, but once we're all circled up and ready to go, Kristi looks around.

"Where's Sloane?" Wariness has entered her voice, and I feel my pulse pick up.

"She went to the marina's restroom," the other PA answers.

"By herself?!" The question is more of a squeak before Kristi turns tail and starts running up the dock toward the front of the marina. Without thinking about it, I take off behind her. Our steps pound across the pavement until we reach the small, blocky building with a door marked "Women" on one side. Kristi whips it open, and I have at least enough brainpower to recognize I should wait outside. After a few seconds, in which I can hear her calling Sloane's name and flinging open bathroom doors, she reemerges.

"She's not there," she says, the cool control she had on the boat now gone.

I turn in a circle, looking all around us. She could only have gone so far, right? She doesn't have a phone to call a car. The marina connects to a parking lot on one side and a boardwalk with shops and restaurants on the other. Acting on instinct, I take off running in that direction.

"Liam!" Kristi calls after me, but I don't have time to wait and strategize with her as I start weaving through the crowd of people milling about. Before long, I glimpse a head of dark, wet hair ahead of me and the red tank top Sloane was wearing at the start of the date today, and my heart flips over in my chest. *If I can just keep eyes on her . . .*

But she's moving fast, and her small stature makes it easier for her to disappear within groups of walkers. I don't know if she's even thinking about being followed right now, or if she's just trying to get away.

"Hey, watch yourself," a guy spits at me after I accidentally shove him to the side with an elbow. Contrary to the behavior I've displayed today, I'm actually not an aggressive person, so I start to turn and apologize. But before I can, I see a flash of red darting to the left.

"Sorry," I yell over my shoulder as I set my course for the pier that Sloane just turned down. It's a long wooden walkway that stretches out on stilts over the ocean. There are fewer people here, some taking pictures, some fishing, than on the main boardwalk's thoroughfare. But Sloane doesn't seem to notice any of them, continuing to jog straight ahead until she gets to the very end and leans against the ledge.

I slow my pace and try to control my breathing before I reach her. She doesn't even seem to hear my approach, so I come to a stop a few feet away in an effort not to startle her.

"Sloane," I pant. So much for breathing normally. "Are you okay?"

She looks to me in surprise, but it turns quickly to anger. "Are you seriously asking me that?"

I swallow the lump in my throat, nodding as I come up beside her. "Okay, yeah. I guess what I mean is that I know you're not okay and I'm sorry for my part in it. Do you want to talk about it?"

Sloane faces forward again, looking out at the ocean. Her chin wobbles and I want to reach for her. Pull her in and hold her and apologize until "sorry" doesn't feel like it's a real word anymore. But I don't think she'd welcome that right now.

"I don't know." Her voice is steady, the threat of tears seemingly pushed away. "I . . . I don't understand you, Liam."

It feels like she's got my heart clutched in her fist. "What do you want to know? I'll tell you anything, seriously."

"Will you, though?" She turns her whole body to face me, eyes narrowed. But I can tell she's hurting more than anything else. "Because apparently you've been keeping plenty from me."

"Sloane—"

"Coming on this show," she interrupts, holding a hand up to me as she takes a step closer. "I thought it would be something fun to do, and obviously, I wanted to have fun. Wanted to help your dad, and get what I could in return. But along the way, I realized I needed to do it for myself, too. Get closer to my writing dreams, indulge a little along the way in a TV drama fantasy. I wanted to feel, for once, like . . . like the main character in my own life, not a side character in the McKinney Family Sitcom. You know?"

The words pain me, but I can tell she needs to keep going.

"And maybe I should've expected this, even though it's 'reality,' because we all know these shows are so contrived. But I didn't expect it from you. I feel like a fool, like I'm more of a side character in someone else's plot than ever, with you and the producers and Aspen all pulling my strings."

She pauses, then adds more quietly, "I made it to the final four, at least. Someone else is finally gonna support me in making my dreams come true, so yay for that. But I'm . . . so tired. Of the process but also of—of putting my heart through this."

I shake my head, feeling every word cut through me. "I only agreed to help Aspen because I thought it would help get you what you wanted. And I think—well, at least I thought—that he genuinely liked you and his intentions were good, and you deserve a guy who really cares about you. I don't know what the hell I think now. But Sloane . . ." I reach out to take one of her hands in mine. "You've always been the main character to me."

Okay, what was that plan about not sharing too many of my feelings? The words are out, though. She lifts her head to look me in the eyes, her own widening. Nothing to do now but keep going.

"You never had to do this show to become anything 'more' than who you already are. You're amazing, and anyone who can't see it, well, it's their fault. And I'll always do anything I can to help your writing dream happen. Supporting you was never—is never—a transactional thing for me. You're not trapped here— not now or even before you made the top four. Say the word and we'll go. I mean, we *did* escape a couple times, and it was pretty amazing."

Her lips have parted, and a wash of pink comes over her cheeks. "Liam . . ." She takes her hand back from mine, and my heart sinks. "When you say things like that, when you helped me sneak out or took me home from the hospital and you—and *we*—" She huffs out a breath and turns to face the sea again. "What are we doing here? I keep thinking there's something more going on than Sloane and Liam, Best Friends Forever. But then you pull away, or I find out you've been trying to push Aspen and me together all this time, and none of it makes any sense. *You* don't make any sense."

I'm speechless for a few moments. I can't believe we're finally, truly putting it out there. A small laugh escapes me. "I could say the same thing about you, flirting with Aspen like you're actually into him—"

"Because I was trying to get this far, and you were—"

"—never telling me in actual words what you're feeling for me—"

"—oh, like you've been any better!"

"Sloane." I put a hand to her waist, and she spins to face me, fire in her eyes and both of us somehow standing closer than ever. Her hand comes up to rest on my chest. Her gaze flits down to my lips, then up to my eyes again, and shit, now I really can't breathe. Is she . . . ? Are we . . . ? I want to, that's for damn sure. But against every instinct in my body, I pull back.

Her face falls.

"No, wait," I say with a shake of my head, giving her waist a squeeze. "I need you to know, if we're ever going to do that again, it can't be a practice kiss."

The words seem to hit her like a blow, her mouth dropping open.

"I know what I want," I go on, a surreal sort of calm settling over me as the truth comes out. "And it's you. I didn't know when you got here for the summer. I didn't know when we started this whole show thing, or when I agreed to help Aspen. But I know now."

She's still gaping at me, and I guess I really haven't been as obvious about my feelings as I worried I was. I want to turn away, to look at the ocean or run back to the boardwalk and buy an ice cream to eat my feelings, but I force myself to stay present with her as she takes in what I've said.

"You—you do want me. As more than your friend," she says, processing out loud. I give her a barely there nod.

We're silent for a few moments, nothing but the sound of the waves and sea breeze. The longer the silence goes on, the more discouraged I get that Sloane's response was not an immediate, enthusiastic "I want you, too." I hate that a small part of me hoped that would be the case. I mean, she literally just detailed how and why my betrayal upset her so much. Of course we're not on the same page, even if she likes cuddling when she's drowsy on drugs or wants to kiss me after I've said some nice stuff to her. That doesn't mean she wants *me.*

I'm about to say something, anything to put an end to the painful nothingness, when another voice ends it first.

"Sloane! Liam!"

We jump apart from each other instinctively and turn to see Kristi jogging down the pier.

She's still a ways out, and Sloane looks at me nervously before whispering, "I . . . I just can't right now, okay? I need time."

My stomach feels like it sinks past my feet, through the planks below us and dropping to the ocean. But I nod, put my hands in my still-soggy pockets, and turn to squish-walk back to land.

"Liam . . . ," she murmurs half-heartedly after me.

"It's fine, Sloane. Don't worry about it. *I'm* fine," I say. I risk one more glance at her over my shoulder, and she looks as lost as I've ever seen her. I guess that's really it—all the answer I need. Before I resume walking and leave this whole miserable conversation behind, I add for her sake, "You're my best friend, okay?"

She nods just as Kristi reaches us, and that's it. The end of our episode, fading to black.

CHAPTER NINETEEN

What are you supposed to do when everything seems to be
crashing down? Earthquake drills didn't prepare us for this shit!
—*THE COVE*, SEASON 3, EPISODE 12

Sloane

If anyone had told me when I agreed to my first foray into TV
World that it would include two near-death experiences and getting my heart broken in the span of a few days, I would have
thought they were confused. This was a *reality show* I was going
on, not an episode of *The Cove*.

What's that saying about truth, fiction, strangeness?

The day after my disastrous SPD—after Kristi found Liam
and me before I could settle on what to say back to him, and we
all ended up in an awkward van ride back to the mansions—the
eerie quiet on set reflects my state of mind. A numbness has
settled over me, and I've sort of forced myself to stop thinking about everything that happened. I sit in the living room at
Chelsea's house relaying the whole story I was too tired to tell the
night before to Bree, Alicia, and, surprisingly, a subdued Peyton.
The latter interrupted my story to explain that while she told
Aspen she thought I had a thing for Liam, she didn't tell him we

kissed and, overall, would like her name excluded from the narrative of me getting pushed into the ocean. I'm too emotionally exhausted to hold it against her. She couldn't have known that Aspen would seek a watery revenge to "mess with" me.

We haven't been mic'd up yet today, nor have we seen a single producer around the house. Normally they'd have been here already, rounding people up for dates, OTFs, or B-roll. Bree heard whispers from some of the crew last night, when she was outside looking for her beach towel, involving Ty's name and the word "suspended." I haven't seen Aspen since the boat nor Liam since we pulled into the cul-de-sac. Peyton came back over from Brock's house because it creeped her out being left totally to her own devices. It's unclear if some kind of pause has been put on filming in light of everything, or if Aspen's quit in a rage after being pushed around by the EP's son, or what. But I'm trying to fill in the blanks that I can for the other girls.

When I get to the part of the saga about Aspen seeking out Liam's help to win me over, I'm met with three identical gasps.

"Whoa," Bree breathes out.

"That's . . . a lot," Alicia says.

I nod, and there's a prolonged pause before Peyton pipes up. "So . . . both guys are, like, in love with you? I'm sorry, I'm just failing to see why this is a problem on your end." She crosses her arms over her chest and sinks back into the couch cushions. "Like, it obviously sucks for the rest of us that we've been made fools by Aspen effing Woods, but don't you just have to choose which one you want?"

I frown at her, unsure how to reply to that, but I don't have to.

"Heeey, ladies," a soft voice calls from the kitchen, and we all turn in surprise to see Kristi standing there, a couple other producers flanking her. The three come into the living room, looking almost cautious as they take seats on the rug and in chairs, joining our circle.

"Sorry if everything's been a bit . . . confusing the last day or so," Kristi continues, and I'm startled by how not startling her voice is. It's like her energy has been turned down twelve notches overnight. "The crew was given this morning off while production regroups and we figure out next steps for the rest of filming. I imagine Sloane's told you all about yesterday?"

We nod, still confused as to what's going on here.

The producer who "supervised" my phone call with my mom, who I've since learned is named Mellie, nods back and speaks. "We wanted to touch base with you all in an unofficial way, kind of debrief. See how you're doing."

"First of all, there's no excuse for what happened yesterday," says the third, Nina. "It came to light that one of our crew members, Ty, encouraged Aspen to push Sloane into the water to stir up some drama and suspense on their date. It's unclear how much he knew about Sloane's fear and swimming abilities, but he and Aspen never should have put her in harm's way like that. Ty is currently suspended while our EPs investigate and decide how to go forward. Consequences for Aspen are . . . to be decided."

Okay, well, that sounds like code for *Aspen's untouchable but we're doing our best.* I'm glad at least that shit stirrer Ty is getting some punishment.

"In general, we feel that what happened yesterday was symptomatic of a bigger issue throughout our filming," Kristi goes on in her cool, understanding-therapist voice, "with you, the contestants, being treated as tools for creating drama rather than real humans with feelings. On the set of *The Cove*, where the three of us normally work, we're a family. We take care of each other, and we thought we'd be able to foster that same environment here, but obviously, it hasn't quite worked out that way. We're sorry if you feel you have been manipulated or used, and if you want to talk anything out, we're here. If we can do anything to help you all going forward, we want to do that. The floor is open."

She holds her arms out to indicate the actual floor between us. The other girls and I look back and forth between one another.

"I guess I do feel a little used," Alicia says. "Like, have I been wasting my time? Has Aspen's apparent interest in anyone but Sloane just been fake?"

There are echoing sentiments from Bree and Peyton, everyone hurt and confused and kind of Over It. When a hush falls across the room, I clear my throat, ready to add my bit.

"I guess I'm confused about why Aspen picked me out in the first place. Like, I don't even mean it in a self-deprecating way— I know I can be cool enough." Peyton rolls her eyes, but I ignore her. "But there are tons of gorgeous girls here, and he still barely knows me. So what was it about me that made Aspen want to go through the effort to try and 'win' me, as he so tactfully put it? Something feels off, and it has the whole time."

"I might be able to answer that one."

At the sound of a new voice, our heads whip toward the front foyer where a tall, gorgeous redhead is sauntering in, heels clicking on the tile.

"Riley Cartwright?" Peyton squeaks. It's the first time I've seen her look obviously intimidated, which is fair because same.

"Hi, girls," the actress says with a smirk. "Care if I join you?"

If this was a TV show I was writing, this would be a great moment for the episode to end. Leave audiences with this shocking cliff-hanger. Cut to a voice-over saying, "Next week on *Sloane's Weirdest Summer Ever . . .*" as a cryptic preview starts to play.

Fortunately, we don't have to wait for answers. Bree and Alicia scoot to make space on the couch they're sitting on, and Riley plops down like she owns the place. I mean, in a way, via her fictional alter ego, she does.

"Like coming home," she sighs wistfully as she looks around the room. But then she snaps out of it, her attention falling on me. "So I have a little story for you that might clear things up."

"Riley . . . ," Kristi says with a note of warning.

"It's fine, K. I know what I'm doing." Riley winks at the producer, and the smiles they exchange are familiar, trusting. "I guess I should begin with the fact that Aspen was my boyfriend when he was offered this show."

Jaws drop around the room—everyone's but Kristi's.

"You—he—didn't he date *Evie*?" Peyton voices what everyone's thinking. Did real-life Dorian seriously date real-life Mara *and* real-life Chelsea? Seems messy.

"That's what the show always wanted you to think, yeah," Riley says with a smirk. "Dorian and Mara got together before

Aspen and I started anything, and the showrunners had already decided that Aspen and Evie needed to be the perceived It Couple in order to get fans more invested in the fictional ship. But no, they never really dated. It was always Aspen and me, and it was always the best-kept secret in town."

I think all our jaws are on the floor, but Riley inspects her cuticles, unmoved. "Yeah, so that wasn't great. Your secret boyfriend of over a year getting an offer he's not really allowed to refuse to be the star of his own reality dating show. I knew the reasons he felt like he had to do it, the pressure he was under to be a good little leading man, but I still wanted him to turn it down and finally tell everyone we were together. Mara and Dorian were broken up, so why would anyone care anymore if he got with Chelsea? But he signed the contract anyway and promised he would 'figure something out.'"

I feel a pit in my stomach growing at the confirmation that my instincts were correct. Something *was* off about Aspen's interest in me.

"A day before filming was supposed to start, he told me he'd found this girl, one of the contestants, who didn't even want to date him. She was a last-minute addition doing someone a favor, so he would just pick her, then obviously they wouldn't really be together or stay together. She was never invested in him from the start, so he just had to keep her around, and then she wouldn't be heartbroken when it was never real in the end."

She pauses, and all eyes in the room now land on me. I give a disbelieving laugh, trying to understand everything I'm hearing. "Okay, well, I guess he wasn't totally wrong. Congrats on getting your boyfriend back, because he's all yours now."

Riley shakes her head, a smirk playing at her lips again. I want to tell her to just spit it out, no need for the theatrics. But she is an actress, after all.

"I'm not done yet. I was skeptical of this plan—I mean, obviously—but agreed to bear with him as filming began. But we were fighting all the time about everything to do with the show. He said he wouldn't kiss anyone, for example, but some of my friends on the set"—her eyes flit to Kristi briefly—"told me he was kissing basically everyone *but* the girl he'd set out to pick in the end."

I blush at that, oddly self-conscious that now everyone knows I'm the only girl who's never kissed Aspen. But screw it, obviously I don't want to kiss him now. Bree and Alicia are both pointedly avoiding eye contact with anyone, gazing up at the ceiling and out the windows guiltily. Not that they have anything to feel guilty for, but it almost makes me laugh anyway. Peyton continues to sit with arms crossed and a sour look on her face, waiting for Riley to go on.

"He was being shitty in every way, so I ended things. And with everything I've heard from this set, I've only felt worse and worse for keeping quiet about our relationship in the first place, and letting his whole charade go on as long as it has. I'm sorry for any hurt you all have experienced in the process, and I want to help you make it right."

Silence falls over the room before Alicia is the first to speak up. "This is . . . a lot to process. And honestly, it seems like a quick turnaround from dating a guy and lying to protect both of you, to deciding you're over him and wanting to help his other girlfriends . . . what, take him down? I guess I have a hard time trusting that you want to side with us when we're the reason your relationship ended."

I expect Riley to bristle at this, but she just angles her body to face Alicia. "I get it. But *Aspen* is the reason our relationship ended, not you all. You didn't set out to date somebody who was already taken. You were played at least as much as I was. More, really. And I feel bad for my part in it. You can trust me."

"Riley's good people," Kristi offers softly. I'd almost forgotten she was there.

"I'm sorry, Kristi, but I don't exactly trust you the most right now, either—you knew Riley and Aspen were dating from the start, right?" Bree asks.

Riley shakes her head vigorously. "Kristi didn't know until I came to her wanting the scoop on what he was really up to during filming. Believe me, she wasn't thrilled when she found out." Riley winces, and Kristi gives her a smile that says they've gotten past the issue. "But she's been a good friend to me and has always been looking out for you all, too."

Peyton, having at last rediscovered both her confidence and attitude in Riley's presence, heaves an exasperated sigh. "So even if we decide to trust all of you shady bitches—which I'm not yet convinced on, FYI—how exactly would we 'make it right' at this point? We've come this far, he's played us all, and we'll go home looking dumb in the end, dumped by our gorgeous, slimy celebrity boyfriend on national television. What are you even imagining here?"

Riley's smirk isn't quite so annoying when it takes on a newly devious quality—and when it's aimed at Peyton, not me.

"I'm not imagining any of you getting dumped. I've been toying with an idea, if you all are ready to hear me out. . . ."

"I'm listening," Bree says. Alicia nods. Peyton sinks lower into her seat, which seems like as much sign as we're gonna get that she's open to hearing Riley's idea. Then all eyes turn to me.

I bite my lip, feeling like my head hasn't stopped spinning in so long that I might be dizzy for the rest of my life. But how much messier could things get?

"Sure," I say finally. "Tell us what you have in mind."

CHAPTER TWENTY

You can't put a price on revenge. But if you could,
I'd send my nemesis the bill.
—*THE COVE,* SEASON 1, EPISODE 19

Liam

The day after Sloane low-key rips my heart in two, I don't feel like I've been hit by a dump truck full of feelings. Maybe just a pickup truck. One with a lot of horsepower, going way over the speed limit.

Compared to the events on the yacht and the pier after, it wasn't even so bad getting yelled at by my dad back on land. Sure, he was pissed I'd been "conspiring" with his show's star behind his back, even if—though I knew it wasn't the time to point this out—it probably helped his show in the long run. And yeah, he threw out an ominous "You'd better hope this doesn't ruin everything" warning as he stormed off to "deal with" Ty. But what could he do to me that would make me feel any shittier than I do right now?

Please, universe, don't take that as a challenge.

When everyone's back on set for the next pre–Casting Call

party, I'm just trying to hold it together. Both the teetering house of cards that is this show and my entire self, which feels dangerously close to falling to pieces, too. I'm also holding the cooler in which we keep the freeze pops for a toast while I follow a weirdly quiet Kristi from place to place, doing whatever she asks me to.

I'm not sure what it's all for, how much longer we can keep this circus up and running anyway. Everything seems a little off, like if this whole production is a car, it's currently being held together by duct tape and running on fumes. In theory, tonight is the last Casting Call, at which Aspen will choose his final two girls. In the next and final episode, one will become his Leading Lady. But is anyone even interested in the role at this point?

Is Sloane?

Surely not, or so I tell myself, remembering what he did to her, too. And I'm positive she's told the other remaining girls what went down by now. But at the same time, I can see all four are present down on the beach as we approach, smiling and chatting with each other like nothing whatsoever is amiss. Bree and Alicia, standing closest to me, look extra fancy tonight in semi-formal dresses and hairstyles. When Alicia shifts as Kristi and I step onto the sand, Sloane comes fully into view.

And I choke on my own spit.

"You okay?" Kristi turns to pat me on the back as I cough.

"Fine," I croak, though that isn't true. Sloane is wearing the black dress she bought on our shopping trip, and she looks even better in it than I remembered. Her hair is down in soft curls, her lips painted dark red, and something shimmery around her eyes makes their blue-green color pop. It feels suddenly ten degrees hotter on this beach, and I want to run away—maybe also drag her with me, see if she knows of any especially comfortable car hoods around here where we could—

"Okay, people, Aspen's on his way," my dad bellows through my headset from where he's watching tonight's events in the control room. He might as well have dumped the cooler of freeze pops over my head.

Speaking of which . . . "Liam," Kristi says, waving me over. "Freeze pops."

I scramble to offer the open cooler to the girls, letting them each take one. Alicia grabs an extra to offer to Aspen. I look at Sloane—eyes deliberately trained on her face and nowhere lower—but she doesn't meet my gaze. When everyone has what they need, I close the cooler and stand with Kristi behind one of the cameras, then pick up an apple box I left there to carry around for any camera operators who need it.

"Ladies," Aspen says as he saunters down the sand, cool as can be appearance-wise. But am I the only one who hears the touch of fear in his voice? The foursome gifts him with matching bright smiles.

Yeah, I would be scared if I was him.

"So lovely to see you all tonight—and wow, you look amazing." He takes a good, long look at each in turn, and I have to fight not to grind my teeth together when his gaze lands on Sloane. But before he can ask her—or ask her chest, more likely—to go talk, Alicia hands him a freeze pop.

"Ah, of course! Let's make a toast, shall we?" Everyone holds the pops aloft. "To the four kind, compassionate . . . *understanding* girls I have with me tonight. I'm grateful for the chance you all have given me to get to know you, and for you to see me, flaws and all, for who I really am."

There's the slightest pause, one in which I can almost hear everyone thinking, *Was that a weird toast, or is it just me?* But then the girls snap into action, tapping the frozen treats together with a resounding "Cheers!"

Alicia, again, wastes no time in keeping things rolling.

"Aspen, can we have a chat?" she asks sweetly. More sweetly than her straightforward way of speaking ever sounds, really.

But Aspen, seemingly sensing nothing amiss, smiles and takes her hand. "Of course."

They start up the stairs with the camera in front of Kristi and me following, so we fall into step behind them. On the lowest deck, they make their way to one of the patio tables tucked away between some plants, and Aspen begins his usual repetitive small talk. Alicia is perfectly polite and pleasant, but after a couple of minutes of this, she gets a new twinkle in her eye.

"So, I know you're really into *The Cove* references," she starts, and Aspen's smile looks a bit less certain. "And something you might not know about me is that I'm really into making jewelry."

"Hey," a voice at my side suddenly whispers, and I turn to see Bree. "Can I borrow this? Thanks!" She doesn't wait for my answer before taking the apple box from my hands and running off with it in the direction of Dorian's house. *Huh?* Hopefully no one needs that, I guess, until I can get my hands on a replacement.

I turn my attention back to Alicia as she pulls something out of a hidden pocket in her dress—a bracelet. Aspen's expression clears, like something's clicked into place for him.

"Ah yes, when Mara gives Dorian a bracelet she made . . ."

Alicia continues, "And she tells him, 'I want you to look at this. Look at it whenever you want to remember how I feel about you. . . . It's my heart in these beads.'"

One of the more ridiculous "romantic" lines, but it triggers my memory, too, and I know the scene Alicia is paying homage to. The bracelet Mara makes for Aspen contains beads spelling out "love u." Is . . . is Alicia telling Aspen she loves him with a bracelet? After everything she's probably learned in the past day?

She reaches out and places the offering into Aspen's open palm, and I see a slight tremor in his hands as he starts to turn the beads over. He clearly doesn't want a love declaration.

But then he coughs. No, laughs? Some kind of disbelieving, breathless sound, and I find myself leaning closer, trying to see whatever he's reading.

"This . . . ," he croaks. "This says—"

"Fuck you. Yeah, it does." She stands then, towering over Aspen, who still sits there in shock. My own mouth is hanging wide open as I watch the scene play out, but when I dart a glance at Kristi, she's smiling. Not a hint of surprise in her face, either.

"And that's from the heart, Aspen. You've wasted my time, taken advantage of me, and that's messed up. Maybe if you wear that thing, it'll remind you of the shitty person I see when I look at you. I'm out of here."

Alicia struts away then, and I almost feel like applauding. That was epic. But my time on the yacht has already resulted in more than enough screen time for me, so I stay quiet.

"What a *bitch*," Aspen spits out after a few more moments of stunned silence, then gets to his feet and throws the bracelet down onto the table before stomping off. The camera operator hurries to follow, Kristi and I close behind. Aspen keeps muttering as he goes, things along the lines of "Such bullshit" and "Who does she think I am?"

"What the hell was that?" Dad barks over the radio, and I'm tempted to pull the headset out of my ear. "Do we have eyes on Alicia? Someone get eyes on that girl! Do not let her leave like this—at least let Aspen confront her. Hello? Does anyone copy?"

There are some murmurs in my headset from other confused PAs and producers about going to find Alicia, but Kristi looks unconcerned as she and our camera guy continue to follow Aspen, so I stay quiet. I'm not sure where Aspen thinks he's marching off to, but before he gets far, another girl is calling his name.

"Aspen!" All heads in the vicinity turn to see Bree standing at the top of the trellis on the side of Dorian's house, smiling ear to ear. Sure enough, at the bottom sits the apple box that she snatched from me, clearly used to give her a boost.

"Oh my God," I say quietly to Kristi. "Should we go help her, or have a medic ready, or—"

"Shh." She shakes her head, looking like she's enjoying this night a bit too much, too. "It's reinforced. Someone twice her size could climb that thing just fine."

So I shut my mouth and keep watching, ignoring my dad as he starts blustering about whether he needs to come down here and get things under control himself.

Bree climbs about three-quarters of the way down, and Aspen jogs closer, all of us on his heels. There's only a couple feet between the bottom of Bree's shoes and the top of Aspen's head when she leans back, taking one hand and one foot off the trellis so she's swinging from one side. Smiling down at Aspen, she says with over-the-top enthusiasm, "I knew you'd be here. I knew you wouldn't leave me hanging."

"Ohhhh," I whisper, getting it now. Sort of. It's an iconic Dorian-Chelsea scene from season one, when Chelsea is trying to sneak out of her house—with its own matching trellis—for the first time and gets scared to jump the last little stretch over the bushes to the ground. After she hangs there for a while in limbo, Dorian comes to her rescue, catching first the shoes she tosses down to him, then Chelsea herself. There are a few moments of staring into each other's eyes, rife with sexual tension, but then he sets her down. And they remain friends for the next million episodes of *The Cove*.

Not that I'm bitter about an arc like that.

Aspen gets what Bree is doing, too, as he smiles up at her and holds his hands out. She slips off one of her heavy-looking wedge high heels, then the other.

And promptly hurls them down one at a time with the power and precision of a major league pitcher, nailing Aspen in the shoulder, then stomach. He bends back at the first hit before doubling over from the second, staggering a couple of steps before landing on his widely coveted backside with a thud.

"What the hell?" he wheezes, looking up in time to see Bree jump the rest of the way on her own, clearing the bush with ease and landing gracefully before sauntering over to her practice target.

"Yeah, I didn't actually need you. Nor do I want you and your shady ass anymore. Oh, but before I go, I'm gonna need my shoes back." She slides one foot daintily into the wedge lying on the ground beside Aspen, then holds a hand out. I watch in awe as he realizes he's clutching the other to his middle, then, in a daze, hands it up to her. Bree slides it on, blows a kiss to Aspen and then straight into the camera, and walks away.

Aspen sits there, breathing heavily as he recovers from the unexpected shoe assault. I almost feel bad enough to try to go help him up. But only almost.

When he finally stands again, he's seething. His menacing gaze sweeps the whole backyard area as he calls out, "Anyone else have any surprises for me? Huh?"

The stunned crew says nothing. Everyone seems frozen, unsure of what to do with these brutal surprise exits. Everyone except Kristi and a couple of other *The Cove* producers, who all seem to be hiding smiles behind clipboards and cupped hands. Aspen doesn't appear to notice them, focused on finding his remaining two girls.

"That's it," Dad growls in my ear, and I can hear chairs scooting out and muffled, upset voices in the control room around him. "I'm coming down there."

Aspen is starting off across the patio. A couple producers rush off in the direction Bree and Alicia left in while others scramble out of the path of Aspen and the cameras. Kristi, hand pressed to her earpiece as she's just heard my dad's angry declaration, looks to me with nervousness in her eyes for the first time tonight.

I still don't fully get what the hell is going on here, but

whatever it is, I'm not about to let my dad stop it. That's when the idea hits me, and I spring into action. "I'll be back," I tell her, then I turn tail and run for Chelsea's house faster than Aspen runs from responsibility for his actions.

Chelsea's is the closest to the control room trailer. Therefore, it's the first place I sprint to, and I bolt the front door before running to the gate between Chelsea's and Dorian's to make sure its padlock is in place. Then I continue on to lock Dorian's front door, and so on until every entry to the back decks is locked up. Sure, there are keys somewhere, but I don't know if Dad keeps any on him. This should at least slow him down by a few minutes, while whatever is happening here gets to play out further.

When I make it back to Kristi on the uppermost deck behind Dorian's house, out of breath and all too aware that I need to introduce more cardio into my life, her attention, like that of the rest of the crew and cameras around, is fixed on Dorian's hot tub. A zen-looking Peyton sits there with her red hair up in a ponytail and a black bikini on, the waterline hitting just below her top. Aspen, having apparently changed into swim trunks while I was gone, is stepping into the tub with the confident smirk of a guy who hasn't just been dumped by two of his girlfriends in the same half hour of TV. He sinks down into the hot water with a world-weary sigh and floats over to sit right beside Peyton.

Nothing gets this guy down, does it?

"I heard it's been a rough night," Peyton coos, laying a hand on his shoulder. "Can I do anything for you?"

She reaches out her other hand and starts to massage Aspen's shoulders, earning a satisfied groan from him.

"That's perfect," he says, leaning back. "Keep doing what you're doing."

As she massages, Peyton gets him to tell her his version of events, which contains enough swearing that I'm not sure the network will bother with airing the footage. She makes enough believably sympathetic noises that I start to wonder if I was wrong to be skeptical—if Peyton is actually still into Aspen. She was never friends with Sloane and her roommates, so I'd get it if she wasn't exactly on their side.

"Mmm, all right, I'm feeling better," Aspen says eventually, turning to sit beside her again. He leans against the back of the Jacuzzi and spreads his arms along the length of the edge, giving Peyton what I think is meant to be a seductive look. I don't know; I'm still seeing him getting nailed with Bree's shoes on repeat in my mind.

"Good," Peyton whispers, then she swings a leg slowly over Aspen's underwater and straddles his lap. His eyes widen, but he certainly doesn't look mad about it as she leans in closer, her head dipping nearer to his, and if I never saw Aspen Woods make out with another girl in my life, I'd be good with that. I'm close to turning away when he brings one hand to her waist, she cups his head in both of hers, and this looks eerily similar to a Mara-Dorian make-out in Dorian's hot tub, which is when my suspicion flares back up and—

Peyton dunks Aspen's head under the water.

He comes up spewing and coughing and immediately irate, while she calmly climbs off his lap and out of the hot tub before wrapping a towel around herself.

"I'd say it was nice knowing you, but I'm big on honesty. Bye, Aspen." She gives a little finger wave then sets off toward Chelsea's house, jostling my shoulder as she goes. Aspen is ranting and angrily splashing the water as he gets to his feet and out of the tub. He dries himself vigorously before jerking the towel about his waist and looking around frantically.

"Where's Sloane?" he yells. "Where the hell is Sloane?"

At the same time, my dad's yell echoes through all the crew headsets. "Where the hell are the house keys? Someone *better* come let me in!"

No one moves. Is this what unionizing feels like?

Aspen's wet hair is matted over his head like a helmet, but he doesn't even attempt to fix it as he scurries around, barefoot and half-clothed, in search of his last girl standing. I'm starting to wonder where she is myself, but then I hear her voice behind us, down on one of the lower patios, and it makes my heart do a backflip in my chest.

"Looking for me?" she says with a mischievous glint in her eyes. My pulse picks up as she ascends the next patio and keeps walking our way. Partly because she really does look amazing tonight, but I think mostly because I can't wait to watch how she's going to hand Aspen his ass.

"Yeah, I am," he barks, appearing less put together than I ever thought possible. He's a man scorned, and he is *not* okay. "Let's hear it. Whatever you have to say to me. You got something to say, don't you?"

His eyes are wild, his knuckles white around the towel where he holds it at his hip. Sloane, in contrast, gives him a serene, gorgeous smile, through red lips that I'll probably see in my dreams.

"I might. But this is what you wanted, isn't it? Me, in the end."

Aspen runs a hand through his wet hair, causing it to stick out in every direction. "Yeah, it was. And I don't see what's so wrong about that. What's wrong with knowing what I want—who I want—and going after you with everything I have? I wanted to be with you and no one else at the end of all this."

She gives him a measuring look, cocking her head to the side. "No one else?"

Aspen swallows, nods. Sloane purses her lips before shaking her head.

"See, I recently heard differently. From a new friend of mine."

Huh? But before I have time to parse that out, Riley Cartwright brushes past Kristi and me, past Aspen, and turns to face him side by side with Sloane. The two make a formidable pair, all crossed arms and black lace and red lips and heels. Which I guess would be exciting, not frightening, if they didn't also look so pissed off.

All at once, Aspen seems to deflate. His anger vanishes, replaced by exhaustion, resignation. He knows it's time to face his fate.

Whatever that fate is. I still don't know what Riley's doing here. But she promptly explains, for me, for the cameras, for all the viewers who will watch this in a month or two, whenever it hits their TVs—if the network actually decides to air any of this.

"That's right, Asp. I told everyone that you and I were dating when you started dating the rest of them for your little show here. That we'd been together for a year, actually. We said we loved each other. Then you did this." She holds her arms out to signify, I presume, everything about *AWFLL*.

"You told me that you'd still be with me at the end no matter what. That you wouldn't even kiss anyone, that you'd found a girl"—she gestures at Sloane—"who you didn't think even wanted to be here. You said she probably wouldn't be heart-broken when it wasn't real, but you wouldn't really care if she was. I thought that was almost kind of romantic, stupidly.

"But I realized your feelings for me were as fake as your spray tan. And I finally told your girls—way later than I should have—who you *really* are. So we're all done with you, and we truly feel sorry for Aspen Woods's Future Leading Lady, whoever she may be."

Aspen has no words, and honestly, I don't either. He was dating Riley *all along*? He picked Sloane out knowing he would break up with her as soon as the show ended? I can't believe I ever thought his interest was genuine, that he might come any-where close to being what she deserved.

With a response from Aspen clearly not forthcoming, Riley waves a hand. Alicia, Bree, and Peyton all come to stand beside the other two girls, arms thrown around each other.

Riley looks directly into the camera when she speaks next. "But don't think these amazing ladies are going home empty-handed. In fact, they're all going to be *my* dates to the next sea-son premiere of *The Cove*. And when filming starts back up, all four are invited back to have guest roles on the show."

The girls apparently didn't know about these offers yet, and lots of hugs and squealing ensue while Aspen quietly slinks away, a single camera and producer hurrying to follow him.

The rest of the crew and I *do* clap then, for the least expected but most entertaining finale we could have possibly gotten from this mess. Cameras stop rolling and Kristi runs over to embrace the girls, but I still hang back. I don't know where I stand with Sloane, and I don't want to bring the mood down with my presence.

Suddenly, a hand grabs my shoulder, jerking me backward so hard I almost fall. "What the—"

I stop short when I'm faced with my red-faced, fuming father.

"You," he starts through gritted teeth. "You screwed this all up for me. If you hadn't put yourself in the middle, conspiring with my star to determine the outcome of my show, none of this would've happened. You took the opportunity I gave you and threw it in the trash, meddling and interfering where you had no business doing so, and now it's resulted in this whole spectacle. Are you proud of yourself? Are you?"

He's yelling in my face now. His question doesn't seem to warrant an answer, so I don't make any effort to offer one. But someone else does.

"Hell no," a voice says from beside me, then Sloane is stepping into the thin space left between my dad and me, her back nearly pressed to my front as she puts a gentle but firm hand to Dad's chest and pushes him backward. "You do *not* get to talk to your son like that. He's done nothing but work his ass off to make you happy. He only ever did this show because you pushed him to, and he never wants to let you down. But you never give him an inch of pride or appreciation or any of the good things he so completely deserves, and I'm sick of it."

Dad's brows have lifted in surprise, his jaw slackening. I don't know if it's the shock of his pseudo-daughter talking to him this way or the beginnings of some much needed self-evaluation, but he can't get a word in edgewise either way.

"Liam didn't cause any of this," Sloane continues. "If anything, Liam's involvement left us all better off in the end. Including you, most likely, when people go nuts over the Most Dramatic Finale in Reality Television History. So step off, cool down, and think about how you'll apologize to your absolute gem of a child once you're ready to do so with the level of sincerity and love that he deserves. Come on, Liam."

Now my dad's gaze shifts to me, something in it that looks surprisingly like regret. With my mouth hanging open, I don't get to consider him for long before Sloane takes me by the hand and pulls me away—from my dad, from Dorian's house, from everyone on the *AWFLL* crew. I don't know where we're going, but it doesn't matter when I'm following her.

CHAPTER TWENTY-ONE

If we don't have love, what do we have? Good looks, sure, but those are gonna get more expensive to keep up.

—*THE COVE,* SEASON 3, EPISODE 6

Sloane

There isn't much time for Liam and me to talk that night after the non–Casting Call, but it's for the best. I'm hopped up on anger and excitement and sugar from the gigantic Coke I get at a gas station once Riley takes the girls, Liam, and me off the set in her big SUV—none of which are a recipe for having a heartfelt, important conversation.

But we have a hell of a good time, eating all kinds of junk food over four different stops; walking on a beach lord knows where; driving through the city with the windows down, music up; enjoying the glittering LA night. Liam is pretty quiet the whole time, but the smiles he gives me every so often say he's enjoying himself, too, if still a little uncertain on where we stand.

It's late, or rather, early the next morning when Riley returns us all to set after we've exchanged numbers and talked future hangouts. She zooms out of there, then the girls and I head up to

Chelsea's house to gather our things and check out with Kristi. Liam, apparently, heads home. I find a text as soon as I get my phone back that says he didn't know how long I'd be and didn't want to rush me, and he's waiting for me at home whenever I get there.

Despite everything that's happened in the last few days, it makes me smile.

I hug the other girls goodbye in the driveway of Chelsea's house, even Peyton, my newly minted ally. Then Kristi packs us all into rideshares to our respective destinations—airports, hotels, or, in my case, the mansion owned by the executive producer of this disaster show.

After dropping my stuff in the guest room back in a quiet Daniels house, I check Liam's room. He's not in there, but then I hear the telltale scraping sound of his plane cutting across wood, coming from above. I take the stairs to Liam's workshop quietly, then knock on the door. It takes a couple of tries for him to hear me, and when he opens the door, his cheeks are flushed and his eyes are wide. He pushes his safety goggles up on his head, sending his hair out in a messy halo, and I bite down on my smile.

"Hi," I say. *Killer opening, Sloane. Revolutionary.*

Liam lets out a soft laugh. "Hi. Uh, yeah, come in." He steps back and turns in a circle before grabbing the stool by his workbench and pulling it out for me. "Have a seat, if you want."

It's quiet except for the whir of a fan in the corner as I take the offered seat and he leans against the bench. His posture is casual, but I can see the tension in his forearms and hands where he grips the benchtop at his sides. I look around the sawdust-covered room as I think about how to begin, when a beautiful table near the wall opposite us catches my eye. I don't think I saw it the last time I was up here—I would have remembered. It has four legs that look sturdy but also delicate, covered with carvings of flowers and vines that wind from bottom to top. There's a wide, flat tabletop with a drawer half pulled out underneath it. One of Liam's planes sits atop it, a wood shaving curled over the end that suggests this is what I heard him working on when I came up.

"That looks stunning," I say, standing again to cross the room to the table. I run my hand along the surface, mostly smooth with a few rough patches here and there.

"Oh." Liam clears his throat, coming to stand at my side. "Yeah. I mean, thank you. It's not quite finished, obviously. Still surfacing it, then I'll have to scrape, sand, and varnish it."

I crouch to look at the legs more closely, and the carvings are even more intricate than I thought. "These are amazing," I murmur, letting my fingers trace the flowers' outlines and along the twisty lengths of the vines. "Are you going to sell it?"

"No," he says quickly, and I look up at him in surprise as I stand again. He sighs and pushes a hand through his hair, knocking his goggles off his head. He doesn't even look to where they've tumbled onto the floor. "It's . . . Well, I was going to wait until it was finished, but I guess I'll just tell you."

My brows knit together. "Tell me . . . ?"

His eyes finally meet mine as he says plainly, "It's yours."

My breath catches in my throat. "What? I couldn't possibly take—"

"No." He shakes his head. "It's a writing desk. I made it for you. Of course, I didn't know when I started it months ago that I . . . well, that we'd . . ."

Liam trails off, and I find myself dying to know how that sentence was going to end. But when he picks up again, it's on a different thought. "Anyway, the legs are oak and the top is cherry. I can make the legs shorter if you want, too, once you know what chair you'll use with it. The surface has breadboard ends here, which makes it so the wood has more ability to expand and contract in different weather and humidity, so you can take it with you anywhere you end up without worrying about that kind of damage. Oh, and uh, we can ship it to Tennessee or I can hang on to it until you move here, whatever you want. There's also this drawer here for you to keep pens and stuff—the dovetails on it are a little gappy, but they're the first ones I've ever done, so—"

I put my hand over his where it's touching the drawer and its supposedly gappy dovetails, whatever that means. But my touch shuts up his rambling. Since he's pulled out the drawer all the way, I now see a stack of papers sitting in it, which I pull out upon seeing a familiar logo. It's a brochure for the Los Angeles Film Academy. Stacked with it are more brochures for other screenwriting programs, business cards for various deans and admissions counselors and even some working screenwriters, and more.

"Liam," I breathe as I flip through them all.

He exhales heavily. Clearly this is another thing he wasn't planning on showing me today. "I've been gathering this stuff for a while, but I got a little more deliberate about it this summer.

There's the card of the writer you met from *The Cove,* for one, but also an admissions officer for UCLA's screenwriting program, and some scholarship information here. . . ." He keeps explaining the papers as he points to them from over my shoulder, saying things like "They said they'd be happy to mentor you" and "There's always my house if you need a place to stay." But I'm barely tuned in to the specifics, turning my head so I'm looking at his face, now a few inches from mine. Appreciating this boy and what he's done for me. The way he's always been here, the most consistent, most supportive, most *loving* person in my life.

"Liam . . . ," I say again, and he drops off midsentence, turning his head and seeming to realize how close we are. He licks his lips, then bites on the bottom one anxiously.

"I'm so sorry, Sloane, again. Sorry that I went behind your back, and that I ever thought helping a guy like Aspen Woods was the way to make you happy. If I'd known his real reasons for doing the show, I'd have told you in a heartbeat. I just . . ." Liam turns and walks back over to his workbench. "I meant what I said on the pier. About knowing what I want—who I want. But what I want even more is for you to be happy."

"When did you know?" I ask, so soft it's almost inaudible over the fan.

"That I want you to be happy?" he asks, his lips quirking up on one side. I give him a pointed look, and he runs a hand over his face. "I started to recognize it when you first got here. But I wonder if part of me had those feelings awhile before that. I mean, I know you joke about my inability to commit to anyone I date, but I've started to think maybe it's because I've been committed for a long-ass time to someone else. I always compare my connections with people to how I connect with you, how natural and easy it is between us. And then we kissed and, well, that was that."

My face is so flushed I consider sticking it in front of the fan, but my feet stay glued in place. I think for more than a few moments about how to respond, because I don't want to screw this up. But before I can get there, a nervous Liam keeps going.

"I don't want to pressure you, though. Seriously. Our friendship is the most important one in my life, and the last thing I want is to mess that up with anything more complicated if you're not feeling it, too. I'll figure out how to—"

"Liam." I cut him off yet again as I cross the room toward him. His wary gaze never leaves mine, even as I'm standing close enough that he has to look down at me. Then it's time to come out with it. "I love you. In the friend way, obviously, but I'm also pretty sure I'm *in* love with you. And not because you built me a desk, or saved me after an unhinged celebrity pushed me into the ocean, or had a Hot Simba glow-up over the last few years—"

"Hot Simba glow-up?"

Definitely didn't mean to say that part out loud. "Don't worry about it. Anyway, all those things are wonderful. But I've loved the person you are for a long, long time."

His chin falls and his eyes close as he lets out a sigh of what I think is relief. When his eyes open again, their brightness and warmth match the smile that takes over his lips.

"Sloane, I'm pretty sure I'm in love with you, too."

The words send an explosion of sparks through my chest—sparks of excitement, joy, and more than a little desire.

I give him an answering smile and bring a hand up to his cheek. "I would very much like to mess up our friendship with something more complicated now."

I stand on my tiptoes, and a soft laugh escapes his lips just before I cover them with mine.

It's the best our friendship has ever been.

EPILOGUE

Endings . . . they're like mirrors for beginnings. But sometimes
you have to shatter the mirror and say, "It's not over yet!"

—*THE COVE*, SEASON 3, EPISODE 21

Sloane
Two months post-*AWFLL*

"Riley!"

"Riley, look this way!"

"Girls, all five of you, this way please!"

I've never been particularly sensitive to lights and sounds,
but this red carpet experience feels like watching a *Star Wars* ship
going through hyperspace on a glitchy projector while a bunch
of people yell at you.

"Come on, let's head inside," Riley Cartwright says from the
middle of our lineup, the rest of which is made up of Bree, Alicia,
Peyton, and me. Riley is the only one who doesn't look completely overwhelmed by our entrance to the season premiere of
The Cove, and as such, she is the mama duck to our lost baby

ducklings. She's paraded us down the red carpet so smoothly that I'd love to believe the photographers can't tell it's the first time the other four of us have done this.

And now, finally, blessedly, she seems to think we've posed and smiled and stepped and posed for long enough. I let my cheeks relax, trying to rub at the soreness as we turn our backs to the crowd and walk into the theater. But I only make it a few steps before I look up and my smile returns all over again—and this time, it's real.

"Nice dress," Liam says, appearing in front of me with that warm grin that, no matter how many times I've been on the receiving end of it over the past couple months, still turns my insides all melty. I stop a few feet from him, the crowd in the theater lobby fading away as I take in the dark suit that's perfectly tailored to his tall frame and the way his hair has been styled mostly into submission, save for one blond lock that always finds its way to his forehead.

How did I ever *not* see him as the most handsome guy in existence?

I put my hands on my black-lace-covered hips and give him a mischievous look in return. "Thanks. There was this really unhelpful shopping companion who lost his ability to speak when I tried it on. Thought that was a good sign."

Liam laughs softly as he steps closer, pulling me into a hug and kissing the top of my head. "Still speechless over here, McKinney."

"I am *so* single," Riley sighs, bringing our attention to the fact that my real dates are still standing around us.

As far as anyone else in the world is concerned, I'm technically here, along with my fellow *AWFLL* top four, as Riley's date. The finale episode of *Aspen Woods's Future Leading Lady* aired this week, and the viewing public is still buzzing. The saving grace for what was largely a train wreck for *The Cove*'s image is the way it's put Riley in the spotlight as a girl-power icon.

So we're here, a united front, showing off how the best part of *AWFLL* really was the friends we made along the way.

But Riley was kind enough to score my boyfriend an invite, too. What better way to make our official semipublic debut as a couple than to canoodle in a dark theater with a bunch of Hollywood types who don't care about our existence, and hold hands in a popcorn bucket while we watch my sort-of-ex's face in Technicolor?

"Ugh, get a room," Peyton gripes.

"Don't you all get enough of each other at home?" Bree adds in a more playful tone. We've gotten so much shit from this group since we officially got together about the fact that we're already "shacking up"—along with a scarce Mr. Daniels—for the rest of the summer. We let it roll off us—it's not like we sleep in the same bed. Not *every* night, anyway.

"Hey, we're about to be in a long-distance relationship here. Gotta pack it all in while we can," I answer, squeezing Liam. This is my last weekend in California before I fly home to Tennessee to start the school year. I'm nervous, especially considering my unexpected turn to reality TV notoriety, but excited to keep moving toward the next chapter.

"Good for you guys," Alicia says, giving a chastising look to the other three. "The rest of us are just jealous."

"Nah, not me. Somebody had to find love on *Aspen Woods's Future Leading Lady,* and it wasn't gonna be Aspen Woods," Bree offers. "Speaking of, is he coming tonight?"

Riley shakes her head. "He had a 'scheduling conflict,' aka he's probably hiding in his house and hoping everyone forgets he exists."

"Good luck to him," Peyton says dryly. "Now where can I get some popcorn?" We follow Riley as she leads us toward the line for concessions, and the others start to pepper her with questions about season four.

What they don't know yet is that I probably have more answers about what's to come on *The Cove* than our actress friend does. With Liam's push, I reached out to Priya, the writer from my first SPD, and she's already brought me as her guest to a couple of meetings in the writers' room. I got to hear plans for the *AWFLL* girls' guest starring roles, which they'll fly us all back here to film in a couple months. We'll be portraying a Roller Derby crew called the Derby Devils who get to beat up Dorian in the skate rink's parking lot. I can't wait to see Peyton's delivery of the line "That'll teach you to roll on our turf again, punk-ass kid!"

I feel for Aspen a little, punk-ass kid though he may be. The reception of his reality show persona was divided, even before it all went up in flames in the end. The whole time *AWFLL* has aired, he's had some support from his longtime fans, but he's also gotten shit for just about everything he did, from seeming inauthentic to kissing too many people too quickly. I haven't exactly been proud of everything I've seen of myself, watching it back, but at least I have people to support me through it, including Liam and four of the closest friends I never expected to meet this summer.

My family has also been surprisingly excited to watch me on TV. We always video call to discuss the episodes after they air, and oddly enough, it feels like they're learning more about the real me from watching an hour of TV each week than they probably have in years of living together. There's been more B-roll than I expected of some of my day-off heart-to-hearts with my roommates, me writing in my notebook, all of us playing games. Plus the unique experience of watching me date Aspen Woods while realizing I'm in love with my best friend.

Come to think of it, I've learned more about myself than I had in years, too. And somehow, in the midst of all of it, I've gained the confidence to start talking with my parents more about my dreams for after college, plans of coming back out here, and the kind of support I need—and feel I've missed out on— from them. It's been tough, and it's a work in progress, but we're getting there.

"We're up next." Liam links his fingers with mine as the concessions line surges forward. "Know what you want?"

I look at him with an eyebrow raised, and he lifts his free hand defensively. "Hey, I figure I should always ask, just in case. Your preferences could change."

Tugging him toward me, I laugh before dropping a kiss on his shoulder. "They haven't this time, but thank you for checking."

At the counter, Liam orders us popcorn, Cokes, and a pack of sour straws. Have I mentioned how amazing it is to date someone who knows you inside and out?

"We should have a standing movie date next year," I say while we wait for our order. The other girls have already gotten theirs and left to find us all seats.

"Deal," he answers with a smile. "There's a really cool theater by LAFA. . . ."

He goes on about the better movie-viewing experiences in the greater Los Angeles area, and I feel like my heart is in my eyes. Since *AWFLL* wrapped, we've started talking about next year like it's a sure thing—I'm coming to California, I'm studying screenwriting, and we'll be together. This all felt even more certain and exciting after Mr. Daniels came through and had the dean of the Los Angeles Film Academy over for dinner. We hit it off amazingly, which was helped by Mr. Daniels selling me as if I'd already written six Emmy-winning productions.

He and Liam have been working on their relationship, starting with family therapy, and he's still earning back my respect as a dad to the boy I love. But as far as helping me with my future, he's surpassed expectations. After the meeting with Dean Kelly, he arranged for me to meet with an admissions counselor to figure out how to optimize my college applications. Combined with all the options Liam had been gathering for me, it really feels like I have the screenwriting world at my fingertips and the Daniels family in my corner.

"Daniels!" a concessions worker calls out, and Liam and I pick up our order. He gets the candy and popcorn, taking the latter over to the butter station to prepare it just how we like it, while I grab the drinks. Sustenance secured, we head toward the theater to find our friends and get ready to watch the show.

We're halfway down the long hallway when Liam whispers, "Hey, come here for a second."

Confused, I follow him into this curtained-off alcove. It's darker in here than the hallway, but I see him set the popcorn down then straighten back up. Before I can ask what he's doing, he puts one hand on my hip, the other coming up to cup my jaw as he pulls me in for a kiss.

Our kisses are usually soft, loving, easy. This one is still loving, sure, but there's nothing easy about it. It's hot, eager, claiming. I wish I didn't have two gigantic soft drinks in my hands so I could pull him closer, maybe mess up that near-perfect hair a little more. But it's probably for the best that I can't.

We spend a couple minutes like that, his hands moving all over his favorite dress in the whole world and mine getting frozen from Coke condensation while we kiss like we won't have many, many chances to do this again. When we finally pull apart, I'm breathless and, honestly, unopposed to skipping the premiere part of the premiere.

"What was that for?" I say as I hand one Coke to Liam, then wipe around my mouth for smudged lipstick, a futile effort with no mirror to look at.

Liam picks up the popcorn, then looks down at me with a smirk. "I wanted to check 'Make out in a movie theater' off my new list, but it seemed awkward to do it surrounded by our friends and a bunch of celebrities."

I'm already laughing as I ask, "Your new list?"

"Yeah," he says, pulling the curtain back and holding it for me as we step back into the bright hallway. "Sloane and Liam's Lifetime of Fun."

ACKNOWLEDGMENTS

Many, many authors before me were not wrong when they said the second book is hard! It's been different from the first in so many ways, and I'm more grateful than ever for all the people in my corner, without whom this book never would've made it into your hands. They include:

My agent, Laura Crockett, and editor, Hannah Hill. Thank you both so much for continuing to believe in my stories, make them better than I ever could on my own, and keep me (relatively) steady in the process. I feel so fortunate to have you as supportive, empowering teammates in my publishing life.

The rest of the team at Delacorte Press and Random House Children's Books, who have been such a wonderful publishing home! Special thanks to Beverly Horowitz, Wendy Loggia, Barbara Marcus, Tamar Schwartz, Colleen Fellingham, Alison Kolani, Lili Feinberg, Regina Flath, Cathy Bobak, and Ray Shappell. Thank you to Monique Aimee for the beautiful cover illustration that so perfectly captures this book's spirit!

My writing friends who keep me going on the days when words are the hardest. Thank you to Elora Ditton, Claire Ahn, and Thais Vitorelli for the humor, inspiration, and love you always provide. Thank you to my fork family—including LC Milburn, Emily Varga, Chandra Fisher, Anna Sortino, Molly Steen, Briana Miano, Katie Bohn, Sami Ellis, and more whom I wish I had the space to name—for being there every day over the last couple wild years, making me laugh, lifting me up, and letting me learn from all of you.

My fellow '22 debuts. Thank you to all who shared the ups and downs of debut year and have given me so much fun reading material, including Susan Lee, Anita Kelly, Emma Ohland, Torie Jean, Brian Kennedy, Ava Wilder, Mazey Eddings, Angela Velez, Karina Evans, Samantha Markum, Rimma Onoseta, JC Peterson, Gigi Griffis, Victor Manibo, Tanvi Berwah, Vaishnavi Patel, and Kate Dylan.

Other authors who have been so kind, generous, and supportive, even as I ask some of you a million questions and/or melt down in your DMs. Thank you especially to Auriane Desombre, Rachel Lynn Solomon, Martha Waters, Kelsey Rodkey, Nina Moreno, Heather Walter, Chloe Gong, and Jenna Evans Welch.

All the reviewers, booksellers, teachers, librarians, and other readers who have found my work. Thank you for giving me a reason to write, sending so much love my way, and helping others find my books! I feel so incredibly lucky because of you.

The friends who keep me grounded in the world outside of books and are the best cheer squad at every milestone. Thank you to Katie and Aaron Cambron, Daniel Cambron, Sydney Norman, Megan Wall, Jamie Vescio, Trevor McNary, Abby Slucher, Senait Nuguse, Barton Lynch, Lee Kiefer, Gerek Meinhardt, Maggie Garnett, and Jillian Madden.

My family. Thank you to all sides, Hill, Tudor, and Parsons, for your unflinching love and belief in me, and for mostly letting me pretend you all haven't read my kissing scenes.

Stephen. This is the first book in which I can call you my husband! Thank you for being my big adventure and safe place to come home. I love life with you.

RIVALRY HAS NEVER TASTED THIS SWEET.

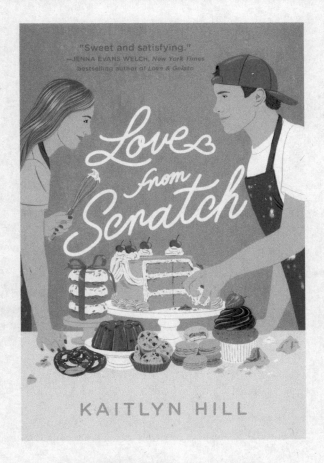

Turn the page to read more!

Chapter One

The man in front of me has a bee in his bonnet and cat hair on his coat. I know these things because from where I stand—smooshed into the back of a crowded elevator in the downtown Seattle skyscraper where my internship is located—the sleeve of his suit is only inches from my face. As such, I can see the white strands plain as day against the black fabric while he grunts at the phone in his hand—plus feel the tickle in my nose that says I'm dangerously close to a sneeze.

Lordhavemercy, I think, one big compound, catchall word I inherited from my mamaw and so many other Southerners, religious or not. It's what you say when you're in company too polite to say something worse.

Mr. Business is testing my limits, though. He just couldn't be bothered to use a lint roller, could he? Nor to give me any personal space back here, in the midst of whatever turmoil he's dealing with in his email inbox. I hope my nose breath is making him hot. I press my tongue to the roof of my mouth, a trick I saw online somewhere to help put off sneezing, watching the floor numbers tick higher.

Finally, the *ding ding* is for my floor and I adjust my grip on the tray of to-go cups I'm balancing in the crook of my arm, reaching for my badge to swipe into the office with the other hand as I make the quiet, "pardon me, sorry" noises required to edge my way out of the crush of bodies. It's made a little easier today by the human Grumpy Cat, whose office must also be on floor forty-two, thus allowing me to slink through the wake left by his wide frame.

That plan is working flawlessly, right up until he steps off the elevator and—I don't know—needs a moment to collect himself, or realizes he forgot to feed Fluffy or something. He stops short, with no regard for my or anyone else's presence a half step behind him.

And because I do not stop short, I run smack into his cat-hair-covered backside, coffee tray first, sending hot brown lava into the air, onto the floor, and all over myself.

"Whoa, careful there," the man grumbles with an errant glance over his shoulder. He's already turning to head down the hall toward the entrance of some investment firm, leaving me gaping and covered in gourmet bean water.

I should be careful? Oh, for the love of—

"Reese! Oh my God, are you okay?"

Teagan, receptionist at Friends of Flavor, comes rushing out of the glass double doors that face the elevators, through which I guess she just witnessed the accident.

"I'm fine," I say in the least grumbly voice I can manage, peeling my once-lavender shirt away from where it's clinging to my stomach and chest. I'm never dressed in the blacks and grays of most of the businesspeople who work in our building, but of course I had to go all-pastel today. "Can't say the same for the drinks, though."

I peer over the to-go cups, which have all miraculously stayed in their designated slots, and to my relief find that my own hot tea might be the only total loss. *Gourmet leaf water,* I mentally correct myself, with regard to what's soaked me. I've never felt so betrayed by my favorite beverage. The bean waters kept their lids on and lost a little foam at most. Small victories.

"What an asshole," Teagan blurts, nodding in the direction of my new nemesis, who has by now disappeared. I nod my agreement but keep my mouth shut; she's been here a couple of years and is so well liked that I don't think anyone would bat an eye at her outburst. I've been here less than two weeks and would rather not be tossed out on my tea-soaked rear for losing my temper.

"You go on in, I'll wipe the rest of this up," she continues, shooing me away. I would argue, but she probably knows the time and therefore realizes that I'm already cutting it close, so I thank her profusely and get on my way.

Rounding the lobby corner, I shift the ill-fated tray to my other hand just in time to hold it out of the way of someone passing with a wheel of cheese so massive he nearly has to walk sideways to fit it through the hall. I pass by one of the ingredient pantries and catch a guy who looks like he stepped straight out of the Discovery Channel dropping live crabs into a tank. When I've almost reached the little alcove off Prep Kitchen 2 where my team works, a cooked strand of spaghetti sails just past the end of my nose and sticks to the wall beside me.

"Sorry! Didn't see you there," calls out an embarrassed kitchen assistant. I wave him off and bite my bottom lip to keep myself from saying something snippy. Not seeing me there seems to be the theme today, doesn't it? But honestly, they seldom "see me there," and that's fine. So long as I'm noticed by the people who matter—the people with my future in their hands.

This is how it goes at Friends of Flavor. It's the second full week of my internship, and I'm only just getting used to the organized chaos that characterizes these "culinary content creators." There is constant hustle and bustle, chefs and kitchen assistants and art directors and camera crews and more rushing around to get the next recipes made, the next episodes shot for the various series, the kitchens cleaned so it can start all over. I'm merely a background player, an intern on the marketing team, and I have no desire to be anything more attention-grabbing—for now. If I can just keep my head down, work hard, learn from the pros, and do a good job on the tasks I'm given this summer, it could be the beginning for me. My entry into their flagship semester-long culinary internship in the fall, and from there . . . who knows what else? Once I have my degree, I'm angling for something full time in marketing or maybe on the production side—wherever my skills can be best put to use. If all goes according to plan, hopefully I'll have a chance to stay in this weird and wonderful world long term.

Working at FoF has been my dream for years now, ever since my best friends back home in Kentucky, Natalie and Clara, pulled me out of a seriously self-pitying funk our freshman year of high school and into the home theater at Clara's house with a dozen FoF videos queued up. It was the start of our shared obsession with the channel and the charismatic chefs who make its culinary magic. On countless nights when our schoolmates went to parties and football games, we stayed in, smooshed together on someone's bed or couch, catching up on all the episodes of FoF's cooking series. We fell in love with Katherine's easygoing competence on *Fuss-Free Foodie*. We got to travel the US with Rajesh in *Cross-Country Cookery.* We dreamed of one day competing against other amateur chefs on *Good Chef/Bad Chef.* The prep kitchens and studio where most shows took place seemed like Narnia to us, as aspirational and dreamy and seemingly out of reach as that wonderland through the wardrobe.

I never imagined Narnia having quite so many copy machines, though. After rounding the corner near one of the mechanical beasts, I'm finally in the marketing team nook. I hand off the surviving cups to each of the team members I work with, who mumble their under-caffeinated thanks, then take a seat at my makeshift TV-tray desk. If anything, I suppose I can be thankful that the shock of the hot liquid down my front has given me the jolt of energy that I won't be getting from a beverage this morning. I see a lock of dripping blond hair hanging in my periphery and try my best to discreetly wring it out above the trash can before pushing it back into place. I snap a quick picture of the results of the spill to Natalie and Clara with the caption "#OOTD #professional." Their responses come quickly and are highly on-brand.

> **Clara:** yikes! hope you have stain-fighting detergent. my mom uses tide

> **Natalie:** Wet t-shirt contest?? LOVE that for you!

Laughing as I pocket my phone, I decide to put the annoyance of the coffee-tea-tastrophe to rest so I can get on with my day. I take out my laptop and open it, tucking my backpack neatly against the wall—as neatly as it will go, anyway, in a space barely big enough for a small trash can, let alone a whole human and her possessions.

Dream internship, I remind myself. Living the dream.

The dream that wasn't so out of reach, as it turns out. Friends of Flavor is a real business, with real offices, where they hire real people to do real work. I had no idea the extent of the labor it takes behind the scenes to make twelve minutes of "Rajesh Prepares Chef Grant's Deconstructed Chicken Cordon Bleu" look so clean and flawless. But the world of food media is complex, with many cogs that keep the machine running. It's appealed to me since I first started watching FoF's shows, and they're producing the best work in the business. I love food and enjoy cooking, but my culinary chops are mostly collected from time spent in my mamaw's kitchen throwing extra butter into everything and learning her recipes and techniques by example. Without any professional kitchen experience, I always figured that my graphic design skills from years on the school newspaper staff would have to be my in.

And when I started browsing internships for the summer before college and saw that the big streaming service that hosts Friends of Flavor had a spot open in its marketing department for a recent high school grad with minimal experience to their name? A chance to get away from my hometown and to my new city as soon as possible before I go to the University of Washington in the fall, to start anew away from all the people and baggage of my past, to work with some of my favorite creators in the whole wide web? I barely even considered what the day-to-day would look like, or that it might be anything other than a dream come true. Truly, I don't think I've ever clicked a button so fast in my life.

I've done quite a bit of clicking buttons since then, though, like I do now as I open up the usual tabs in my browser. Button clicking is one of my main responsibilities here, along with getting morning coffee when the boss decides to splurge on some from outside the staff break room. Every Friends of Flavor social media page is at the ready on my computer, waiting for me to tend to the replies and reposts and favorites appropriately. In other words, to click some buttons.

On Instagram, I like everyone's comments that I can. This is a never-ending task, as there are thousands of comments per post and they are constantly multiplying. Half of them are just people tagging their friends so they'll see the post, but as my boss Margie says, we still have to show that we "appreciate their engagement." I reply to a handful that I deem reply-worthy, like if they ask a genuine question to which I can find an answer—

> **@sw3et.c4rolin3e3:** What brand of brown sugar did Nia use in her drop cookies?

> **@friendsofflavor:** Domino, but any kind will do!

—or if they say something that gives me a chance to be quippy—

> **@MrZtoA1:** I accidentally melted my butter instead of softening it OOPS

> **@friendsofflavor:** BUTTER luck next time! ;)

Quippy comments always get more engagement and are the most fulfilling for me personally. My food pun repertoire is vast and always growing. Those almost balance out all of the comments I have to delete and users I have to block for inappropriateness. Why anyone would come to a page for a *cooking channel* to post racial slurs is beyond me, but then so is posting that garbage anywhere. I think of it as my daily taking out the trash, and it's sort of cathartic. Block, delete, block, delete, block, block, block.

Twitter and Facebook are more of the same, though the latter is increasingly bogged down with accidental comments by older folks who were clearly trying to type in the search bar, bless their hearts. Where we get the most engagement, and therefore where I spend the bulk of my time, is in the comments on our actual video content.

It's impossible to keep up with all of the comments on the Friends of Flavor channel on our host streaming service, Ulti-Media. The UltiMedia website is busy as it hosts a wide variety of original scripted and unscripted content on its different channels. There are channels for every interest—sitcoms, dramas, romantic movies. But Friends of Flavor's culinary reality series make it one of the most popular channels of all. Everyone likes food, right? And honestly, most people seem to like our videos.

UltiMedia has a comments section under each video, and each channel has an account that can monitor and reply to comments—a lot of my job is managing Friends of Flavor's. But there are so many episodes within each of the different series getting a minimum of thousands of new views daily, it's all I can do to give the occasional "Thanks for watching!" to every 217th commenter. Anything to show we care, I guess. It's one of

Friends of Flavor's biggest priorities to remain as approachable to the over four million viewers of each new video as they were to the first fourteen, and as a loyal longtime fan myself, I appreciate it.

I've been at it for a couple of hours when I hear Margie abruptly scoot her chair back behind me. I peek over my shoulder, though I know she's likely only taking a bathroom break. But to my surprise, she's gazing at her cell phone as she gets to her feet and gestures for me to get up, too.

"Aiden texted. Impromptu meeting in PK 1. Why don't you join me, see what's up?"

I nod, knowing it's more of an order than a suggestion, and close my laptop. I fight the urge to tuck in the flyaway strands of Margie's long, gray-brown braid as I trail her down the hall. While Margie has her shit together more than most people I know, the state of her braid always suggests otherwise. And somehow, I seem to be the only one who notices. It's like these people didn't grow up with a mama who would lick her fingers and pat into submission any individual hair that dared to step out of line.

When we reach Prep Kitchen 1, I'm pulled out of my hair reverie by the tall, stressed-out head of operations of Friends of Flavor—and cohost of *Good Chef/Bad Chef*—looking even paler than usual. Aiden, whose blond-haired, surfer-bro looks I might find attractive if not for every word that comes out of his mouth, paces back and forth. He has one hand on his hip and the other scratches aggressively at his neck, his intense gaze snapping toward us—well, toward Margie—when we enter.

"We have a problem," he announces.

"So I gathered," Margie replies coolly. She has at least a couple of decades of age and experience on Aiden and the rest of the Friends, and it mostly stands out when anything has gone wrong.

"The six of us have to fly to Chicago this afternoon. Jules Veronique had an opening in his schedule come up for tonight, and his assistant just called me, and they've finally agreed to let us film the crossover episode at his new restaurant. Everyone's schedule is cleared, the suits okayed it, and flights are booked, so we're going. Because we have to go, right? So we're going. We need to leave any minute."

He pauses, giving Margie an opening. "So . . . what's the issue?"

Aiden sighs, pulling a hand through short, platinum locks. "We were going to film a regular episode of *Piece of Cake* this afternoon, but Nia will be with the rest of us in Chicago. We have advertisers already scheduled and expecting an episode tomorrow, but now we won't have our pastry chef here to *film that episode.* Since you're marketing and have experience in the saving-face stuff, I thought you might . . . I don't know, have an idea."

Margie nods slowly, sucking her cheeks in. I feel a bit touchy on her behalf at the clipped way Aiden talks to her. Maybe it's my respect-your-elders upbringing. Maybe I'm still thinking of Mr. Cat Suit and I'm projecting onto Aiden. Or maybe it's just that I'm over men's condescension toward women who are their equals—not that I'd ever express such opinions to these two.

After a moment of staring blankly into mid-distance, Margie opens her mouth to speak.

"Yo, A, was this the sourdough starter you were looking for? It kinda looks like a baby vommed in this bowl. Kinda smells like it, too, but—"

The speaker who isn't Margie stops short and sets the bowl he's holding on the counter, looking at our small crowd in confusion. I haven't seen him before. He's definitely an intern; if the fact that he looks about my age hadn't given him away, the general air of doesn't-know-what's-going-on-in-this-office-or-the-world would.

"He could do it."

It's Margie who speaks this time, and it feels like all eyes in the room turn to her in surprise.

"Our *intern*?" sputters Aiden.

Sourdough Guy crosses his thick arms over his apron-clad chest, looking a little defensive even though he doesn't know why yet. He's significantly shorter than Aiden, barely my height, but a lot bulkier. It'd be hard not to notice that he clearly works out when he's not in the kitchen. I try not to judge appearances, but muscles combined with the backward baseball cap on his head are making it difficult. Another dude-bro.

Margie shrugs. "Sure. It'll be different. '*Piece of Cake* Makes Macarons, Featuring the Intern.' Better than nothing."

Aiden steps closer and lowers his voice nowhere near enough to keep Sourdough Guy from hearing him. "I don't think so. He really—he's not ready to do a video. Not on his own, anyway."

"Reese can do it with him."

I don't even register at first that Margie is talking about me. The stressed-out chef doesn't either, but that's because he hasn't bothered to learn my name.

"Who?" he asks.

"Reese. Marketing intern." Margie puts a hand on my shoulder and nudges me forward as if presenting me for inspection. I open my mouth to protest, but I can't seem to produce any sound.

Aiden barely glances at me before wiping a hand over his face. "Margie. Please. Intern plus intern does not equal chef."

She matches Sourdough Guy's stance, though it looks less aggressive on her. "No, but it does equal a solution to your problem, which is what you asked me for. It'll be fun and different, and if it's a bomb, we'll never have to try it again. Don't you have a plane to catch?"

The expression on Aiden's pale face is grim, and I'm sure my own is similar, because what the *devil*? After another tense moment, Aiden sighs heavily. "I'm trusting you with this, all right? Can you manage this for me?"

In spite of my reluctance to do what Margie has suggested,

I'm secondhand offended again when he speaks to her like a child. But she just pulls her braid over her shoulder and starts smoothing it with her hand like she has all the patience in the world.

"I've got it. Give Jules my best."

Chapter Two

The next couple of hours are a blur of following Margie around the office as she makes the necessary preparations and adjustments for the sudden change of plans for Nia's baking show, *Piece of Cake*. Consulting people in various kitchens and cubicles, and even a few over the phone, she makes a bunch more decisions than it seems should be needed for a video of two people doing some baking. But I imagine I don't even understand the half of it.

My eyes have glazed over and my head is spinning when Margie finally turns to me, sometime after the lunch break we've skipped. It's the first real acknowledgment I've gotten since we were standing in front of Aiden.

"Have you seen the other intern recently?"

I look around and shake my head. "I can go look for him if you want."

She just turns and waves for me to follow her, calling out as we walk back through the prep kitchens, *"Intern!"*

In Prep Kitchen 3, a backward-cap-covered head pops up from beneath the counter.

"Me?"

Margie beckons him over with two fingers. "Yes. I assume you have a name?"

He flips a kitchen towel over his shoulder and wipes his hands on his apron before holding one out to her. "I'm Benny."

"Margie." Their hands meet in one brisk shake before he drops his and offers it to me.

"Reese," I say, still in a daze. I am totally dead-fishing our handshake, but he doesn't seem to notice.

"Like Reese's Cups, the best candy in the history of the world?" He gives me a lopsided grin and I blink back at him.

"Uh . . . no. Like Reese Witherspoon, patron saint of Southern ladies who watch too many romantic comedies."

Benny laughs so loud, it startles me.

"Right." Margie smirks between us. "You two ready to get started?"

This is the closest anyone has come to asking if I *want* to be in a video to be viewed by millions on one of my favorite cooking shows of all time. But still, it doesn't feel like I have much choice. I nod as Benny gives an enthusiastic "Let's do this!" He's like the FoF equivalent of the spirit chair on my high school's student council, who had to get the crowd going at pep rallies. I hated pep rallies.

Margie leads us to a counter in Prep Kitchen 2 where

some kitchen assistants have set out bowls of ingredients. A videographer—Charlie, I think—sets up a camera on the opposite side of the counter. There are a couple of other people bustling around the kitchen testing recipes or something of the sort, and no one seems too interested in the fact that two inexperienced teenagers are about to be trusted with the most precious of Friends of Flavor content.

"First, these. You're both eighteen, right?"

Margie slides some forms toward Benny and me. Waivers, consent to be filmed, and all that. We both nod—we have to be eighteen to work here in the first place. Benny barely even looks at the papers before dropping his signature onto the designated line. I'm reminded of the scene in *The Little Mermaid* when Ariel signs her voice away to Ursula, and I try to skim for any major life-altering clauses. But I feel the pressure of everyone waiting on me and quickly sign my name, kissing my fins goodbye.

"Great," Margie says. "So this should be pretty easy. The premise is that—true to reality—Nia had to step out for the day with the rest of the Friends, but she left you with all these ingredients already on the counter and asked you two to take over. À la *Chopped* but with fewer ingredients and less direction. That's all we give you to go off, and we'll see what you two come up with. We're calling it *Piece of Cake: Amateur Hour.*"

Benny crosses his arms again, and his thick brows knit together under the edge of his hat. "Gotta say, as the *culinary* intern, I resent the word 'amateur' a little."

Margie looks amused. "We'll talk about a title change once you've had any formal training whatsoever."

I clear my throat, sensing an out. "As the *marketing* intern, I accept that word. Completely. Like, are you sure you want me to be part of this? Because my kitchen skills aren't too refined just yet, and—"

"I think it's even better that way, honestly. But that reminds me"—Margie's eyes flick down to my shirt, which now looks like the result of a sad attempt at purple-brown tie-dye. "We do need to grab you an apron. Lose the sweater. Be right back."

I blink at her retreating messy braid before sense returns to me. I slip my cardigan from my shoulders and hang it on a coat hook on the wall. There's a dress code at Friends of Flavor and I'm careful not to push the boundaries. Fortunately, today's tea-stained top at least has short sleeves. I feel Benny watching, which makes me self-conscious about my—*gasp*—scandalously bare arms. I must have forgotten to check my internalized self-consciousness from years of sexist school dress codes at the door today. That shit runs deep.

I feel fabric brush my arm and turn to find Margie holding out what looks at first glance like a burlap sack but is actually an ugly brown apron. Still an improvement over what's currently happening across my torso.

"All we had left are the ones we give to guest stars. Sorry," she adds with a shrug that suggests she's less than concerned. I take the apron anyway and pull it over my head, freeing my hair from the neck strap before I tie the strings behind my back. It fits much like a burlap sack would, too. Feeling better and better about my first and probably only brush with internet fame.

Maybe I can come up with a fake name for the video so it won't follow me forever when anyone Googles "Reese Camden." Better yet, if people who already know me stumble across the video, they'll just think I have a doppelgänger.

As Benny and I wait for further direction, I notice that his apron actually looks good on him. It should, since he has to wear it every day, but does it have to look *that* good? The off-white accentuates the tan on his muscular arms, and the muscles themselves are accentuated by the second skin that is his tight T-shirt.

I mean to look away, but my eyes catch on his, and on the cocky smirk playing over his face. *Ugh.* He knows he's objectively attractive, and now *he* knows that *I* know. I narrow my eyes at him, but his prideful look doesn't falter.

"Now just relax and have fun with it," Margie tells us. "Introduce yourselves however you want, then, Benny, why don't you explain the scenario and kick off the rest of the show? It's okay if it's awkward or you fumble with words or whatnot, just keep going. We'll edit all the extraneous stuff out later. Ready?"

No. Not even close. Those are the vaguest instructions that have ever instructioned. And I have to carry them out with a guy who, as far as I can tell, is a tool. Who thought this was a good idea?

Margie. Margie, my boss, who I very much want to like me.

"Yep!" My voice comes out as a squeak.

Benny's gaze slides to me before he answers. "Lights, camera, action, baby."

Okay, Spielberg. I barely curb my eye roll before Charlie the cameraman mumbles something that sounds like "That's my line," then starts counting down from three on his fingers.

The camera's red light comes on.

We're rolling.

"Hey, y'all, I'm Reese, marketing intern here at Friends of Flavor," I say with a wave. I'm shocked that I'm even saying words. I have essentially mimicked the way my favorite Friend, Katherine, does her intro on *Fuss-Free Foodie*. Plus a "y'all," because I can't help it.

"*Hey, y'all,*" Benny says in a high-pitched, exaggerated Southern accent. My eyes dart to him and my jaw drops, but he just laughs and eases back into his normal voice. "I'm Benny, culinary intern. We're stepping in today because Nia and the other Friends had to run off to tend to some very important . . . food . . . things. But don't worry: we are total nonprofessionals with very little experience, and they left us with zero direction."

He's good at this. Too good. I feel the instinct to clam up coming on and do my best to fight it. *Channel Katherine.*

"We met just a few minutes ago and he's already making fun of how I talk," I say. "All required ingredients in a recipe for success."

"Don't get your petticoats in a twist, Scarlett O'Hara," Benny shoots back. "I'm twice as rude to people I actually know. Now, let's check out our ingredients."

Oh, this is a game he wants to play, is it? Scarlett O'Hara? I just—I won't even begin to engage with that. Nope. This guy is getting nothing from me. Only the minimum amount of interaction to get through this video and not make myself out to be a total bitch. And maybe afterward I'll figure out a literary character to whom he would least like to be compared and throw it back at him. All in due time.

"Looks like we have some eggs," I start, naming the most obvious ingredients first. "Green food coloring . . . flour . . . sugar . . . or maybe it's salt, I can't tell."

Benny takes a pinch and tosses it in his mouth. "Sugar," he declares, then reverts to his imitation accent and adds with a wink, "Darlin'. And some other not-yet-identifiable stuff, but from first pass, I'd guess they want us to make green eggs and ham."

I cross my arms, ignoring his cheekiness. "There's no ham."

"Ah, good catch. Back to the drawing board."

"What if we—"

Before I can finish my thought, Benny plunges his fingers into the remaining bowls and licks the contents off one at a time.

"This one's powdered sugar, not flour," he says, then licks a different finger. "This one's flour."

Lick. "Vanilla"—lick—"salt"—lick—"*butter*, yum"—lick—"mmm, cream of tartar?"

I don't even know what that is, let alone what it tastes like. With a flourish, he uses his clean hand to reach over and pluck a nut out of the last bowl. "Pistachio," he declares, smiling obnoxiously at me with gross bits of green smeared across his teeth.

"Please go wash your hands," I reply with a frown.

He turns to the sink, remarking over his shoulder, "You won't get my cooties, Reese's Cup."

I roll my eyes at the camera. "We're not at nickname level yet."

Benny returns to my side, wiping his hands dry on his apron. "I'm sorry to report that we are. Benny's my nickname."

"Really? Then what's your re—"

"Let's get started on these macarons, eh?"

He doesn't want to talk about his real name. Duly noted. I'll bring it up if he calls me Reese's Cup again.

"How do you know that's what we're making?" I ask.

He puts a hand to his chest. "Chef," he says in the same tone with which you would say *duh*. When I raise a skeptical eyebrow, he adds, "In training. And it was a hunch based on the stuff laid out for us. Plus, it's the example Margie used when pitching the video earlier. Enough chitchat, let's shake 'n' bake!"

Benny rubs his hands together excitedly and starts pushing bowls my way. I have no idea what to do with any of them, and while I hate to look like the student in this little production, he seems to actually know what he's doing. Or he's confident enough to fake it well.

"So I should probably just tell you I'm about as green as these pistachios when it comes to macaroons. I've never even eaten one, let alone made—" I begin self-consciously, but Benny cuts me off.

"Macarrr*ons*," he says, throwing his hands up emphatically and rolling the *r* for longer than seems necessary. "Not macar*oon*s. Important distinction, Reese's Pieces. Two different cookies."

I shake my head on an exhale, trying hard to keep my composure. "Right, well. Painful as it was to admit it the first time, I'll repeat that I've still never had a macar*on,* so you've gotta, like, tell me what to do."

Benny grins at me, then looks directly into the camera. "It would be my honor."

He shuffles around more bowls and I mock-whisper to the imaginary audience, "Apologies in advance to, well, feminism as a whole."

"Did you say something?" Benny teases, pushing the pistachios toward me with finality. "There are just so many recipes, so much knowledge in my head that sometimes it's hard to hear anything outside it, you know?"

"Keep it up, Benjamin," I say in the warning tone that my mamaw would use to tell my papaw that he should very much *not* keep it up.

"Not my name," he says, pointing a finger at me. "Blanch those nuts."

I cock my head to the side. "Do what now?"

He reaches for the flour and a sifter. "You're in charge of the filling, and first you'll need to make pistachio paste. Fill a pot with water and bring it to a boil."

Something tells me this is going to be a long and involved process. I've always known that even a supershort episode on Friends of Flavor is a highlight reel of footage that can take anywhere from hours to days to prep and film. But this is the first time I've considered what that could mean for Benny and me. I'd feel better about the prospect if I'd eaten lunch.

Benny tells some stories about trying macarons in France when he visited while spending the summer in Italy with his grandparents. I'm half listening while I wait for the water to boil. But mostly, his stories add to the insecurity I'm feeling right now. He knows complicated recipes off the top of his head; he's traveled around Europe. I'm good at button clicking, sure, and I can handle my familiar comfort food recipes, but I don't have his ease around a kitchen. And so far, I've felt in over my head in Seattle. I've never resented the fact that I haven't been far out of the Southeast before, not when I've had the internet at my disposal for all kinds of armchair travel and self-education. For most of high school, I was desperate to leave—it's why I applied to UW, just about as far as I could get in the States without having to fly over an ocean—but that was because of the people around me, not the place. I love Kentucky and dare anyone to hate on it to my face. But I have to admit to myself that right now, my upbringing makes me feel like some country bumpkin who's out of her depth.

Benny recaptures my attention once the water is boiling and gives me the next few instructions. Put the pistachios in the pot, take it off the heat, let it sit a couple of minutes before draining. Then I should be able to rub the flaky brown skins off with ease.

"Easy there, Girl Scout, you're not trying to build a fire. Gentle." He puts his big, floury hands over mine and delicately flicks the skin off a pistachio to demonstrate. I flinch at the contact, momentary as it is, then let up on the pressure I've been applying to the cluster of nuts between my palms. They really do come apart with the lightest touch.

I'm pouring the nuts into the food processor when I notice Benny is already pulling a bowl out from under the stand mixer and starting to fold in dry ingredients by hand.

"Why do I feel like you're way ahead of me?"

He gives me that lopsided smile. "Mine still have to bake. Relax, it's not a competition. But if it were, I'd probably win."

I push the processor button aggressively, like I'm trying to tune out his voice, but in my haste make a fatal mistake. Okay, not fatal, but messy.

I don't get the lid fully locked in place.

It's secure enough that the food processor still starts, but in the two seconds my finger is on the button, the lid goes flying across the counter, sending pistachio bits in every direction. Mostly, it seems, toward me. They're in my eyes, nose, mouth, and all across the front of my ugly apron. Forgetting the nuts are edible and probably even taste good, I sputter and try to spit them out, stepping back from the counter as if the damage isn't already done. As my senses return, I hear Margie, Charlie, and Benny . . . well, losing their shit.

After a moment, I drop my head and start to laugh too. The tears that come to my eyes help flush out some of the stray pieces that are stuck in my lashes, and I try to wipe off the rest of my face with the bottom of my apron. It takes a couple of minutes for everyone to regain composure. Benny is the first one to address me.

"You good, Hurricane Reese?" he asks, stepping closer and swiping once at his own eyes.

"Aside from being covered in green chunks and hugely embarrassed? Sure," I offer with a reluctant smile.

He takes another step closer and my smile drops. Our faces are less than a foot apart. But before I can react, he reaches up and his fingers are on my face . . . pulling a piece of pistachio from my eyebrow.

"There," he says softly, stepping back. "There's still more where that came from, but mostly in your hair. And might I say, green is your color."

I let out a choked cough, still surprised by the close contact with this near stranger and not impressed by his poor attempt at flirtation. I turn away and gather my blond-with-temporary-green-highlights locks up into a high ponytail. I can write off any remaining chance of looking cute in this video.

Clearing his throat, Benny asks, "Would this make you feel better?"

I look over in time to see him dipping a finger in his light green batter and smearing it like war paint in a single stripe under each of his eyes. I laugh in spite of myself and shake my head.

"You look like you're fixing to play a St. Patrick's Day football game, while I was caught in an explosion at the Planters factory."

His head falls back as he laughs and before I know it, he has more batter on his fingers and reaches over to put two stripes under my own eyes. "When the nut factory explodes at noon but you have to play in the big game at one."

I shake my head, but I'm fighting a laugh, too. I notice Margie twirling a finger in a "wrap it up" motion, so I try to regain control of the situation.

"Okay, we can do this," I say, shaking myself to refocus on the task at hand.

Benny takes a deep breath and turns back toward his side of the counter. "Yep. Your 'stach stash is down by about half, but that's fine. They'll just be more creamy than nutty."

I finish processing the pistachio paste with the lid fully on, and Benny starts piping his batter onto a cookie sheet in neat little circles, giving me further instructions as he goes.

The rest of the prep goes off pretty smoothly. He supervises cream production while the cookie parts of the macarons bake, and both finish almost simultaneously. While the cookies are cooling, the camera keeps rolling. Margie and Charlie are talking with each other and not really paying attention, so Benny and I both relax a bit. We use the time to pick at the cookies with air bubbles that cracked while baking, popping little bites in our mouths. They are light, sweet, and delicious.

"These are good," I admit before I can stop myself. I clear

my throat and try to backtrack. "I mean, seriously, did they give you a recipe before this? Believe me, I'm not trying to pump your tires any more, but there's no way you just knew all the steps on the fly."

One side of his mouth quirks up, a dimple appearing in his cheek. I blink back down toward the cookies quickly. Up close like this, the boy's face is dangerous. Which he absolutely knows.

"No recipe, thank you very much. My parents own an Italian restaurant in San Francisco, where I'm from. Pops runs the kitchen for the most part, all the entrées and stuff, but desserts are all Ma. Her specialty is cannoli because, y'know, Italian, but she went through a French pastry phase a couple of years ago. Our kitchen at home was like a macaron factory for months while she perfected her recipes, and my brothers and I were her line workers. I'll probably remember how to make macarons even if I get to be old and decrepit and forget my own name."

I smirk at that. "So what you're saying is that you got lucky."

"Oh, extremely. No matter what ingredients were here, we would've had to find a way to make 'em into pasta or pastries. It's all I got." He pauses, then adds, "But with your newfound skills at putting the lid on the food processor, who knows what we're capable of?"

"Cute," I deadpan, feeling around my hair for a piece of debris. When I find one, I throw it at him.

Benny laughs as he dodges, then leans over to check on his cooling cookies. Margie and Charlie return their attention to us.

"All right," Benny says finally, rubbing his hands together. "I think we're ready to pipe."

I hold the frosting bags while he spoons the cream in, then we each take a bag and half the cookies. I watch as Benny does his first couple, hesitant that I might mess something up again.

"Learning from the master, eh, Reese's Cup?" he says cockily without lifting his head from his work.

I roll my eyes and lean over to start doing my own. I'm about to squeeze out the first dollop when Benny's voice cuts the silence again. "The trick is to be fearless. The macaron can smell your fear."

"I think my only fear was making a fool of myself, and that one already came true, so . . ."

"Nothing to lose!" He fist-pumps with the hand not piping.

I start piping, *fearlessly.* In a matter of minutes, we've each made our own share of little cookie-sandwich-y macarons. Without planning it, we both pick up one of the delicate desserts and turn to each other.

"Cheers, *y'all*," Benny says with a wink that looks to be more for me than the camera. I narrow my eyes again, but tap my macaron against his and we each take a bite.

And for a dessert made by one near-novice and one semi-apprentice working entirely from memory? They turned out damn good.

I say so through a mouthful, then slap a hand over my mouth, cheeks reddening. "You probably can't say 'damn' on a video, right? Cut that out, please. My mama will fly to Seattle to stick a bar of soap in my mouth."

Benny makes a sound halfway between a cough and a laugh. "Wait, are you serious? That's a little 1800s. She never actually did that, did she?"

"No." His shoulders relax before I continue. "'Cause we never swore in front of Mama. But I don't want to try my luck now."

He looks appalled. I don't *really* think Mama would wash my or my siblings' mouths out with soap, but it was her favorite threat. Truth be told, she used it way more often for all my lord-have-mercies and oh-my-lords, especially after I stopped going to church with my family a few years back. But it's kinda funny to see Benny riled up, so he can think what he wants.

"I think we've got about enough, if one of you could just tie it all together for us," Margie says.

Benny looks to me. He did do the introduction, and I am feeling a little more used to the whole camera thing now. I nod.

"Thanks for watching as we made a total mess of the kitchen, and some macarons to boot. I'm Reese, he's Benny, and this has been *Piece of Cake: Amateur Hour.* We'll see y'all . . . well, probably never again, because we weren't hired for this and we're kind of a train wreck. Have a flavorful day!"

I wave after dropping the signature ending line, and Benny chuckles beside me as he lifts a hand, too.

"That was excellent," Margie declares, surprising me with her praise. "Editing will have fun with it, huh, Charlie?"

He grumbles in agreement as he starts to disassemble the camera, and I'm gathering that grumbling is just his standard mode of communication. Some of the kitchen assistants appear to whisk away the dirty dishes, and Benny and I clean up our workstation. Margie says we can go home for the day whenever we're finished, then retreats to the marketing office.

Once the mixers and processors are put away and the counter clean of flour and pistachio debris, we stand there looking around and seem to mutually decide there's nothing left to do.

"Well," Benny says, turning to me with a hand outstretched. "It's been a pleasure, Reese."

He adds my name as an afterthought, deliberately not using an annoying variation of the only nickname he's come up with. I shake his hand, meeting his strength instead of limp-noodling this time. The macaron batter stripes on his face are cracking, even more so when he smiles and gets little creases around his eyes. The whole effect is . . . a lot. I feel the beginnings of a blush coming on but hope the mess on my own face distracts from it.

"Likewise, Benvolio."

He laughs. "It's short for Beneventi, actually. My last name."

I notice we're shaking for an oddly prolonged time, and I slip my hand out of his. "So you're not going to tell me your real first name?"

"We don't speak of it" is his mock-stern reply.

"Mysterious," I deadpan.

"Keep the ladies wanting more, I always say."

I roll my eyes, unable to come up with an appropriately snarky retort. "Well, um . . . see you around, then." I turn away from him to retrieve my sweater, untying the apron as I go.

"I hope so," he says, and it's like I can hear the crooked grin in his voice. "Hey, actually, what are you doing this weekend? We should have lunch."

My arm slips through my cardigan sleeve and I pull the sweater tight across my front before turning back to him.

"Lunch?" I say, the word loaded with as much skepticism as if he'd suggested we hit up a nightclub. *What's your angle, Beneventi?*

"Yeah," he says, eye-smoldering at me. "The meal in the middle of the day. Or dinner, which happens in the evening. They have those where you're from?"

I feel my upper lip curl and I'm sure my face is the least attractive thing right now, but that's for the best. "Yes, we do. Just usually with people I actually want to spend time around."

There. That's for the Scarlett O'Hara comment. And it's true, anyway. I barely know the guy and what I know so far, I'm not sure I much care for. He's cocky, which I hate, whether it's earned or not. And perhaps even more frustrating to me is it probably *is* earned. He knows his stuff, and I don't like being made to look ignorant while he mansplains the difference between baking powder and baking soda. Logically, I know I can't blame him for being good in the kitchen nor for the fact that I'm less so. But I'm not trying to out-logic my intuition about this boy.

Benny puts one hand over his heart and stumbles back like

I've shot him. "Oof. You wound me, Reese's Cup. But c'mon. I don't really know anyone around here and—no offense—I doubt you do, either. We're the only interns, as far as I know. Don't you think we should be . . . I don't know, at the very least, allies?"

That's actually the very most I want from him. But his point reminds me of something important—we *are* the only two interns. I don't know if he's trying to work here long term, but as far as I know, we're the only two in-house candidates eligible for the fall culinary internship—the application for which states that "preference will be given to in-house applicants." He clearly has the upper hand in culinary experience, having done the restaurant thing. I've always played more of an assistant role for my mamaw, who works through the same recipes time and again and usually tells me what to do at every step.

So *is* he going for the fall culinary spot? That seems like something I should know. Something I could find out over, say, lunch. Along with other things about him that might be useful to me if we're in competition with one another. Like his weaknesses. Keep your enemies close, and all that.

Goodness, I'm thinking like a movie villain. Or maybe I'm just thinking like a woman who wants to get ahead and won't lie down and let her future happen without doing anything to sway it.

Benny interrupts my thoughts, adding, "My treat. Please?"

I scrunch my nose. Even a movie villain can cover her own bill, thank you. "No."

"No? That's it?" he scoffs. I get the sense he's not rejected often, and I want to make him sweat it out a bit more, but . . .

"No, you won't pay. I'll go, but I'll pay for myself. Lunch Saturday. Do you have your phone?"

That smug smile is back and I find myself regretting my decision already, but it's my own fault. He pulls his phone from his back pocket and hands it to me, and I enter my number.

"Reese Camden," I say as I hand it back to him. As if he has seven other Reeses in his contacts already. "Text me and we'll pick a time and place."

"No need to beg, now," Benny teases, leaning against the counter and folding those annoyingly nice arms over his chest.

I turn on a heel and start to leave the kitchen without another word.

"Looking forward to it!" he calls after me, and I feel my frown deepen. That sure makes one of us, bud.